DON'T MESS

In the distant d   Buckalew cursed for it
had been his mou   l his
Colt, kicking his h   was
possible in the rai   bove
his head, he bega   f his
lungs. There were   oined
in. But Buckalew and his companions were in for a surprise. The Texans, who had weathered more than one
stampede that had been planned by outlaws or Indians,
did not limit their return fire to muzzle flashes. Lead
whipped through Buckalew's hat and another slug
burned the flank of his horse. The animal screamed and,
despite the darkness, lit out in a gallop. Buckalew found
himself caught up in the stampede—in a veritable sea of
flailing horns . . .

THE OREGON TRAIL

RALPH COMPTON

St. Martin's Paperbacks

This is a work of fiction, based on actual trail drives of the Old West. Many of the characters appearing in the Trail Drive Series were very real, and some of the trail drives actually took place. But the reader should be aware that, in the developing of characters and events, some fictional literary license has been employed. While some of the characters and events herein are purely the creation of the author, every effort has been made to portray them with accuracy. However, the inherent dangers of the trail are real, sufficient unto themselves, and seldom has it been necessary to enhance their reality.

THE OREGON TRAIL

Copyright © 1994 by Ralph Compton.

Cover illustration by Bob Larkin.
Map illustration on cover by Dennis Lyall.
Cover type by Jim Lebbad.
Map on p.v by David Lindroth, based upon material supplied by the author.

ISBN: 0-312-95547-2
EAN: 9780312-95547-2

Printed in the United States of America

St. Martin's Paperbacks edition/June 1995

20 19 18 17 16 15 14 13 12 11

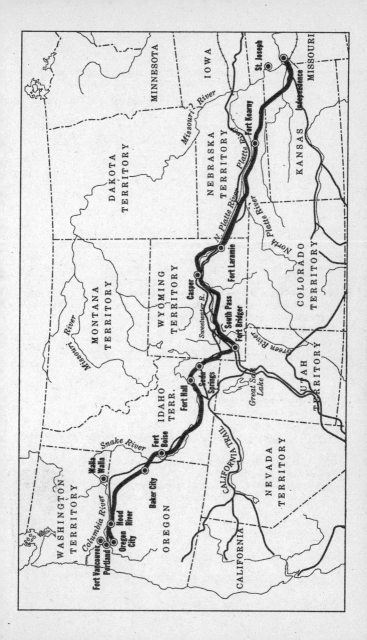

AUTHOR'S FOREWORD

In the 1830s the Oregon Country was opened to settlement and the Oregon Trail—a distance of more than two thousand miles—was blazed to what was to become new settlements along the Columbia River and the Willamette Valley. In May 1843 the migration began in earnest. Emigrants gathered on the banks of the Missouri River in Independence, and from there the wagons rolled westward. Thousands of men, women, and children trudged beside ox-drawn, canvas-covered wagons along the well-worn trail that led toward the faraway Rocky Mountains. Prior to departure, emigrants were told to "bring seventy-five pounds of bacon and two hundred pounds of flour" for every adult. The journey took as long as six months, and seldom was there a train of less than twenty-five wagons. In fact there were many trains of 250 wagons or more. For drawing the wagons, oxen were preferred over horses or mules because oxen were patient, far less likely to stampede, and never had to be shod.

At the time the migration began, Oregon was a vast area stretching from the Rocky Mountains to the Pacific Ocean, and from California—claimed at that time by Mexico—to Alaska, owned by Russia. There is speculation that the thousands of emigrants who surged west might have prevented war between the United States and England, for the English had their eyes on this coveted territory so conveniently bordered on the west by the Pacific Ocean. There was a negative side to this westward expansion, however, for it was the coming of the white man that planted the seeds of distrust, suspicion, and hatred that led to the bloody Indian wars. But there were some who were critical of the migration. Horace Greeley, then editor of the *New York Daily Tribune*, called the endeavor "an aspect of insanity. . . ." The British vowed the trek was impossible, while an official of the Hudson Bay Company said the foolish Americans "might as well undertake to go to the moon."

While there were many ways of dying along the trail, the biggest killer was disease, cholera taking the greatest toll. Death resulted from accidents with firearms, dangerous river crossings, rattlesnakes, fights, and from an occasional Indian ambush. Eventually more than twenty thousand would die along the treacherous trail. At least half the deaths occurred within the first six hundred miles, before reaching Fort Laramie. By 1850 there were as many as four graves per mile. The Oregon Trail has been called "America's longest graveyard." Near South Pass, a rocky ridge—7,412 feet above sea level—marked the halfway point. Here the springless wagons bounced over unyielding granite, and rarely did anything breakable survive the climb. At that point it has been estimated that the trail climbs a thousand feet in five miles. Emigrants were forced to use double or triple teams. Near present-day Atlantic City, Wyoming, massive amounts of broken glass can still be seen. Almost every wagon was overloaded, making it all but impossible for weary oxen to draw the heavy wagons up the steep trail. Travelers were forced to discard all but the bare necessities. Left behind were family heirlooms, clothing, spare parts, tools, medicine, axes, plows, spades, stoves, bread, beans, flour, bacon, hams, and furniture.

Many of the emigrants owned livestock and took it with them to Oregon. Some who had no cattle bought herds, with an eye toward ranching in the rich Willamette Valley. The irony of it was, in the late 1870s there was a sharp decline in mining, and Oregon became cattle country. Tens of thousands of Shorthorn-bred cattle were driven east along the Oregon Trail to range in

Idaho, Nevada, Montana, Wyoming, the Dakotas and Colorado. In 1880, two hundred thousand cattle were trailed eastward from Oregon cattle towns, while the little railroad town of Winnemucca, Nevada became another Dodge City. Thus the Oregon Trail has the distinction of having been the *only* trail on which cattle were driven west, and thirty years later, having herds driven eastward to the high plains.

PROLOGUE

❧

Independence, Missouri. May 20, 1843.

"*T*ake your hands off me," the girl shouted at the burly man.

She had long corn-silk-blond hair, wore a light blue skirt and a white blouse with ruffles at the wrists and throat. Her tormentor seemed to tower above her, each of his huge hands imprisoning one of her slender ones. His hat was black, flat-crowned. He wore an expensive blue suit with coat and vest, a black string tie, and polished flat-heeled teamster's boots. Black shaggy hair curled down to the collar of his white boiled shirt. It was near the noon hour, and but for a pair of Texas cowboys coming down the boardwalk, the street was almost deserted. Both men were in high-heeled riding boots, rough range clothes, and high-crowned, wide-brimmed hats. While each had a tied-down Colt on his right hip, the oldest of the duo wore his butt forward for a cross-hand draw. It was he who spoke.

"By God, Waco, the skunks grow almighty big in Missouri. You goin' to teach that bastard the error of his ways, or you want me to?"

"Lou," said Waco Tilden, "you know skunk smell makes me sick to my gut. You just do what needs doin' on the lady's behalf, and I'll side you. That varmint looks like the kind that's likely got a pistol under his coat or a pepperbox up his sleeve."*

"Mister," Lou said quietly, "let the lady go. Then you will apologize for havin' bothered her."

"Like hell," the big man snarled. "This is between me and her. It ain't none of yer business."

"Ma'am," said Lou, "would you like for me to make it my business?"

"Yes," the girl cried. "Oh, please. I want nothing to do with him, and he's hurting me."

"You heard her," said Lou. "Do you aim to turn around and face me like a man, or do I have to bust your skull with the muzzle of my Colt?"

The stranger released the girl, turned on Lou and charged like a bull. Lou stepped aside, brought a right up from his knees, smashing the big man on the point of his chin. The blow, coupled with his own momentum, left him dazed. He stumbled off the boardwalk and sat down in the dusty street.

"You can end this now," Lou said, "by apologizin' to the lady."

"Damned if I will."

"You're damned if you don't. I'm Lou Spencer. I always introduce myself before I beat hell out of a gent that's needful of it. That's so he can come lookin' for satisfaction if he's of a mind to. Now get up."

But when the big man moved, it wasn't to get up. His hand dipped under his coat, but it froze short of his pistol. Waco Tilden already had him covered.

"Go ahead," said Waco. "It'll give me a chance to do what I've wanted to do ever since the lady hollered for help."

"I'm all right," the girl said. "Let him go."

"We can't do that, ma'am," Lou said. "Not without an apology."

"Nobody kicks Jap Buckalew around and lives to talk

* Derringer

about it," the big man snarled, getting to his hands and knees. He staggered to his feet, his hands where they could be seen.

"I'll stomp hell out of any varmint that abuses a woman," said Lou, "and that includes you. Now you tell the lady you're sorry, or we'll take up where we left off."

"They's two of you bastards agin' me," Buckalew snarled, "but I ain't one to fergit. Fer now I got no choice, Sandy Applegate. I'm plumb sorry, Miss Uppity, that I laid a hand on you."

"That's an insult," said Lou, "and you don't sound a bit sorry. You'll have to do better than that. Try again, and this time you'd better get it right."

Buckalew deliberately faced the girl, and she paled at the fury she saw in his eyes. He spoke slowly, forcing out the words.

"I'm sorry I bothered you, ma'am."

"Now," Lou said, "get going and don't look back."

"Damn you," said Buckalew, "there'll be another time, another place."

"Thank you," the girl said after Buckalew had stomped angrily away. "I'm Sandy Applegate, and he's bothered me before. I shouldn't have come to town alone. I'm sorry you had to get involved. I've heard he's awful handy with a pistol and that he's killed before. He'll kill you if he can."

"He won't be the first or the last to try," Lou Spencer said. "On the frontier a man takes his chances. We just brought a herd of longhorns up the trail from Texas, and we got some gun throwers there who could have this Buckalew for breakfast. I'm Lou Spencer and my pard is Waco Tilden."

The pair removed their hats and the girl smiled. "I'm pleased to meet both of you," she said. "You have renewed my faith in mankind."

"We'll just walk with you a ways," said Waco, "in case this Buckalew ain't got the sense enough to quit while he's ahead."

"Thank you," Sandy said. "I left my horse tied at the mercantile and walked down to the mail facility to post some letters to our kin in Indiana. That was foolish of me. I won't do it again. I hope I'm not prying into something that's none of my business, but have you sold the cattle that you brought from Texas? That is," she added hastily, "if you intend to sell them."

"We aim to sell 'em," said Lou. "Some other herds got here ahead of us, but we've got five thousand head, the largest herd yet. We're hopin' to sell to the folks takin' the Oregon Trail. The rest of the outfit's bedded down ten miles south of here. Waco and me rode in to look things over and maybe find some buyers. Are you with the train bound for Oregon?"

"Yes," said the girl, "and Jesse Applegate, my father, wants to buy a herd. I don't believe he can take them all, but I'm sure he will buy some."

"In that case," Lou said, "I think we'll ride back with you and talk to your daddy. Waco, get our horses. I'll walk Miss Applegate back to the store."

"He's always doin' that," said Waco, looking as sorrowful as he could. "Taking the pretty girls and leavin' me with the horses."

The girl laughed. "Call me Sandy," she said.

The trio rode west along the Missouri, Waco on one side and Lou on the other. They listened while Sandy Applegate talked.

"There'll be two hundred and fifty wagons," she said, "and there's been some cuss fights already. Father hoped to become wagon boss, but he only got sixty votes. Would you believe the rest of them elected that brute Jap Buckalew? They're the ones who want to reach Oregon as quickly as they can, and since all they have to worry with is their wagons and teams, Buckalew's promised to get them there in far less than the six months we've been told it takes. Buckalew's convinced the majority—those without livestock—that livestock will slow down the train, that we might be on the trail even longer than six months."

"I reckon this Buckalew fancies himself the bull of the woods, then," Waco said.

"He does," said Sandy. "He's been bothering me ever since we joined the train."

"Then he'll be hounding you all the way to Oregon," Lou said.

"Maybe not," said Sandy. "Since those of us with live-stock aren't wanted, sixty wagons are going to fall back. Father will be wagon boss, and that suits the rest of them —those who chose Buckalew. They're laughing at us, calling us the 'cow column,' saying we'll still be trying to cross the Rockies when snow flies."

"Buckalew and his bunch may be in for a surprise," Waco said. "If most of the stock is Texas longhorns, they'll be trailwise. Even on a bad day they'll cover ten miles. Wagons ain't goin' to do any better, and there'll be days when they don't do as well. That's why we packed all our supplies on mules."

"Our camp's near the head of the column," said Sandy.

She waved to the other emigrants once they approached the wagon camps. Most of them were several hundred yards north of the river, and in most of them, crude canvas shelters or tents had been erected as protection from the elements. The wind was from the west and brought with it the odor of roasting meat.

"If all these folks have livestock," Lou said, "there's gonna be one almighty big herd. Where *is* the stock?"

"Most of us have been here a week or more," Sandy said, "and we've had to keep moving the stock north to find graze. When I said these sixty families had livestock, I didn't mean they all had a herd of cattle. Only Ezra Higdon and Jonah Quimby have large herds. They each bought half the three thousand head that came up the trail ahead of you. Besides the oxen needed to draw the wagons, the others have a few cows, horses, and mules. One family has some goats and two others have sheep."

"Sheep," Waco grunted. "My God."

"They plan to raise sheep when they reach Oregon," said Sandy. "How else would you do it, except to take them with you?"

"I wouldn't do it," Waco said. "The varmints eat the grass down to the roots. Give 'em a few years, and this Oregon Territory will be a desert."

The girl turned to him, her eyes twinkling. "What about the goats?"

"I got no opinion on goats," said Waco. "I'm a cowboy and there's a lot I don't know, but there's one thing I'm sure of: sheep don't belong in cow country."

"We're a mite one-sided when it comes to cows," Lou said with a grin.

When they rode into the Applegate camp, the Texans were impressed with the family's apparent affluence. The Applegates—including the mother, the son, and another daughter—were all better dressed than the emigrants Lou and Waco had seen along the way. The wagon and its canvas was new, and a pair of Hawken rifles leaned against a rear wheel. Beyond the wagon was a large tent, and before it, a fire pit. Sandy dismounted first, followed by Lou and Waco. After she had introduced the Texans and told their reason for being there, she turned to them and introduced her parents.

"This is my father, Jesse Applegate, my mother Sarah, my brother Jud, and my sister, Evangeline. She hates that, so we just call her Vangie."

The Texans tipped their hats to Sarah and Vangie and then shook hands with Applegate and his son. Applegate stood about six-two, broad-shouldered and lean. His flaming red hair and beard were streaked with gray, and unless life had been unusually hard on him, he looked much older than Sarah. The woman had light brown hair, brown eyes, and a smile much like Sandy's. The younger daughter—Vangie—had blue eyes and hair that one day might be as red as her father's. Jud had the brown hair and brown eyes of his mother. He looked about sixteen and was trying mightily to look much older.

"We were waiting dinner until Sandy returned from town," Applegate said, "and it'll be ready in a few minutes. You gentlemen are welcome to join us. Sandy, you and Vangie go help your mother."

"We're obliged," said Waco. "It'll be a pleasure to eat somebody's cooking other than our own."

"Lord A'mighty," said young Jud, "do all Texans carry tied-down pistols?"

"Son," the senior Applegate said, "mind your language and your manners. It's impolite to inquire into things which are none of your business."

"It's all right, Mr. Applegate," Lou said. "It's a fair question." He turned to the boy with a grin. "Not just in Texas, Jud, but just about every man on the frontier. You'll be ready for one yourself by the time you reach Oregon. Maybe sooner."

"I've never seen one with the butt turned to the front," said Jud. "How do you get it out in a hurry?"

"Every man makes his own decision about that," Lou replied. "I carry mine butt-forward for a cross-hand draw because it gains me a second or two. But the most important thing you must learn about pulling a gun is never to sacrifice accuracy for speed. If you can't hit what you're shootin' at, a quick draw can get you shot dead."

"Hell's fire!" Jud shouted. "I want me a pistol, and I want to wear it just like he does."

"Jud," his father said, "you're just about an ax handle away from having your mouth washed out with soap. Excuse him for bothering you," he said, turning to Lou, "but I share his awe in your ability with that weapon. When you move that fast, do you hit what you're shooting at?"

"Most of the time," said Lou. "It's kept me alive. You

first learn to hit what you're shootin' at. Then you work on speed. Makes no difference if you're fast as forked lightning if you miss. Many a man who had nothing but speed has grass growing over him."

Sarah ended the conversation by announcing that dinner was ready. The men had their plates filled first. There were slabs of fried ham, potatoes, onions, beans, and corn bread. There was no further conversation until the men had finished eating. Finally they trooped back to the huge coffeepot that hung over the fire from an iron spider, refilling their cups. Jesse Applegate and his son sat on the wagon tongue while Lou and Waco hunkered down facing them. The women went about washing the tin plates, cups, and eating tools, but they did it quietly so they might hear the conversation between Applegate and the two Texans.

"I think," said Applegate, once they got down to business, "that I can take half your herd. Twenty-five hundred head. Those ahead of you went for thirty dollars a head. Will you accept that?"

"I reckon we can accept that," Lou said, "if it's the going rate, but we'll need to talk to the rest of the outfit first. There's nine of us, and we all own a piece of the herd. Do you know of anybody else in this train who might be willing and able to take the rest of our herd?"

"I could name several who would like to," said Applegate, "but they do not have the money. Our holdings in Indiana were such that, while I'm not a rich man, we're better off than most. Like I told you, most of this train consists of people who have no livestock except the oxen to draw their wagons, and that's all they want. The others, who will be part of the 'cow column,' will be farmers. That requires only a plow, some hand tools, and seed. So your problem, gentlemen, is not that nobody will want the balance of your herd. They just can't afford it."

"This emigration has just started," Waco said. "You got any idea when there'll be another wagon train to Oregon?"

"No," said Applegate. "We plan to leave here on June first so we can get across the Rocky Mountains no later than August. By September they'll be impassable, I've been told."

"My God," Lou said, "that means there may not be another train for months. Maybe not until next spring."

"We can't afford to winter here," said Waco. "Mr. Applegate, while we ride back to our outfit and tell them of your offer to buy half the herd, will you do us a favor? Ask around and see if there's any chance that we can sell the rest of our herd, even if we have to do it a few at a time."

"I will," Applegate said, "but like I've told you, the rest of the families in my part of the train simply don't have the cash. May I suggest something that might solve your problem as well as one of my own?"

"Go ahead," said Waco. "We'll listen."

"I've already told you that Higdon and Quimby each bought half the last herd that came up the trail from Texas. There were seven riders. Higdon and Quimby were smart enough to hire the lot of them to trail the cattle on to Oregon. I'd like to hire you and your outfit for the same purpose."

"That would solve your problem," Lou said, "but what would you suggest we do with our twenty-five hundred head of unsold cattle?"

"Take them with you," said Applegate, "and carve out a ranch for yourselves in the Willamette Valley. I'll pay each of you forty dollars a month and feed you. Sarah and the girls will do the cooking. All you'll have to do is see to the cattle and keep them moving. Will you consider it?"

"We'll consider it," Lou said, "but I'm making no promises until we talk to the rest of the outfit. I don't think we'll have any problem with your offer of thirty dollars a head, but as for the bunch of us hirin' on for a drive to Oregon, I just don't know."

"I hope you go with us," Jud cried excitedly. "I want you to teach me to draw and fire a pistol."

Lou grinned at the boy. "Perhaps I will if we decide to go, and if your daddy approves."

Applegate laughed. "I'll consider that while you're considering my offer. I'm beginning to learn that life on the frontier is different from anything we've ever experienced. We're going to have to learn to adapt."

"Until tomorrow then," Lou said, "adios."

The Texans tipped their hats to Sarah, Sandy, and Vangie, mounted their horses and rode back the way they had come. When they looked back, Sandy raised her hand in farewell.

Waco laughed. "That was for you," he said.

Lou Spencer said nothing, but he found himself half hoping that Waco was right.

1

Lou and Waco didn't talk much as they rode back to their herd and the rest of their riders. Eventually it was Lou who spoke.

"I reckon it'll take both of us to explain this situation to the rest of the boys, so don't just stand there lookin' at me. Speak up."

Waco laughed. "I don't aim to say a word. You're the talky one. Just make believe these seven ugly jaspers is all purty females with corn-silk hair and shapes only God could have created. You'll have 'em eatin' out of your hand."

"Once in a month of Sundays you come up with a sensible idea," Lou said, casting him a sour look. "Just shut the hell up until it's time to say yes or no to Applegate's offer."

The rest of the outfit had been watching for them, and there was an unspoken question in the eyes of every man as Lou and Waco dismounted. Lou wasted no time. He first told them of Applegate's offer to buy half the herd at thirty dollars a head. There were unanimous shouts of approval, but Lou held up his hand.

"I'm not finished. We have more than one decision to make. Hear the rest, and then I'll want some answers. But from one of you at a time."

First he explained that the only emigrants with money

to buy cattle had already done so. He told them there
might not be another Oregon-bound wagon train for
months because of the near impossibility of crossing the
Rocky Mountains in winter. Finally he concluded with
Applegate's offer of forty and found and the suggestion
they use the unsold half of the herd to carve out a ranch
for themselves in the Willamette Valley. He allowed
them a little time to digest what he'd said. They were
Texans to the bone. Their boots were rough out, their
trousers dark homespun, and their shirts faded blue or
red flannel. Their wide-brimmed hats were in varying
stages of deterioration as a result of dust, sweat, rain,
and the merciless Texas sun. Lou spoke first to Red Brodie. His hair was red, his eyes green. His Colt was tied
down on his left hip. He hailed from San Antonio. At
twenty-four he was the oldest man in the outfit, a year
older than Lou Spencer.

"Red," said Lou, "you're the oldest. How do you
feel?"

"Thirty dollars a head is a fair price," Brodie said,
"and I'll go along with that. But how do you know Applegate's levelin' with you when he says there's nobody
else to buy the other half of the herd? This old pilgrim
needs cowboys, which he ain't goin' to have if we sell the
rest of our herd and ride back to Texas."

"Because Waco and me rode past most of the wagons
in Applegate's train," said Lou, "and those who haven't
bought cattle for ranching are going to be farmers."

"Except for them with sheep and goats," Waco added
helpfully.

"Sheep and goats?" the seven riders bawled in a single voice.

"Wasn't no hogs that we could see," said Waco.

Lou turned furious eyes on Waco, and if looks could
have killed, the twenty-one-year-old rider would have
been buzzard bait. Finally Lou had to face the seven
riders who glared at him in varying stages of indignation.

"There are a few goats and some sheep," Lou said,

"but that won't be a problem. All we'll be concerned with will be the cattle. The last herd to come up the trail from Texas—three thousand head—were bought by families in Applegate's party. The riders who sold the cattle have hired on for the drive to Oregon."

"By God," said Brodie, "it ain't my ambition to have a cow ranch within a day's ride of a damn sheepman. Not in Texas, Oregon, or nowhere else."

There were shouts of approval from all the riders except Waco.

"In the morning," Lou said, "we'll deliver Applegate's twenty-five hundred cows. Of the unsold half of the herd, I figure 277 head belong to me. I'll want to cut them out and drive them along with the Applegate herd. I believe I'm entitled to two bulls, if nobody has any objections. I've got kin in Texas, but nothin' else. If I don't like it in Oregon, the trail runs both ways. The rest of you can do as you like with your part of the herd, and no hard feelings on my part."

"I reckon I'll cut out my cows and go with you," said Waco. "Hell, if we don't like it in Oregon, we can always drive the cows south to Nevada and sell 'em to the miners."

"So you're just goin' to leave the rest of us here on our hunkers till another wagon train comes along," said Sterling McCarty. He was from Austin, with black hair and deep brown eyes. He was twenty-three, and carried his Colt on his right hip.

"You can sit here, go west to St. Louis, or back to Texas," Lou said.

"I sure as hell don't aim to winter here," Vic Sloan said. "We got no way of knowin' if the next bunch of emigrants will be buyin' cows or not." Sloan was just nineteen, the youngest man in the outfit. From Laredo, he had sandy hair and pale blue eyes. He carried his Colt for a right-hand draw.

The six undecided riders turned their questioning eyes on Red Brodie, and he responded with a shrug of his shoulders. He was having some trouble facing them, for he had committed them and himself to a hostile position from which there seemed no retreat. Having no alternative to what Lou had proposed, Brodie was forced to pull in his horns. Each man must make his own decision, and Sterling McCarty was the first.

"Well, hell," he grumbled, "just because a man don't like the trail he's bound to ride don't mean he ain't got the sand to do it. Havin' no other choice, I'll throw in, but by God, no sheep, you understand? Keep them damn woollies away from me."

"I don't like sheep any better than the rest of you," Lou said, "but that don't give us the right to round 'em all up and drive them off the edge of the world. We're cattlemen and we'll keep our distance. I reckon there's enough territory in Oregon so's we don't have to build our spread right next to a sheep ranch. You got my word on that."

Waco grinned in appreciation of Lou's ability with words. Not only had he overcome their hostility, he had allowed them a means of backing away from their hasty negative decisions without too much damage to their pride.

"I'm already sick of this camp," said Vic Sloan, "and I couldn't last out the winter if I was of a mind to try. I'll take Applegate's offer."

"Reckon I will too," Del Konda said. He was twenty-one, from San Angelo, had brown hair and hazel eyes. His Colt was tied down on his right hip.

"I'm in," said Josh Bryan. From Uvalde, he was a year older than Del. His hair was black, his eyes gray, and his Colt was belted for a right-hand draw.

All eyes shifted to Alonzo Gonzales and Black Jack Rhudy. Alonzo was Mexican and had been the outfit's cook all the way from Texas. He had black hair and eyes, and carried his Colt beneath the waistband of his trousers. There was a Bowie knife down the back of his shirt, attached to a leather thong about his neck. While he

looked younger, he claimed to be twenty-one. Black
Jack had said he was twenty-three, and he looked it. He
too was from Mexico. While he had the black hair and
eyes of a Mexican, he had the high cheekbones and the
coloring of an Indian. His Bowie was concealed as was
Alonzo's, but strapped about his lean middle were twin
Colts in a buscadera rig.* Nobody knew Black Jack's
given name. The handle he used had been taken from
the game that kept him broke most of the time. Alonzo
the Mexican spoke first.

"If I am make this drive, I be cowboy, no?"

"You'll be a cowboy, yes," said Lou. "Applegate's wife
and daughters will do the cooking for the family and for
us."

"I think I go with you," Alonzo said, "if I no have to
cook. I start to feel like female servant."

"Damn good thing you don't look like one," said
Black Jack, "or you'd of been in big trouble by now. If
there's goin' to be honest-to-God females doin' the
cooking, deal me in."

"Since we ain't carryin' grub," Waco said, "we won't
be needin' five pack mules. What will we do with the
extra ones?"

"They'll all go with us," said Lou. "We'll still need our
cooking and eating tools when we reach Oregon. Besides, I have the feeling this will be one hell of a drive.
All the mules might not survive, and the extra ones
won't be extra anymore. We'll move out tomorrow at
first light. From what Applegate told us, the train won't
be moving out until June first. We'll have to drive them
far enough north of the river so they'll have decent
graze, and we may have to move them to new graze
every day. For sure we'll be driving them to the river to
water."

"My God," Sterling McCarty said, "we got to loaf
around these parts for two more weeks?"

* A buscadera belt had holsters for right- and left-hand pistols.

"Loafing hell," said Lou. "Except for Applegate and his family, we don't know these people. We'll have to watch the herd day and night. One good thunderstorm and they'll scatter from here to yonder."

"Like they done three times on the way from Texas," Waco said.

"But they're trailwise now," said Vic Sloan, "and not so skittish."

Red Brodie sighed. "Lou's right. Cows never get *that* trailwise. You drop enough thunder and lightnin' on a herd and they'll just run like hell wouldn't have it. If I got a choice, I'd ruther spend the next two weeks keepin' a close eye on the varmints than trackin' 'em down and draggin' 'em out of the brush."

"By God, Red," said Josh Bryan, "ever' once in a while you say somethin' so sensible, so smart, it just plumb amazes me."

"Damn it, Josh," Del Konda said, "now you've gone and done it. You'll have him thinkin' he's somethin' more than just a cow nurse, and he'll just be more impossibler than ever."

The rest of the outfit laughed at Brodie's expense, and it even drew a grudging grin from the redhead. "You sarcastic bastards," he grunted. "I hope you all get throwed and stomped in a patch of prickly pear."

Independence, Missouri. May 21, 1843.

"Move 'em out," Lou shouted.

While they had been a considerable distance south of the Missouri, the terrain was level, and they crossed the river an hour past noon. Riding point, Lou led them north. They would drive the herd several miles beyond the river and then west, avoiding the emigrant camps. Somewhere to the south they could hear the bawling of the cattle bought by Higdon and Quimby. When Lou believed they were somewhere due north of the Applegate camp, he reined up and waved his hat. It was time to bunch up the herd. The graze was good and the long-horns wasted no time taking advantage of it. Lou waited until the rest of the outfit caught up to him.

"We're near enough to Applegate's camp," he said. "We'll need to let Applegate know we're here with his herd and that we're accepting his offer to trail the rest of our cows to Oregon with his. Since we can't leave the herd unattended, we can't all take our meals together. I'll need to talk to Applegate about it, so I'll ride in first. I want all of you to meet the Applegates, so I'll take some of you with me. When we've had our supper, we'll ride back, and Waco can take the rest of you with him. Del, Vic, Red, and Sterling, you'll ride with me. The rest of you will ride in with Waco when we return. We'll stand two night watches. The first until midnight and the second from midnight to dawn. As you all know, if there's trouble with the herd, it usually comes at night, so five of us, including me, will stand the second watch. There'll be time enough to set up the watches after all of you have met the Applegates and we've all eaten. I don't look for any trouble, Waco, but if it comes, you know the warning. Three quick shots. Those of you going with me, let's ride."

Lou discovered they had driven the herd too far, and reaching the river, they had to ride half a mile back to the Applegate camp. Applegate saw them coming and walked out to meet them. Lou reined up, his riders fanned out on either side of him. He was blunt and to the point.

"Mr. Applegate, we've brought your herd and ours. They're several miles north of here. We're accepting your offer of forty and found for trailing your herd and ours to Oregon. We'll need to eat and return to the herd so Waco and the rest of our outfit can ride in for supper. I think it's only proper that your family meet the rest of our outfit, and your womenfolk need to be warned they can't feed us all at one time. I don't know how you feel about it, but we wouldn't dare leave the herd unattended, day or night."

"Nor would I want you to," said Applegate. "I respect men who take their responsibilities seriously. Come along and introduce your men to my wife and daughters. They'll have some food ready in a few minutes. Then you can eat, ride back to the herd, and send in the rest of your men. We'll keep their supper hot."

Lou and his riders dismounted, following Applegate into the camp. The rest of the Applegates were waiting, and Jesse wasted no time announcing the good news.

"Yipeee," young Jud shouted. "Texas cowboys."

Sarah, Sandy, and Vangie were all smiles, and Lou's four companions were staring at the girls in open admiration. These young riders had none of Waco's bashfulness where women were concerned, and Lou felt a sudden surge of jealousy. Sandy seemed to have forgotten him, smiling invitingly at his four companions.

"Sarah," said Applegate, "these men need to be fed so they can relieve those who remained with the herd. We'll save supper for them."

"Ma'am," Lou said, "I know this means more work for you all, having to feed our outfit twice, but I reckon there's no help for it. We just don't feel comfortable leavin' the herd unattended. When we return to the herd, Waco and three more hungry hombres will be along pronto."

"We understand," said Sarah. "Really, there's no extra work. Once we've cooked the food, we'll just have to wait longer to start cleaning up, until all of you have eaten. We're just thankful you're going with us, and we'll do whatever we must to feed you plentifully and quickly."

The meal was soon ready. Lou and his four companions hunkered down with full plates and big tin cups of scalding coffee. There were slabs of fried ham, potatoes, onions, beans, corn bread, and dried apple pie. When they had finished, the women collected their empty

plates, cups, and eating tools. Before anybody could ut-
ter a word of thanks, Sterling McCarty spoke up.

"Ma'am, when Lou Spencer was tellin' us about this
drive to Oregon an' suggestin' we throw in with your
wagon train, I just naturally thought he'd lost what little
sense he had. But after that feed, I got to admit ol' Lou
is a hell . . . er, whole lot smarter than I thought he
was."

His slip of the tongue bothered the Applegate women
not at all, but McCarty's face flamed with embarrassment. His companions roared with laughter and Applegate grinned. Lou caught Sandy's eye and winked. To his
delight, she winked back and something passed between
them. All too soon the moment passed and it was time
for the cowboys to return to the herd.

"First breakfast at first light," Sarah said as the five
men mounted, "and the second when the rest of your
riders get here."

The riders tipped their hats and rode north. When
they reached the herd, Waco, Alonzo, Black Jack, and
Josh were ready.

"Waco," said Vic Sloan with a straight face, "I ain't
sure what kind of welcome you hombres will get. Mc-
Carty's been cussin' before the women."

"Damn you," McCarty howled, "I didn't mean to, it
just—"

The four who had witnessed the event again roared
with mirth as they recalled McCarty's discomfiture.

"Don't let it worry you, Waco," said Lou, drying his
eyes on the sleeve of his faded shirt. "Just keep in mind,
if you ever take McCarty to be fed, see that he only uses
his mouth to eat his grub."

The night passed uneventfully, and the following
morning, Lou and his four companions from the second
watch got first choice at breakfast. Reaching the Applegate camp, they found three riders already there. One of
them Lou immediately recognized as Jap Buckalew. The
pair with him wore rough clothes, flop hats, and tied-

down Colts. The trio stood facing the incoming riders, their thumbs hooked in their pistol belts. Lou and his men reined up just shy of the Applegate camp.

"Mr. Spencer," Applegate shouted, "you and your riders are welcome. I have asked Mr. Buckalew and his men to leave. They are not welcome here."

Lou and his companions dismounted, ground-reining their horses where they stood. Slowly the five began walking toward the Applegate camp, Buckalew and his men directly in their path. Without slowing his pace, Lou spoke.

"You men have been asked to leave. Mount up and ride."

"Applegate don't own this land," Buckalew sneered, "and neither do you. I'm here to court Miss Sandy, and that's between me and her."

"Then we'll let her decide whether you stay or go," said Lou. "Sandy?"

"I wouldn't have Jap Buckalew if he was the last man on earth," Sandy said furiously. "I want him to go, and if I never see him again, it'll be too soon."

While Buckalew and one of his men hesitated, the third became victim of poor judgment. He went for his gun, and before he cleared leather, Lou's slug tore into his shoulder. He stumbled backward, his companion catching him before he fell.

"I allow a man one mistake," said Lou quietly. "Draw on me again, any one of you, and I'll kill you. And Buckalew, when you're tempted to ride back this way, keep in mind that from here to Oregon me and my outfit are part of Mr. Applegate's train. There's nine of us, and not a damn one that's opposed to shootin' a skunk that's needful of it."

The trio mounted, the wounded man doing so with difficulty. Without a word they rode west, none of them looking back.

"I'm sorry it came to this," Applegate said when the five men reached camp.

"He pulled on me," said Lou. "With Buckalew's kind, it had to come sooner or later, and I'd as soon have it out in the open. In Texas you aim for somebody to dance to your tune, you'd best be a damn good fiddler. The varmint siding Buckalew should of stayed out of the dance."

"Buckalew has eight men just as rough as the two he had with him today," Applegate said, "and they're all armed. Yet he has only one wagon. Perhaps I'm being unfair to the man, but I suspect he has something far more devious in mind than just getting those hundred and ninety wagons to Oregon."

As Sandy filled Lou's breakfast plate she said, "I'm so glad you're going with us. I just want all of you to be careful. That man was about to shoot you, just as Buckalew tried to yesterday."

Applegate raised his eyebrows. "What about yesterday?"

"I didn't tell you," Sandy said, "because I didn't want you to worry. That's how I met Lou and Waco. Buckalew was bothering me, and Lou knocked him down. He reached for his gun but Waco had him covered."

"Waco should of shot the snake-eyed bastard," said Jud.

"Jud," Sarah cried, "you watch your . . ."

But her reprimand was drowned out. Sandy and Vangie laughed while the cowboys roared, some of them spilling their coffee. When the laughter died down it was Lou who spoke.

"Dying is almighty permanent. You don't kill a man unless he won't have it any other way. I've seen better men than Buckalew cash in with a belly full of lead or at the business end of a rope. I hear it's a long trail to Oregon. Ever'body won't make it, and if this Buckalew don't mend his ways, he may be one of them."

All too soon the meal was finished and the cowboys had to ride back to the herd so the rest of the outfit could eat. They tipped their hats to the women and swung into their saddles. Lou looked back and Sandy smiled.

Vangie giggled. "Sandy's got her bonnet set for Lou."

"I hope she has," said Jud, dead serious. "Marry him, Sandy, so's he won't ride away when we get to Oregon."

"Jud," Sandy cried, blushing furiously. She ducked her head, hiding her face, but there was a smile on it.

In the days that followed, Lou and his outfit took turns riding among the rest of the emigrants in Applegate's party. In addition to the teams of oxen drawing their wagons, most families had only two or three cows and two to four mules. The family with the goats had only a dozen, and to the relief of the cowboys, there were just thirty sheep. Each family had two or more sons to tend the extra stock. Just as Applegate had said, the seven riders who would trail the Higdon and Quimby herds were Texans, and it turned out that Lou and his outfit knew three of them. One of them was a half-breed known as Indian Charlie, another was Tobe Hiram, and a third was the trail boss, Dillard Sumner. The others— Kage Copeland, Pete Haby, Tull Irvin, and Dub Stern— were typical Texas cowboys.

"Ezra Higdon and Jonah Quimby are feedin' us from the same camp," said Dillard Sumner. "Since we're going to be trailing the herds together anyhow, why don't we go ahead and combine your five thousand head with our three thousand? There's sixteen of us, and with us all taking one watch and your outfit the other, it'll be easier on both outfits."

"I'll buy that," Lou said. "There's nine of us, so we'll take the second watch. Seems if there's trouble with a herd, it always comes in the small hours of the morning. That's when extra riders are needed."

"That be good," said Indian Charlie, "but there be somethin' better. With two outfits, there be no rush to eat. When you hombres be done with second watch, we be awake, watching the *vacas* while you enjoy your meals. Then we eat. There be no hurry."

"By God," Waco said, "he's got somethin' there. Unless all hell breaks loose during the night, every man of us will start the day with at least five or six hours of sleep."

"Damn it," said Sterling McCarty, "I hate to admit it, but this drive to Oregon may not be half bad. In all my days of cowboyin', I can't recollect ever havin' enough sleep or enough grub all at the same time."

"Lou," Dillard Sumner said, "the mercantile in town just got in some more long guns from St. Louis. You'd do well to arm all your outfit with one, like we have. They're .50 caliber Hawkens. Ain't none better."*

"So I've heard," said Lou. "We'll take that advice. We don't know what lies ahead. I don't much like the idea of standin' off a bunch of outlaws or a band of hostile Indians with Colts."

"There must be Injuns between here and where we're goin'," Tobe Hiram said, "and if they're anything like Comanches, they'll be givin' us hell. Has anybody heard what the situation is, Injunwise?"

"Applegate hasn't said anything to us about it," said Lou. "I doubt that he knows, one way or the other. Except for the several wagon trains that have already gone, this is somethin' that nobody's ever done before. I expect we'll just have to go prepared for trouble."

The four riders with whom Lou's outfit were unfamiliar—Kage Copeland, Pete Haby, Tull Irvin, and Dub Stern—had been listening with interest but had contributed nothing to the discussion. Dillard Sumner sought to include them.

"You gents don't know Lou and his outfit yet," he said, "but by the time we reach Oregon, they'll be some

* The .50 caliber Hawken weighed 9½ pounds and had a 38½-inch octagonal barrel with one inch outside dimensions. Double-set triggers were standard, as was iron trim, a rounded buck-horn rear sight slightly slanted to the rear, and silver-blade front sights set in a copper frame. Many mountain men, including Kit Carson and Jim Bridger, owned Hawkens.

of the best pards you ever had. If you got anything to throw in, or maybe questions for Lou and his boys, speak up."

"I got a question," said Dub Stern. "I reckon you fellers know we've been kicked back to the tail end of the train into what's bein' called the 'cow column.' How do you feel about that?"

"Fortunate," Lou said, "considerin' the varmint the folks at the head of the train have picked for their wagon boss."

Kage Copeland laughed. "I see you've met the tall dog in the brass collar who reckons he's nine feet tall. We don't think much of him either."

"He could take slop with the hogs and be in better company than he's deserving of," said Sterling McCarty. "Him and a pair of his pet coyotes was at Applegate's camp when we rode in for breakfast one mornin'. Lou winged one of the fools that tried to pull a gun. He should of killed the dirty lowdown sidewinder. It would of been one less we'll have to shoot somewhere along the trail."

"Lou always be softhearted," Indian Charlie said with a straight face. "He let sidewinder bite him twice before he shoot."

Appreciating the cowboy humor, they all laughed at Charlie's exaggeration, and it seemed to draw them closer together.

"We ain't seen this Buckalew but once," said Pete Haby, "and that was when he rode back and told us we was to keep our cows a decent distance behind his part of the wagon train. I reckon he's handed you gents the same warning, huh?"

"We haven't given him the chance," Lou said. "After that time one of his men reached for a gun, we ran the three of them out of Applegate's camp and told them not to come back."

"By God," said Tull Irvin, "I'd of give a month's wages

to of seen that. You hombres are Texans born an' bred, and I'm mighty pleased to be ridin' with you."

"We're pleased to have you with us," Lou said. "All of you."

"Damn right," Waco agreed. "I got me a feelin' about this drive. Long before we reach the end of this trail, ever' man of us is goin' to need a pard at his side with a Colt in his hand."

None of them ever forgot his words, for it was a prophecy that would be fulfilled. In spades. But Lou had something more to say.

"I have some serious doubts about trailing a herd of Texas cattle after a bunch of wagons. I look for trouble, and I look for it to involve every man of us."

"Then why don't we corral Applegate, Higdon and Quimby right now," said Dillard Sumner, "and straighten this out?"

"Give it a little more time," Lou said. "I've been wrong before, and I don't aim to jump the gun. When the time's right, I'll talk to Applegate. I want to see how quickly Buckalew gets those wagons across the river."

2

Independence, Missouri. May 28, 1843.

*H*aving liquidated all his holdings in Indiana, Jesse Applegate had built a false floor beneath his wagon box, and it was there that he had secreted his gold. When Lou presented him with a bill of sale for the cattle, Applegate had a suggestion that necessitated him taking Lou into his confidence.

"Take as much of your gold as you need," Applegate said, "but for the peace of mind of you and your riders, you are welcome to leave the bulk of it concealed beneath the wagon box."

"I'll talk to the men," said Lou, "but I see no reason why they won't go along with that. Otherwise, we'd have to use pack mules, and that would mean loading them every morning and unloading them at the end of the day."

After supper, after Dillard Sumner and his outfit rode out to begin the first watch, Lou told his riders of Applegate's offer as they rode into the Applegate camp for supper. To a man they agreed to the arrangement.

"I'd been wonderin' about how we was goin' to handle all them double eagles," Waco said. "My God, what if we had it all packed on mules and there was a stampede?

This is goin' to be unfamiliar territory all the way, and we might never find them damn mules."

"I think," said Lou, "we should each take maybe three hundred dollars. That should cover anything we'll need from town, including the Hawkens."

During supper Lou explained what they wished to do, and Applegate nodded his approval. "We'll wait until it gets dark," he said. "I'd as soon some of our traveling companions didn't see the gold changing hands."

"I won't fault you for that," Lou said. "When you're done diggin' out what we need, blow out your lantern. We'll come to the wagon's pucker one at a time."

The riders waited almost half an hour before the dim glow behind the wagon canvas was extinguished. Lou went first, quickly collecting his fifteen double eagles. Once he had vanished into the shadows, the rest of the riders came one at a time, following his lead. Applegate waited until the nine of them had mounted and ridden north before he exited the wagon.

"It was generous of you to allow them to leave their gold in the wagon," said Sarah, "but you're taking a terrible risk. I know there are men ahead of us, and perhaps some within our own company who would murder us for a lot less than what's under the wagon bed."

"Not if they don't know it's there," Applegate said. "Nobody's going to know that Spencer and his men haven't taken payment in full. Not unless they hear it from one of us, and that isn't going to happen, is it?"

"No," said Sarah, "and it would be foolish of Mr. Spencer and his men to speak of it. But there's already been talk of how much Higdon and Quimby paid for their cattle, and nobody's going to expect us to have paid any less. With Mr. Spencer and his men having no wagon and no pack animals, don't you suppose a devious mind might conclude that all or most of their gold is still in our wagon?"

Jesse Applegate sighed in frustration. "Damn it, Sarah—"

"Don't swear at me, Jesse. I have followed you, leaving all my kin and giving up the only home I've ever known. I don't often question any of your decisions, but when I have cause, I expect to be heard."

"All right, Sarah," Applegate said quietly, "there is some risk. But suppose Spencer and his riders had taken all their gold, loading it on their pack mules? Don't you suppose Buckalew's gunmen and others like them would be smart enough to conclude the mules were carrying gold from the sale of the cattle? Some dark night they could attack Spencer and his riders and murder them all. I don't believe our risk is that great."

"Mother," said Sandy, "Lou and his riders have stood up for us against Buckalew and his men. We can't be sure Buckalew won't have them murdered at first opportunity, gold or not. Even if we are taking some risk, don't we at least owe Lou and his outfit that much?"

Vangie laughed. "Nobody will get to Lou without shooting Sandy first."

"And me," young Jud said angrily. "Shut up, Vangie."

Sarah said no more, but stared nervously into the shadows beyond the glow of the dying supper fire.

"Before we move out," Applegate said, "I am going into town and purchase enough pistols to arm us all. Spencer was right. This frontier is a hard land, and if we don't adapt to it, we'll die."

"No, Jesse," said Sarah. "I have never fired a weapon in my life."

"Neither have Sandy and Vangie," Applegate said, "but all of you are going to learn. The time may come when you'll have to shoot or be shot. We are at risk with or without Spencer and his riders, and I intend to minimize that risk. Tomorrow each of us will have a new Colt revolver. God forbid that we should ever have to use them, but God help us if the need arises and we are unprepared."

Just after midnight lightning flared in the northwest, revealing for an instant a gray mass of clouds. While there was no moon, there was dim starlight, with no clouds overhead.

"Heat lightning," said Waco, "but we're overdue for a storm. Maybe not tonight, but sometime tomorrow night, for sure."

"Thanks," Red Brodie grumbled, "I needed that. We ain't had a good ground-thumpin' stampede in near a month. That's all we need, havin' this bunch scatter from hell to breakfast the day before we have to move 'em out."

Lou laughed. "The luck of the draw. With two thousand miles of God knows what ahead of us, it's a mite early to worry about what might happen."

Normally the riders circled the herd, but to break the monotony of a long night, they had gathered for a moment of conversation. It came suddenly to a halt when a horse nickered somewhere to the north, beyond the slumbering herd. Without a word the riders split. Lou, Sterling, Vic, and Red kicked their horses into a gallop, circling the herd to the east. Waco, Black Jack, Alonzo, Del, and Josh galloped away, circling the west flank. By the time the two groups of riders met to the north of the herd, there was no sound except the chirp of sleepy birds in the pines overhead.

"Damn," Waco said. "Who could that of been, and why was he here?"

"Nobody friendly to us," said Lou. "He hightailed it when his horse gave him away. I reckon we'd better avoid bunching, not more than two of us ridin' together. Half a dozen good shots could have gunned down the whole damn lot of us."

"Maybe it was somebody from the Applegate camp, or from the Higdon and Quimby camps," McCarty said.

"I'd like to believe that," said Lou, "but I know better. I've told the Applegates to keep shy of the herd at night, and Dillard Sumner has told the Higdon and Quimby families the same thing. Nobody else has any business near the herd, after dark or otherwise. I'll talk to Dillard in the morning. I reckon he'll talk to Higdon and Quimby, and I'll talk to Applegate, but I doubt any of them would have ridden up here in the middle of the night after being warned not to. If these people don't learn anything else before we take the trail, I want them to learn to stay in camp after dark, to stay the hell away from the herd. This drive is going to be mean enough without us havin' to look twice before we shoot, lest we gun down somebody from one of the wagons. In the dark we can't count on anybody bein' our friend."

The following morning, Lou told Dillard Sumner of the midnight intruder. It was a while before Sumner spoke, and when he did, his prediction was as grim as his lean face.

"I think some hombres in Buckalew's party is takin' an almighty deep interest in these cattle."

"I agree," said Lou. "But why? If we're to believe what we've been told, the last thing Buckalew needs is eight thousand longhorns. The bunch that named him wagon boss don't aim to be slowed down by a cattle drive. If he aims to rustle the herd, why not just wait until we get 'em to Oregon?"

"That's what I'd expect of him," Sumner said. "But for now, amigo, and likely along the trail west, I think he has something far more deadly in mind. You backed him down, shamed him, and I hear even some of his own gun toters are lookin' slanch-eyed at him. He ain't the bull of the woods he was before you come along. I think the hombre you heard last night was just waitin' for you and your riders to begin circlin' the herd again. The first rider comin' close enough would of been shot out of his saddle."

"And the varmint would of been gone before a man of us could have pulled a gun," said Lou.

"Exactly," Sumner said. "At night you got nothin' to shoot at except a muzzle flash. Nothin' but a damn fool is goin' to cut down on one of you at night if there's another rider near enough to return the fire. Maybe this

Buckalew varmint just has a mad on for you and your riders. Then again, he might gun down me and my outfit to lessen the odds for some other devilment he has in mind somewhere down the trail. I don't aim to take any chances. I'll be pacing my riders just as I'm wantin' you to pace yours."

Lou grinned. "I underestimated this Buckalew, and I feel like a damn fool, having you point out the obvious."

Sumner laughed. "That's the problem with Texans. We get to thinkin' we're so by God mean, we can face down any man. I'd almost have to agree with that, in daylight, when you're facin' the varmint. But when a no-account scutter back-shoots you in the dark, you bleed and die just like everybody else."

"Thanks for reminding me," Lou said. "You know the feeling. A man gets pretty damn good with a Colt, and he's just a short and sometimes fatal step away from thinkin' he's the best there is. Who was it said there never was a hoss that couldn't be rode and never was a rider that couldn't be throwed?"

"Damned if I know," said Sumner, "but it would pay us all to keep that in mind, whether we're mountin' a bronc or pullin' a Colt."

When Lou and his riders went to breakfast, he told the Applegates of the rider who had approached the herd during the night.

"You can rest assured it was none of us," Applegate said. "We don't own a horse. All we have are the oxen and two teams of mules. Besides, you told us to stay away from the herd at night, and I can see the need for that. Who do you believe this rider was, and why was he there?"

"We doubt he was concerned with the cattle," said Lou. He then told them of the possible motive he and Sumner had discussed.

"This is what I was afraid of," Applegate said, "and it's pretty much what I would expect of Buckalew. I'm going into town tomorrow and buy enough Colt revolvers to arm every one of us. You've stood up for us, and now you have Buckalew trying to kill you and your riders. The least we can do is be prepared to protect ourselves."

"*Bueno,*" said Lou. "You have to meet the frontier on its own terms."

Independence, Missouri. May 30, 1843.

"Well," said Josh Bryan as the outfit was eating breakfast, "it looks like we might get the herd on the trail without any more trouble from Buckalew's bunch."

"Maybe," Lou said, "but don't count on it. A failed ambush usually just makes a bushwhacker a little careful."

They learned the truth of his words that very night, for the bushwhacker struck.

"Everything's been quiet," said Dillard Sumner when Lou and his outfit took the second watch at midnight. "I reckon Buckalew's bunch will get to us eventually, but for now they have a mad on for you gents. Ride careful."

"We aim to," Lou said.

They began circling the herd in opposite directions, five riders one way and four the other. They paced themselves so that if any man was shot at, he had a companion close enough to return the fire. They were in the third hour of their watch when the bushwhacker fired. Waco became the target. The first slug grazed his left cheek while the second whipped away his hat. There was no third shot. Waco's Colt was blazing, firing at the muzzle flash. Behind him, Del Konda threw lead to the left and right of it. When the firing ceased, the silence seemed more profound than ever. Waco and Del had dismounted when the rest of the riders reined up.

"No sound of a horse," said Waco. "We got the varmint unless he slipped away afoot."

"He could be playin' possum," Lou said, "wounded maybe, but just waitin' to cut down the first man gettin' close enough. If he managed to get away, he won't be back tonight. If he's wounded, he can't afford to lay there and bleed. Come first light we'll have a look. Let's get back to the herd."

Warily they circled the herd until first light, but there was no more trouble. They waited until Dillard Sumner and his outfit arrived before investigating the fate of the bushwhacker.

"We heard the shots," Sumner said, "but they ended damn sudden. We was pretty sure you didn't need any help."

"We didn't," said Lou. "Now that it's light, let's lope down there and see if we nailed the varmint."

When they found the bushwhacker, he had been drilled twice. Lou had no trouble recognizing him.

"Buckalew's man," Lou said. "I wounded him one morning in Applegate's camp, when he drew on me."

"Let's find his horse," Waco said, "and take him back to Buckalew belly down over his saddle."

"I aim to do exactly that," said Lou.

"You boys have had a long night," Sumner said. "Why don't you ride in for breakfast and then come back for this skunk? We'll find his horse and have him ready to ride. We'll side you against Buckalew's bunch if you see the need."

"Thanks," said Lou, "but I think Waco and me can handle this. Before we get to Oregon, I reckon we'll need your help. We're obliged for the offer."

Lou and his riders were nearing the Applegate camp when Waco spoke. "I reckon we'll have to tell Applegate about this."

"I don't see how we can avoid it," Lou said, "or why we should. Don't be surprised if Buckalew raises hell and uses this as an excuse to come down on Applegate."

"Hell's fire," said Red Brodie, "this varmint was salted down while he was tryin' to ambush us in the dark. That's self-defense, by God, whether you're in Texas, Missouri, or New York City."

Applegate angrily uttered an almost identical statement when told of the killing. "Of course Buckalew will deny any responsibility for this," said the wagon boss. "He purposely sent the man you had already wounded, in case the ambush failed. Now he can claim the gunman was acting on his own, seeking revenge."

"That's about what I expect," Lou said, "but he won't be able to hide behind that the next time. And there *will* be a next time. We're going to leave Buckalew with some things to think about. Some unpleasant things."

When Lou and his outfit returned to the herd, Dillard Sumner and Indian Charlie were tying the hands and feet of the dead bushwhacker beneath the belly of a skittish bay horse.

"Thanks," said Lou when Sumner passed him the reins of the bay. "Rest of you get some sleep," he said, turning to his riders. "Waco and me won't be any longer than it takes to deliver this buzzard to Buckalew, along with some hard words he purely ain't goin' to like."

"I'm bettin' this hombre wasn't the only back-shooter in Buckalew's outfit," Dillard Sumner said. "You gents better back your horses away from that bunch till you're out of gun range."

Lou rode out leading the burdened horse, Waco following. Lou rode southwest, intending to miss the Applegate camp. Reaching the river, they rode a mile before reaching the first of the emigrant camps that was with Buckalew's train. Men, women, and children stood beside their wagons watching in silence. It had exactly the effect Lou had expected. Several of Buckalew's emigrants, mounted on mules, began following. They wished to know where the dead man was being taken, and by the time Lou and Waco reined up facing Buckalew, the curious followers numbered a dozen or more. They paused, close enough to hear what might be said. The arrogant Buckalew stood there, hands on hips, saying nothing. Four of his men had fanned out, two on either side of him. Thirty yards away, Lou and Waco reined up. Lou wrapped the reins about the saddle horn of the dead man's horse and slapped the animal on the flank. It trotted forward, slowing uncertainly as it neared Buckalew and his men. When Lou spoke, it was loud enough for the emigrants who listened to hear his every word.

"This bushwhacking varmint took a shot at us last night, Buckalew. He missed. We didn't."

Buckalew responded as expected. "He wasn't actin' on my orders. He had a mad on for you after you shot him. I had no idea he was gunnin' fer you."

"I'm sure you didn't," Lou said, his words dripping with sarcasm. "I only toted him here to tell you what you can expect the next time one of your gun dogs cuts down on me or any man in my outfit."

"Speak your piece," snarled Buckalew, "and then get the hell out of my camp."

"I'm coming after you, Buckalew," Lou said. "I'll bring my riders to side me, in case some of your bunch decides to do something foolish, so you can't hide behind them. It'll be just you and me. *Comprender*?"

Buckalew said nothing. Unwilling to turn their backs on Buckalew and his men, Lou and Waco backstepped their horses until they were out of range.

"Mister," one of the emigrants asked as Lou and Waco rode past, "is that gospel, what you just said, that you was shot at in the dark?"

"Every word," said Lou grimly. "You and your folks are drivin' your ducks to a bad market, friend."

The man shook his head, turned to his friends, and the lot of them looked uncertainly at Buckalew and his men. Two of them were removing the body of the dead man from the horse.

"We ought to ride back by Applegate's camp," Waco said. "They'll all be wonderin' what happened when we faced Buckalew."

"I aim to have another serious talk with Applegate sometime today," said Lou, "but first we need to talk to

Dillard Sumner and his outfit. They'll be neck-deep in the fight when Buckalew comes down on us. Higdon and Quimby own three thousand head of this herd, and I want Dill to find out how committed they are to this 'cow column' foolishness Buckalew's trying to enforce."

Waco laughed. "If I'm gettin' your drift, you aim to tell Buckalew to take his orders and stick 'em. Knowin' you, I reckon we won't be playin' by his rules."

"You got it," Lou said, "but I don't aim to say it but once. So you'll have to wait till we reach the herd, when I tell the others."

Once they reached the herd, Lou and Dillard Sumner gathered his riders.

Except for Lou and Waco, their outfit was asleep, having been off the second watch not more than two hours. They awoke grousing and grumbling.

"Hell," McCarty growled, "we ain't slept more'n an hour."

"What I have to say won't take more than a few minutes," said Lou, "and after that you'll have the rest of the day. Before we move out tomorrow, there's a question we need answered and a decision that's got to be made. Dill, the question involves you and your boys. The decision will depend a lot on how you answer the question. Just how committed are the owners of your herd—Higdon and Quimby—to this foolish demand of Buckalew's havin' the cattle follow the wagons?"

"They don't like it," Sumner said, "but I think they've mostly been followin' Applegate's lead. Are you sayin' Applegate's about to tell Buckalew to take his cow column ideas and go to hell?"

"He will after I explain to him just how foolish and dangerous the whole thing is," said Lou. "If Higdon and Quimby won't stand behind us, tell them how it is on the trail. Tell them how it is when thirsty cows smell water somewhere ahead, how they're goin' to run like hell wouldn't have it, that it'll take more than emigrant wagons to stop a stampede. Wagons will be destroyed, oxen gored, and people will die."

"If Applegate defies Buckalew," Sumner said, "I can just about promise you Higdon and Quimby will side him."

"I want to be sure of that," said Lou. "I want you to talk to both of them today, because come tomorrow there'll be a showdown of some kind with Buckalew. By the time you've talked to Higdon and Quimby, I will have found a place for us to cross the river somewhere north of the usual crossing. The one Buckalew's wagons will be using."

"By God, you're right," Sumner said. "He'll be crossing the Missouri about where it bends to the east, and I think I see what you're gettin' at. With all them wagons, it'll take Buckalew's bunch all day, just gettin' 'em across the river. Longer, if anything breaks."

"You're damn right it will," said Black Jack Rhudy, "and our cows will be settin' on their hunkers waitin' for Buckalew's wagons to get out of our way. If he can shove us to the rear so's our cows don't slow down his wagons, then we can feed him a dose of his own medicine."

"That's the decision we have to make," Lou said. "Do we waste two days waitin' for Buckalew's wagons to get ahead of us, or do we find our own crossing and take the lead?"

"We take the lead," they shouted in a single voice.

"I'll take Waco with me," said Lou, "and by the time we have word from Higdon and Quimby, we'll also have a place where we can get our cattle and wagons across the river without following Buckalew's train. Then we'll ride back to Applegate's camp and have some serious talk."

Lou and Waco rode north another mile and then west until they reached the Missouri well above the crossing earlier wagon trains had taken.

"We'll ride upriver first," Lou said. "I want us distant

enough so that Buckalew can't possibly claim we're interfering with his crossing."

"Pard," said Waco, "you know damn well it ain't goin' to matter a whit how far away we are. We'll have a fight with Buckalew because we're gettin' ahead of him. He's made a brag about gettin' his train to Oregon first, and we're about to make him out a liar."

"Buckalew has a bigger problem than that," Lou said. "He's used to pushing people around, and nobody's resisted. That's about to change."

They found a suitable crossing almost immediately. For twenty yards the river flowed over a bed of almost solid rock that extended beyond the banks on either side.

"Shallow water," said Waco approvingly. "Why, that won't even reach the wagon hubs, and the cows can walk across. This may be an even better place than the earlier trains have used."

"It couldn't be better," Lou said. "We can cross the horse remuda, the cattle, and the wagons in maybe two hours. Now we'll talk to Applegate."

The Applegates watched them ride in. "We've been listening for gunfire," said Applegate. "Thank God we didn't hear any."

Waco laughed. "Too many witnesses. Some of Buckalew's emigrants heard what we had to say to their wagon boss. I reckon we left 'em with something to think about."

"Mr. Applegate," Lou said, "I've sent Dillard Sumner to tell Higdon and Quimby what I'm about to tell you. What we have in mind will likely bring on a fight with Buckalew before we're out of Missouri."

Lou spoke earnestly while Applegate and his family listened. When Lou had finished, Applegate stood there for a moment, tugging at his red beard. Finally he spoke, and Lou didn't like his indecisive tone.

"Yes," he said, "I can see there will be an immediate confrontation with Buckalew. We more or less agreed to this cow column idea of his, and I feel as though I'm going back on my word."

"Mr. Applegate," said Lou, exasperated, "even if there was no danger of stampedes, this damn fool idea of Buckalew's won't work. His train has three times as many wagons as yours. In some rivers we'll have to cross, there may be quicksand. Bog down a few of Buckalew's wagons ahead of us, and you won't have to worry about crossing the Rocky Mountains, because we'll never reach them."

"Jesse," Sarah said, "you never gave Buckalew your word. You just took his orders without argument. Those of us who had cattle or who didn't want Jap Buckalew as wagon boss were ordered to the rear. If we cross the Missouri ahead of Buckalew and take the lead, how can he or any of his selfish people claim we're slowing down the train? His wagons will be guilty of that."

"Lou's right, Father," Sandy said hotly. "Buckalew's making fools of us."

Applegate flushed, his lips tightening into a thin line. "You're right," he said. "All of you. I've justified Buckalew's foolish charges by allowing him to shove us around like pawns. Go ahead, Spencer, and I'll back you every mile of the way. If Buckalew wants his wagons ahead of ours, then damn him, he'll have to catch up and pass us."

"I'm right pleased to hear you say that, Mr. Applegate," said Lou, "because that's exactly what we would of done anyway. We're Texans, and we'll get these longhorn brutes to Oregon, come hell or high water. All you got to do is keep them wagons movin' and follow the drag riders."

"Yippeee," Jud shouted. There was excitement in the eyes of Sandy and Vangie, and obvious satisfaction in Sarah's. Clearly they had resented Buckalew's domination and Applegate's apparent acceptance of it.

When Lou and Waco returned to the herd, Dillard

Sumner said, "Higdon and Quimby are with us. What about Applegate?"

"He's solid," said Lou.

Lou and his outfit reached the Applegate camp early, and supper wasn't quite ready. Lou wanted time for some final instructions before they took the trail the following morning.

"Have all your wagons ready to move out in the morning after breakfast," he told Applegate. "All of you will drive due north until you see the herd. Follow the herd but rein up before you reach the river. We'll take the cows across first, bed them down well beyond the river, and some of us will ride back to see your wagons across. That's in case Buckalew rides up there with intentions of enforcing his demands."

They were well away from the Applegate camp when Waco spoke. "I'd bet my share of the herd that Buckalew shows up before we get them wagons across the river. Why don't we force him to draw, shoot the no-account sidewinder and be done with it?"

"I'm not opposed to that," Lou said, "if he won't have it any other way. But he won't go that far. Not yet. He's had Applegate and his people pretty well buffaloed, but a bluff's only good till somebody calls it. Buckalew's got that pack of easterners convinced he can back up his brag. Before they get to Oregon—if they ever do—the whole damn lot of them will be cussin' the day they ever named Buckalew their wagon boss."

3

On the trail. June 1, 1843.

*W*hen Lou and his companions rode into the Applegate camp for breakfast, there was nothing left unpacked except the utensils necessary for cooking and eating. Within sight of Applegate's camp were emigrant wagons being prepared for the trail. Teams of oxen had been yoked and were being harnessed to the wagons.

"They'll all be ready to move by the time we are," Applegate said.

When Lou and his companions were finished eating, Sarah and the girls had washed the pots and pans and packed them in the wagon. There were only tin plates, cups, and eating utensils to be washed and packed.

When Lou and his outfit were mounted, he turned for a final word with the wagon boss. "Come on when you're ready, and we'll move out the herd."

From somewhere beyond the Applegate camp came the plaintive bleating of sheep. "Damn woolly buzzards," Red Brodie growled in disgust.

Lou looked back and Sandy waved. He noted with approval that she and Vangie wore men's trousers and shirts. Only Sarah Applegate didn't seem dressed for the hazardous trail that lay ahead.

Applegate didn't waste any time. Within minutes after

Lou Spencer and Dillard Sumner had their riders posi-
tioned, the Applegate wagon rumbled into sight. Applegate strode beside the teams on the near side. Looped
over his wrist was a rope attached to the lead animal's
halter. Sarah followed her husband, while Jud, Sandy,
and Vangie walked on the opposite side of the wagon.

"By God," said Vic Sloan, "they're armed. Even the
kid and the girls."

Applegate had a Colt belted to his right hip. Sandy
and Vangie had followed his example, but not young
Jud. His Colt was slung low on his left hip, butt forward.
Some of the riders grinned at Lou, and Waco laughed.

"You'd better talk to the kid," he said. "First time he
pulls that iron, he'll likely gut-shoot himself."

Lou wasn't amused. "Move 'em out," he shouted.

The drag riders began shouting and popping the
rumps of the cattle with doubled lariats. While the
brutes hadn't lost their trail savvy, they just weren't anxious to leave the good graze and plentiful water. Many
of them bawled in fury when prodded from behind by
the horns of their companions, and in their frustration
hooked the animals ahead of them. Cowboys shouted,
ropes popped longhorn hides like pistol shots, and a
horse screamed when its flank was raked by a horn. It
was a bawling, horn-clacking commotion that Buckalew
and his bunch couldn't possibly overlook.

"Damn it," Sandy said, "I was hoping we could go
quietly."

"You've taken to swearing as badly as Jud," Vangie
said disapprovingly. "I ought to tell Mother."

"Go ahead, you snitch," said Sandy. "I'm too big to
spank, and all the soap's packed away in the wagon."

"I heard my name," Jud said. "What are you she-
males sayin' about me?"

"It's your prude sister, Vangie," said Sandy. "She says
I swear damn near as bad as you, and she's going to
snitch to Mother."

"You're pretty good, for a girl," Jud said approvingly.

"Vangie, we're goin' to Oregon, and everything's different. If you wanted to of been a Miss Priss, you should of stayed in Indiana. You go whining to Ma, I'll pull your britches down and hold you while Sandy takes a switch to your behind."

"You wouldn't dare," Vangie cried, her seventeen-year-old indignation getting the best of her. "You're just a little . . . little . . ."

"Bastard," said Jud cheerfully.

Sandy laughed, and Vangie ran to catch up to her mother.

Despite a few ornery bunch quitters, the cowboys had the herd under control by the time they reached the river. The first steers reaching the water were allowed to drink, but they were soon prodded on across, for the cattle behind were thirsty too. The crossing was orderly and the longhorns were driven far enough beyond the Missouri to make room for the wagons to cross. Once the herd was bunched and grazing, Lou selected some riders to join him in seeing the wagons across, to foil any scheme Buckalew might conceive to deter the crossing.

"Waco," said Lou, "you and Black Jack come with me. Dill, bring two of your boys and let's get those wagons across."

"Indian Charlie and Tobe," Sumner said.

The rest of the cowboys from the combined outfits were left with the herd. By the time Lou, Dill, and their men reached the river, seven riders had reined up before the Applegate wagon. Nobody had any trouble recognizing the bull voice of Jap Buckalew, but Applegate wasn't alone.

"By God," said Tobe Hiram, "there's Higdon and Quimby."

True to their word, the owners of the lesser herds had taken their stand with Applegate. Both men were heavy, bearded, and more roughly dressed than Applegate. Each had a Colt revolver hung on his right hip, and a thumb hooked in his belt near the butt of the weapon suggested that both men were willing and able to fight. Applegate seemed equally defiant, as did Jud, Sandy, and Vangie. Only Sarah Applegate seemed afraid. In view of this opposition, and despite his angry shouting, Buckalew seemed indecisive. As Lou and his riders splashed their horses across the river, Buckalew turned angrily on them.

"Damn you, Spencer, this is your doin'. The rule was made for this cow column 'fore you and your hardcases ever showed up."

"Wrong, Buckalew," said Applegate. "You told us how it was going to be, and we didn't have the guts to say no. These Texas cowboys have helped us to see just how dangerous and impractical your cow column is, and we are now doing what we should have done in the first place. We're saying no."

It was an impossible situation, and Buckalew knew it. He and his men faced a dozen Colts, three of them in the hands of Applegate's son and two daughters, all of them yet in their teens. Buckalew and his riders were forced to take water, and they did so with poor grace, backstepping their horses away from the Applegate wagon. But Lou Spencer wasn't finished with them.

"Buckalew!"

The burly teamster reined up, facing Lou.

"You're welcome to go ahead of us, Buckalew, if you can, but don't ever expect us to slow our drive for you. And if there's trouble—gun trouble—we aim to give as good as we get. Now get the hell back to your wagons, the lot of you."

They rode out, none of them looking back. Higdon and Quimby laughed, slapped Applegate on the back and strode toward the mounted riders.

"Well said, cowboy. I'm Ezra Higdon." He extended his hand and Lou took it.

"I'm Jonah Quimby," the second man said. "It pleasures me to have you with us."

Lou shook his hand. "These are my riders, Waco and

Black Jack. The others are with the cattle, and you'll be meeting them later. Now let's get these wagons across the river."

But the pair insisted on shaking the hands of Waco and Black Jack before returning to their wagons.

"Thank God that's over," said Applegate, wiping his brow on the sleeve of his shirt.

"It's not over," Lou said. "Just put off to some better time when this Buckalew reckons he's got an edge. Keep your eyes open and your gun handy. Now move that wagon."

The cowboys backstepped their horses, allowing Applegate's teams to go forward into the water. The Applegates splashed into the river alongside the wagon, the cowboys grinning as Sarah hoisted her dress above her knees. The wagons crossed rapidly. The Texans tried to hide their disgust when the two emigrant families crossed with their small flock of sheep.

"By God," said one of Buckalew's men when they had ridden away, "them Texans don't foller your orders too good."

"Just shut the hell up," Buckalew snarled. "There's always another time and another place."

"But the *same* damn bunch of gun-totin' Texans."

Buckalew shifted in his saddle, turning cold eyes on the man, but the man didn't flinch. Instead he just looked at Buckalew with an insolent grin, and the big wagon boss experienced a moment of silent panic. Each time he allowed himself to be backed down by the Texans, he was losing ground with his own men. Already he had heard rumbles of discontent among the emigrants in his train, for they'd seen a pair of the cowboys deliver one of his men belly down over his saddle. He'd been shot dead in a failed ambush, and there was open talk that the man's motive had not been revenge, as Buckalew claimed. That placed full responsibility on Buckalew, and he had caught some of his emigrants looking dubiously at him. Some eyed him with fear, many with

disgust, and not a one with respect. Reaching the bend
in the river where his train was to cross, he found only
five wagons had done so. A sixth had slewed sideways in
midstream, having slid off a rock shelf and ruined the
right rear wheel. The rim had cracked, spokes had been
snapped from the hub, and the wide iron tire had disap-
peared into the water. A hapless emigrant stood in the
water staring helplessly at the shattered wheel, his disabled wagon blocking the crossing.

"Get that damn wagon out of the way," Buckalew
bawled.

"It won't move on three wheels," the man cried helplessly. "The bottom side of the wheel's split and there's
just a spoke or two holdin' the hub."

A dozen emigrants waiting on the farthest bank were
watching, making no effort to assist their unfortunate
companion. Buckalew turned on them in a fury.

"Damn it, get in the river and take hold of that axle, as
many of you as can find a grip. Raise that side of the
wagon up, so's the team can pull it out of the water."

"Hell," said an observer, "it ain't my wagon." He
yelped when a slug from Buckalew's Colt kicked up sand
at his feet.

"Next time," said Buckalew venomously, "it *could* be
your wagon. Now some of you git in there and take holt
of that axle, or by God, the next slug will draw blood."

Five of them scrambled into the water and began
groping for the submerged axle. The owner of the wagon
scurried to his lead animal, taking the rope attached to
the halter. But there was no room for the desperate five
to grasp the wheel hub at the same time, and the sagging
corner of the big wagon remained where it was.

"One of you take an ax," Buckalew said, "and chop
down a tree the size of your leg. Trim it to a pole twenty
feet long. We'll have to jam it under the axle and move
the wagon a little at a time. Move, damn it."

In contrast to the difficulty Buckalew's people had
encountered, the Applegate train crossed the Missouri

without difficulty. Applegate followed Lou's suggestion and the wagons were lined up two abreast, Applegate's being one of the lead wagons. Applegate waved his hat, and the drag riders got the herd moving. Again there were some bunch quitters, but the herd was rested, watered, and well-grazed. Eventually they settled down, and Dillard Sumner rode to the point position, trotting his horse alongside Lou's.

"Higdon said Applegate has some kind of map of the trail," Sumner said. "We need to have a look at it, so's we'll know where the next water is."

"Here," said Lou, taking a folded paper from his shirt pocket. "Since we're taking the lead, he let me keep the map. With two trains gone ahead of us, I doubt we'll need it."

"If this is even close to right," Sumner said, looking at the crude lines, "we're in luck. We'll cross the Kansas River just short of where the Little Blue flows into it from the northwest. From there we follow the Blue all the way to Fort Kearny, Nebraska Territory."

"I'm figurin' that at something like 325 miles," said Lou. "From Kearny we'll follow the North Fork of the Platte all the way to eastern Wyoming Territory. I'm countin' that as another four hundred and fifty miles. That means for a good eight hundred miles we'll not be plagued with a lack of water."

"That's hard to imagine," Sumner said, "but I believe I can get used to the idea. Anyhow, with all these wagons, I reckon what problems we don't have with water, we'll make up for somewhere else. I'm wonderin' about that shot from downriver. You don't suppose we could be lucky enough for somebody to of shot Buckalew?"

Lou laughed. "I doubt it. I suspect he's havin' some trouble convincin' his emigrants he's the bull of the woods they thought he was. It purely won't help when they all learn we're ahead of them."

Buckalew's inept easterners didn't seem to understand how the wagon boss intended for them to use the heavy pole to advance the crippled wagon. Buckalew dismounted, cursing them for their ignorance.

"Mr. Buckalew," a man shouted from the opposite bank, "there's women and children present."

"Just shut the hell up," Buckalew bawled, "an' git in the water. We need help mannin' this pole."

He stomped angrily into the river, seized the heavy pole and rammed the butt end under the axle of the disabled wagon. "You," he shouted at the emigrant owner, "be ready to lead the team forward as far as you can when we heave the wagon level. By God, I hope the rest of you can use your backs better'n you use your heads. Git your shoulders under this pole, an' when I give the word, heave."

Tired of Buckalew's abuse, the men scrambled to obey. Nearest the wagon, Buckalew stooped, getting his shoulder under the pole. Six men behind him followed his example. Buckalew swiveled his head around enough to see that they were with him.

"Heave," Buckalew shouted. "Heave."

Slowly the wagon came level, but before the team could move it forward, the wagon slewed to one side. The axle slipped off the pole and the wheelless rear of the wagon chunked back into its original position. The men stood there panting, sweating, and it was a moment before Buckalew caught his breath enough to begin swearing again.

Fed up, several of the men seized the pole and again jammed the butt of it beneath the crippled wagon's axle. Buckalew shut his mouth, put his shoulder to the task and they tried again. This time the pole held steady and the emigrant urged his team forward. The wagon advanced a little, but settled back into the river when it was free of the pole.

"Again," Buckalew panted. "It's movin'."

Time after time they repeated the procedure, gaining but a few inches for their efforts. Finally the exhausted teams dragged the wagon free of the river, and the men who had poled it out fell on the ground, heaving for breath. Except Buckalew. He stood there panting, his hands on his knees until he caught his breath enough to speak.

"Git up," said Buckalew. "We ain't done. We got to move this wagon to the side far enough so's the others can cross."

"Go to hell, Buckalew," one of the exhausted men snarled. "You want that wagon moved any farther, move it yourself."

Buckalew responded with a boot aimed at the man's head, but the emigrant was big and burly as Buckalew himself. He caught the foot and with a mighty heave flung Buckalew belly down in the river. Buckalew rolled over and tried to sit up, but the water was over his head. Finally he got to his knees, spitting water, and found everybody laughing at him; even his own men, who hadn't dismounted from their horses. The man who had flung Buckalew into the river was unarmed, but Buckalew didn't give a damn. He reached for his Colt, only to freeze when a slug slapped the water just inches from him.

"You got what was comin' to you, Buckalew," said a man from the other side of the river. "Get out of there and start actin' like a wagon boss. We voted you in, and we can vote you out."

There were shouts of approval from men on both sides of the river, and Buckalew didn't like the way his own men were looking at him. Slowly he got to his feet, stumbling out of the water toward the disabled wagon.

"Now," said the man who had chunked Buckalew into the river, "we'll get the wagon off to one side, out of the way, but you'd best remember somethin', Buckalew. We're almighty fed up with you swearing at us and talkin' down to us like we was dogs." There were growls of approval from the rest of the men, and cries from some of the women who had crept close enough to hear. Buckalew seized the pole without a word, shoving the butt of it under the wagon's sagging axle. Other men took their places, shoulders under the pole, and a few inches at a time the wagon was moved to one side.

"Bring the others across," Buckalew shouted, "and don't git as far downstream as he did."

The Kansas River proved as shallow as the crossing Lou had found on the Missouri. Once the herd was across, Lou Spencer and Dillard Sumner waited for the trailing wagons. When the wagons had crossed, Lou headed the herd due west until they reached the Little Blue. From there they followed the river northwest, bound for Nebraska Territory. There were animal droppings in abundance, proof enough they were following the trail taken by earlier caravans. An hour before sundown Lou found abundant graze, and there he and the riders bedded down the herd. Lou then rode back and halted the wagons.

"Still some daylight left," he told Applegate, "but with all our livestock, it's best to take good graze when you can find it. We've had a good day. I'd judge we've come more than ten miles."

"I'm thankful we took your advice," Applegate said. "We thought we heard another shot. Do you suppose Buckalew got all his wagons across?"

"I doubt it," said Lou. "He's had some trouble. I think he'll be lucky to get all those wagons across the Missouri by sundown tomorrow."

Lou Spencer's prediction proved more than accurate. Buckalew's train had lost almost half a day freeing the disabled wagon from the river, and when darkness caught them, only fifty wagons had crossed. There were supper fires on both sides of the river, and gathered around them were angry men and fearful women. Children hunkered quietly in the shadows. The only sounds of revelry came from Buckalew's camp, for his men had bought an ample supply of whiskey before leaving Independence.

"Put them damn bottles away," Buckalew growled.

"We're rollin' out at first light. Besides, some of them easterners is Bible thumpers. All this drinkin' and hell-raisin' won't set well with 'em."

"Haw, haw," said one of the men, "what can we do that you ain't done already, and worser? They're already talkin' about replacin' you as wagon boss."

"You'd better hope they don't," Buckalew snarled. "I'll cut the whole damn lot of you loose with nothin' but horses an' saddles, wherever we are."

"You ain't scarin' us," said another of the group. "Way you started out, wherever we split the blanket, we'll be a hell of a lot closer to Independence than you'll be to Oregon."

They laughed, and there was so much truth in the statement, Buckalew could think of nothing to say. He sat there brooding, looking into the fire, while his men continued passing around the bottle. He too had a rough map of the trail ahead, and the many river crossings that awaited them did little for his peace of mind. It was costing him two days—perhaps longer—to get the wagons across the Missouri, and he feared that rivers that lay ahead might be far more treacherous. There had been a spare wheel to replace the splintered one, and they were still near enough to Independence for the man to drive back to replace his spare. But what would happen when a wheel or axle broke, was replaced with a spare, and the replacement broke? What was he to do with a disabled wagon when they were hundreds of miles from the nearest fort or town where help could be found? For the first time he was forced to consider the immensity of the task before him. He had actually believed what he had told the emigrants, that without herds of cattle to slow them down, their trek to Oregon would take far less than the customary six months. Now, damn it, by this time tomorrow Applegate's train would be two full days ahead. With him were those gun-handy Texans and the enormous herd of cows he himself had predicted would slow down all the wagons. Somehow, by

God, he had to catch up and pass Applegate, or face up to the lie he had so cunningly sold these dumb easterners. While in the river, when he had gone for his Colt, one of them had slung lead painfully close to him. To his dismay, they had more sand than he'd expected. His bluff had been called, not just by Applegate and his cowboys, but by the emigrants in his own caravan.

The fire went out and Buckalew's men had drunk themselves into stupors, leaving him alone in his frustration. While he had no idea what tomorrow held in store, he dreaded the possibility that it might be as bad or worse than this miserable day he had just put behind him.

There was laughter among Applegate's emigrants. They had not only the satisfaction of having traveled a good ten miles on their journey, they had defied Buckalew, taking the lead.

"I was afraid, at first," said Vangie during supper, "but not anymore."

The cowboys were sitting cross-legged, balancing their plates, while the women were just beginning to eat. Young Vic Sloan caught Vangie's eye and winked. The girl blushed, her eyes on her plate, but the devilish Sandy hadn't missed a thing. She laughed, digging an elbow into Vangie's ribs, and the younger girl retaliated by grabbing a handful of Sandy's hair.

"The two of you behave yourselves," Sarah Applegate said sharply. "Your conduct is disgraceful."

Sandy giggled. "Vangie's got herself a cowboy."

The rest of the Texans howled at Vic Sloan's expense, and he ducked his head, his face almost as crimson as Vangie's. The Higdon and Quimby camps were nearby, and they had taken supper earlier, so that Dillard Sumner and his riders could begin their first watch. Both Higdon and Quimby had taken a liking to Lou Spencer and his riders, and the two men stepped out of the shadows, hunkering down with the cowboys.

"I can't help feeling we got off too easy with Buckalew," said Jonah Quimby. "Lou, how do you and your riders feel about it?"

"About the same as you," Lou Spencer said. "When him and his bunch challenged us at the river crossing, I don't think he expected any of you to side us against him."

"He had every reason to be surprised when we stood up to him," Ezra Higdon said. "Until Dillard Sumner talked some sense to us, we let Buckalew tell us what to do."

"I reckon that's what we didn't understand," said Waco. "You don't have to be around Buckalew for long to take his measure. How long had the bunch of you been with his train when we showed up?"

"Only a few days," Applegate said, joining the conversation. "You see, we never actually trailed with Buckalew. When we reached St. Louis, we learned he was somewhere ahead of us. We caught up to him at Independence, and we originally were going to be part of his train. Then Sumner and his riders showed up with three thousand head of Texas cattle. When Ezra and Jonah bought the herd, that's when Buckalew kicked us out. Or at least to the back of the wagon train. The more I thought of it, the more sense it made, buying a herd and driving it to Oregon. When you and Lou rode into our camp with Sandy, and I learned you had a herd for sale . . ."

"I never understood why we had to wait for June first to move out," Del Konda said. "We could of left Independence two weeks sooner."

"I know," said Applegate, "and again we allowed Buckalew to intimidate us. It was his idea to leave June first. I believe he was hoping that more emigrants would arrive from St. Louis. People without cattle."

"That," Ezra Higdon said, "or he needed time to hire that bunch of gun toters that follow him around. I don't recall seeing them until we'd been here a few days. I think he got them out of the saloons in Independence."

"About all we can say in our behalf," said Jonah Quimby, "is that we thought Buckalew had some experience as a wagon boss. None of us had ever undertaken a journey such as this, and we believed we needed someone with experience."

"I reckon," Lou said, "you've changed your minds about Buckalew."

"My God, yes," said Quimby. "Don't rub it in."

They all laughed, including many other emigrants who had gathered close enough to hear the conversation.

"Now," Jonah Quimby said, "let's go back to what I said that started all this talk. So far we've stood up to Buckalew and his bunch, and they've backed away. I see Buckalew as a vengeful man who will get even, if he can. What can we do to protect ourselves?"

"When Dillard Sumner and his riders are with the herd on the first watch," said Lou, "all of us will be here in camp, getting what sleep we can. When we take over the second watch at midnight, Dill and his boys will be in camp. But you can't depend entirely on us, because if there's trouble with the herd, we'll have all the trouble we can say grace over. When the day's drive is done, don't leave your wagons strung out. Circle them two or three abreast, and then do your cooking and sleeping within the circle. Establish a first and second watch, just as we've done. Put four men on each watch, outside the wagon circle. Two of them should circle the camp in one direction and two in the opposite direction. Nobody leaves or enters the wagon circle after dark, except when watches are changed at midnight."

"That's terrible," Sandy Applegate said. "Suppose I . . . we . . . have to . . ."

Everybody knew what she was trying to say, and the Texan had to wait for the roar of laughter to subside before he could respond.

"It'll be dark," said Lou. "Hunker under one of the wagons. Unless you'd rather risk being shot."

· Again there was laughter, but it was brief. The cowboy was dead serious.

On the Little Blue. June 2, 1843.

During the night, clouds had rolled in from the west, and the dawn broke gray and dismal. Applegate's train barely had time for breakfast before the rain started. By the time Lou and the riders got the herd on the trail, a strong west wind swirled the rain into the faces of the longhorns and they became ornery. It was their nature to turn their tails to a storm and drift. The patient oxen slogged through mud that was hub-deep on the wagons, and the train slowed to a crawl.

But Jap Buckalew's train faced a far more serious problem. The rain had become a downpour and there seemed no end in sight. With less than half his wagons across the Missouri, Buckalew stood on the bank and cursed the rising water. . . .

4

The rain continued throughout the day, and as the Little Blue began to rise, Applegate's train had to move farther away to escape the backwater. Thanks to the continuing windswept blasts of rain, the herd was lagging, and Lou could no longer see the horse remuda ahead. He was considering catching up to it, having Alonzo and Black Jack slow the gait, when the sound of a galloping horse caught his attention. It was Josh Bryan, who had been riding drag.

"Trouble with the wagons," said Josh, trotting his horse alongside Lou's. "We looked back and they wasn't nowhere in sight. We reckoned you'd need to know."

"You're right," Lou said, "and with this damn herd fighting the storm, we're gettin' nowhere in a hurry. Do me a favor. Ride ahead and catch up to the horse remuda. Tell Alonzo and Black Jack to pick some high ground with graze and bed down the remuda. When we get there with the herd, we'll bunch the varmints and wait out the storm. Some of us can ride back and see what's wrong with the wagons."

"Knee-deep mud," said Josh.

"I reckon," Lou said gloomily.

The young rider galloped ahead and Lou looked back. Through the gray curtain of rain he couldn't even see the forward flank riders. It was the kind of day that, whatever little progress they made wouldn't be worth the strain on men and animals. Even when they bunched the herd, it would be a fight just to keep the brutes from turning their backs on the storm and drifting back the way they had come. He was beginning to wonder what had become of Josh when he again heard the horse coming.

"They've bunched the horses," Josh shouted. "Maybe two miles ahead."

He rode on back to the drag, joining his companions in their fight to keep the longhorns moving into the driving rain. They pushed on, and though it wasn't yet midday, the low-hanging clouds made it seem as though night was upon them. When Lou was finally close enough to see the first of the horses, he and the riders had to alter the course of the herd. Alonzo and Black Jack had taken the remuda almost a mile east of the Little Blue, and not just to escape the rising water. There was a large stand of trees, mostly sycamores. While the emigrants would not be able to circle their wagons among the trees, they would serve as a shelter of sorts for the horses and cattle. The animals would be less likely to drift before the storm. Lou breathed a sigh of relief as the lead steers surged into the forest.

"Won't be no graze under them trees," said Dillard Sumner, reining up beside Lou, "but that ain't what they're needin'. It purely ain't the nature of a cow to walk headlong into a storm, and they been givin' us hell. Why, we could of pushed 'em till them and us was ready to drop, and we wouldn't of made five miles all day."

"I couldn't see we had any choice," Lou said. "Besides, one of my boys rode in from the drag and said they could no longer see any of the wagons. I reckon Applegate and his bunch are in trouble back yonder. I reckon you and me had best ride back and see what's wrong."

"Damn," said Sumner, "you *know* what's wrong. They got them wagons loaded to the bows, and they're sunk axle-deep in mud."

The rest of the riders rode in behind the last of the herd, watching as the animals sought the shelter of the trees.

"Waco," Lou said, "there's trouble with the wagons. Dill and me are ridin' back to see what's wrong. The rest of you begin circlin' this herd as best you can. Just keep 'em under the trees so's they don't try to turn tail and drift back the way they come."

The two cowboys rode what Lou judged to be three miles before they saw the first of the wagons. The Applegate and Higdon wagons were beside one another and were indeed mired down to the axles. Other wagons, attempting to bypass the stalled ones, had also bogged down. Men tugged vainly on lead ropes while teams of oxen strove unsuccessfully to move the heavy wagons.

"Damn it," said Sumner, "that's a wet weather seep emptyin' into the Little Blue. They're caught in a slough that'll be mud for three days after the rain stops. If it ever does."

The cowboys reined up and dismounted a few yards ahead of the stalled wagons. Applegate and some of the other men stared at them helplessly.

"We've bedded down the cattle and the horse remuda about three miles ahead," Lou told them. "Your folks might as well unhitch your teams, find some high ground and put up whatever shelter you can. When the rain stops, you can likely get the wagons across one at a time, usin' double or triple teams. This will likely get worse before it gets better, and you're just punishing yourselves and your teams for nothing."

"If we don't circle the wagons," Applegate said, "we'll be out in the open, unprotected."

"Those wagons won't be goin' into a circle or anywhere else for a while," said Lou impatiently. "Now unhitch those teams and lead them to graze. When you get that shelter up, you start lookin' for wood—pine knots or anything that'll burn—for supper fires. Dark will come early. We'll have to eat in two shifts, because we can't leave the herd and the horses alone."

"Unharness your teams," Applegate shouted to the emigrants behind him. "Put them out to graze, find some high ground and erect whatever shelter you have." He then turned to Lou Spencer and Dillard Sumner. "When do you want supper?"

"Soon as possible," said Lou. "There won't be a first and second watch. As long as the storm continues, we'll all be circling the herd."

"Give us three hours," Applegate said, "and we'll manage to feed half of you. Then you can ride back and send the others."

He said no more, and went about unhitching his oxen, Jud helping. The Applegate women stood beside the mired wagon looking like a trio of half-drowned sparrows. The cowboys wheeled their horses and rode back toward the herd.

"They're a sad lot," Sumner said. "I feel kind of sorry for them."

"Save it," said Lou. "They have as much to learn as Buckalew's emigrants. I got me a feelin' this drive is goin' to be hell with the lid off and all the fires lit. It's hard not to laugh when I think of Buckalew convincing those poor souls followin' him that Texas cattle would slow them down. Hell, if we wasn't burdened with these damn wagons, we'd cut the trail time to Oregon by two months at least."

"Them longhorns' hooves will take 'em places no wagon will ever go," Sumner said. "Even Buckalew ain't fool enough to believe that, ignorant bastard that he is. He just needed an edge to get himself named wagon boss, and jumped on our herds because he didn't have nothin' else."

"Startin' today—or maybe yesterday," said Lou, "he's gonna have to blame his troubles on somethin' besides us and our cows. I'd bet my share of the herd less than half of Buckalew's wagons ever got across the Missouri, and with the risin' water likely over the wagon boxes, what do you reckon Buckalew's doin' about it?"

They laughed, slapping their sodden thighs with their equally sodden hats. But in their certainty that Buckalew could do nothing to improve his perilous situation, they were overlooking the possibility that the vengeful wagon boss might not content himself with waiting for the water to recede so that he might cross the rest of his wagons.

Buckalew had managed to get seventy of his 190 wagons across the Missouri before the swollen river prevented further movement. As a result, he had men on both sides of the river swearing at him.

"Damn you, Buckalew," a man shouted from the opposite bank, "if we'd of moved out two days sooner, we'd of crossed ahead of this storm."

"You'd be mired up to the axles in mud," Buckalew shouted back, "and you'd *still* be goin' nowhere."

"We'll name a new wagon boss," someone shouted.

"Haw haw haw," Buckalew laughed. "See if I give a damn. If he gits the rest of them wagons across in this flood, the job's his, and welcome."

The truth of Buckalew's statement overcame their hatred for the man, for the river had become a raging torrent hurling debris, broken limbs, and uprooted dead stumps before it. The emigrants had long since unhitched their teams. Men, women, and children huddled under tents or beneath their wagons, and those who had been fortunate enough to find something dry enough to burn had fires going. Buckalew had a piece of canvas the length of his wagon and a dozen feet wide. One long side of the canvas had been lashed to the wagon bows where they peaked. Stretched tight, the other side had been secured to oak poles driven deep into the soggy ground. On the lee side of the wagon, with the wagon canvas bearing the brunt of the storm, it was a better shelter than most. Somewhere, Buckalew's men had found wood for a fire, and the seven of them hunkered around it, drinking coffee from tin cups. They all seemed perfectly content doing nothing, and several of them grinned insolently at Buckalew when he stepped in out of the rain. It irked Buckalew, and he spoke more harshly than he'd intended.

"The lot of you had best better be oilin' and checkin' yer weapons while there's plenty of light to see. Later on t'night we got some ridin' and some gun work ahead of us."

"Hell," grunted one of the men, "come dark, it'll be black as the underside of a stove lid. Whatever you got in mind, why don't we do it now? With this rain, nobody kin see ten feet in front of his nose."

"Because," Buckalew sneered, "we're gonna pour some lead amongst them longhorn cows and see how fast the varmints kin run. You hanker to go up agin' them Texas gun throwers in daylight?"

That silenced them, and Buckalew laughed. "We ride at midnight, after this bunch of wagon jockeys has turned in."

Buckalew turned away and, hands on hips, stood looking into the storm. Behind his back his men grinned knowingly at one another, for they had taken his measure. The Applegate train was now two full days ahead, and his claim that the Texas cattle would slow the trek to Oregon was fast becoming an obvious lie. Even Buckalew's gun toters saw his plan for the night as the mean, low-down scheme it was. Buckalew aimed to make good his brag and buy himself some time by stampeding the cattle. The seven now eyed one another, and their smirks had vanished, for they recalled the grim-faced Texas cowboys with their tied-down Colts. . . .

Allowing Applegate the three hours he had requested, Dillard Sumner and his six companions rode back to the stranded wagons for supper. Applegate's tent had been set up, while others—including Higdon and Quimby— had set up canvas shelters either behind or to the sides of the wagons. Beneath the shelters, the men had cut and laid poles side by side, getting them out of the axle-deep mud that trapped the wagons. Since Higdon and Quimby had no children, they and their wives had gathered at the Applegate supper fire.

"With Higdon, Quimby, and me all owning cattle," Applegate said, "we've decided to share provisions and a common fire. It'll be easier on our women, especially at times like this."

"Glad to hear it," said Sumner. "You'll have to help one another, else this Oregon Trail will be bigger an' meaner than any of you can face alone. Once this rain lets up, it'll take your oxen and those of your neighbor just to free one wagon."

"Well said," Higdon replied. "We've learned something today."

Despite the rain, the mud, and a shortage of dry wood, the emigrant women had turned out a meal that dazzled the Texans. There were broiled slabs of bacon, beans, fried onions, corn bread, and plenty of hot coffee.

"Sorry there was no apple pie," said Sarah Applegate. "We're saving that to celebrate the end of the storm and the freeing of our wagons."

"Ma'am," Dub Stern said, "was we on this trail by ourselves, providin' our own grub, we'd all be chawin' jerked beef and drinkin' rainwater. I never et this good at my own mama's table."

None of the riders could top that, so they tipped their hats and rode back to the herd, the laughter of the women ringing in their ears. Reaching the herd, Sumner and his men dismounted. Red Brodie studied them critically before he spoke.

"Must of been some hell of a meal. Here we all stand, in mud nigh to our boot tops, an' you varmints looks as content as a bunch of corn-fed geese."

"Reason fer that," said Tull Irvin, "is that we et it all. We told them emigrant women the rest of you jaybirds wasn't hungry, and they didn't want to throw it out."

He had spoken as seriously as he could, but the laughter of his six companions gave him away.

"You hombres mount up and ride," Dillard Sumner said. "You won't believe the grub these emigrant women is dishin' up, knee-deep in mud and in the midst of a storm. The Applegates, Higdons, and Quimbys is sharin' grub and a common fire. I don't know about them emigrants in Buckalew's train, but I'd say there's hope for the folks in ours."

Lou and his riders could only agree. The food was all any cowboy had the right to expect, without the stranded wagons and the storm-inflicted misery, and the cheerfulness of these people was unmistakably genuine. Lou was hunkered beneath the shelter, his plate on his knees, when Sandy Applegate knelt beside him.

"Somewhere along the trail," she said, "when everything's not wet, muddy, and the wagons mired down, I'd like to ride ahead and see the cattle. Will you take me?"

Her hair and clothes were soaked, while soot—probably from the cook fire—streaked her face. Lou almost choked. He put down his tin plate and admired her for a moment before he spoke.

"I'd be glad to," he said. "As often as you want to go."

When Lou and his men rode out toward the herd, the rain seemed to have gotten harder.

"By the time we get back to the herd," said Waco, "it'll be dark."

"Hell," said Sterling McCarty, "it's dark now."

"Damn it," said Waco, "it'll be night. More dark. Stop actin' so blasted ignorant."

Black Jack Rhudy laughed. "He ain't actin'."

It was cowboy humor, and not having much of a sense of humor, McCarty pulled his sodden hat over his eyes and bore their laughter as best he could.

"I reckon," said Lou as they neared the herd, "there's no point havin' two watches tonight, unless some of you figure you can sleep in the mud with rain in your face. Anybody arguin' with that?"

"Not from me," Waco said. "I can pull down my hat and doze in the saddle."

"Won't be near as bad as it might of been," said Del Konda. "We got a mighty good feed under our belts."

Reaching the herd, they found Dillard Sumner and his cowboys already nighthawking. Sumner and Indian Charlie reined up.

"We'll be ridin' with you," Lou said. "We reckoned we'd get more sleep in the saddle than layin' in the mud with rain in our faces."

"That's kinda the way we feel," said Sumner. "When the rain finally quits, it'll take them folks a day or two just to free their wagons. We can take turns sleepin' then."

"Suits me," said Kage Copeland, who had just reined up. "I purely ain't wantin' to leave the saddle again until this damn mud dries up. Besides, we can't take the herd on, leavin' them folks and their wagons stranded. I'd not be surprised if Buckalew don't figger some way to give 'em hell."

"I doubt it," said Lou. "With all this rain, I reckon Buckalew's got his hands full. While the rain and mud is costing us some time, it's costing him more. With all this rain, God knows when the river will drop enough for him to cross the rest of his wagons."

"Yeah," Sumner agreed, "and he'll still have ten miles of mud ahead of him to get where our wagons are now. We'll still be ahead of him."

Because of the driving rain and low-hanging clouds, it had been dark all day, but when what had passed for daylight was gone, the blackness became so intense, a rider couldn't see his companion at arm's length. They circled the drowsing herd and the horse remuda, Lou's outfit riding in one direction and Dillard Sumner's in the other. They had to depend entirely upon the savvy of their horses, for they could see nothing. Weary of the constant rain, some of the cattle became restless, and in the black of the rainswept night their bawling was the only evidence of their existence. Time stood still, for there were no stars, no moon, no sky. Ten miles eastward, Buckalew and his riders were having their own problems.

"By God, Buckalew," said one of his disgruntled riders, "you're as lost as a blind mule in a root cellar. I can't see my hand in front of my face."

"We ain't lookin' fer your hand in front of your face," Buckalew growled. "Just keep your mouths shut and listen fer them cows. We're downwind from 'em, and with this storm, they'll be makin' some noise."

"Hell," said another rider, "if'n that map of yours is worth a damn, all we got to do is ride to the Little Blue an' foller it. You know they ain't that far ahead."

"I also know the damn cows is ahead of the wagons," Buckalew said, "and I ain't wantin' all the Applegate people suspectin' who we are and where we're goin'. We bypass the wagons, an' with this rain to cover our tracks, them Texans can't prove nothin'. They sure as hell can't see us."

"No," said a rider, "but they can sure as hell see our muzzle flashes."

"God Almighty," Buckalew snarled, "what kinda shorthorns are you? All you got to do is hold yer damn pistols over your head. All you got to do is scare hell outta them cows, not shoot 'em betwixt the eyes."

That silenced them. They rode on, able to follow Buckalew only because they rode single file and one horse followed another. Occasionally Buckalew ordered a halt to rest the horses and to listen. Finally, from somewhere ahead came the lowing of a cow. There was a second and then a third.

"Good," Buckalew grunted in satisfaction. "We're far enough off the trail so's we missed Applegate's wagons. Now we got to git on the far side of them cows. I want the varmints runnin' back the way they come, maybe all the way to the Missouri."

One of the riders laughed grimly. "Like hell. Dark as

it is, and with this rain, when them cows scatter, you won't know where they are."

"Or where *we* are," said another rider. "We'll be damn lucky to find the Missouri ourselves, 'less we find the Little Blue and foller it."

Buckalew didn't bother responding. He kicked his horse into motion and they followed him in silence. He *did* have some doubts as to how they would find their way back to camp unless they followed the Little Blue to its confluence with the Kansas. Or they might simply ride eastward—provided he could be sure of his direction—until they reached the Missouri. Then it would be simple enough to follow the river south to the wagons. Once they had stampeded the herd and the horses, he wanted as much distance as possible between himself and the furious Texans. They would delay only until it was light enough to see where they were going. Then they'd come down on him and his men like the wrath of God. Under the circumstances, there was no way he and his men could be identified, and with the rain, there would be no tracks to follow, but would that spare him the wrath of the cowboys? But it was a thing to which he had committed himself, and he rode on, uneasy. Once more he reined up, this time for some final instructions.

"Nobody fires until I do," he said. "Yell your heads off, empty your pistols and then git the hell back the way you come."

He rode on, not allowing them opportunity to complain further. He was as anxious as they to have it over and done. Again they heard the lowing of restless cattle, and the sounds seemed to come from the direction Buckalew believed was south. He had to be sure they were west of the herd. The wind and rain still blew out of the west, and would make the hell-raising he had planned all the more effective. They rode on. The wind was in their faces, carrying the lowing of the restless cattle away from them, diminishing the sound. Finally it became so faint, Buckalew was certain they were well west of the longhorns. He reined up.

"Follow me," Buckalew said. "We'll ride south till we can hear the river, and from there we turn back toward the cattle. We're only goin' close enough to scare hell out of the herd. When you've emptied your pistols, git goin' toward camp."

"Lord A'mighty," said Waco, "the Little Blue sounds ten times bigger'n it was. It near drowns out the bawlin' of the cows."

"I wish to God it would," Red Brodie said. "Them damn cows is bawlin' like they was in dry camp, an' water's knee-deep ever'where."

"I reckon this is the most rain they ever had fallin' on 'em without a letup," said Black Jack Rhudy. "It's startin' to get on my nerves too."

Suddenly a horse nickered, loud and clear.

"Somebody's comin'," Black Jack said.

"Aw hell," scoffed Red, "not in this kinda weather. It's likely one of the remuda."

"Like hell," said Waco, cocking his Colt. "That come from the west, on the wind."

In the distant darkness, Jap Buckalew cursed, for it had been his mount that had nickered. He cocked his Colt, kicking his horse into as much of a gallop as was possible in the rainswept darkness. His Colt held above his head, he began firing, screeching at the top of his lungs. There were other Colts roaring as his men joined in. But Buckalew and his companions were in for a surprise. The Texans, who had weathered more than one stampede that had been planned by outlaws or Indians, did not limit their return fire to muzzle flashes. Lead whipped through Buckalew's hat and another slug burned the flank of his horse. The animal screamed and, despite the darkness, lit out in a gallop. Buckalew found himself caught up in the stampede, and a horn raked his thigh. It was a veritable sea of flailing horns, and when one tore along the flank of his horse, the animal began to buck. The horse crow-hopped its way clear of the stampede, and Buckalew could hear the roar of the river. In a final frenzy of bucking, his horse pitched him off, and Buckalew went belly down in the surging brown water of the Little Blue. He came up winded, spitting water, and unable to fight the powerful current. He was only able to keep his head above water as he was swept downstream. Without a horse, and unarmed, he wished only to get as far from the vengeful cowboys as he could, and the fast-moving river was better than stumbling through the darkness afoot. . . .

While Buckalew had no way of knowing, the stampede had been far more successful than he could ever have imagined. Already restless, the herd had lit out to the east like hell wouldn't have it, taking the horse remuda with it. Many of the Texans, endangered by the stampede, had been unable to return the fire of Buckalew and his riders. The cowboys barely had time to save themselves and their mounts, and few of either escaped without some hurts from the wicked horns. The receding thunder of the stampede was soon lost in the roar of the Little Blue. Lou Spencer dismounted, leading his trembling horse well beyond the river.

"Texans," he shouted, "where are you, and how bad are you hurt?"

"Skint up a mite," Waco responded, "but some no-account lowdown skunk owes me a horse. Mine took a horn in the belly."

Dillard Sumner's mount had met a similar fate, and while the horse was still alive, it had to be put out of its misery. One by one the riders made their presence known. Sterling McCarty, Black Jack Rhudy, Indian Charlie, and Pete Haby led limping horses. The animals had stumbled in the darkness, and to a man their riders were killing mad, for they had been pitched off in the mud, belly down.

"I don't personally give a damn if we *never* git to Oregon," said McCarty. "We got business right here. Killin' business."

"Bueno," Indian Charlie said, "an' the quickest it happen not be too damn soon."

"We can't do a blasted thing," said Dillard Sumner, "until daylight—or whatever passes for it—finally gets here. Then I reckon we'll doctor ourselves and our horses. We can't even do that in the dark."

"Hell," Waco said, "we got nothin' in our saddlebags but a few tins of sulfur salve. I feel like I got some busted bones in my left wrist."

There were other complaints, but as Alonzo Gonzales pointed out, "We all be alive."

"Come daylight," said Lou, "we'll ride back to Applegate's camp. He has a medicine kit. When we've patched up our horses, ourselves, and had some breakfast, we'll decide what's to be done next."

"Maybe *you* got to decide," Red Brodie said, "but I don't. I aim to find this Buckalew an' gut-shoot the varmint. Him and them yellow coyotes that's follerin' him."

"None of us saw him or any of his men," said Lou, "and by morning there won't be any tracks. We have no proof. You can't kill a man on suspicion."

"The hell I can't," Brodie said. "Who else besides Buckalew had cause to stampede them cows? Who, by God?"

"I don't know," said Lou, "but we can't shoot anybody on suspicion. I think you're right, that it was Buckalew, and when the time comes, he'll get his. But not on suspicion."

"We're so damn sudden with plans for killin' Buckalew," Sumner said, "we ain't considerin' the possibility that them stampedin' longhorns might of overrun that emigrant camp, maybe killin' some of them people."

"My God," said Lou, "you're right. We sent them away from the wagons, to pitch their tents on high ground. Dark as it is, we can still find their wagons by followin' the river. Even if the stampede missed them, you can bet it went close enough that they didn't sleep through it. We can see to our own hurts, those of our horses, and maybe get some hot coffee."

"Just a damn minute," Waco said. "Dillard and me ain't got a horse at all, and four others are lame."

"Some of you can ride double," said Lou. "It's maybe three miles, and we won't be ridin' faster than a walk."

Jap Buckalew was still caught up in the rushing water of the flooding river. Several times he could have seized roots or overhanging limbs, dragging himself out of the water, but to what avail? He would be afoot, stumbling in knee-deep mud, lost in pitch-black darkness.

Instead, he allowed himself to drift with the rushing current. Somewhere along this river would be the Applegate camp, and what better way to reach it than have the river take him to it? If the Applegate camp was near enough to the river for him to know when he was approaching it, he might slip ashore and steal a horse, a mule, or even an ox; an animal he could ride back to his own camp. There was, however, the unpleasant possibility that all or most of the Applegate train's livestock had been caught up in the stampede. For sure, the Applegates and their companions had been aroused, for ahead, on the sheltered sides of a pair of wagons, fires blazed. Even above the storm-fed gurgle of the river, Buckalew could hear angry voices. The water slammed him into the underwater root of a sycamore that overhung the bank. Buckalew used the root to reach the trunk of the tree, and grasping it, dragged himself out of the rushing river.

5

The Texans rode in to find most of the emigrants gathered at the Applegate, Higdon, and Quimby camps under the canvas shelters stretched from the wagon bows. There was a fire near each of the three wagons, and over each a huge coffeepot simmered.

"My God," Applegate said as the men rode into the light of the fires, "are any of you badly . . . injured?"

"Skint up some," said Lou. "We'll need the use of your medicine kit. But I think some hot coffee would do us more good than anything else. Were any of you hurt in the stampede?"

"No, thank God," Applegate said. "I believe the animals had slowed and begun to scatter before they reached us. Anyway, we wouldn't have been caught by surprise. The wind being from the west, we were all awakened by the shooting. We knew something had happened, but we recalled what you said about not leaving camp after dark. We had no doubt that someone deliberately frightened the herd."

"And we know who that someone was," said Ezra Higdon angrily.

"But we have no proof," Jonah Quimby said. "What are we to do?"

"Come daylight," said Lou, "we'll have some better idea as to how much damage was done. We lost two good horses, and maybe more. We won't know until we round up the remuda. We may have lost some cows too. All we have going for us is that the varmints who rode in shootin' wasn't able to get off that many shots. Like Mr. Applegate said, the longhorns had begun to run out of steam before they reached your wagons. Cows have short memories, and when they get spooked, they won't run far. Not unless there's somethin' or somebody on their heels keepin' 'em spooked."

"You didn't answer my question," Quimby said. "Buckalew's behind this. You know that as well as we do. Are we going to let him get away with it?"

"I'm open to suggestions," said Lou. "Buckalew's camp is within hollerin' distance of Independence, there's a sheriff, and we don't have one damn shred of evidence. Are you suggesting we ride in at daylight and gun down Buckalew and his bunch?"

"Well," Quimby said, "I, uh . . ."

"What the hell else *can* we do?" growled Red Brodie.

"We be in Texas," Indian Charlie said, "law be ridin' with us."

"But we ain't in Texas," said Dillard Sumner. "What we're in is a bad position. I'm with the rest of you. I want Buckalew to pay, but Lou's right. We can't just ride in and start shootin'."

"As much as I hate to admit it," Jesse Applegate said, "I believe we're going to have to gather our stock and allow this incident to pass. Am I being a fool, Mr. Spencer?"

"No," said Lou. "Buckalew will have a hundred witnesses to any act of vengeance. I'm not saying Buckalew and his bunch won't pay for last night. I'm saying that between here and Oregon, we'll catch him and his bunch with their britches down. Like Buckalew's fond of sayin', there'll be another time and another place. He's goin' to regret those words."

"You're sayin' that between here an' Oregon, somebody's bound to shoot the varmint," Red Brodie said.

"I expect somebody will," said Lou, "but it may not be us. I reckon he's in big trouble with folks in his wagon train, and he's about half hopin' we'll show up with fire in our eyes and guns in our hands. He could use that to turn the anger of his emigrants away from himself and toward us."

"When we don't ride in and create a diversion," Jesse Applegate said, "Mr. Buckalew will still be stuck with most of his wagons on the wrong side of the Missouri and many, many angry emigrants on his hands."

"I know it rankles hell out of all of you, allowing this to pass," said Lou, "and no more so than it does me, but that's what we have to do. At least for now. Come daylight, we begin our gather. Mr. Applegate, Mr. Higdon, and Mr. Quimby, do whatever you must to free those wagons. When you finally do, move them—the entire train—to higher ground, farther from the river. Until we get some sun, the ground anywhere even close to the river will be one long, continuous bog. Double or triple your teams of oxen, freeing one wagon at a time."

Nobody complained, not even the cowboys. Despite their anger and desire for retribution, they understood Lou's reasoning. There was a scattering of applause from some of the emigrants, especially the women.

"By God," Waco said admiringly, "if we ever settle down someplace where folks is allowed to vote, you oughta run for Congress."

"Oh, shut up, Waco," said Lou, embarrassed.

After escaping from the river, Jap Buckalew stumbled on, knowing he could follow the Little Blue to its confluence with the Kansas and from there to the crossing at the Missouri. Time after time he paused, hoping to hear a horse—or even a mule—cropping grass. But he heard nothing but the patter of rain and the continuing roar of the wind. His weary body drove everything from his mind except the fact that he was ten long miles from his wagon. His sodden boots quickly blistered his feet, and every step became agony. He cursed the wind, the rain, the darkness, his riders, his own fool horse for throwing him, and finally, the Texans and their cows. Buckalew fully expected the cowboys to confront him with drawn guns as soon as it was light enough for them to find their way back to his wagon, and he hadn't even the faintest idea where his men were. Had the damn fools allowed themselves to be caught up in the stampede and trampled? Buckalew wanted only to collapse and sleep, even in the rain, but he could not. As it was, he'd be lucky to reach his wagon by daylight, and he dreaded facing the hell-raising emigrants even more than the armed Texans. Since the Texans were with the "cow column," part of the Applegate train, Buckalew had hoped to use that to his advantage. When the Texas outfit had shown up, furious and armed to the teeth, that should have turned the farmer emigrant faction against Applegate and the cattle-raising emigrants, uniting Buckalew's train behind him. It would take some of the pressure off Buckalew if his emigrants believed their enemy was Applegate and the cow column riders. It had been a serious blunder on his part, not getting his wagons across before the storm flooded the Missouri. As he stumbled through the rain-shrouded darkness, he consoled himself with the assurance that the Texans would live up to his expectations, creating a diversion that would buy him some time.

Two hours before first light, the wind died and the rain became a drizzle. It soon ceased altogether, and the clouds began to drift away, revealing the last few stars in a purple sky.

"Thank God," Applegate almost shouted.

"I reckon this is goin' to work out about right," Dillard Sumner said. "I figure it'll take us a couple of days to round up the cattle, and I'll be surprised if it don't take at least that long to free these wagons."

"Soon as it's light, we'll begin moving the wagons," Applegate said. "Sarah, it's not too soon for you and the ladies to start breakfast. We have to make up some time. We've lost one day and may lose two more, but I believe we can still stay ahead of Buckalew's train."

"Damn right we can," said Red Brodie. "After this, they just ain't no way we're lettin' that varmint get ahead of us."

There were shouts of approval from the rest of the riders and from the emigrants as well. By the time the first gray of dawn touched the eastern sky, breakfast was over. The emigrants began hitching three teams of oxen to the first of the stranded wagons at the head of the column. But before the Texans could ride out in search of the scattered longhorns, they first had to find their horse remuda. Pete Haby, Indian Charlie, Black Jack, McCarty, Dillard Sumner, and Waco were without mounts.

"Those of you needin' horses will just have to wait here until we can find the remuda," Lou said. "The rest of you mount up and let's ride."

The ten cowboys rode out, following the wide swath the hooves of the stampeding longhorns had pounded into the muddy ground.

"Just our luck," said Del Konda. "The brutes had to run headlong into the horse remuda. We can't go lookin' for the herd until we find the horses, and the horses are likely grazin' with the cows."

"I doubt it," Lou said. "If you was a horse and them eight thousand varmints was rakin' your behind with their horns, would you keep runnin' with 'em? The remuda was at the head of this stampede. The horses could have swung out of the path of those cows. All of you fan out, keepin' to the outer fringes of this trail, and look for horse tracks."

They spread out in a three-hundred-yard line, and it was Vic Sloan who found where the horse remuda had separated from the stampede.

"By God," Vic shouted, "Lou was right. Them cows is

headed toward the east, but the horses cut loose and went north."

The cowboys followed the lesser trail left by the galloping horses, and soon found the entire remuda grazing peacefully.

"Some of 'em got a bad rakin' over," said Josh Bryan as the riders reined up. Some of the grazing animals had wicked horn slashes along their flanks.

"We'll drive them all back as far as Applegate's camp," Lou said, "and before we do anything else, we'll lay on heavy doses of sulfur salve. We don't want the blowflies gettin' at them."

Within an hour after departing Applegate's camp, the cowboys rode in with their missing horse remuda.

"Waco," said Lou, "when you and Dillard ride back for your saddles, drop a loop on your dead horses and drag them a mile or so north of the Little Blue. When we take the trail, the smell of death could spook the herd all over again. While they're gone, the rest of us are goin' to salve the wounds of our remuda. Now what about the four lame horses we led in after the stampede?"

"They'll all have a sore leg," Black Jack said, "but nothin' worse. We looked 'em over while the rest of you was gone after the remuda."

The cowboys set about doctoring the hurts of their horses, while Jesse Applegate toiled with his emigrants to free the big wagons from the mud slough. By the time Dillard Sumner and Waco returned, the Applegate and Higdon wagons had been moved to hard ground. Lou and the rest of the riders had applied healing salve to the wounds of horses raked in the stampede, and the Texans were at last ready to begin their gather. They rode out, sixteen strong, taking the trail of the stampeded herd.

"Without thunder and lightnin' to keep 'em runnin', I purely don't believe them cows would of run very far," said Pete Haby.

"*Si*," Indian Charlie said, "but they have their tails to the wind and they drift with the storm."

"Charlie's right," said Waco. "They was stampeded sometime after midnight. Between then and the time the storm died, they had a good four hours to just drift. We may have to foller the brutes all the way to the Missouri."

"I doubt that," Lou said. "They drift on the open plains, but give 'em any kind of shelter and they'll bunch, their tails to the wind. I hear there's plenty of open plains in Kansas and Nebraska, but we're still in Missouri. There's plenty of woods and thickets."

They almost missed the dead man. He lay on his back, and having been trampled into the mud, only one leg and a boot was visible.

"My God," said Del Konda. "My God."

The Texans reined up, and for a long moment looked upon the grisly thing in horror. Waco uncoiled his lariat, dropped his loop over the extended leg and dragged the remains out of the mud.

"One of Buckalew's bunch," Dillard Sumner said.

But they would never know the identity of the dead man, for what had been his face was bloody, unrecognizable pulp. It was more than they could stomach, and they backstepped their nervous horses.

"God," said Black Jack, "I wouldn't wish that brand of dyin' on nobody. Not even Buckalew."

"Mebbe that *be* Buckalew," Alonzo Gonzales said.

"Oh hell," said Red Brodie callously, "we couldn't be that lucky."

"Waco," said Lou, "you got a loop on him. Take Red with you. Wet as the ground is, you won't have any trouble findin' some arroyo with a bank you can cave in on him. Whoever he was—whatever he was—he deserves buryin'."

"Yeah," Dub Stern said, "and we don't need him layin' here to scare hell out of the herd when we drive 'em back."

"God," said Waco, "that's what I like most about

Texas cowboys. They're just so kind and thoughtful toward their fellow man."

"Enough, damn it," Lou said. "You and Red get it done and catch up. There may be more of them."

"Somebody else plants the next one, then," said Red Brodie.

Waco half-hitched his lariat around the horn, and Red beside him, they rode away. Their horses, fully aware of the macabre thing at the end of the rope, shied nervously. Lou and the rest of the riders continued along the muddy path left by the stampeding cattle. The sun had risen and its golden glow fanned out across the eastern horizon.

"*Dios,*" Indian Charlie cried, pointing. "I know how Senor Noah be feeling when he get off the boat."

"Hell, Charlie," Tobe Hiram said, "it ain't rained but one night an' two days."

"Mebbe," said Charlie, "but it seem hell of a bunch longer when it blow in your face, sag the sombrero over the nose, fill the boots with blisters, an' gall the behind from the always so wet saddle."

Red and Waco soon caught up. The Texans topped a slight rise and reined up, looking into a valley in which the heavy rain had created a temporary river. There was oak, sycamore, pine, and thickets of head-high underbrush.

"Plenty of water down there," Lou said, "with all the briars, thorns, and bushes any Texas longhorn could ask for."

"Damn," said Waco, "the varmints is likely down there, strung out all the way to the Missouri."

"Yeah," Kage Copeland said, "and look at them thickets. Hell on a man tryin' to swing a rope. Reminds me of them damn brakes along the Trinity and the Brazos."*

* Two major rivers in Texas. In the years following the Civil War, thousands of wild longhorns were driven from the brakes and trailed north.

"We ain't facin' nothin' we ain't faced before," said Dillard Sumner. "Let's ride down there and chase the brutes out, before they forget they're a herd bound for Oregon Territory."

When the rain finally ceased, Buckalew leaned against the trunk of a tree, exhausted. Dawn couldn't be too distant, and he dared not be absent if the Texans rode in, blaming him for the stampede. He stumbled on until at last he saw the welcome glow of what proved to be several fires. One of them, he discovered as he drew nearer, was next to his own wagon, and he could see men moving back and forth. Apparently his men had fared better than he. Reaching the wagon, Buckalew slumped down on the tongue. Five men hunkered around the fire, drinking coffee from tin cups. They stared at Buckalew, saying nothing, and it was he who broke the silence.

"Where's Wilson?"

"Dunno," said one of the men at the fire. "His hoss come in without him. Hell of a slash on his left flank. One of them cows hooked him an' he likely pitched Wilson off."

"Damn," Buckalew said. Wilson's fate didn't concern him. What did bother him was the possibility the Texans might identify the unfortunate Wilson as one of his men. Buckalew got up, went to the rear of the wagon and fumbled around inside until he found a tin cup. From the blackened pot hanging over the fire, he poured himself scalding hot coffee. Returning to the wagon tongue, he again sat down, saying nothing. His five remaining men—Kincer, Logan, Bender, Hawkins, and Gatlin—only looked at him, and their expressionless faces told him nothing. Across the Missouri, Buckalew could see other fires. Apparently, the disgruntled emigrants hadn't slept, reason enough to expect them to begin raising hell as soon as it was light enough to see.

"Any of you seen my horse?" Buckalew asked, turning his attention back to the five men around the fire.

"Naw," said Bender. The others said nothing.

The dawn came, and with it, activity among the emigrants on the other side of the Missouri. They were harnessing their teams. The river still ran bank full, muddy and turbulent. It was enough to bring Buckalew to his feet, and he stomped down to the water's edge.

"You people!" he shouted. "Where the hell do you think you're goin'?"

The emigrants across the river ignored him, while his men laughed behind his back. "Looks like they're goin' to Oregon without you," Kincer said.

It was true. Buckalew watched in dismay as first one wagon and then another turned north, following the Missouri. Adding insult to injury, the emigrants on Buckalew's side of the river cheered.

"Damn it," Buckalew snarled, turning to the five men still hunkered around the fire, "saddle up and let's ride. I got to see where they're goin'."

Logan laughed. "Hell, they're lookin' fer a place to cross the river. Just 'cause they can't cross here don't mean they can't somewheres upstream."

"Yeah," said Hawkins. "Damn shame their wagon boss didn't think of that."

"By God," Buckalew bawled, "I said saddle up and let's ride."

Refusing to be intimidated, the five took their time, aware that Buckalew had no horse except the injured one that had been ridden by Wilson. Buckalew turned on them in a fury.

"Where the hell is Wilson's saddle and bridle?"

"Bridle's in the wagon," said Gatlin. "Hoss come in without a saddle."

"I ain't believin' that," Buckalew growled. He dropped his hand toward the butt of his Colt and found the holster empty. He had lost the weapon when his horse had thrown him. The five mounted men laughed. Finally Hawkins spoke.

"If it ain't askin' too much, take a look at Wilson's

hoss. It's been raked pretty bad. It's likely a horn caught an' broke the cinch."

Buckalew said nothing. He went to the wagon, taking the bridle, and went after Wilson's horse. Without regard for the animal's wound, he caught and bridled it. Mounting bareback without stirrups was difficult, and Buckalew failed three times. His fourth attempt was successful, and he kicked the horse into a gallop, riding upriver. His five riders followed, grinning at one another. They didn't have far to ride. The emigrant wagons had crossed the Missouri. Several of the emigrants had poles and were testing the depth of the water. While the river ran bank full, the banks were low, with a flat, stony surface that extended into the water. Buckalew reined up, glaring at the men who were measuring the depth of the river. The emigrants ignored their wagon boss, wading into the rushing water.

"By God," one of the men shouted, "it ain't all that deep, an' the bed's solid rock. We can cross here."

"I ain't said you can cross here," Buckalew bawled. "Long as I'm wagon boss, I give the orders."

"Then you ain't wagon boss no more," somebody shouted.

There were yells of approval as other men led their teams in line for the crossing. Furious, Buckalew turned to his men, and they sat with their hands on their saddle horns. Hawkins nodded toward the river, suggesting that Buckalew observe what was taking place. Buckalew turned and found himself facing six of the emigrants, each with a cocked Colt.

"Turn your horse around," said one of the angry men, "take your gunslingers and ride back the way you came."

Without a word, Buckalew turned his horse and rode downriver. His men followed, exchanging questioning looks. Kincer passed the flat of his hand across his throat like the blade of a knife, and his companions nodded their understanding.

* * *

Lou's prediction proved even more accurate than he'd dared hope. By the time the sun was two hours high, the riders had five hundred of the stampeded longhorns gathered and grazing.

"Hell," said Waco, "this ain't gonna be no trouble at all. They went in the thickets to get out of the storm, but with all them trees, there can't be much graze in there. Come high noon, that sun'll be hotter than Hades. Then the varmints will drift out lookin' for grass."

"You're likely right," Lou said, "but what do you aim to do between now and then? Pull your saddle and catch forty winks?"

"By God, that's a good idea," said Red Brodic. "We didn't git no sleep last night."

"Hombre bet cow do any damn thing for sure be damn fool," Indian Charlie said.

"Truer words ain't never been spoke," said Sterling McCarty. "Let's ride in there an' run the rest of the varmints out here with them we already got. I don't know what'n hell Oregon's like, but I'm plumb sick of Missouri."

They all laughed, and shouting, rode back among the trees and into the thickets. An hour before sundown they drove more than a thousand head onto graze just north of where Applegate had begun gathering the wagons. When the Texans rode in for their supper, they found Applegate and his emigrants jubilant. Most of the wagons had been freed of the mud, and a day of continuous sun had hardened the once sodden ground to a noticeable degree.

"We'll be ready to move out sometime tomorrow," Applegate said.

"Unfortunately," said Lou, "we won't be. Reckon there's some truth to Buckalew's claim that cattle will slow down the train. Stampedes are part of trail driving, and there's never any way of knowin' how long it'll take to round the varmints up."

"This was Buckalew's doing," Applegate said. "Do you think he'll do it again?"

"I doubt it," said Lou. "One of his riders was trampled last night, and when we didn't play into his hands by going after him this morning, he won't gain much by stampeding the herd. Anyhow, he had a storm for cover. Otherwise, him and his bunch wouldn't have ever got that close."

"Man-made stampedes ain't usually the problem," Dillard Sumner said. "The varmints can run for any reason or no reason at all. A clap of thunder or a ball of ground lightning can scatter 'em from here to yonder."

"That's all too true," said Lou. "We had three stampedes on the drive from Texas. Comanches caused one, but thunder and lightning laid the others on us."

"Under normal conditions," Applegate said, "the herd should stay well ahead of the wagons, should they not?"

"I can't answer that," said Lou. "On a trail drive, I'd find it hard to say what normal conditions are. If nothing goes sour, we can usually take the herd a dozen miles a day, but you can't set your day's travel by that. You'll have wagon trouble, such as busted wheels and axles, and we'll end up waiting for you. If it hadn't been for the stampede, we'd be waiting for you now."

"Buckalew was just half right, then," Ezra Higdon said. "We can't necessarily blame our delays on the cows or the wagons. We may each delay the progress of the other."

"You're dead right," Lou said. "Buckalew's a fool to try and fix the blame on anybody or anything before he even takes the trail. Don't cuss the cows for bein' slow, because tomorrow the herd may be waitin' while you fix a broke-down wagon."

6

When Buckalew reached his wagon, it stood alone. The wagons that had crossed safely had moved out, and somewhere along the Little Blue they would again join their companions who had used the Applegate crossing. Buckalew reined up and sat there looking morosely at his lonely wagon. His teams of oxen had wandered near, seemingly anticipating their following the other teams drawing the departing wagons. Buckalew's remaining men rode past him, dismounting near the wagon. Kincer let down the tailgate and climbed inside.

"Damn you," Buckalew snarled, "git out of my wagon."

"After we get what belongs to us," said Logan. "That's all we want. Then we're ridin' on."

"Like hell you are," Buckalew said. "You're bein' paid all the way to Oregon."

"We're bein' paid by the month," said Bender, "and we're into June without seein' no money. We're givin' you them three or four days, 'cause we just decided we ain't goin' to Oregon. At least not with you."

Buckalew choked on his response, words failing him. From within the wagon Kincer passed rifles belonging to himself and his companions. He then dropped to the ground and closed the wagon gate. The five men mounted their horses and rode away, following the Missouri north. They would cross back to the east bank, where the emigrant wagons had crossed heading west.

"Damn them," Buckalew hissed. "Damn them all." They would ride back to Independence and return to the saloons where he had found them. The more Buckalew thought about it, the less inclined he was to hitch up his teams and catch up to the train. He had become wagon boss with the intention of using the position to his advantage, but thanks to his bungling and lack of experience, the task had been more than he could handle. Slowly, a plan began to take shape in his mind. Who needed the responsibilities and problems of wagon boss? He would catch up to the wagon train and go on to Oregon, but not immediately. The men Buckalew hated most were Jesse Applegate, Ezra Higdon, and Jonah Quimby, for their having bought cattle. The damn cows had surged ahead of the wagons, contradicting all his predictions to the contrary, causing him to lose face. These owners of the herd had money. A lot of money. Enough to make Jap Buckalew a rich man after he reached Oregon, if he played his cards right. But if his scheme was to succeed, he needed men. Not saloon hirelings, but men as devious and unscrupulous as himself. Men who were not content to work for wages, but hard men who chose to share the spoils when all the dying was done. With that thought in mind, he rode upriver, where emigrant wagons were still crossing and heading west. Ignoring the men leading their teams, Buckalew crossed to the east bank of the Missouri and followed the river eastward toward Independence.

On the trail. June 6, 1843.

Near the end of the third day after the rain ended, the Texans gathered the last of their scattered longhorns. Many of the emigrants from Applegate's train had watched the cattle the Texans had already gathered, allowing all the cowboys to devote their time to finding the rest of the missing herd. But despite all their efforts, the wagon train once bossed by Buckalew caught up and passed the Applegate party the day before the gathering of the cattle was finished. Although the train passed to the south of where the cowboys were working, the wind was from that direction. They paused, listening to the rattle of the wagons and the shouts of the teamsters.

"Damn it," Waco said, "they're gettin' ahead of us."

"It not be so much bad," said Indian Charlie, "if that skunk, that *bastardo* Buckalew, not be wagon boss."

"I ain't too sure that he is," Dillard Sumner replied. "Them wagons had to cross upriver, where Applegate's party crossed, and I doubt Buckalew has the smarts for that. If they'd been able to cross where Buckalew had started, they'd have followed the Little Blue, like we did. Then they'd have been too far south of us for us to hear 'em."

"Dill's right," said Lou. "We still have another day's work here in the brush, and that means they'll be two days ahead of Applegate's party. I expect Applegate will have some word for us as to who the wagon boss is. Whoever he is, he'd need horns, hooves, and a spike tail to equal Buckalew."

When they had finished their day's gather and rode in for supper, Applegate did have some interesting news.

"Their wagon boss is Landon Everett," Applegate said. "Buckalew's men deserted him, and Buckalew rode back toward Independence. Landon admitted they'd been fools, naming Buckalew wagon boss, and wanted us to rejoin their party."

"Maybe you should have," said Lou. "We'll be another day in the brush, rounding up the herd. They were smart, riddin' themselves of Buckalew."

"I agree," Applegate said, "but it's going to take more than that. The hard truth is, not a man of us has the experience for such a journey as lies ahead. You men—you Texans—have the knowledge of the trail that we lack. While I respect Mr. Everett, any one of you would make a better wagon boss than Everett or me."

"Whoa," said Dillard Sumner. "Not a man of us has ever been to Oregon. Our savvy of this trail is no better than yours or Everett's."

"No," Applegate said, "but you've come up the trail from Texas. You've faced hostile Indians and you've crossed rivers. Can the trail to Oregon be any more treacherous than those you've ridden already?"

"As far as the longhorns are concerned, I reckon not," said Lou, "but you can drive a cow where a wagon ain't got a prayer. You've seen how long it takes to gather the herd after they've stampeded. We can't promise there won't be more stampedes, more worse ones than what we just had. Now do you still think our trail savvy is worth the wait, everytime the herd runs?"

"I do," Applegate said.

"And I," said Ezra Higdon.

"That goes for me too," Jonah Quimby said. "Just because the other trains crossed the Missouri at one particular ford, you didn't bog us down behind Buckalew's train. You had the good sense to find another crossing. I fear that Landon Everett will make the same mistakes Buckalew did, blindly following the emigrants who have gone ahead of us."

"We've discussed this with every man in our party," Higdon said, "and we've reached the same conclusion. We'll gladly accept any delays caused by the cattle in return for the guidance of all of you on the trail ahead. Don't follow those who have gone before us if there's some better way. We want you to take the herd ahead of the wagons, choosing a trail the wagons can follow with the least difficulty."

"That still brings it back to one of us bein' wagon boss," said Dillard Sumner.

"I think not," Applegate said. "You must choose the trail over which you will take the cattle. All we're asking is that the trail not be so steep or so rough the wagons can't follow."

"We know as little of what lies ahead as you do," said Lou, "and there may be times when the only choice we'll have is the best of a bad lot. You may be forced to use three teams just to move one wagon. I can promise you only one thing, and I reckon the rest of the boys will side me. Keepin' your wagons in mind, we'll lead out with the herd, findin' the best trail that we can."

"That's all we're asking," Applegate said. There were shouts of agreement from the rest of the emigrants who had gathered to listen to the discussion.

Despite the lost time and the prospect of more, supper was a relaxed and happy occasion. For the first time, all the emigrants accepted the Texans, and the cowboys found themselves talking to many who had previously avoided them. This was most gratifying, for most of the families had at least one comely daughter of sixteen or more. Almost everybody seemed regretful when supper was over, especially the cowboys, but it was time for the first watch to ride out, and the second had to get whatever sleep they could.

"My God," said Del Konda when they had ridden away, "did you hombres see *that*? Old Waco was actually talkin' to a female, an' actin' like he knowed what he was doin'. I always reckoned anything in a skirt just purely scared hell out of ol' Waco."

"She was wearin' britches," Sterling McCarty said gleefully. "Now tell it true, Waco. You didn't know it was an actual she-male, did you?"

"God, Waco," said Red Brodie, "I never knowed you was like *that*." He rolled his eyes heavenward in mock disbelief.

"You skunks just keep your tongues a-trottin'," Waco said coldly, "and I'll lay my sweet nature on the shelf and stomp hell out of the bunch of you. One at a time or all at once."

They all laughed, swatting their hats against their thighs, forcing Waco to laugh with them.

Reaching Independence, Jap Buckalew bought himself a saddle, a Colt, a belt and holster. He then purchased a new suit and went in search of a bathhouse. His boots had dried and were stiff as barrel staves, but a good greasing would fix that. His bath finished, he stalked into a saloon and ordered a shot of whiskey. It was still early and there were only two patrons. Kincer and Logan sat at a table nursing a bottle, and Buckalew tried to ignore their smirks. He downed his whiskey and walked out. Damn them and their kind. He had found the whole sorry lot of them in the saloons, and obviously the pickings weren't going to improve until he raised his standards.

He strode down the street to the Golden Spoke, the most prestigious hotel in Independence. It boasted second and third floors and had its own restaurant in the lobby. There was a dark maroon carpet on the floor, matching drapes on the windows, heavy oak chairs, and every table had a red-and-white-checkered tablecloth. Breakfast was still being served to those who could afford to dine leisurely, and Buckalew studied the clientele. He avoided the men who wore derby hats or looked as though they had town jobs. He settled finally on a table where two men sat with their backs to him. While they were well-dressed, their hats were broad-brimmed, and there was the unmistakable bulge of pistols on their right hips beneath their coats. Buckalew avoided the waiter who was approaching, taking the table next to the pair of men who interested him. He appraised them boldly, and their hard eyes never left his. They had the look, Buckalew decided with satisfaction, of men who had run afoul of the law in more civilized places, for they looked upon him with suspicion. They were finishing their breakfast as he ordered his. While Buckalew waited, he continued to stare at the strangers, a half smile on his cruel lips.

"Pilgrim," said one of the men coldly, "I don't like bein' stared at like you got some plans for me I don't know about."

"Maybe I have," Buckalew said just as coldly, "and maybe you ain't measurin' up. I'm needin' men to side me on the trail to Oregon, but I'm wonderin' if the two of you ain't just a little too green. I've seen you somewhere, maybe in Illinois or Ohio. Or was it Indiana? I disremember what the occasion was, but you boys left town in a hurry."

The pair eased back their chairs just a little, allowing their coats to slide away from the butts of their pistols. But Buckalew had his arms crossed on the checkered tablecloth, and kept them there. He laughed and then he spoke.

"By God, didn't I say you was green? Was I the law, I could of took the both of you without firin' a shot."

With angry scowls the duo relaxed a little, dropping their hands away from the butts of their guns. It was the second man who finally spoke.

"We don't take orders an' we don't work for wages. Not to Oregon or nowheres else."

"I ain't payin' wages," Buckalew said. "The gents that rides with me gits theirs at the end of the trail, when I git mine. A share of a quarter of a million in double eagles an' a good eight thousand head of Texas cattle."

"And what would a man have to do for a share of that?" one of the strangers asked quietly.

"Somewhere along the trail," said Buckalew just as quietly, "he'd have to kill some folks, includin' a gun-handy bunch of Texans."

"We're not opposed to that," said the first man who had spoken, "long as the stakes are high enough. Up to now you said all the right things. We got a room here and we can talk in private. That is, if you got the patience for greenhorns like us."

The sarcasm wasn't lost on Buckalew, nor the fact that this pair were likely killers, fugitives from the law. "I'm a real patient man," he said with an evil grin. "Let's go."

He followed them to the second floor, and nobody spoke until the three of them were in the room and the door closed. "I'm Jap Buckalew," he said then, and kept his thumbs hooked in his pistol belt, not offering his hand.

"I'm Cope Suggs," said the heavier of the two. He remained as aloof as Buckalew. He nodded to his partner, and the other man spoke.

"Jedge Gerdes." The pair sat down on the bed, leaving the only chair to Buckalew.

Buckalew sat down, studying them. Both were at least six feet. Suggs weighed about 250, while Gerdes was twenty-five or thirty pounds shy of that. They were clean-shaven, but their hair was black as a crow's wing. Their eyes were a deep brown, almost black, while their mouths curved down at the corners, like they didn't smile much. They could be brothers, and Buckalew wondered if they were. They stared at him with no friendliness, still not fully trusting him, and Buckalew's thick lips curled in what passed for a smile. They were exactly what he was seeking. Men evil enough and unscrupulous enough to suit his purpose, and outlaws nobody would mourn when he was through with them. . . .

The fourth day after completing the gather, the Texans led out, trailing the herd northwest, along the Little Blue. There wasn't a trace of the mud that had plagued them following the storm. There was dust in abundance, however, and the emigrants quickly discovered a powerful disadvantage in having the cattle lead the wagons. Dust clouds descended on wagons, oxen, and humans.

"My God," said Ezra Higdon, "our first day on the trail—before the rain—the dust was nothing like this."

"We've had four days of sun," Applegate said. "I look for it to become worse as we travel farther west because of less rain at higher elevations. I've read about these mountainous regions, and they depend on snow, not rain."

Lou Spencer dropped back to see how the wagons were faring. Men and women trudged along, heads down, their faces just muddy, sweaty masks.

"Applegate," said Lou, "you're followin' too close. Drop back some and give the drag dust time to settle. If anything goes wrong, fire three shots. Our drag riders can hear them."

Applegate nodded, saying nothing, but Lou received grateful smiles from the Applegate women. Lou caught up to the drag, grinning at the sweaty, dust-encrusted riders.

"I reckon them wagons is still a-movin'," Sterling Mc-Carty said.

"Yes," said Lou, "but they're eatin' as much drag dust as you are. They're followin' too close. I reckon they're afraid to fall too far behind."

"No damn wonder they're willin' to put up with stampedes," McCarty said. "Applegate don't know doodly about bein' a wagon boss. Him an' all the rest of 'em is dependin' on us to lead this bunch to Oregon."

"Muy Dios," said Indian Charlie, "we not know hell of a bunch about this trail ourselfs. Mebbe we git lost lak hell."

"That's likely the only thing we won't have to worry about." Lou said. "We just follow the setting sun. I reckon there'll be trouble a-plenty. We'll just have to face up to it when it comes."

It was a prophecy that was fulfilled even more quickly than Lou Spencer expected. Applegate's party was an estimated sixty miles west of Independence, following the Little Blue, when they first became aware of somebody on their back trail. It was just getting dark when the Texans saw the glow from a distant fire.

"Not more'n a mile behind us," said Dillard Sumner. "Some of us had best ride back and see who it is. I don't like somebody at my back when I don't know who he is or why he's there."

"Exactly how I feel," Lou said. "Let's you and me ride back and see who it is. Waco, you and Tobe come with us."

No frontiersman rode up to a strange fire at night, and the four riders reined up in the shadow of some trees, three hundred yards from the fire. There was enough light from the fire so they could see the gray of wagon canvas, but nothing more.

"Hello the fire!" Lou shouted. "Who are you?"

"None of yer damn business," a voice bawled, "an' you ain't welcome here."

"By God," said Dillard Sumner in disgust, "it's that varmint, Buckalew."

"It sure as hell is," Lou sighed. "Buckalew," he shouted, "you're not welcome in our camp, or even close to it. If you or any of your bunch rides within gun range, you'll be shot out of the saddle. Is that clear?"

"Yeah," Buckalew responded. "We ain't interested in you an' that bunch of pumpkin rollers. We're peaceful gents on our way to Oregon. We'll just tag along behind, lettin' you damn fools break trails fer us. Much obliged, cow stink."

There was an evil, taunting laugh, and then silence.

"Come on," said Lou. "We still don't know how many men he has with him, but we've learned enough. We know he's up to no good, but we can't shoot him on suspicion."

"Damn shame," Waco said. "Sometimes I do fool things. One of 'em was that day in Independence when Buckalew was botherin' Sandy. You recall, he reached for his gun and I threw down on him. Damn it, I should of let him pull it and then shot the dirty sidewinder."

"I'd have to agree with you," said Dillard Sumner. "Now I reckon none of us will get that good a chance again. He's got somethin' in mind that we purely ain't goin' to like."

Applegate and most of his emigrants were anxiously awaiting the return of the cowboys, and Lou's report left them looking worried and uncertain.

"We can't stop him from followin' us," Lou said. "All we can do is keep him at a distance. That likely won't be a problem except at night. It's goin' to take all of us to see that he doesn't stampede the herd again. That means you men will have to continue circling your wagons and posting a watch from sundown to first light. Don't let anybody out of the wagon circle after dark except those of us taking the second watch. In Texas we used it against the Comanches, and there is no more effective defense. Isolate your own people and then gun down anything or anybody moving along the outer perimeter."

Lou and his riders unrolled their blankets to get what sleep they could before taking the second watch at midnight. To avoid the dewfall, Lou took refuge under a wagon. He had begun to doze when something awakened him, and he sat up, a cocked Colt in his hand.

"Lou, it's me," Sandy Applegate whispered.

"Lou eased the Colt off cock. "What are you doing here?"

"You said wher. we have to go to the bushes at night, to squat under one of the wagons."

"Damn it," Lou hissed, "not one with a cowboy sleepin' under it."

"It's so dark you can't see your hand in front of your face," she said defiantly. "Besides, I want to talk to you."

"Then talk," said Lou, "and then you get out of here."

There was a soft giggle somewhere in the darkness. "Oh, damn," Sandy groaned. "Vangie, you little sneak, why did you follow me? You knew where I was goin', and why."

"Yes," said Vangie, with an exultant giggle, "but I didn't know you was going to squat under the wagon with Lou. Caught you, didn't I?"

"You don't have a thing on me," Sandy snapped. "It's

so dark, you can't see a thing. I could be stark naked and you'd never know."

"Oh, but I would," said Vangie, trying mightily not to laugh. "You've already told Lou why you're here, and it's not just to talk to him. Already he's so flustered, he can't wait to be rid of you."

"You little hussy," Sandy all but snarled, "forget anything I said. I'm here only because I want to talk to Lou."

"Oh, I can't forget. If Daddy knew, he'd take a strap to your backside and you'd be sleeping on your belly the rest of the way to Oregon."

"You little snip," said Sandy venomously, "you tell, and I'll rip your hair out by the roots. So help me, I will."

Vangie only laughed, while Sandy all but sobbed in frustration.

Despite himself, Lou laughed. "Vangie, I saw you making eyes at Vic Sloan around the supper fire. I reckon he's sweet on you, and I'd not be surprised if we found you cozied up next to him, listenin' to him telling you how pretty you are. Might even find you, some dark night, squattin' under a wagon with him."

"No," the girl stammered. "I . . . I . . ."

She withdrew in confusion, and Sandy laughed. "Thank you, Lou. I think she needed that. I know I did."

"She's right about one thing," Lou said. "Your daddy would raise hell if he knew you was here, whether your britches was up or down."

"I'll risk that," Sandy said. "With the storm, the stampede, and the wagons mired down, I haven't had a chance to talk to you since that day in Independence, when you rescued me from Buckalew."

"A cowboy don't have much to talk about," said Lou.

"We could talk about Oregon, what you plan to do when you get there. You have a fortune in gold, your own herd of cows, and there'll be land—as much as you want—for the taking. Why, you could become a king. A king of the range."

"That's the last thing I'd ever want to be," Lou said. "I remember some men in Texas, gents with more money, cows, and land than any one man deserves. They built their big houses, hired their servants, and got so almighty puffed up with their own importance, nobody could stand bein' around 'em. If I ever end up like that, I'll do the world a favor and shoot myself. Anyhow, I don't know that I'll like Oregon. I might not stay."

"Would you if . . . if you had a reason?"

He felt her hand on his arm, felt her moving closer in the darkness. She said no more, taking one of his big hands in both of hers.

"I reckon I'd stay," he said huskily, "if there was somethin'—somebody—strong enough to hold me."

"By the time we reach Oregon," Sandy said, "perhaps there will be."

Suddenly her lips met his, and chills galloped up his spine like a herd of lightning-spooked longhorns. Just as suddenly she was gone, and he was still awake when his watch began.

7

Northeastern Kansas. June 9, 1843.

*A*round the breakfast fire, Applegate studied the crude map they were following. He shook his head before he spoke.

"If this map means anything, we're still a good three weeks out of Fort Kearny." He turned to Lou. "Is there any way we can make up some time?"

"That depends on the wagons," Lou said. "Long as we're followin' a river, we can push the herd right up to sundown, and likely cover fifteen miles. Once we're away from the rivers and have to bed down at the first water, that'll slow us down."

"These oxen seem to have only one gait," said Ezra Higdon, "and I doubt they'd cover fifteen miles from sunup to sundown, if we whipped them every step of the way."

"You got the straight of it," Dillard Sumner said. "Lose a day, and all you can do is add it on at the end of the trail."

Suddenly their attention was diverted to the sound of a galloping horse approaching from the west. Coming within sight of the camp, the rider slowed his mount to a lope.

"That's Landon Everett," Jonah Quimby said. "Something must have happened up ahead."

Something had. Everett dismounted, saying nothing until Applegate had introduced the Texans. When the wagon boss spoke, he came straight to the point.

"Nels Jacobs was killed last night. Had his throat slit."

"Great God," Jesse Applegate exclaimed, "you have three times the men we do. Aren't you posting sentries?"

"Why hell, yes," Everett said, irritated. "Nels *was* one of them. We think it might have been Indians."

"I doubt that," said Applegate. "According to the newspaper in Independence, Kit Carson and Jim Bridger claim there's no trouble with Indians along the trail."

"There must have been tracks," Dillard Sumner said. "Some sign."

"Damn it, no," said Everett. "When Nels was found, there was so much confusion, nobody thought to look for sign. By the time all the crying was done, any sign had been lost."

"If it was the work of Indians," Lou said, "they'd have taken something. One of your women, some of your stock, or your weapons. Was anything missing?"

"Nels had been robbed," said Everett. "His missus says he had two hundred dollars in gold on him."

"Indians don't care a damn for gold," Waco said. "You're lookin' for a white man. Likely somebody from your own party."

"I find that hard to believe," said Everett stiffly.

"Well," Applegate said with some heat, "you can rule out anybody from our camp. Our sentries do not allow any of us outside the wagon circle after dark."

"There were the riders watching the cattle," said Everett.

"I had charge of the watch until midnight," Dillard Sumner said, "and you have my word none of my men rode anywhere except for circling the herd."

"Me and my outfit took over at midnight," said Lou, "and I don't aim to waste my time tryin' to convince you we didn't ride to your camp and slit anybody's throat."

"I'm not accusing anybody," Everett said hastily. "The truth is, we don't know what to do, how to protect ourselves. Jesse, this wasn't my idea. I'm here on behalf of my people. We have all agreed that excluding your wagons from the original train was a mistake. We were fools for listening to Buckalew, allowing our haste to reach Oregon to overrule our common sense. I'm here to ask you and your people to trail with us, cattle and all."

"I don't think so," said Applegate. "As things now stand, you don't know who murdered Nels Jacobs. Suppose we did rejoin your train and there was another killing? You would then have a right to suspect one of us, just as you now must suspect those in your own party."

Everett sighed. "I feared you would say that. I suppose I will have to be more honest with you."

"I would appreciate that," Applegate said coldly.

"It's true that we want you and your wagons with us," said Everett, "but we want your Texas cowboys too. We've seen how they stood up to Buckalew, how they've stood by you, and we're sorely in need of that kind of loyalty and guidance."

Before Applegate could respond, Lou Spencer spoke.

"Just rein up right where you are. Me and my outfit signed on to trail Mr. Applegate's cattle to Oregon. We stood up to Buckalew because the varmint got in our way, and we've stood by Mr. Applegate because he's payin' us wages. It's the Texas way to side the man who pays your wages. We purely don't believe our loyalty to Mr. Applegate includes takin' on the protection of your people and your wagons."

"That's the sentiments of me and my outfit," Dillard Sumner said. "Mr. Quimby and Mr. Higdon are payin' our wages, and we wouldn't be fair to them was we to take on anybody else."

Landon Everett turned to Jesse Applegate, but Applegate had nothing to say. His anger obvious, Everett mounted his horse and rode out.

"Thank you," said Applegate, turning to the cowboy trail bosses. "You said almost exactly what I was thinking, but I feel better, having him hear it from you."

"A Texan will throw down on the devil himself," Lou said, "if he's fightin' for the brand, but only a fool gets himself gunned down in somebody else's fight."

"This whole affair is most disturbing," said Applegate, "because I fear it may be the start of something beyond our control. We've barely begun our journey. We've hundreds of miles ahead of us, with no law other than our loaded guns."

"Well hell," Waco said, "that's all we Texans has ever had. Welcome to the outfit."

Despite the grim circumstances, they all laughed at the laconic cowboy humor. But Applegate was worried, and he turned to Lou Spencer with a question.

"Suppose they just linger ahead of us until we catch up? Our oxen are no faster than theirs, and we'd be forced to trail with them."

"We'll keep the herd between their wagons and yours," said Lou. "You'll circle your wagons as you have been doing, and not become part of their camp. Unless it's a bad night and all of us are nighthawking, there'll be at least one of our outfits sleeping within your circle of wagons, but security is mostly up to you and your sentries. Texans are cautious by nature and sleep with one eye open, but you can lose all of us in a hurry if the herd stampedes."

"We understand that," said Applegate. "What's happened in Everett's camp should be warning enough for us."

"The killer's a white man," Dillard Sumner said, "so that's in your favor. Indians can kill quick and quiet. They could murder every man on watch, strip your camp and be gone before you knowed they was there."

"Dear God," Sarah Applegate moaned, "we are in danger of being murdered by our own people, and we were told all we had to fear were Indian savages."

"Senora," said Indian Charlie, "all savages not be Indios."

"I'm sorry," Sarah said, embarrassed.

"Not be sorry," said Charlie cheerfully. "You know Indio, you know Indio way."

"That's the same message Kit Carson an' Jim Bridger's been preachin'," Pete Haby said. "They ain't no Injun trouble where we're goin'. Not yet, but it'll come, an' when it does, it'll be the whites that's the cause of it."

It was a profound statement, and nobody wished to argue with it. The Texans saddled their horses, wagon owners harnessed their teams, and the women loaded cooking utensils. The cowboys bunched the longhorns, pushing them northwest, along the Little Blue.

It was Lou Spencer's turn to ride point, and the sun was noon-high when he first saw the dust ahead. He took off his hat and with three downward movements signaled the flank riders to mill the herd. He then galloped his horse ahead, catching up to the horse remuda. Indian Charlie and Alonzo Gonzales had already seen the dust ahead. They looked questioningly at Lou.

"Bunch them where they are," said Lou, "and hold them here until I get back to you. I know what we're goin' to do, but I need to talk to Dill and Applegate."

The rest of the cowboys had the herd bunched and grazing. Suspecting what lay ahead, Dillard Sumner was already riding to meet Lou. Together they trotted their horses back to meet the oncoming wagons. They rumbled along, three abreast, the terrain being level. The Applegate, Higdon, and Quimby wagons were in the lead, and their stopping immediately halted the rest of the caravan. Lou didn't waste words.

"You were right. We're catching up to Everett's wagons. They've either slowed their gait or deliberately made a late start. They aim for us to be part of their trail whether we want to or not."

"I expected that," Applegate said. "What do you propose to do? They have three times as many wagons, so there's no way we can get around them."

"No," said Lou, "but we can make it damned uncomfortable for them. We're going to do exactly what I said we'd do. I'll drop the horse remuda back behind the drag, and we'll see how they like a passel of longhorns loping among their wagons."

Lou rode ahead to where Alonzo and Indian Charlie were holding the horse remuda.

"Drive them half a mile north," Lou told the wranglers, "and when the herd passes, take them in behind the drag riders."

Lou rode back toward the herd, waving his hat as a signal to the riders to get the longhorns moving again. Lou then trotted his horse out of the path of the oncoming herd, meeting Dillard Sumner at left flank.

Sumner grinned. "I thought you was ridin' point."

"Not for a while," said Lou. "Everett's slowed his wagons, figurin' we got no choice but to trail with him. That's the same bunch that forced the cows out of the original wagon train and into a cattle column. Well, by God, we're about to convince 'em they was right the first time."

"They could shoot some of our cows," Sumner said.

"Maybe," said Lou, "but I doubt it. Everett needs us, or thinks he does, but he's about to learn something, and it may cost him."

"You aim to increase the gait of the herd?" Sumner asked.

"No," Lou replied. "We'll hold them to their usual gait. I've had enough of this bunch gettin' in our way ever since they got bogged down at the Missouri, listenin' to Buckalew."

The herd again took the trail, and within an hour the lead steers were nearing the slow-moving wagons. The terrain allowed them to travel four abreast. The herd split, some of it trailing to the farthermost side of the fourth wagon. But some of the longhorns, aggressive brutes that they were, loped between the moving wagons. Some of the wagons were drawn by teams of mules rather than oxen, and some of the mules began to bray in fear as the longhorned interlopers ran loose among them. One old bull, annoyed by the braying mules, reacted in typical longhorn fashion. He hooked one of the offending mules, raking its flank with the tip of a murderous horn. The animal screamed and the rest of the team lit out like retribution with the fuse afire. Women screamed, men shouted, and there was a grinding crash as a rear wheel of the runaway wagon ripped off the rear wheel of another. Teamsters with oxen managed to hold them, but two other mule-drawn wagons followed first, wreaking havoc as they went. The first wagon came to a shuddering stop when a left front wheel smashed into an upthrust of stone and the lathered mules could drag it no farther. Before the other mule teams could be halted, their wagons had smashed into other wagons. When the run finally ended and the dust settled, six wagons had been disabled. Four of them had been toppled and dragged, double trees ripped loose, wheels torn from the hubs. By some miracle, nobody seemed to have been hurt. Men and women got shakily to their feet, dusted themselves off and stared unbelievingly at their damaged wagons. The wagons ahead had halted as men tried to calm their teams.

"Come on," Lou Spencer shouted, "let's get those cows out of there."

Incredibly, only a dozen longhorns had wrought all the destruction. The crazed braying of the mules and the clatter of runaway wagons had spooked the rest of the herd, and the brutes had veered north, bypassing the strung-out wagons.

"Lou," Waco shouted, "look out."

The shot came from somewhere behind Lou, the slug

ripping through the crown of his hat. Lou wheeled his horse, his Colt drawn and cocked, but Waco already had the angry teamster covered.

"Damn you," the man snarled. "Damn you."

"Put the gun away," said Lou to the man who had fired the shot. He holstered his own Colt and then he spoke to the many whose angry eyes bored into him. "If you're looking for somebody to blame, then blame your wagon boss. He deliberately slowed you people down, believing he could force us to become part of your train. When you made the decision for the cattle to follow you, it became your responsibility to stay ahead of the herd."

The last of the herd, followed by the drag riders, had passed the wrecked wagons when Landon Everett came galloping back to the scene of the disaster. Dillard Sumner, Waco, and Dub Stern had joined Lou in separating the longhorns from among the emigrant wagons. The four cowboys now lounged in their saddles, thumbs hooked in their pistol belts. After glaring furiously at them, Landon Everett turned his eyes to the rising cloud of dust that marked the arrival of Jesse Applegate's wagons. Ignoring the Texans, Everett rode to meet the approaching wagons. Lou nodded to his three companions and they followed. If there was an account to be settled, Applegate wouldn't have to settle it alone. Applegate saw them coming, and when he nodded to Higdon and Quimby, the three lead wagons stopped, halting the train. Forty yards away, Landon Everett reined up, and when he spoke, his voice shook with anger.

"Jesse Applegate, how could you allow this to happen?"

"You *know* why it happened, Landon," Applegate said mildly, "and it wasn't our doing. We've maintained the same gait while you slowed yours. You wanted a cattle column, with the cattle trailing your wagons, and that's what you have. You were two days ahead of us, and if there's anybody to blame, it's you."

"We'll be a week repairing these wagons," Everett growled.

"Take your time," said Applegate coolly. "That will give us time to get well ahead of you, and I promise you we'll stay ahead."

He said no more, veering his teams past the tag end of the Everett wagons. The Higdon and Quimby teams followed, the rest of the Applegate train trailing behind. The cowboys riding drag had already reclaimed the errant steers that had run rampant among the wagons. Lou Spencer and his three companions rode on ahead to catch up to the herd.

"Jesse," Sarah Applegate said reprovingly as she walked beside her husband, "that was a terrible thing to do. Some of those people could have been killed."

"Their choice," said Applegate. "I refuse to be intimidated."

Reaching the point position, Lou guided the herd well away from the strung-out wagons. The Applegate wagons followed, and behind them came the horse remuda. Soon they had left Landon Everett and his crippled wagons behind, and Lou led the herd back to within sight of the Little Blue. Come sundown, the Texans bedded down the herd and the horse remuda half a mile north of the Little Blue, while Applegate circled his wagons near the river. The emigrants were subdued, their minds still on the near disaster that had taken place earlier in the day. During supper there was an uneasy silence, while some eyed Applegate accusingly. But Lou Spencer had something to say, and he set down his tin coffee cup.

"I reckon it's time I reminded you folks that Mr. Applegate, with all of you in agreement, asked us to lead the way with the herd. Now you're all hunkered around the fire feelin' guilty, thinkin' that if we'd tried, we could have kept them cows away from the tag end of Everett's wagon train. You're right, damn it, we could have. But is there a man or woman among you that don't know why Everett's wagons suddenly got in the way of our herd?"

"They slowed down a-purpose," said young Jud Applegate, "so we'd have to throw in with 'em."

"Exactly," Applegate said, getting to his feet. "There was no way our teams could get past theirs as long as they were on the move, because our teams are not faster than theirs. It's been a hard lesson, but I'm learning. This is the frontier, and we do what we must, even if it means somebody gets hurt."

While some of them plainly didn't like Applegate's hard-bitten attitude, they seemed to understand the wisdom of his words. Dillard Sumner and his outfit rode out to begin the first watch. Lou hadn't been in his blankets long enough to fall asleep when he found Sandy beside him.

"Some of the things about the frontier I don't like," she said softly.

"There'll likely be a lot more before you get to Oregon," Lou said.

"They wanted us to trail our wagons with theirs because they're afraid," said Sandy. "We all fear the unknown, and they don't know what lies ahead. They want you and your cowboys taking the lead for them as you're doing for us."

"Damn it," Lou said, irritated, "we hired on to trail these cattle to Oregon, not to wet-nurse two hundred and fifty families. We've never been to Oregon, and there's not a man of us that knows any more about the trail ahead than any of you."

"But you're not strangers to the frontier. Can this be any more dangerous than driving hundreds of wild cows from Texas to Missouri? Would it be all that bad if you and your riders took the cattle on ahead, like you're already doing, and allowed all the wagons to follow?"

"It would for us," said Lou. "I've talked to my outfit, to Dillard Sumner and his riders, and we're all of the same mind. We already got all the responsibility we can handle, and we don't aim to take on any more. Landon Everett's bunch booted you out. Now they got a killer within their ranks, they've discovered the trail's a hell of a lot tougher than they expected, and they're wantin' somebody to hold their hands from here to Oregon."

"It seems I've misunderstood you," she said hotly. "You are a selfish, insensitive brute."

"I reckon," he said coolly, "but it's kept me alive."

She slipped away in the darkness, and from somewhere nearby Vangie Applegate laughed softly.

With Buckalew's horse tied to the tailgate of the wagon, and Cope Suggs and Jedge Gerdes mounted on good horses, the trio took the trail. Suggs and Gerdes generally rode ahead, occasionally looking back at Buckalew striding beside the oxen. He was well aware that Suggs and Gerdes were impatient, being held to the plodding pace of the oxen, but Buckalew had plans for the wagon, and since he wasn't sure how long his alliance with the two would last, he hadn't told them any more than he'd had to. They followed the Little Blue in the wake of the other wagons, and at sundown Buckalew estimated they had traveled not more than ten miles. Around the supper fire Suggs came up with the suggesion Buckalew had been expecting.

"With that much gold at stake—if there is any gold— why in hell don't we just take the gold and vamoose? Who needs that bunch of cows?"

"I know damn well the gold's there," Buckalew said. "Them cowboys sold old Applegate five thousand head at thiry-one dollars a head. You reckon them Texans is carryin' that gold in their saddlebags, or maybe their pockets? By God, it's somewhere in Applegate's wagon. Now do you understand why I'm takin' this wagon?"

"You're accountin' for five thousand head," said Gerdes. "Where's the gold for the rest of the herd?"

"I ain't sure," Buckalew said. "Higdon and Quimby bought fifteen hundred head each from the herd that come up the trail ahead of the one Applegate bought.

Just fer them three thousand cows, that's more gold than them cow nurses can tote around in their saddlebags."

"Damn it," growled Suggs, "what you're sayin' is the rest of the gold is likely in the Higdon and Quimby wagons. Instead of one wagon, we got three of 'em to rob."

"I told you I wasn't sure about where the rest of the gold is," Buckalew snarled. "All them wagons is part of the Applegate train. We got to catch up to 'em and somehow figger out where the rest of the gold is. By my reckonin', we'd best learn fer sure where all the gold is, but not make our move until we're already in Oregon Territory."

"God Almighty," said Gerdes, "that'll be six months."

"The Applegate train is likely seventy miles ahead of us," Suggs said. "I done some bull whacking in my time, and there ain't one damn ox team in the world that's any faster than any other. How you expect these tail-draggin' varmints of yours to ever catch up?"

"They couldn't," Buckalew admitted, "unless somethin' went wrong and slowed down Applegate's train. Fer instance, if all them cows was to scatter, it'd take maybe three or four days to gather 'em up."

"If them cows had some encouragement, they'd just naturally be more likely to scatter to hell an' gone," said Suggs.

Buckalew grinned. "That's kind of what I was thinkin'," he said. He didn't bother telling them what the first stampede had cost him. Try as he might, he could think of no other means of catching up to the Applegate wagons. There had to be some less risky way to scatter the herd. Gerdes came up with one.

"I don't aim to get myself shot full of Texas lead," said Gerdes. "Cut loose with a Colt in the dark, and the muzzle flash from the first shot sets you up as a prime target. Suppose we was to bag some black powder, light some short fuses soaked in coal oil, an' throw 'em amongst that herd of cows?"

"I like the idea," Buckalew said, "but we ain't got that much black powder."

"Hell," said Suggs, "we ain't more'n a hour's ride out of Independence. In the mornin' I'll go back after some."

Four days ahead of Buckalew and his companions, Landon Everett had set about repairing the damaged wagons. First he had been forced to quell a rebellion, for those whose wagons had not been damaged wanted to press on, leaving their unfortunate companions to fare as best they could.

"We'll build fires," said Everett angrily, "and work at night. We'll circle the wagons as usual and double the guard."

The men labored far into the night, handicapped by the poor light from the fires. Finally they retired to within the circle of wagons to sleep, but the dawn brought new terror. Despite a doubled guard, yet another man had been murdered and robbed. Men and women surrounded Landon Everett, their faces reflecting fear, anger, or a combination of the two. Landon Everett's mind was in turmoil. These were his people and they were looking to him for answers, but he was only a farmer from Indiana, and he had none.

8

Southeastern Nebraska. June 24, 1843.

*T*he weather held, the brutal sun baking the prairie
hard as stone. Even the proximity of the Little Blue
became less assuring as the water level diminished. The
emigrants discussed the situation around the supper fire.

"For all the trouble that plagued us after the last
storm," Ezra Higdon said, "I'm ready for another. Another week of this and the river will be mud."

"Another week without delays," said Applegate, "and
we should reach the Platte."

The herd took the trail, followed by the horse remuda
and finally the wagons. Two hours before sundown, a rim
of dirty gray hung above the western horizon. Twilight
came early as the sun dipped behind the gray mass, its
crimson rays fanning out in a final display of grandeur.

"Rain mañana," Indian Charlie said. "She rain lak
hell."

It was a safe enough prophecy.

"Circle the wagons on high ground tonight, well beyond the river," Lou told Applegate. "When the rain
comes, the nearer you are to the river, the more mud
there'll be."

By dark there was lighning flicking golden tongues

into the western sky, and two hours into the first watch the riders could hear the rumble of distant thunder.

"Been dry too long," said Dillard Sumner. "When she hits, I look for lightnin' like hell with the lid off an' all the fires lit. None of us gets any sleep tonight."

It was true. There would be no first and second watch, but one long continuous watch, with every rider in the saddle.

"Storm's comin' out of the west," observed Waco, "meanin' if the herd runs, they'll light a shuck back the way we come. I just hope Landon Everett and his bunch ain't got themselves rollin' and caught up too close to us. Instead of just a couple dozen, they could wake up to eight thousand longhorns stompin' through their camp."

"That ain't likely," Vic Sloan said. "Thunder and lightnin' will die out, and the herd won't run after that. They'll turn tail to the wind and drift maybe, but nothin' worse."

"That's about it," Dillard Sumner agreed. "Let's just hope that if the varmints run, it won't be 'fore sometime near dawn. Last time they run, they had most of the night to drift with the wind and rain."

"Last time they took a run," said Lou, "they had a bunch of two-legged skunks firin' Colts over their heads. That stampede had nothin' to do with the storm. Bucka-lew's been kicked out as wagon boss, and I can't see where he has anything to gain by stampeding the herd. But we can't afford to take any chances. We can't help the thunder and lightning, but we can damn sure look out for any strange riders."

"Mebbe 'fore storm come, Gonzales an' me take horse remuda far from *vacas*. Them run, they no spook horses," Indian Charlie said.

"Do that, Charlie," Lou said. "It's worth a try. There'll be enough of us to head the herd, if it can be done."

"I just hope we got these longhorn varmints bedded down far enough beyond Applegate's wagons," said

Kage Copeland. "If they decide to run and fan out too much, they could flatten the Applegate camp."

"After we moved north of the river," Lou said, "Applegate was to take all the wagons on west for a ways. Unless the herd stampedes into the storm, Applegate's camp will be safe enough."

The lightning had come closer, and the thunder that accompanied it was already causing slight tremors in the earth. Some of the cattle were on their feet, lowing uneasily. It was a scenario the cowboys had witnessed often enough to know they were in for it. Once a few cows got the feel of the oncoming storm, it spread like a prairie fire to the rest of the herd. There was clacking of horns as other steers lunged to their feet, unsure as to what was coming, but preparing to become part of it.

"Dill," Lou shouted, "take six riders to the north and cover the far side. The rest of us will stay here to the south. Look for them to run to the east. Head 'em if you can, but if they can't be turned, stay out of their way."

Sumner and his riders galloped their horses west, circling eastward on the far side of the restless herd. Lou and his men rode eastward along the southernmost flank. If the herd ran, riders from both flanks would ride madly ahead, seeking to turn the lead steers. Only if the desperate riders could force the herd into a horseshoe turn could a stampede be averted. It was possible in daylight, near impossible in the dark, for riders who got close enough to head the leaders risked having themselves or their horses gored. Worse, they might be thrown into the path of the rampaging longhorns and trampled. On the wings of a rising west wind came the first few cooling drops of rain. Riders were lashing down their hats with rawhide thongs against the force of the coming storm. There was no time or need for words. The nearness of the lightning and the continuous roll of thunder had so spooked the herd that their combined lowing had become a force almost the equal of the storm. They were of a single mind. The fuse had been lighted and they only waited for the explosion. There was a clap of thunder that caused the very earth to tremble, and a jarring sizzle as lightning struck fire somewhere close.

"There they go!" a rider shouted, his words caught and torn away by the wind.

The longhorns lurched from a standing start to a dead run. Predictably, toward the east, away from the force of the storm. The other riders on his heels, Lou Spencer was riding neck and neck with the lead steers. He emptied his Colt into the air, the shots sounding dim and far away. He shouted until he was hoarse, but the herd thundered on. In flashes of lightning he tried to see the riders on the far side of the herd, but could not. The brutes hadn't converged into a manageable column, but had lit out in a mass of such proportions he couldn't see the other side. Heading them would be impossible. He reined up, sparing his horse, the riders behind drawing up beside him. Wind slapped sheets of rain against their backs with such force they leaned forward on the necks of their horses.

"God," said Waco, "they tore out at exactly the same second. Them front ranks must of been a hundred cows wide."

"Maybe more than that," Lou replied. "We couldn't turn the flank steers because they had nowhere to go. Nowhere but straight ahead."

"Wasn't no horses gallopin' at the tag end," said Del Konda, "so that means Charlie and Alonzo was able to hold the remuda."

"Don't count your chickens too quick," Red Brodie said. "The critters could of took off north or south."

"You're a real comfort, Brodie," said Josh Bryan. "How would we ever get along without you?"

Ignoring them, Lou wheeled his horse and rode back the way he had come. The others followed, none daring to hope that the horses had been spared. Thunder had died to a distant rumble, and the lightning had ceased altogether, making the darkness seem all the more intense. The wind no longer slashed at them, and the rain had become a steady downpour that might subside in an hour or two or continue for the rest of the night. The nickering of a horse warned them they were nearing the remuda.

"Texans ridin' in," Lou shouted, warning Indian Charlie and Alonzo Gonzales.

"We hold 'em," Indian Charlie shouted. "By damn, we hold 'em."

"*Bueno,*" said Lou. "*Bueno.* Wish we'd done just half as well with the herd. We'll start the gather at first light. Let's drive the horses nearer Applegate's camp. Maybe we can find some shelter and hot coffee."

"Sumner and riders," came a shout from the darkness.

"Come on," said Lou. "Charlie and Alonzo held the horses. We're drivin' 'em nearer to Applegate's camp, hopin' for some hot coffee, with a few minutes under a canvas so's the rain don't dilute it."

"We didn't have a prayer," Sumner said as they drove the horse remuda toward Applegate's camp. "We caught up to the lead steers and even got ahead of 'em, but the bastards wouldn't of turned if we'd shot off a cannon."

"That's about the way it looked from our side," said Lou. "We'd as well give Applegate the bad news, granted he's up and about."

Everybody was up and about. Three fires were going, each of them with a huge coffeepot dangling over it. Canvas shelters had been secured against the sides of the wagons, and the riders gratefully escaped the pouring rain. The Texans were all handed steaming cups of coffee. After downing half the coffee, Lou spoke.

"Another roundup, folks, startin' at first light."

"No help for it," Applegate said. "You warned us."

"Yes," said Lou, "but that's not makin' us feel any better. Alonzo and Indian Charlie managed to hold the horse remuda. We got that much in our favor, but the horses are never that much trouble. It's gathering the damn cows that'll cost us two, maybe three days."

"If this rain don't let up," Jonah Quimby said, "we may be losin' more time than that. We'll be up to the wagon hubs in mud again."

But the rain slacked to a drizzle before first light, and early rays of the rising sun flamed gold in a blue sky. While there was mud, a day's sun would harden it enough for the wagons to roll without difficulty. When it was light enough to see, the Texans rode out in search of the scattered herd.

"Damn it," said Sterling McCarty, "I just hope the varmints ain't had time to hole up in the thickets an' briar patches."

"Hell, McCarty," Red Brodie said, "you wrastled enough longhorns t' know better'n that. If they's a thicket er river brake in fifty mile, they'll find it. Even in pitch-dark."

To Texas cowboys, that often meant days of hard, sweaty work, but to them it was gospel, and they laughed in appreciation of McCarty's cow wisdom.

"It's still better than that other stampede," said Waco. "With all that rain, there was water ever'where. This time there won't be. Give that sun till noon an' it'll have all the water sucked out of the wet weather water holes. Them cows will go lookin' for water, and closest is the Little Blue."

"That's sound thinkin'," Dillard Sumner said. "Just maybe we'll surprise them wagon people and have this herd on the trail sometime tomorrow. I reckon we owe 'em somethin' for lookin' after the horse remuda so's we got all our riders to gather the herd."

Sumner's optimism was justified. After three or four miles the stampede had slowed and the cattle had begun to scatter. The tracks told the cowboys the longhorns had begun to graze, that with the lessening of the wind, they hadn't drifted.

"We'll split up in pairs," said Lou. "Just get behind a

bunch and start them movin' west. The river will be a
barrier to the south, and once we have two or three
hundred, a couple of us can drive them back beyond the
horse remuda."

They rode east until they no longer saw grazing cattle,
and fanning out over several miles, began riding westward. They met with little resistance, for the herd was
trailwise, and by the time the sun was noon-high, several
thousand of the cattle had been gathered.

Buckalew, Suggs, and Gerdes made good time along the
Little Blue, and the freshness of animal droppings told
them they were not too far behind the emigrant wagons.
Near where the emigrants had camped by the river was a
new-made grave, the dirt mounded high to discourage
predators.

"They done started havin' trouble," Buckalew observed.

"I don't see nothin' but wagon an' ox tracks," said
Suggs. "You said this Applegate train was trailin' eight
thousand head of cattle."

"They are," Buckalew said, "but they somehow took
the lead. There's near two hundred wagons follerin'
'em."

"Hell," said Gerdes, "both trains is likely together by
now. You made it sound like that gold was ours for the
takin'. Now you're sayin' there's more'n two hundred
wagons in this train. How in thunder do you aim to get
rid of all them other people while we rob the wagons
with the gold? Damn, we could of rode to Fort Leaven-
worth an' robbed an army payroll with less risk an'
bother."

"Like I told you," Buckalew said irritably, "these people ain't goin' to be t'gether forever. Just to Oregon.
Somewhere, them damn Texans is goin' to turn over
them cows to the men that bought 'em. That's when we
take the cows. Them emigrants, once they reach Oregon, is goin' to spread out."

"Yeah," said Suggs, "an' if you know what you're talkin' about—if the gold belongin' to them cowboys is in the wagons—then that bunch of Texans ain't goin' nowhere without their gold. There's three of us, bucko, an' sixteen of them. Where I come from, not even a damn fool takes on odds like that."

"I got a .50 caliber Sharps buffalo gun in the wagon," Buckalew said. "Once we git a little closer, I figger to cut down the odds some."

"By God," said Gerdes, "it takes a low-down, no-account sidewinder to bushwhack a man with a buffalo gun. There may be hope for you, Buckalew."

The three laughed, more at ease with one another, for they were of the same stripe. Near sundown they reached the scene of the disaster in which six of Landon Everett's wagons had been wrecked. They camped there, observing the twisted wagon bows, splintered wheels, and broken axles, wondering what had happened.

"God," Suggs said, "looks like some of 'em got in the way of a buffalo stampede. At least one was kilt. There's another grave yonder."

"Buckalew, you said there's two trains," said Gerdes. "Is this the one we're after?"

"It's almost got to be Applegate's train," Buckalew said. "His bunch was first across the Missouri, but durin' a bad storm, all them cattle decided to run. Must of took three er four days to round 'em up again."

"That means the biggest train—maybe two hundred wagons—is somewheres ahead of the bunch we're after," said Gerdes. "If they're far enough ahead, they ain't likely to pay no attention to what happens along the back trail. One of us might just ride ahead, stalkin' 'em with that buffalo gun. Cut down a rider ever' day er two, takin' the Texans first. With them out of the way, we can pluck the rest of them pilgrims like geese."

"Yeah," Buckalew said, "and that leaves just the three of us to drive eight thousand head of cows to Oregon."

"Wrong," said Suggs. "We get our hands on that gold,

them cows can all rattle their hocks back to Texas, for all I care."

"Damn right," Gerdes agreed. "Or you can just take 'em on to Oregon by your lonesome, Buckalew, and have all that dinero for yourself. Haw haw."

Buckalew gritted his teeth, saying nothing. He had talked himself into a bad situation, for he wanted the cattle *and* the gold. For the sake of getting the cattle to Oregon, he *needed* the cowboys. Suggs and Gerdes, damn them, wanted only to get their hands on the gold that had to be hidden in the emigrant wagons, and that necessitated killing the cowboys. Buckalew set his devious mind to work, seeking some means by which he might delay going after the gold until he no longer needed the Texans to drive the herd. He decided a word of caution was in order.

"Once we catch up to the Applegate train," said Buckalew, "I want one thing understood. It'll be my decision as to when we go snipin' after them Texans. This ain't a bunch of shorthorns. First time we cut down on 'em with a buffalo gun, they'll take our trail like a pack of lobo wolves."

"Fourteen feet tall an' a yard wide," Suggs said. "So tough they wear out their britches from the inside."

"You're damn right they are," said Buckalew, not liking the sarcasm.

Gerdes laughed. "Scared of 'em, ain't you?"

"I am when it comes to close work with a Colt," Buckalew said. "I seen one of 'em pull a pistol in a cross-hand draw an' kill another hombre that drawed first. Me, I'll stay with a long range buffalo gun. They're a salty bunch, by God, an' if the time comes when either of you pulls iron agin' 'em, I want to see it. They'll cut you down before you clear leather."

Buckalew's countenance did nothing to soften his words, and his companions eyed one another dubiously. Buckalew's words had the ring of truth, and neither of his companions spoke. Every man was born with the seeds of death within him, and it was only a matter of time and place. Gerdes and Suggs were thieves, and had killed when it could be done without endangering themselves, but neither fancied facing better men in a stand-up fight.

"If them Texans is such a bed of rattlers," said Suggs, "we got enough black powder to run them cows to hell and gone. While they're roundin' up the herd, why can't we just take the gold? You think them farmers wouldn't give up the gold if we was to grab some of their women, threatenin' to slit their throats?"

"Yeah," said Buckalew in disgust, "but you're forget-tin' one damn important fact. Them Texans sold the cat-tle to them emigrants, and the gold stashed in the wag-ons belongs to the Texans. We take that gold while they're alive, and the whole bunch of 'em would trail us to hell and fight the devil for our souls. Like I been tellin' you, damn it, them Texans has got to die, an' if we're goin' that far, why not hold off until they git the herd to Oregon an' take the herd too?"

It was a telling argument, Buckalew's most successful so far, and he was gratified when it left his troublesome companions without rebuttal.

Landon Everett's troubled train lost four days repairing the badly damaged wagons, and when they again took the trail, they left behind yet another of their number in an unmarked grave. Fortunately, the second murdered man, like the first, left behind a son who took over as head of the family, but that was small consolation. Every man, women, and child faced each approaching night with new dread, lest the killer strike again. Far into the night, Everett's wife Mattie found him seated on the wagon tongue, his Colt in his hand.

"Landon," said Mattie, "you haven't slept since this . . . this awful thing began. You've doubled the guard. What else can you do?"

"God, Mattie, I don't know. I just don't know. There's

a cold-blooded killer within our ranks, and I have no idea who he is or how to flush him out. All I know for sure is that he's killing for gold, and he seems to know who has the most of it."

"Would you accept a suggestion from anybody, if it might bring this to an end?"

Everett nodded his assent.

"Have every man in our party bring his valuables to one of our wagons, and then post a heavy guard on that wagon at night."

"Bless you, Mattie," Everett said. "It might work. Before we take the trail tomorrow, I'll call a meeting and suggest it."

The cowboys gathered the herd in two days, and Applegate's party again took the trail. They covered an estimated ten miles before the Texans bedded down the herd for the night. It had been more than three weeks since Sandy Applegate had left Lou Spencer in anger after Lou had refused to consider allowing the Landon Everett train to rejoin Applegate's. Vangie, Sandy's sister, had taken to spending as much time as she could with Vic Sloan, the cowboy nearest her own age. Sandy always worked the serving line when the cowboys took their meals, and her eyes began to soften each time she faced Lou. He said nothing, giving her no encouragement, and he was surprised when one night she spoke to him from the darkness as he lay beneath a wagon.

"What do you want?" Lou asked, sounding as gruff as he could.

"What do you *think* I want?" she snapped.

"Likely more than your daddy would approve of," said Lou.

"And likely more than you'd be willing to give," she said.

"You haven't spoken to me for three weeks," Lou said, "and when you went stompin' off, I wasn't in much of a givin' mood."

"And you still aren't," said Sandy.

"Why should I be?" Lou asked. "I'm an insensitive, selfish brute."

"I'm sorry," she said softly.

"You're sorry I'm an insensitive, selfish brute? That makes me feel a mite better."

"Oh, damn it," Sandy hissed, "you . . . you're impossible. I said I was sorry. What do you want? Do I have to sleep with you?"

"No, ma'am," he said, doing his damnedest not to laugh. "I thought of that, but if I was to give in that easy, I'd lose my status as an insensitive, selfish brute."

She had become a victim of cowboy humor, and finally it dawned on her. She rolled over on top of him, blankets and all, planting a kiss that all but suffocated him before she backed off. It was a while before she caught her breath enough to laugh. Finally she spoke.

"I was wrong, being critical of you for not wanting to allow our wagons to join Landon Everett's train. Back in Indiana, some of those people were our neighbors, and I . . . I couldn't see this as . . . as any different. But it is. Oh, God, it is, and I've been sick . . . miserable . . . since I disagreed with you. Everbody said you were right. Vangie has practically persecuted me. Even Jud and Mother have barely spoken to me."

"You can't lay that on me," Lou said. "I didn't say a word. I'd not want everybody else knowin' I was an insensitive, selfish brute."

"Can't you please forget I ever said that?" she all but sobbed. "It was Vangie that told, damn her."

"I reckoned as much," said Lou. "She's doin' her best to grow up, but she ain't quite knowin' how. She's a mite envious of you, trying to learn from you. I reckon she's been listenin' to us all the time. It wasn't a good idea, you offerin' to sleep with me."

"You know I didn't mean that literally," she said.

"You did so," said a soft voice from the darkness, "but

I won't tell. But just you remember, big sister, you owe me."

"Why, you rotten little sneak," Sandy snarled. She went scrambling off into the darkness toward the sound of soft, exultant laughter. Lou grinned to himself, feeling better than he'd felt in three weeks.

After an uneventful night, Landon Everett visited the breakfast fires of his people. While he didn't relish the task that lay ahead, he knew he had to take some action to eliminate the late night robberies in which two of his party had died. Called together, there were more than five hundred people. Some of the younger children cried or complained. Otherwise, it was a silent, solemn occasion, all the emigrants suspecting the reason for the meeting.

"I won't beat around the bush," Everett said. "Starting tonight, I want all of you with gold to consolidate it in a single wagon. That goes for jewelry of value as well. We'll then post a heavy guard over that wagon. Is there any one of you who doesn't understand the need for this action?"

"Hell," a man shouted, "I don't trust my valuables to nobody but me. We got no promise the damn thief or thieves won't murder all the guards an' take ever'thing in the wagon. I ain't leavin' the little I got in nobody's wagon."

There were angry shouts of agreement, and Landon Everett sighed. He had a thankless job. None of his charges respected his judgment.

9

"*T*oday or tomorrow," Buckalew predicted, "we'll be catchin' up to Applegate's wagons."

"I just can't wait," said Suggs. "I reckon they'll welcome you with hugs an' kisses."

"It'd surprise the hell out of me if they did," Buckalew said. "It was me that forced them emigrants with cattle to the rear. They're bein' called the cattle column."

"I got me a feelin'," said Gerdes, "you ain't told us all you know about this damn situation."

"I told you all you *need* to know," Buckalew said sharply. "In case you ain't figgered it out, none of these pilgrims will be thinkin' much of us once we gun down their cowboys, take the gold, and rustle the cattle. So what damn difference does it make what they think of us now?"

It was the day following the storm, and Buckalew's prediction proved correct. The wind was out of the west, and less than an hour before sundown they smelled wood smoke.

"That ought to be Applegate's bunch," said Buckalew. "We'd as well ride up there and let 'em know they got comp'ny. We'll make camp here."

Buckalew unharnessed the oxen and turned them out to graze. He then untied his horse from the wagon's tailgate, mounted, and the three of them rode west along the Little Blue. All the wagons had been circled four abreast, and cook fires had been started within the circle. Although it wasn't yet dark, Landon Everett already had men circling the wagons afoot. Buckalew and his companions reined up, and Buckalew was astounded when Landon Everett emerged from the maze of wagons. There was no friendliness in Everett's eyes, and when he spoke, even less in his voice.

"What the hell do you want, Buckalew?"

"Well, now," said Buckalew with a devilish grin, "we're on our way to Oregon just like you. You know me an' I know you, so I just figgered we'd keep you comp'ny."

"You're not welcome in my party, Buckalew. If you or your friends come sneaking around here after dark, you'll be shot on sight."

"Well, Lord A'mighty," Buckalew said, feigning shock, "I ain't never seen such an inhospitable varmint. Gents, I reckon we'll just have to drive on an' join my friend Mr. Applegate."

"I'm sure Applegate will welcome you," said Everett, his voice dripping sarcasm.

"Hell," Buckalew said, "we wouldn't trail with you, Everett, if you went belly down an' begged us. Truth is, we was expectin' Applegate's train. Where is he?"

"Two or three days ahead of us," said Everett grudgingly.

Buckalew laughed. "That must of been your wagons that took a smashin' back yonder. That's what comes of havin' a wagon boss with all the smarts of a blind mule in a root cellar."

Landon Everett bit his tongue and said nothing, watching the trio as they rode back the way they had come. He would have willingly died rather than have Jap Buckalew know the extent of his troubles and the precarious position in which he had found himself. Now, with another long night in store, he must make the rounds of the wagons, trying to inspire his people with a confidence he lacked. Most of his emigrants had wives and one or more children, but in some of the wagons there was but a single parent and a son or daughter. Since the killing and stealing had begun, he'd been mentally separating his people into two groups. In one group, he placed those he thought least likely to be guilty of thefts that resulted in grisly murders; in the other, he placed those who might be capable of such a crime. He'd narrowed down his suspects to five wagons, in none of which there was a women. He had his wife Mattie to thank even for that small bit of inspiration.

"Think, Landon," Mattie had said. "Every Sunday afternoon we have our Bible study, and every married woman is included. Could you slip out at night and murder a man for his gold without me knowing or suspecting? Look to the wagons where there are only men. There are men—fathers, sons, brothers—who haven't spoken a civil word to any of us since we left St. Louis. Put mind to them, Landon. . . ."

While a man's Bible-reading wife didn't guarantee his innocence, the theory had a kind of sensible feel to it, and for the lack of anything better, Landon Everett began ticking off in his mind the suspects. There was Jules Dewees and his sons Hamby and Isaac. They rarely spoke to anybody if they could avoid it. Sol Menges and his son Daro were no better. Then there were the Schmidt Brothers, Ab, Jenks, and Rufe. The three had made themselves unwelcome at most of the other wagons with their constant attention to the unmarried daughters of other families. There was Gus Shondell and his sons Jasper and Grady, and finally, a foreigner, Upshur Hiddenbrandt. Twelve men, and Landon Everett had to admit he had no real reason to suspect any of them. The Schmidt brothers had been involved in fistfights over various women, but that didn't make them thieves and murderers. Damn it, how had the killer left his wagon, committed his grisly act, and escaped without one or more of the men on watch seeing him? Then a thought struck Everett that sent chills up his spine. If the killer had been one of the men on watch, his being up and about in the night wouldn't have aroused anybody's suspicion. Could he, Landon Everett, have assigned the killer to a watch, allowing him to roam freely among the wagons without being suspect? Landon Everett allowed his mind to drift back to the nights of the killings and the men who had been on watch. Slowly a plan began to take shape. . . .

"You sure as hell wore out your welcome with that bunch," said Suggs as he and Gerdes followed Buckalew back to their camp.

"The high an' mighty Landon Everett has been brung down a notch er two," Buckalew said. "You saw how bad he wanted rid of us. He's in big trouble of some kind, and I aim to enjoy it. We ain't in no hurry to catch up to Applegate, so maybe we'll just trail along behind Mr. Landon Everett fer a while. Might be kind of interestin', knowin' how deep a hole he's dug fer himself."

"Damn it, Buckalew," said Gerdes, "I ain't of a mind to poke along behind these sodbusters while you enjoy their misery. You come to us talkin' gold an' cattle. You heard the man. The gold an' cattle is two or three days ahead."

"An' you know damn well it's too soon to make our move on Applegate's wagons or to grab the cattle," Buckalew said, "so why bust our britches catchin' up? I'd bet ten years of my life that Everett's train is split seven ways from Sunday, an' that most of his bunch is chawin' on his carcass day an' night. Now, if I'm rememberin' right, a bunch of them sodbusters, as you call 'em, sold out back east. There's likely thousands in gold stashed in them wagons, if we can figger a way of gettin' our hands on it. There's a bunch of right handsome women in Everett's train too."

"Likely not a one that'd spit on you if you was afire,"

said Gerdes. "A woman don't pleasure me much if she hates my guts."

Buckalew laughed. "A man takes his pleasure when an' where he can. I had more'n one that wasn't in the mood fer me, but got me anyhow. Nights is mighty dark out here on the plains."

"Buckalew," Suggs said, "it's one thing to steal a man's gold, but it takes a low-down skunk-striped son of a yellow coyote to violate his woman."

"Well, by God," Buckalew said angrily, "I ain't got ankle chains on either of you. If that's how I look to you, then ride on, an' keep ridin'."

"Shut up, Buckalew," said Gerdes. "You got the scruples of a sneaking, egg-sucking dog, and that's all you got goin' for you. That's what this job calls for. Why else would we of took a hand in your dirty game?"

Fort Kearny, Nebraska. July 6, 1843.

It was early afternoon when the Texans bedded down the herd and the horse remuda near the confluence of the Little Blue and Platte rivers. Applegate halted the wagons, mounted his horse and rode ahead to confer with the cowboys.

"If your map means anything," said Lou, "we're somewhere within shoutin' distance of Fort Kearny. I reckon some of us ought to ride ahead and make ourselves known to the commanding officer and the men who garrison the post."

"An excellent idea," Applegate said. "Choose another man and I'll ride with the two of you."

"Dill, ride with us," said Lou.

Sumner joined them, and the trio set out to find the military post, if there was one. They found it, such as it was, on the south bank of the Platte. It consisted of three large tents pitched on a knoll to escape high water. Beyond the tents there were a dozen horses grazing. At first there was only one soldier in sight, but when he sounded the alarm, the others appeared. The cowboys raised their hands to shoulder level, and Applegate followed their example. It was a friendly gesture, moving their hands far from the butts of their holstered Colts. Riding closer, the men became identifiable by rank. There was a lieutenant, a sergeant, a corporal, and nine privates. Reining up a dozen yards away, Lou introduced himself and his companions, explaining that they were on their way to Oregon.

"I'm Lieutenant Emmet," said the officer. "This is Sergeant Davis and Corporal Harter." He didn't bother introducing the privates.

"We just wanted you to know who we are and where we're headed," said Lou. "Is there anything helpful you can tell us of the trail ahead?"

"Very little," said the officer, "except that there'll be some rugged country west of Fort Laramie. You'd better lighten your wagons, leavin' anything you can do without. We have word that Jim Bridger will be at Fort Laramie, and he knows something about the territory in western Wyoming Territory and what lies beyond. You're a little more than three hundred miles west of Independence and maybe four hundred out of Fort Laramie."

"Much obliged for the information," Lou said. He rode out, followed by Sumner and Applegate.

"I don't see how in tarnation they can get by with callin' that a fort," said Dillard Sumner. "Three tents?"

"From what I have read," Applegate said, "there are plans for a fort, including a stockade. I believe this is a temporary measure, probably to reassure those of us on our way to Oregon."

"I appreciate their efforts," said Lou, "but I wouldn't rest too easy. Keep your Colt handy."

Applegate laughed. "I am inclined to agree. It's still early. Since we'll be following the Platte River and there'll be no water problem, shall we move on?"

"Yes," Lou said. "Dill, how do you feel?"

"Let's move on," said Sumner. "If there'd been a

store or maybe a saloon, we could have spent the night here. But with a dozen soldiers and three tents, why bother?"

There was some disappointment among his party when Applegate told them Fort Kearny was a fort in name only. The cowboys took the trail with the long-horns and the horse remuda, the wagons following. The caravan traveled another four or five miles along the Platte before sundown. Millions of stars winked silver against a purple sky, while a mellow glow announced the eventual arrival of a full moon. Sandy Applegate sat with her back against a wagon wheel. Lou Spencer knelt beside her and spoke softly.

"I aim to walk down the river a ways. Will you come?"

Silently the girl got to her feet. Nobody said anything, but there were knowing grins from Lou's riders. Sarah Applegate looked at Jesse, raising her eyebrows. Applegate winked at her.

"It took you long enough," Sandy said when they were well away from the camp. "I've been looking at my reflection in the river every morning, wondering if my teeth had gone bad or if my hair was falling out."

"Your hair looks right good," said Lou. "I'll have to wait for daylight to check your teeth."

"Thank you for asking me to walk with you. This looks more honest than having Vangie spread the word I've been spending my nights with you under a wagon."

"Vangie's got nothin' on you," Lou said. "Your daddy ain't as blind as you think he is."

"Has he spoken to you . . . about me?"

"No," said Lou, "and I reckon he would have if he thought I was havin' my way with you under a wagon. But just for the sake of appearance, I don't think you ought to come slippin' around in the dark after I've spread my blankets."

"I won't," Sandy said, "Now that you've decided you're not ashamed to be seen with me."

"I've never been ashamed to be seen with you. You're

mighty pretty, and I have the same weaknesses of other men. I'd find it easy to spend every spare minute with you. Then what do you reckon would happen was I to find I didn't care a damn about this Oregon Territory an' decided to ride back to Texas? You'd hate my guts for leadin' you on, and I'd be so god-awful lonesome, I'd spend all my nights out howlin' with the coyotes."

She started to laugh, but the seriousness in his voice silenced her. When she finally spoke, her voice trembled.

"Then it's . . . it's not Oregon that bothers you. You're just not that sure . . . of me. . . ."

"I *am* sure of you, damn it," said Lou, "but you're not bein' fair. You've pulled up stakes back east, and this Oregon country will be home to you, come what may. That's not the case with me. I was born and raised in Texas and I got kin there. Can't you see I'm shyin' away from you 'cause I don't want to hurt you by maybe ridin' away? I'm bein' honest, Sandy, hurtin' you a little now instead of hurtin' you a lot at the end of the trail."

She stopped, head down, and he turned back to face her. He put a finger under her chin, lifting her eyes to his, and even in the dim starlight he could see the tears streaking her cheeks.

"Don't you . . . know," she sobbed, "that if . . . if you rode back to Texas . . . or anywhere else . . . that I'd go with you?"

It was the very last thing he expected her to say, and it hit him hard. He was immediately ashamed, for he had thought of her as a young girl whose infatuation with him might not last the months it took to reach Oregon Territory. But her reaction had been that of a woman, true to her feelings, willing to follow him without question. She said no more, and it was he who broke the silence.

"Sandy, I . . . you'd do that . . . for me?"

"I would," she cried. "I will." She threw her arms around him, her body shaking with sobs. He held her close, until her sobs became an occasional sniffle. Then he lifted her chin, kissing her until she gasped for breath.

"Sandy Applegate," he said, "if you feel that strong about me, then you got yourself a cowboy."

She threw her arms around him and they went through it all again, this time without the tears. It was he who backed away.

"Now," he said, "I reckon we've gone far enough. It's time we was gettin' back to camp."

"So soon?" she cried. "We were just about . . ."

"To get in too deep, too soon," he finished. "In just about another minute, I'd have stretched you out on this riverbank and had my way with you."

She laughed nervously. "I wouldn't have put up much of a fight."

"I know you wouldn't have," said Lou, "and there would have been a next time, and a time after that. You know the risk, and this trail will be hell at the best. I won't chance makin' it any harder on you. I want you, damn it, but I'm man enough to know I can't have whatever I want, when I want it. I can wait, and so can you. I'd rather spend a little time with you every night or so, than to stay out too long and have your daddy come lookin' for us with a cocked pistol."

"He would never do that," Sandy said. "He likes and respects you."

"I hope so," said Lou, "and I don't aim to do anything to change his opinion."

Landon Everett told nobody, not even Mattie, but he would harness his own suspicions to Mattie's theory and put them to the test that very night. For the first watch he chose a dozen men, all of them with wives and children. For the second watch, eleven of the men had wives and children, while the twelfth, Caleb Vandiver, was a widower with a twenty-year-old daughter, Marcie. With none of the dozen unmarried suspects on watch, none of them would have any reason to roam the camp during the night. He prayed that Mattie's reasoning proved correct, that no man with a wife and family could willfully rob and murder others within his own party. While Everett felt guilty singling out the unmarried men in the party, those who had been distant or antagonistic, he had no choice. If his own theory was correct—that one of the men was using his watch to steal and kill—this night and perhaps several others might accomplish one of two things. If the crimes ceased, it might limit the suspects to the twelve men on his mental list. However, if there was yet another robbery and murder, he would be back where he'd started. Any man, in a party of more than three hundred, would be suspect. Eventually somebody would want to know why a certain dozen men were not taking their turns at sentry duty, but by then Everett expected to know if his suspicions—and Mattie's theory —were correct. When the watch changed at midnight, Caleb Vandiver paused at the Everett wagon. Everett was leaning against a front wheel.

"You ain't gettin' much sleep, Landon," said Caleb.

"I'll get by, Caleb," Everett said. "Watch careful."

"I will," said Caleb. "Git yourself some shut-eye." But they were less than two hours away from an event that would change Caleb's life forever.

Landon Everett remained where he was. He had ordered the men to make room within the wagons so that their women might remain inside at night. There had been numerous complaints and grousing, for most of the wagons were heavily loaded. To meet Everett's demand, some wagons had to be partially unloaded before dark and loaded again the next morning. If a man ended up in a fight for his life, he didn't need a terrified woman in the midst of it. Everett looked at the Big Dipper, found it was two A.M., and began to breathe a little easier. That's when the silence of the night was shattered by the scream of a woman. It all but stood Everett's hair on end, and before the sound of it died away, she screamed again, and then a third time, each more agonized than the last.

"Dear God," Mattie cried. She all but fell out of the wagon, but Landon caught her.

The screams had come from the side of the camp nearest the river, and Everett ran that way, all but dragging Mattie through the maze of circled wagons. Men shouted, women and children wept, and above it all the terrified screams had resumed. The moon was full, and with the starlight, they had no trouble seeing the pathetic figure on her hands and knees within the circle of the wagons. She moaned like a wounded animal, the sound rising and falling like the wind on a winter's night. She was stark naked, her golden hair hung down over her face, and even in the poor light they could see the terrible bloody gash on the back of her head.

Within seconds dozens of men and women were there, most of them immobilized by shock. Mattie Everett was the first to kneel beside the moaning girl, and was immediately attacked by a clawing, screeching fury. It took Landon Everett and three other men to restrain the girl. Finally they got her on her back, holding her arms and legs, but unable to calm her.

"Oh, God," said Mattie Everett, "it's Marcie. It's Caleb's Marcie."

Caleb knew. He fought his way to the girl and fell on his knees, weeping. He reached a trembling hand toward her face and she snapped at it like a rabid dog. Mattie Everett took charge.

"Somebody bring some blankets," she shouted, "and get a fire going." Blankets were brought and they managed to roll the kicking, moaning girl in them.

"We'll take her to Caleb's wagon," Everett said. "Some of you men unload it so's the women can get in there and see to her."

Men rushed to do his bidding, while several women returned to their own wagons and brought candles. A fire was soon going, a kettle of water hanging over it from a three-legged iron spider. Women knelt around the blanket-shrouded girl, talking to her, and their words had a calming effect. She said nothing, her eyes wide open, but she had stopped moaning. Caleb Vandiver stood with his head down, his hands trembling.

"The wagon's ready," somebody shouted.

Marcie Vandiver didn't protest when two of the men carried her to the wagon. Landon Everett climbed into the wagon to help them lift her in.

"Now," said Everett, "we'll let the women see to her." He hoisted Mattie into the rear of the wagon, while other women climbed up over the big front wheels. Caleb Vandiver sat down on the wagon tongue, his face buried in his hands.

"Nothin' more we can do," Everett said quietly. "Those of you on the second watch resume your rounds. Hannigan, you take Caleb's place."

Landon Everett stood looking into the fire. The water had begun to boil, and he saw Mattie coming with a wooden bucket.

"Mattie," he asked hesitantly, "what's been done to her? Was she . . . ?"

"My God, yes," said Mattie with a shudder. "She's had a blow to the head that knocked her unconscious, and then she was violated terribly. She's bleeding . . . inside. . . ."

"Has she . . . can she . . . talk?"

"Some," said Mattie, "but she makes no sense. She keeps calling for her mother, and she's been gone since Marcie was nine. Landon, she . . . her eyes look . . . like her very soul is gone. She doesn't know any of us. I'm afraid, Landon. Afraid she's lost her mind."

She said no more, dipping her bucket into the boiling water and returning to the wagon. It was more than an hour later when Mattie and the three other women left the wagon.

"She's asleep," Mattie said. "We've done all we can do. I don't believe we should leave her alone. Caleb won't leave the wagon, but he shouldn't be alone either. One of us should stay the rest of the night with her."

"No," said Everett, "all of you get what sleep you can. Since Caleb's in no condition to be alone, I'll stay with him outside the wagon. If Marcie wakes and you're needed, I'll come for you."

Caleb still sat on the wagon tongue, and Landon Everett left him there. Caleb seemed in shock, unable to accept the tragedy that had befallen him. Landon sat down, his back against one of the rear wheels of the wagon. He didn't worry about falling asleep. He wondered, in fact, if he'd ever sleep again. Several times he heard Marcie Vandiver calling for her mother, and once he thought he heard her moving around. Lost in his thoughts, Landon Everett was shaken to the depths of his soul by the sound of a shot. A shot from within the Vandiver wagon. Fearfully, he lit a match. Marcie Vandiver had taken the Colt her father had bought for her in Independence and put a bullet through her head.

10

❦

The wind being from the west, Buckalew, Suggs, and Gerdes were awakened by the terrible screams from the emigrant camp.

"What'n hell's goin' on?" Gerdes wondered.

"Sounds like some varmint's got the same way with women as Buckalew," Suggs observed.

"Watch yer damn tongue," Buckalew growled.

The three slept, only to be awakened again by a single shot.

"They must of caught the damn fool that was behind all that squallin' a while ago," said Gerdes.

"If we aim to foller that bunch," Suggs said, "I reckon we better keep our distance."

"You finally got somethin' right," said Buckalew. "There's trouble in that camp, and I ain't wantin' no part of it. Once we're past Fort Laramie, it'll be time for us to catch up to Applegate's party."

"In other words," Suggs said, "we trail 'em too far, you're scared that bunch of Texas gun throwers might get curious an' ask some embarrassin' questions."

Gerdes laughed. "I'm startin' to think nobody on this whole damn trail likes you, Buckalew, an' I just can't understand why. I reckon they all know you better'n we do."

"Just shut the hell up," Buckalew snarled. "It's the middle of the night an' I'm tryin' to sleep."

Following the fatal shot that freed Marcie Vandiver's tortured mind, there was total chaos. Women wept, men cursed, and Caleb Vandiver collapsed, unconscious. Dawn was no more than an hour away when Landon Everett managed to restore some order. He did so by promising to at least try to find the man responsible for Marcie's death. Weary of shouldering the burden alone, he decided to rely on Will Hamer and Buck Embler, men he had known for many years. He began by telling them of his suspicions, of the twelve men he had purposely kept off night watch.

"That's somethin' to consider," Will said, "but it could have been almost any man in camp, except those on the second watch. Caleb's wagon is one of them nearest the river, an' there are so many trees, that area's in deep shadow. A cat-footed varmint could get in and out of a wagon without bein' seen, even by the men on watch."

"No chance of findin' any tracks either," said Buck. "When Marcie started screaming, we all lit out for the wagon, spoilin' any sign. Landon, how and where do you plan to start looking for the man responsible?"

"I'm sticking to my original suspicions," Everett said. "I don't believe this is the doing of a man with a wife, and while I have no proof, I still think it narrows down our suspects to twelve men. The only thing we know for sure is that the man who did this knocked Marcie unconscious while he did his dirty work. He all but cracked her skull. Now if you was goin' to bash in somebody's head, what's the first thing—somethin' handy—that you'd think of usin'?"

"A pistol barrel," said Buck.

"I'd have to agree with that," Will said.

"That's all we have to go on," said Everett. "Come daylight, the three of us are goin' to take a look at some revolvers. And I think, since the Schmidt wagon is nearest Caleb's, we'll talk to Ab, Jenks, and Rufe. We'll have to do it quietly, so the rest of our suspects don't know what's comin'. The guilty man, if he did club Marcie with a pistol barrel, might throw the weapon in the river and say he'd lost it."

"We're lookin' for dried blood and maybe a hair or two," Buck said. "With Marcie's blond hair, that should be easy."

"Maybe not," said Will. "All this is dependin' on one thing. If this skunk *did* use his pistol barrel to club Marcie, did he remember—or was he smart enough—to clean the pistol barrel afterward?"

"It's a slim chance," Everett said, "but it's all we have to go on."

"We could split up," Buck said, "each of us going to a different wagon. We might get to them all before any of them discovered what we're up to."

"You might also get shot dead," said Everett. "There's two or three men in five of those wagons. Only Upshur Hiddenbrandt is alone. Buck, you'll examine each man's weapon. Will and me will stand prepared to shoot."

Following Marcie's deadly act, few in the camp had slept. After breakfast the women would prepare the girl for burial, the Word would be read over her, and hers would become another lonely grave along the Oregon Trail. The stars began receding into that faraway realm where they spent their daylight hours, and a golden glow to the east heralded the start of another day.

"It's time," said Landon Everett. "Let's go."

The three men set out for the Schmidt wagon and found the three brothers hunkered around a fire drinking coffee. None of the three offered any greeting and each wore a belted Colt.

"Stand up," Everett said.

"Fer what reason?" Rufe Schmidt demanded.

"Because I asked you to," said Landon Everett, drawing his Colt. Will Hamer followed suit.

Slowly the trio got to their feet.

"Now," Everett said, "stand apart. Fan out."

The three moved away from one another, their bearded faces showing no emotion but anger.

"Get behind them, Buck," said Everett, "and take a look at their revolvers."

"Why?" Jenks Schmidt snarled. "Why you lookin' at our guns?"

"Our business," said Everett. "I'm wagon boss and I have the right. Now raise your hands shoulder-high."

Reluctantly they did so, and Buck Embler lifted Jenks's Colt from its holster. He ran his fingers along the barrel and returned the weapon to its holster. He repeated the procedure with Rufe without finding what he sought. That left only Ab Schmidt, and not a trace of emotion betrayed what was about to follow. Waiting until Buck's hand was on the butt of the Colt, Schmidt reacted violently, so quickly that neither Landon Everett nor Will Hamer could fire. Schmidt seized Buck's arm, drawing Buck between himself and the two armed men. But Buck Embler outweighed Ab Schmidt and seized Ab in a bear hug. Jenks and Rufe dropped their hands to the butts of their Colts but they weren't fast enough.

"Don't do it!" Everett shouted.

The pair froze. Buck Embler and Ab Schmidt fought, Ab trying to reach his pistol. With Buck on top, there was little his friends could do to help him. Ab broke Buck's grip and went for his Colt. Landon Everett and Will Hamer had clear shots, but Everett stepped forward, slamming the barrel of his weapon against Ab's head. Will Hamer had kept his revolver leveled at Jenks and Rufe Schmidt. The commotion had caused a number of men and women to gather around, wanting to know the cause of the confrontation with the Schmidts. Buck Embler was on his feet now, and he carefully removed Ab Schmidt's Colt from its holster.

"You were right, Landon," said Buck. "There's dried blood and a strand of Marcie's hair. That's why he put up such a hell of a fight."

"He never done nothin'," Rufe snarled. "He was with us all night."

"The evidence proves otherwise," said Landon Everett. "The rest of you people, there's somethin' you need to know."

Ab Schmidt sat up, rubbing his bleeding head. "I never hit nobody with that pistol," he bawled.

"Nobody said you did," Everett replied. "In fact, nobody said anything about anyone being hit with a pistol except you. If you hadn't done it, how would you know that was the evidence we were looking for? People, we're going to delay everything—breakfast, the burial of Marcie Vandiver, everything—until justice has been done."

"I want a trial," Ab Schmidt shouted.

"You're going to get one," said Landon Everett, "with a jury of five hundred."

"Hang the scum," somebody shouted.

By now the entire camp had congregated, and there was a scuffle as men fought to restrain a screaming, cursing Caleb Vandiver. They finally wrestled him to the ground, taking away the revolver with which he had intended to kill Ab Schmidt.

"I see no need for choosing a jury of twelve," said Landon Everett. "I am accusing Ab Schmidt of willfully and brutally violating Marcie Vandiver, after first beating her unconscious with the barrel of his pistol. You all heard Ab deny beating anyone before he had been accused of it. If there is just one among you with any doubt, raise your hand. Buck will come to you with Ab's pistol, so that you may see the dried blood and bits of Marcie's hair. Are there any doubters?"

"No," shouted a dozen men. "Hang the murderin' skunk now."

"I ain't killed nobody," Ab Schmidt cried desperately. "I . . . I'm sayin' I hit her an' I . . . I took her, but she kilt herself. Fer God's sake, you all know that."

"Yes," said Landon Everett, "and she did it because

of what you did to her. You couldn't be any more guilty, damn you, if you'd pulled the trigger. I'm recommending that you be hanged for your crime, just as quickly as somebody can knot a noose."

"No," Caleb Vandiver shouted. "Damn you, Landon Everett, hanging's too good for him. I want him stripped, cut like a bull, gelded. *Then* we'll hang him."

There was a brief shocked silence, and then everbody began shouting at once.

"Silence," Landon Everett shouted. "Now," he said, when they had calmed down, "we're going to decide this man's fate like civilized people. We're not going to torture him. I think we're goin' to need that jury. Buck, choose twelve men."

"Just let Ab go," Rufe begged. "We'll leave the train and you'll never see us again."

"You and Jenks *are* going to leave the train," Landon Everett said, "but Ab's going to pay for what he's done."

"Landon, the jury's ready," said Buck.

"Take them to the other side of the camp," said Everett, "and see that they're undisturbed until they've reached some decision."

Ab Schmidt still lay on the ground. Jenks and Rufe stood with their hands shoulder-high, under the guns of Landon Everett and Will Hamer.

"Get up, Ab," Everett said. "Gus, get some rope and bind his hands behind him."

Buck returned with the twelve men who had been chosen for the jury. They had deliberated not more than fifteen minutes.

"The jury's reached a decision," Buck said. He nodded to one of the men who had been chosen. The man cleared his throat nervously before he spoke.

"We find Ab Schmidt guilty. We sentence him to hang."

"No," Ab cried. "No."

His hands had been bound behind him and he was led, weeping, from the circle of wagons. Jenks and Rufe were

marched along behind him, their hands in the air, dis-
armed and still under the guns of Landon Everett and
Will Hamer. Buck Embler brought a rope, at one end of
which was a thirteen-loop hangman's noose. Men followed, but the women remained behind, unwilling to
witness the grisly spectacle. A hundred yards upstream
the group halted beneath an old sycamore. Buck Embler
flung the noose end of the rope over a limb a dozen feet
from the ground. Four men took the loose end of the
rope, drawing the terrible noose head-high. Buck placed
the noose around Ab's neck, drawing the knot tight behind his left ear. Facing the doomed man, Landon Everett spoke.

"Ab Schmidt, do you have any last words?"

"Yeah," said Schmidt. "All of you go to hell." He then
spat in Everett's face, and it was his final act. The four
men at the loose end of the rope laid to, and Ab
Schmidt's feet left the ground. Ab kicked, revolving
slowly, kicking away his life. His face contorted, becoming a death mask, and men turned away. "That's
enough," Landon Everett said. "Let him down."

The men who had hoisted Ab eased him down, and
Buck Embler felt for a pulse. Finding none, he removed
the noose.

Landon Everett turned to Rufe and Jenks Schmidt.
"You want us to bury him, or will you do it?"

"You done enough fer us," said Rufe bitterly. "We'll
take care of him."

"Do it, then," Everett said. "When you're done, take
your wagon out of the circle and take it down the back
trail. If either of you are caught near this camp again, I'll
have you shot on sight. You'll find your guns in your
wagon. Buck, you and Will clear the way for them to get
their wagon out of the circle."

Buck and Will watched Rufe and Jenks Schmidt take
a pair of spades from the wagon and begin their slow
walk back to the old sycamore, the hanging tree. Landon

Everett and the rest of the men who had witnessed the hanging returned to camp.

There was still the sad burial of young Marcie Vandiver. Everett chose a pair of men to help him dig the grave, and they found a grassy knoll almost a mile north of the Platte River. Beneath a huge oak, they dug Marcie's grave. When the grave was ready, the three of them returned to camp. The women had wrapped Marcie's body in blankets, for they had nothing else. Oxen had been hitched to one of the wagons, and it bore the girl to her final resting place. Two men helped Caleb Vandiver up the hill, and he fell facedown before the grave, wailing and weeping. Finally he became silent and lay there trembling. Only then could Landon Everett read the Twenty-third Psalm. When he was finished, several of the men lifted Caleb into the wagon. The men who were to fill the grave waited until the wagon bearing Caleb was well on its way before they began their chore.

"Now," Everett said, when the sad mourners reached the camp, "after breakfast we're movin' out."

On the Platte River, southern Nebraska. June 8, 1843.

Far ahead, the Applegate party was not without its tragedies. The horse remuda leading out, the longhorns followed, and behind them came the emigrant wagons. Mules or oxen, three teams—six animals—were used to draw the heavy wagons.* It was the spooked mule teams of Devon and Nell Hayden that were the cause of the midday disaster. Kage Copeland, Dub Stern, Red Brodie, and Waco Tilden were riding drag, and it was Waco who first saw the runaway mules, the driverless wagon

---

* While oxen were led, mules were controlled by reins, the teamster riding a wide seat atop the wagon box. The front team was the lead team, the middle one the swing team, and the rear one the wheel team. Many of the wagons were built by the Studebaker brothers, beginning in 1839.

thundering along behind them in a cloud of dust. The out-of-control team was headed straight for the tag end of the herd.

"God Almighty!" Waco shouted. He wheeled his horse, kicking it into a fast gallop. As he neared the runaway team, he could see a woman on the wagon seat, frantically trying to recover the lost reins. Waco rode even with the lumbering wagon, turned his horse, and matching the speed of the galloping mules, kicked his feet free of the stirrups. Leaning from his saddle, he threw himself astride one of the lead mules. Gradually he took control of the runaway teams, slowing the wagon. Once the teams had stopped, Waco slid off the lead mule and hurried to the wagon. The woman sat slumped on the seat, her face buried in her hands. As Waco approached, she didn't even look up.

"Are you all right, ma'am?"

"I . . . I think so," she said, "but my husband . . . the wagon wheel hit something and . . . and he was thrown off."

"I'll catch my horse," said Waco, "and then we'll drive back and look for him."

Waco tied his horse to a bow at the back of the wagon, mounted the wagon box and took the reins. But by the time they were headed back the way the runaway team had come, they could see the lead wagons of Applegate's train in the distance. They would have found the unfortunate teamster who had been thrown from the wagon. Waco reined up, waiting for the Applegate train to reach them. Applegate halted the wagons and as he walked toward them, Waco could read the sadness in his weathered face. So could Nell Hayden. She began to weep.

"Nell," Applegate said, "I'm sorry. The wagon ran over him. He's dead. I have him in my wagon."

"Mr. Applegate," said Waco, "I'll take the news to Lou and Dill. I think we'll be makin' camp here for the night."

"Thank you, Waco," Applegate said. "Let's do that."

Waco had seen Devon and Nell Hayden in the emigrant camp many times, but he couldn't recall ever speaking to either of them. Devon had been some years older than Nell. Waco doubted she was more than a year or two older than his twenty-one years, and she seemed so pathetically alone, he felt the need to say something to her. But he didn't have a way with women, and there was an awkwardness about him.

"Ma'am," he said, removing his sweat-stained hat, "I'm real sorry. I'd have got there sooner if I could."

She looked at him for the first time, and Waco's heart leaped into his throat. Her bonnet hung down her back from a chin strap, and her curly dark hair was awry. Tears from big green eyes streaked the dust on her face, but she managed a wan smile.

"You did the best you could," she said, "and what you did was wonderful. Thank you."

Unable to think of anything more to say, Waco put on his hat, mounted his horse and rode ahead to tell Dill and Lou of the tragedy.

"Damn mules," said Dillard Sumner. "Oxen are slow, but they don't get spooked at their own shadow."

"This is likely to create a problem," Lou said. "If I'm thinkin' straight, this is goin' to leave the Widow Hayden with a wagon and no man to drive it."

"Yeah," said Dill, "and with them same blasted jugheaded mules pullin' it."

"Well, hell," Waco said, "we're near four hundred miles out of Independence, and we can't have her walkin' back. They'll have to figure out somethin'."

"Well, I'm goin' to be almighty interested in seein' what she'll do," said Dill. "She sure as hell can't drive them teams of cantankerous mules from here on to Oregon Territory."

The Texans backtrailed the horse remuda and the herd, bedding them down near the circled wagons. Jesse Applegate had men digging a grave near the river. Devon Hayden's body had been wrapped in blankets, and when the grave was ready, he was lowered into it. The emigrants and the cowboys gathered around, the men removing their hats. Jesse Applegate stood at the head of the grave, and under the hot Nebraska sun read selected passages from a worn Bible. Sarah and Sandy Applegate stood with their arms around Nell Hayden as she wept silent tears. She was led away before the grave was filled. When the party reached the circled wagons, the emigrants gathered around the girl, expressing their sympathy. The cowboys had to wait their turn, and Waco was last. Again he removed his hat and speech failed him. Impulsively, Nell took his big left hand in hers and squeezed it briefly, and when her eyes met Waco's, the tears began anew.

Jesse and Sarah Applegate spent several hours with the distraught Nell, and when everybody gathered for supper, Applegate had an announcement to make.

"We are still months away from our destination," Applegate said, "and I am sure all of you have been concerned about the . . . ah, future of the Widow Hayden. The wife and I have talked to her at length, unsure as to what she might wish to do. She has made her decision. She will continue on to Oregon Territory, handling her own teams, taking her wagon."

There was only silence. There was obvious doubt in the faces of some of the men, but the announcement drew a round of applause from the women. The Texans joined in, for it was an act of real courage; it was her kind of woman the frontier needed.

Southern Nebraska, along the Platte River. June 10, 1843.

When the cowboys rode in for breakfast, the emigrants were loading the wagons and harnessing their teams. Waco was the first to finish eating, and when he sought out the Hayden wagon, he found Nell harnessing the mules. She obviously knew how, but she was slow, and several of the animals had decided they didn't wish to be harnessed and were reacting accordingly.

"Let me harness them for you," said Waco.

Nell said nothing, gratefully surrendering the task. Waco harnessed the brutes, and taking the bridle of one of the lead mules, led the teams a ways to be sure they would behave themselves as they drew the wagon. Nell climbed over a front wheel, taking her place on the wide seat atop the wagon box. She took the reins from Waco, thanking him with a smile. The rest of the Texans were watching, and to their surprise as well as Waco's, Nell Hayden handled the team well.

"Keep a tight rein on the varmints," Waco shouted.

The cowboys led out with the horse remuda and followed with the herd. The emigrant wagons came last. Pete Haby, Tull Irvin, Sterling McCarty, and Waco Tilden were riding drag. Waco was there by request, and nobody had any doubts as to his reason.

Sterling McCarty laughed. "Ol' Waco ain't wasted no time gittin' thick with the Widow Hayden, an' her man ain't even cold in the ground. That purely don't seem fittin' an' proper."

"Who the hell are you to say what's fittin' and proper?" Waco growled. "I harnessed her team, and I'll do it again in the morning and the day after that. Mind your own damn business, McCarty."

"Well, ain't *you* touchy," McCarty said, with just a little too much sarcasm.

"I am," said Waco, glaring at McCarty, "and when I'm this way, I generally pick some hombre that's needful of it and beat his ears down to his boot tops."

"Hell," Pete Haby said, "I don't see nothin' wrong with a gent harnessin' the woman's teams. It'll be hard enough on her as it is."

"I know what McCarty's gittin' at," said Tull Irvin. "I got kin back east. Them Yankees—the high sassiety kind —reckons a woman ought to mourn her man fer a year, wearin' black. Boys, it's a whole 'nother world out here in the wilds of the western frontier. A woman needs a man, an' by God, she ain't too bright if she waits a year. You harness that little gal's teams from here to Oregon Territory, Waco, an' time we git there, you'll have a mighty purty bed buddy on cold nights."

Waco went red as a gobbler's wattles, and his companions roared with laughter, but deep down, the sandy-haired cowboy was pleased.

11

After Rufe and Jenks Schmidt buried Ab, they returned to find that other wagons had been moved so that they might remove theirs from the circle. Landon Everett was there to see that they did so, and to drive along the back trail a ways. He didn't want the undesirable duo ahead of him.

"You have two choices," said Everett. "You can head on back to Independence, or you can set out yonder on the back trail until the sun's noon-high. I want you at least half a day behind me if you continue on to Oregon."

Without a word, the two harnessed their oxen and started their wagon along the back trail. Neither spoke until they were well away from the emigrant camp.

"What you think we ought to do?" Jenks Schmidt asked.

"Hell," Rufe said, "we're goin' on to Oregon. Landon Everett don't own this trail. Way I see it, we owe that bastard somethin', an' if we ain't figgered a way to git at him on the trail, we'll git him at the end of it."

"What's the use gittin' us kilt fer what they done to Ab? It was his own damn fault. He'd been after that Vandiver gal ever since we left St. Louis, an' she wouldn't have nothin' to do with him. Ain't no woman worth a man gittin' his fool neck stretched."

"I know," Rufe growled. "I know. But that was always Ab's weakness, like a man has a weakness fer rotgut. So it warn't all Ab's fault, an' by God, he *was* our blood kin."

Rufe and Jenks were four or five miles along the back trail when Rufe, who led the oxen, halted the teams after turning the wagon around.

"I feel like a damn fool, settin' here half a day," said Jenks.

"We ain't waitin' half a day," Rufe said. "Couple of hours, maybe. We'll stay jist far enough behind so's we don't git them farmers gunnin' fer us."

The pair had been there only a few minutes when they heard the rattle of an approaching wagon.

"Buckalew," Jenks said as the wagon drew nearer, "but them two gents in the saddle don't look like none of the bunch he had when we left him at the Missouri."

"They ain't," Rufe replied. "This pair looks like real sidewinders. Buckalew's judgment is improved some."

Buckalew halted his teams next to the Schmidt wagon, saying nothing. He finally spoke when it became obvious neither of the Schmidts intended to.

"Why are you two settin' here like a pair of knots on a log?"

"None of yer damn business," said Rufe.

Gerdes laughed. "These peckerwoods looks guilty as a pair of whores in church. I'd bet my drawers they had somethin' to do with that screamin' and shootin' that busted loose durin' the night."

"And ol' Landon Everett booted 'em out of his train. As I recall, they was three of you ugly varmints. Where's the other one?"

"Ab's dead," said Jenks. "They hung him this mornin'."

"Jenks," Rufe snapped, "jist shut the hell up."

"Damn if I will," Jenks shouted. "Ab's dead, it's his own fault, and there ain't nothin' we kin do about it. You wanta go on makin' like nothin' happened, then you do it, but I ain't."

"Landon Everett thinks he's God," Buckalew said, sounding more sympathetic. "He run us off, told us to stay away from his people. Who the hell does he think he is, Moses?"

"He told us to set here on the back trail till the sun was noon-high. He wants us half a day behind him," said Jenks.

"And you was settin' here waitin'," Suggs said. "Hell, my old granny's got more guts than that."

That stung Rufe, and he turned on Suggs in a fury. "By God, I don't see you three shirttail pistol packers in any hurry to catch up. Everett said scat and the three of you lit out."

"Why not?" said Buckalew. "We ain't married to that bunch of plow pushers in Landon Everett's party. We'll trail behind 'em for a while, but we don't need them. If you aim to go on to Oregon Territory, why don't you trail with us? Might be we can use your help somewhere along the trail, and it'd pay off big."

"Yeah? How big, an' in what way?" Rufe demanded.

"I ain't ready to tell you just yet," said Buckalew. "I'd wanta see the pair of you git a little more cooperative, an' quit takin' your mad agin' Everett out on us. Maybe time we're ready to git ahead of Everett's outfit an' catch up to Applegate's, I'll feel more like talkin'. You're goin' to Oregon anyhow. Convince me I kin depend on you, and you could reach the end of this trail with some gold coin in your pockets."

Jenks looked at Rufe and Rufe shook his head. He turned to Buckalew, and when he spoke, it was without anger.

"You're right, Buckalew. We are goin' on to Oregon, so what do we got to lose? We'll trail with you, an' whatever you got in mind, long as we don't git shot or hung, we'd be int'rested."

"Let's git on the trail then," said Buckalew. He

winked in the general direction of Suggs and Gerdes.
The Schmidts could be used, and disposed of when they
were no longer needed.

Rufe led his teams in behind Buckalew's wagon and
they were on their way. Jenks walked alongside Rufe,
and when he spoke, it was a low hiss, so only Rufe could
hear.

"I don't like Buckalew nor them gunnies ridin' with
him. Why in hell was you makin' deals with 'em?"

"Gold," Rufe said. "Damn it, you think I don't know
they'd double-cross us 'fore it come time to pay up?
They got somethin' in mind, an' if it pays off big, then
you oughta know what we're goin' to do."

"Pull a double-cross of our own, gun the varmints
down and take it all fer ourselves."

Rufe grinned. "Yer damn right, an' when they're least
expectin' it."

Landon Everett's party moved on. Damon Kilmer's son,
sixteen-year-old Danny, had agreed to drive Caleb
Vandiver's wagon for a day or two until, hopefully, Caleb
came to his senses. But there seemed little hope for that.
Caleb lay inside the wagon on a blanket, talking out of
his head, his eyes apparently seeing nothing. Young
Danny had already been complaining about Caleb's ee-
rie behavior. Will Hamer and Buck Embler confronted
Everett with the problem after the wagons had been
circled for the night.

"God, Landon," said Will, "Caleb's talkin' to Marcie
like she was alive, and Danny's spooked. He says he ain't
leadin' Caleb's teams no farther. What are we gonna do
about Caleb and his wagon?"

"Damn it," Everett snapped, "I don't know. If that
was the only problem we had, I'd feel like Moses viewin'
the Promised Land. Marcie's dead, Caleb's lost his
senses, and there's still a killer on the loose. We still
don't know who robbed and murdered Fraser and Hen-

dricks. As wagon boss, I feel I must solve these earlier murders to prevent any new ones."

"We're rid of the Schmidts," said Buck, "and that leaves nine men on your list of suspects. Will you go on keepin' them off night watch?"

"Until somethin' happens to convince me I'm wrong," Everett said. "You got any better ideas?"

"No," Buck said. "We got nothin' else to go on. I guess what's botherin' me is I'm half afraid the killer will strike again, and then we'll be back where we started, not knowin' what the hell to do."

"The biggest problem facin' us right now," said Will, "is who's gonna lead Caleb Vandiver's teams on to Oregon Territory?"

"That may not be the only problem," Buck observed. "What if we get him there and he's lost his mind permanent? What'n hell are we gonna do with him?"

"By God," Landon Everett shouted, "one thing at a time. I will personally see to it that somebody leads Caleb's teams. I refuse to worry about what's going to happen in Oregon until we finally get there. If we ever do." He stalked off toward his wagon to talk to Mattie.

"We got to do somethin'," said Will, "or Landon's goin' to break, if he ain't already."

Buck sighed. "I know. But what can we do?"

Mattie had the supper fire going when Everett reached the wagon. He looked at her from sleepless eyes, his weathered face seeming more haggard than ever. The women always talked among themselves, and Mattie already knew what the immediate problem was.

"Landon," she said, "I want to talk to you. Sit down."

He sank down on the wagon tongue, saying nothing, knowing she would speak her mind.

"Landon, I've found someone to lead Caleb's team until he's right in the head."

"Caleb may *never* be right in the head," Everett said wearily. "Who's going to lead his teams all the way to Oregon Territory? All these people have wagons of their own. Anyway, Caleb's ranting has already scared hell out of Danny Kilmer, and there's no reason to believe he won't have the same effect on everybody else. Damn it, Mattie, we'd have to pay somebody."

"We *are* going to pay somebody," Mattie said calmly.

"Who, for God's sake, and how?"

"Quilla Rowden," said Mattie. "Thirty-five families have agreed to contribute ten cents a week so we can pay her fifty cents a day."

"And she's agreed?"

"Yes," said Mattie. "I spoke to her mother, Flora, and she talked to Quilla's father, Joseph. She handles teams as well or better than any man."

"God," Everett said, "if I didn't know she *is* a woman, I'd swear she was a man. But she's been helping her daddy with his teams."

"Her brother Ned is seventeen," said Mattie. "He'll take Quilla's place helping Joseph lead their teams. I don't mean to pry into your business, Landon, but you have worries enough. I only did what I thought was best, the little I could do to help."

"Bless you, Mattie," Everett said with a sigh. "If there's anybody among all these people worthy of the job, it's Quilla."

Quilla Rowden was twenty-five years old. She looked, worked, dressed, swore, drank, and fought like a man. She apparently had no interest in anybody, male or female. When she wasn't leading her father's teams, she stalked silently along behind the wagon. Her seventeen-year-old brother, Ned, was terrified of her. He had sneaked around and watched her bathing in the creek once, and she had almost drowned him. She had been an embarrassment to Joseph and Flora Rowden most of her life. When only a child, she had set fire to a neighbor's barn, and when the Rowdens were ready to leave Indiana, they'd had to get Quilla out of the local jail. She had gotten crazy drunk in a tavern, broken a man's jaw in a brawl, and had been arrested for public drunkenness and disorderly conduct. There was speculation among those who knew the Rowdens that the unpredictable, hell-raising Quilla had been their reason for selling out and heading for Oregon. The enigmatic Quilla had a trunk in the Rowden wagon. Nobody seemed to know what the trunk contained, and Quilla had the only key.

A hundred miles east of Fort Laramie. July 24, 1843.

"Maybe ten more days to Fort Laramie," Lou said, studying Applegate's map as they waited for supper.

"Good news," said Dillard Sumner. "I been startin' to feel like we'd never reach Laramie."

"I know how you feel," Lou replied. "That looks like maybe the halfway point. We'll still be followin' the Platte River for a good two hundred miles after we leave Laramie. After that I don't see another river on this map until we cross the Green, in southwestern Wyoming Territory."

"That's something that's been bothering me," said Applegate. "Since leaving Independence, we've always followed a river. When we leave the Platte, how do we know where the next water is?"

"I don't know how the trains ahead of us managed it," Lou said, "but on the drive from Texas we sent a rider ahead to find the next nearest water, and we always stayed one day ahead. So when we reach the place where the Platte turns south, before we leave there, we'll scout ahead to the next water."

"I can see the need for that," Applegate said, "but suppose the next water is too far ahead for us to reach it in a single day?"

"Dry camp," said Lou, "but at these higher elevations, I'd not be surprised to find springs and creeks that don't show on the map. I expect these rivers have been drawn on the maps more as landmarks than to show us where the water is. We've just been lucky the trail follows the river as far as it does."

The procedure the Texans had established for nighthawking had worked well, so Dillard Sumner's outfit continued taking the first watch while Lou and his men took the second. Every night after supper, Lou and Sandy Applegate managed to be alone for a few minutes. At seventeen, Vangie was only two years younger than Vic Sloan, and the cowboy had become more aggressive, asking the girl to walk with him. Since the emigrant families had become more friendly to the Texans, several of Dillard Sumner's riders had grown close to girls in the Applegate party. Kage Copeland had become more than a little friendly with Dorrie Halleck, while Dub Stern was taking all his meals with Rosa Wallace. Both girls had former suitors, and smelling trouble in the making, Jesse Applegate spoke to Dillard Sumner.

"Copeland and Stern aren't my riders," Applegate said, "but since I'm wagon boss, Higdon and Quimby thought I ought to talk to you."

"Kage Copeland and Dub Stern are two of my best riders," said Dillard Sumner. "What's the problem?"

"Maybe none," Applegate said, "but I don't want trouble between you Texans and my people. It seems there may be some in the making, and I'm not quite sure how to handle it."

"If it's what I think it is," Sumner said, "I ain't sure I know how to handle it either. Keep talkin'."

"Copeland has become quite close to Dorrie Halleck, while Stern has developed a similar interest in Rosa Wallace. While I see nothing wrong with that, Barney Sandlin and Juno Pender are ready to fight. Barney and Dorrie practically grew up together, and so did Juno and Rosa. I was told the four of them planned a double wedding when they reached Oregon, but the girls have put an end to that. Now I hear Barney and Juno are calling for a fight. With guns, knives, or fists."

Sumner sighed. "Damn. Have you talked to the parents of the girls?"

"Yes," said Applegate, "but they're as confused as I

am. Both women are of age, old enough to do as they please, and as stubborn as balky mules."

"Don't I know it," Sumner said. "For the past three or four nights they've been out there for two or three hours, nighthawking with Kage and Dub."

"They're riding your horses," said Applegate. "Can't you forbid them riding the animals?"

"No," Sumner said, "because they ain't ridin' my horses. Every rider in my outfit has a string of three. They're using their own mounts. You're the wagon boss, damn it. Just tell Sandlin and Pender there'll be no fightin' in camp. For any reason."

"I've done that," said Applegate. "Now they've issued a challenge to fight your riders while we're camped this next Sunday. Somewhere well away from camp."

"Then I have some advice for Sandlin and Pender," Sumner said, "and you'd best pass it on. My boys have fought Comanches with Bowie knives, and they're quicker than chain lightnin' with Colts. If this Sandlin and Pender is hell-bent on a fight, then they'd better stick to fists. Bruises heal quick, gunshot and knife wounds don't. Sometimes never."

"I'll talk to the parents of these two young fools," said Applegate. "Maybe they can stop it."

"I wouldn't lose no sleep over it, Mr. Applegate," Sumner said. "Unless Sandlin and Pender force it, I'll see that my men don't pull knives or Colts. Best way to cure a man of what he thinks he wants is to give him a good dose of it. I've seen these young bucks that reckoned they could go huntin' lobo wolves with a switch, and I never seen one yet that didn't change his mind after somebody purely beat the hell out of him."

Applegate sighed. These Texans were a salty buch, but they were fair. He was weary of trying to talk sense to damn fools who wanted none of it. Maybe Sumner was right. He found himself half hoping Sandlin and Pender insisted on the fight.

"Hell," said Lou when Sumner told him of the conversation with **Applegate**, "you can't blame Kage and Dub. This is the frontier. Stake out your claim, and you'd better be man enough to hold it. If these young roosters are spoilin' for a fight, then let them fight, but let it be with fists. My money's on Kage and Dub."

"I told Applegate he'd better keep the guns and knives out of it, or he'd have a pair of dead hombres on his hands," Sumner said. "I think we can count on him to warn Sandlin and Pender."

Suggs and Gerdes virtually ignored the Schmidts. Buckalew, however, seemed more sympathetic for their having lost Ab, and as Jenks and Rufe began to talk a little more freely, Buckalew learned what was troubling Landon Everett.

"Hell's fire," Buckalew said, "somebody's mighty brave or god-awful stupid, slittin' a man's throat for the gold in his pockets. Let one gent wake up just a second ahead of the knife and he could rouse the whole damn camp. The killer wouldn't stand a chance."

"Whoever's doin' it is cat-footed and slick as a greased pig," said Rufe. "Everett ain't got a clue as to who's doin' it."

"Unless I'm disrememberin', Buckalew," Suggs said, "it ain't been more'n a few days since you was suggestin' we might pick up some gold from them sodbusters in Everett's party."

"Well, by God," Jenks said, "if *that's* what you got in mind, Buckalew, you can just figger me out of it. Everett's got so's he only trusts certain men on night watch, and they're all as jumpy as a bunch of sore-tailed tomcats. You go nosin' around them wagons after dark an' you'll end up with enough lead in yer gut to sink a ferry boat."

"Hell," said Buckalew, "you *know* some of Everett's bunch is got more than what they carry in their pockets. Yeah, I give it some thought, havin' a go at it some dark night. But that was 'fore I knowed about them killings an' robberies. Schmidt's right. With them pumpkin rollers settin' there with loaded guns, afeared fer their lives, we could get our ears shot off without even gittin' close. We'll stick with what we already planned."

"An' you still ain't told us what that is," Rufe said.

"I wasn't goin' to until I knowed how much help we could expect from you," said Buckalew. "You jist convinced me, tellin' us about them killings in Everett's train. We never knowed his trouble was all that bad, and yer right. We could of been shot to doll rags, gittin' too close. I think mebbe you're ready to hear what we got planned."

Quickly Buckalew ran through their plans to take the gold hidden in the Applegate, Higdon, and Quimby wagons, and finally the taking of the herd of Texas longhorns.

"That makes more sense than anything that's ever come out of you, Buckalew," Rufe said with some admiration. "Can't hang a man but once, no matter if he's stole a sheep or a wagonload of gold. I'd foller you to hell for a piece of that."

"Just see that you two jaybirds don't start thinkin' in terms of more'n a piece of it," Gerdes said suspiciously. "Get too damn greedy, an' you'll be goin' to hell all right, but by your lonesome."

"Gerdes," Buckalew said angrily, "this is my idea, my show, an' by God, I'm sayin' what goes an' what don't. Jist be sure *you* don't git too damn greedy. An' that goes fer you too, Suggs."

Suggs and Gerdes said nothing, but the looks they exchanged suggested that before the finish, Jap Buckalew might not be calling the shots. They had killed men with far less provocation and without a wagonload of gold up for grabs.

There was considerable talk and speculation among the Everett party when everybody learned of Mattie Everett's arrangement with Quilla Rowden. While most of the older women looked upon the buxom, friendless Quilla with compassion, some of the younger ones and a few of the men called her names, including "Quilla the gorilla." But never to her face or loud enough for her to hear.

"God," said Will Hamer, "there's somethin' unnatural about a woman lookin' so much like a man she can get drunk in saloons without even bein' questioned."

"That's true," Buck Embler agreed, "but at least she don't smoke or chew plug, and nobody's caught her shaving."

Despite some crude jokes and talk behind her back, nobody bothered Quilla, for her vocabulary of cuss words had become legend. Her tongue could flay a tormentor like a blacksnake whip, and her being a woman —no matter how unwomanly she looked and acted— there was little a man could do to defend himself.

"I just hope nobody says or does anything to anger Quilla," Mattie Everett said worriedly. "Sometimes I think the women are envious of her because she has the audacity to do . . . to do . . ."

"What she damn pleases," Landon finished, "and the men don't like her because she's the best damn bull whacker of us all."

Despite her misgivings, Mattie laughed. "I believe you've discovered the secret, Landon. But something had to be done, and whatever she is or has been, Quilla's the answer to a prayer. Caleb was heard crying and talking to himself last night."

Landon Everett sighed. "I know. Some of the men on the second watch told me. I'm sorry for the man and for poor Marcie, but my God, if we have to listen to him squall and carry on all the way to Oregon, we'll be as out our minds as he is."

"That's a terrible thing to say," Mattie replied, "but Lord, it's so true. But what *really* bothers me is, suppose we reach Oregon and—"

"Caleb Vandiver's still out of his head." Everett

knuckled his tired eyes. "God, Mattie, I just don't know. That's somethin' that only time will tell. What happened to Marcie, Caleb crackin' up, and havin' to hang Ab Schmidt, knocked us all down so low, we're forgettin' that two men have been murdered for the gold in their pockets. The damn killer is still on the loose."

"You still have nine suspects, Landon," said Mattie, "and there's a chance the killings may be over. We may never know who did these terrible things, and nobody's going to blame you, especially if it doesn't happen again."

But it *did* happen again. That very night a third man had his throat slit and his gold taken. It took place in the dead of night, silently, and while none of the men Landon Everett suspected were on watch.

12

Fifty miles east of Fort Laramie. July 29, 1843.

Since the Oregon Trail virtually followed the North Fork of the Platte River for several hundred miles west of Fort Laramie, there was no shortage of water. Emigrants could pause for the night wherever they chose, and it had become customary for Applegate's train to make camp early on Sunday afternoons, when there was still a good three or four hours before sundown. It had become a time to wash clothes and blankets, or to rest. The cowboys had come to enjoy the respite, for unless there was a violent storm, there was little chance the herd would stampede. It was one of the few times when the Texans could socialize with the emigrants, allowing some of the cowboys to make inroads with the party's single women. This particular Sunday, tension ran high, for it seemed there was no way to avoid a fight between cowboys and young easterners over a pair of flighty females. Once the wagons had been circled, Jesse Applegate sought out Dillard Sumner. Lou Spencer was with him.

"I have said all I intend to say to this pair of young fools," Applegate growled, "and that goes for their parents as well. Dorrie Halleck and Rosa Wallace are single, of age, and insist Sandlin and Pender have no claim on them. If Copeland and Stern walk the girls along the river, away from camp, Sandlin and Pender will surely follow. Sumner, your riders may defend themselves in whatever manner may be necessary. You'll get no argument from me."

"I reckon Kage and Dub can handle this pair of roosters without killin' either of 'em," said Sumner, "but they may be so busted up they'll be ridin' in a wagon for a few days. We ain't the kind to start fights, Mr. Applegate, but we finished a hell of a bunch of 'em."

"Mr. Applegate," Lou said, "Vic Sloan and me will walk Vangie and Sandy down that way and look out for them. Just about everybody's aimin' to follow, to watch the fight."

"Just keep my girls out of the way if there's shooting," said Applegate. "This whole foolish affair has been blown out of proportion. You'd think the rest of these people are on their way to a circus."

"Maybe they are," Dillard Sumner said. "Why don't you walk down there with us? You might learn somethin'."

"Maybe I will," said Applegate. "I suppose every other man in camp will be there. They've been placing bets."

Applegate was at his wagon when Lou and Vic came for Sandy and Vangie. Kage and Dub, accompanied by Dorrie and Rosa, had already started their walk upstream. A hundred yards behind them, dozens of men followed, led by Juno Pender and Barney Sandlin. Both men wore belted Colts on their right hips.

"Jesse," Sarah Applegate said worriedly, "Sandy and Vangie shouldn't be attending such . . . such a thing. Why did you allow them to go?"

"Because they're in safe company," said Applegate. "There's not a soul left in camp except us. Are you afraid to stay here alone for a while?"

"You . . . you're not going to witness that . . . that spectacle?"

"I am," said Applegate. "I forbade them to fight, and they laughed in my face. I have every confidence these cowboys won't take unfair advantage, but I intend to witness this entire affair. I suspect Sandlin and Pender are going to learn a painful lesson. Afterward, when they begin to whine, I will know the truth of what happened and what did not. Why don't you go with me?"

"I will," she said, surprising him. "You've done your best to stop this foolish fight. Perhaps it would do me good to see this pair of young ruffians take a thrashing."

The Applegates hurried, catching up to Lou, Vic, Sandy, and Vangie.

"There was nobody left in camp but us," said Applegate. "I suppose we have as much business there as anybody else."

"You should be there," Lou said. "Then if there's any complaining afterward, you'll know the straight of it. That's why Dill and me aim to be there."

Sumner laughed. "That and the fact a Texan never misses a good fight."

The many followers were still within sight of the circled wagons when Kage Copeland and Dub Stern paused, watching the challengers approach. The women —Dorrie and Rosa—moved well away from the river. The rest of those who had come to observe veered away, joining Dorrie and Rosa. Lou, Vic, Sandy, Vangie, Jesse, and Sarah Applegate went on to join the rest of the spectators. Barney Sandlin and Juno Pender paused, aware that they now stood alone. They might have had second thoughts, but it was too late for that. Their big talk and fierce pride had committed them to a battle that seemed less and less appealing, the closer it came. They walked on, while Kage Copeland and Dub Stern waited, hands on their hips.

"We aim to teach you cow-nursin' varmints a lesson," Sandlin bawled.

"Damn right," Pender shouted. "You took our women."

"Wal, I declare," said Kage in an exaggerated drawl, "we looked real close an' their ears wasn't notched."

"We didn't see no brands on their flanks neither," Dub added. "You poor young fellers got any proof?"

The absurd conversation was loud enough for everybody attending to hear, and they roared with laughter. It infuriated Sandlin and Pender, and the two crouched, shaking hands hovering over the butts of their Colts. It was Kage Copeland who spoke, and his voice was steady, cold, deadly.

"You gents had best have a good look at that blue sky. Next time your eyes is turned in that direction, you won't be seein' nothin'. When you pull iron, you die."

His hard words had a ring of finality that wasn't lost on Sandlin and Pender. They paused and their cause was lost. Sandlin cursed and Pender shouted an insult.

"We got cause for the way we feel," he bawled. "It's a low-down, snake-mean thing to do, stealing a man's woman."

"We've stole nothin' belongin' to either of you," Dub Stern replied coldly. "You can't lose somethin' you never had."

"You got burrs under your tails and are hell-bent on a fight," Kage said, "shuck them gun belts and we'll give you as much satisfaction as you're man enough to take."

"Damn right," said Dub. "We don't waste lead on shorthorns we can educate by just stompin' hell out of 'em. If you varmints don't learn nothin' today, we can always shoot you some other time."

Sandlin and Pender unbuckled their pistol belts, passing them to men who came to get them. Kage and Dub unbuckled their pistol belts, passing them to Dillard Sumner.

"Thank God," Jesse Applegate sighed. "At least nobody will die."

Kage and Dub stood their ground, forcing their antagonists to start the fight. Sandlin and Pender were big-boned, outweighing Kage and Dub, and feeling they had

an edge, sought to take advantage of it. They charged
with the intention of taking their opponents in bear
hugs. Kage and Dub, with perfect timing, stepped aside,
tripping Sandlin and Pender. They went belly down, and
eventually arose to a roar of laughter from everybody.
Even their friends. Wary now, they approached more
cautiously. Again Kage and Dub forced their adversaries
to come to them. Sandlin took a swing at Kage, but
Copeland avoided it, responding with a blow of his own.
Sandlin, off balance, took a smash on the point of his
chin that all but lifted him off his feet. He stumbled
backward, his eyes glazed, sitting down abruptly. Juno
Pender let fly with a vicious right, and Dub Stern didn't
even try to avoid it. With his left hand he caught
Pender's right wrist, using Pender's own momentum to
draw him closer. Stern's own right came up with such
force the observers heard it thud against Pender's jaw.
He went down almost beside Sandlin, and the pair of
them looked as though they had taken time out to rest.

"Sandlin, Pender," Applegate shouted, "that's
enough. You've been beaten fair and square. That's
enough."

But for Barney Sandlin and Juno Pender it wasn't
enough. Both men got to their feet, each drawing a concealed knife from his boot.

"Stop it," Applegate shouted frantically. "Drop the
knives, or I'll shoot both of you." He wasn't bluffing, for
his hand was on the butt of his Colt when Dillard Sumner got to him.

"No," said Sumner. "Kage and Dub can handle
them."

Sandlin took a swipe at Kage, slashing his shirtfront
from left to right, but it cost him. Kage caught the wrist
of the hand bearing the knife and, drawing Sandlin
closer, slammed the toe of his right boot into Sandlin's
groin. Sandlin sank to his knees, groaning. Kage seized
the knife, and kicking Sandlin in the behind, flattened
him belly down. Kage got a fistful of Sandlin's shirt and,

starting at the collar, slit it down the back. But he didn't stop there. He slashed Sandlin's belt and then his trousers from waist to boot tops. He then ripped the shredded trousers from the unfortunate Sandlin, leaving him wearing only a slashed shirt and drover's boots. He flung Sandlin's knife into the nearby Platte River.

"My God," said Applegate, "that's enough."

"No, sir," Dillard Sumner said, "Dub ain't finished yet."

While Dub's left arm bled from a knife slash, he had flattened Juno Pender and was in the process of humiliating him in the same manner that Kage Copeland had stripped Sandlin. Finished, he threw Pender's knife into the river. He and Kage then stepped back to admire their handiwork. Those who had come to see the fight stood in shocked silence, and there were only the agonized groans of Sandlin and Pender. Both men sat up, aware for the first time of their terrible humiliation.

"Damn you," Sandlin sobbed, his hate-filled eyes on Kage, "I'm gonna kill you for this."

"You'd best make it good the first time, bucko," said Kage, "because you won't get a second chance. Next time you pull a knife on me, I'll cut off a mite more than your britches."

"The same goes for you, Pender," Dub said. "Next time, if there is one, I won't go easy on you. I don't aim to dirty my hands either. If you still got a mad on and you come after me again, pull your iron."

"You son of a bitch," Pender snarled, "when I'm ready, I'll be comin', and I'll kill you if it's the last thing I ever do."

"You can try," said Dub, "and it *will* be the last thing you ever do."

Dub Stern and Kage Copeland turned and walked away, back to the silent spectators. Dillard Sumner returned their pistol belts, and they buckled them on. The Texans then sought out Dorrie Halleck and Rosa Wallace. The women were white-faced and silent, their eyes on the two virtually naked men who dared not stand while they had an audience.

"Dear God," Sarah Applegate said, "this is terrible. I never saw anything like it."

"It was pretty raw," said Applegate, "but this is a hard land. I did all I could to avoid this, and I can't say I'm sorry."

Sandy Applegate laughed. "I've seen fights before, but this is the first time I ever saw the losers end up naked."

"Sandy, shame on you," Sarah said.

But her reprimand was lost in the laughter following Sandy's remark. Only the parents of Barney Sandlin and Juno Pender had gone to the aid of their offspring. Dorrie Halleck and Rosa Wallace had overcome their initial shock. Dorrie again walked beside Kage, while Rosa accompanied Dub.

"Thank God this is behind us," said Jesse Applegate. "I hope these young men have learned a lesson."

But Kage Copeland and Dub Stern knew it wasn't over. While they did not know when or where the showdown would come, they were all the more sure it would come. Fists and knives had settled nothing; there was no law except the Colt and only two kinds of men: the quick and the dead.

Landon Everett sat on the wagon tongue, face buried in his big hands, waiting for breakfast. They had just buried Luke Wilson, the third man to have his throat slashed and his gold stolen. Luke had left behind two sons old enough to lead the teams, and for that Everett was thankful. He now had three women in the party whose men had died at the hands of the mysterious killer, and he was no closer to solving the mystery. These unfortunate women who had lost husbands eyed Landon Everett with a bitterness that was difficult to ignore, and though Mattie had said nothing negative, Everett could see the worry in her eyes. Every woman in the party existed under a cloud of fear, aware that her man might be the next to die.

"Breakfast, Landon," Mattie said.

They ate together, neither speaking, she knowing what was on his mind. The nine remaining men of whom he had been suspicious had not been on watch when Luke Wilson had died. That didn't mean it couldn't have been one of them, but it lessened the possibility, for a dozen men walked the circle of wagons from dusk to dawn. They were finishing their coffee when Will Hamer and Buck Embler approached.

"We're hearin' some hard talk, Landon," said Will.

"I'm not surprised," Everett said wearily, "and I don't blame them. If it will help, I'll step down as wagon boss."

"It ain't that," said Buck. "There's talk among some of the families of goin' back. Back to Illinois, Indiana, and Ohio."

"I can't stop them," Everett said, "but Mattie and me will go on."

"Me and Will and our women will go with you," said Buck. "I think when we stop at the end of the day, you should call a meeting."

"Perhaps I should," Everett replied, "but what am I going to say? That I'm no closer to putting a stop to these damned killings, and the only possible theory I had has been shot to hell?"

"No," said Will, "Buck and me think you ought to remind them there's as much danger goin' back as there is in goin' ahead. There won't be as many goin' back as will be goin' on to Oregon, and who can be sure that the killer will go on? If some of the party returns East, there won't be near as many men on watch. There's a chance the killer, whoever he is, don't care a damn about goin' to Oregon. Maybe he just saw this as a chance to get away from the law, to kill and rob."

"What you're suggesting," Everett said, "is that the killer, instead of going on to Oregon, might choose to return East with a smaller party."

"That's it," said Will. "They're damned if they do and damned if they don't, so why not just go ahead and take their chances?"

"It makes sense to me," Everett said, "but when people are afraid, I doubt they'll think or act sensibly. When I speak to these people, I will be speaking to the killer too. When I mention the possibility of his returning East with a smaller party, suppose I'm suggesting something that might convince him to do exactly that?"

"Landon," said Mattie, "if some of these people choose to turn back, then they're no longer your responsibility. Dear God, Landon, let them go, without adding to their fears or burdening them with your suspicions."

"Mattie's right," Will said. "If some of these people return East, it's at their own risk. There'll be far more of them going on to Oregon Territory than will be turning back. God knows, we'll have our hands full with those who are going on. Buck and me will side you in every way we can. Go on and call a meetin' tonight before supper, but don't raise any false hopes. Damn it, just admit you don't have any answers. You got this bunch thinkin' you're goin' to stop this killing and stealing, and now they're put out with you 'cause you ain't been able to do it."

"You're dead right, Will," said Everett. "Now what *are* we going to do?"

"Maybe I can answer that," Buck Embler said. "Landon, you've had the men unrollin' their blankets beneath the wagons, makin' room for the women and children inside."

"I think I know what you're gettin' at, Buck," said Everett, "and you know these damn wagons are piled to the bows. Am I right when I say you're about to suggest *all* these people—men, women, and children—crowd into the wagons at night?"

"I was about to suggest that very thing," Buck said. "So what if they have to pile some of their goods outside the wagon every night and then sleep sittin' up? Ain't that better than wakin' up to more dead men? Way it is now, women and kids is inside the wagon, and all this damn killer's got to be concerned with is the men on watch. In the dead of night not a man of us is safe, alone under our wagons. Startin' tonight, no matter how cramped it is, I'll be in the wagon with my woman. Even if the both of us have to squat like toads."

"I feel the same way, Landon," said Will. "By God, let these people do somethin' to protect themselves. It's one thing to knife a lone man under his wagon, and somethin' else to have to go inside, where there's others to cry for help."

"Landon, that's the answer," Mattie cried. "If you can't find the killer, take away the victims. Please call a meeting before supper and do as Will and Buck have suggested. Then there'll be nobody outside the wagons except the men on watch, and they'll be awake."

"I'll consider it," said Everett. "God knows, I have nothing else to suggest."

"Accordin' to the map," Will said, "we can't be more than eighty miles east of Fort Laramie. That's almost halfway. I'd say if anybody's serious about returnin' East, they'd better pull out now."

"I'll talk to them," said Everett, "but I'll not encourage anybody to leave the train. That will be their decision."

At dusk Dillard Sumner's outfit rode out to begin the first watch. The Sandlin and Pender families, while still within the wagon circle, kept to themselves. There was no sign of Barney Sandlin or Juno Pender. Lou Spencer and his riders hunkered around the supper fire, drinking coffee. Jesse Applegate said little, his anxious eyes on the Sandlin and Pender wagons. He caught Lou watching him and finally spoke.

"That disgraceful affair this afternoon has created a rift among us," Applegate said. "I regret that it happened, and I fear it isn't over."

"For Sandlin and Pender's sake," said Lou, "I hope it is. Kage and Dub could have killed those damn fools if they'd chosen to."

"Perhaps they should have," Applegate said. "I doubt there would have been any more bitterness. I am tempted to talk to the Sandlin and Pender families in the hope that this whole thing might be laid to rest."

"Don't," said Lou. "You spoke to them before all this took place and it got you nowhere. By now they know you were right, and they'll take their anger out on you. Dillard Sumner will see to it that Kage and Dub don't do anything to renew the fight, but if Sandlin and Pender decide to pick it up where they left off, Dill will step aside and let them get what they deserve."

Fort Laramie, Wyoming Territory. August 4, 1843.

An hour before sundown the Texans bedded down the horse remuda and the longhorns on the south bank of the Platte, two miles east of the trading post that would soon officially become Fort Laramie.*

"Laramie can't be more than three or four miles ahead," said Lou. He, like the other riders, was concerned with the several dozen Indian tepees almost directly across the river. Applegate had halted the wagons, saddled his horse, and ridden ahead to find the cause of the delay. He reined up beside Dill and Lou. The three of them watched a rider depart the Indian village, splashing his horse across the shallow Platte.

"White man," said Lou, "and no hostile activity among the tepees. I'd say they're a friendly tribe, whoever they are."

As the rider drew nearer they could see he was clad entirely in buckskin, wore a flop hat and a full beard,

---

* Although Laramie appeared on early maps as "Fort" Laramie, it opened in 1834 as a trading post. It had not yet become a U.S. military post when the first emigrants took to the Oregon Trail in 1843.

and had a Colt revolver belted on his right hip. What looked like the stock of a Hawken rifle protruded from a saddle boot. He reined up thirty yards away and, raising his hand, made the peace sign.

"I'm Jim Bridger," he said. "That's a Shoshone camp acrost the river. They're friendly."

"Sixty emigrant wagons," said Lou, "and eight thousand head of Texas cattle. This is Jesse Applegate, wagon boss, and the other hombre is Dill Sumner. I'm Lou Spencer. There's sixteen of us Texans drivin' the herd. I reckon we must be close to Fort Laramie."

"Ain't no fort to it," Bridger said. "Just a tradin' post, started by Sublette and Campbell."

Lou laughed. "Our map calls it a fort, but we'll take your word for it. We hope to spend a day or two here and maybe learn somethin' about the trail ahead."

"Welcome," said Bridger. "Reckon I can tell you somethin' about the trail from Laramie to Bear River, in eastern Idaho Territory. Worst you got betwixt here an' there is South Pass, a little more'n three hunnert miles west of Laramie. I'm 'bout ready to ride west again. Mebbe I'll go along when you leave Laramie. When you git to the post, you'll find me in the saloon. Come in, set, an' we'll jaw a spell."

Without awaiting a response, he turned his horse and rode back the way he'd come.

"That was a strange welcome," Applegate said. "Abrupt too."

"I'm glad he's here," said Lou. "I've heard of Jim Bridger. He's one of the original mountain men, comin' here as a trapper. He has a supply post of his own, somewhere beyond South Pass, on the Black Fork."*

"I've heard of him too," Dillard Sumner said, "and he's a *bueno hombre*. We'll be lucky havin' him with us, far as he wants to ride."

---

* Bridger later leased his post to the government. It became Fort Bridger.

"Mr. Applegate," said Lou, "you can allow your folks to visit the post whenever they want. Dill's outfit or mine will be on watch day and night, for as long as we're here. I've known a bunch of friendly Indians that wasn't opposed to rustlin' a few cows or horses, given the chance."

"Thanks," Applegate said. "This will be a welcome diversion." He rode back and gave the order to circle the wagons, hoping several days' rest and the nearness of the trading post might lessen the animosity that had resulted from the recent fight.

"Dill," said Lou, "I think we'll avoid that tradin' post except during daylight hours. Since we have second watch, you and your boys can ride in for a while in the morning. The rest of us will maybe go in sometime after you return."

"I reckon that's good thinkin'," Sumner replied. "If there's any outlaws, gun throwers, or thievin' Indians within two hundred miles, they'll be hanging around the tradin' post. Especially since there's a saloon."

"I didn't want to trouble Applegate with something that might not come to pass," said Lou, "but that saloon could mean trouble. Those emigrants, men with wives, likely won't be a problem, but there's a bunch of them young roosters that might be. And I don't mean just Sandlin and Pender."

"That's botherin' me some," Sumner admitted. "If all we had to worry us was Sandlin and Pender havin' a permanent mad on, then I'd say to hell with it. But I reckon even they have friends. Get enough of 'em likkered up, and they're likely to start thinkin' ol' Sandlin and Pender's been powerfully mistreated. Kage and Dub can hold their own with anybody in a fair an' face-to-face fight, but a varmint gettin' his courage from a bottle don't see nothin' wrong with shootin' a better man in the back."

"All the more reason for your outfit to stick together," said Lou, "and we'll all stay away from the tradin' post after dark. But us gettin' away from here won't lessen the danger. I expect many a man will take to the trail packin' a bottle or two of rotgut. Time we was gettin' back to the wagon circle. Supper may come early, us bein' so convenient to the tradin' post."

It appeared some of the emigrants had skipped supper entirely, for at some of the wagons there was no supper fire. But the Higdons, Quimbys, and Applegates were there, preparing supper for themselves and the cowboys.

"I see some of 'em couldn't wait for supper," Lou said, "but we didn't meet any of 'em. Which way did they go?"

"Straight across the Platte," said Applegate. "The water's shallow enough. Some of those with only oxen set out afoot."

"That'll take them past the Shoshone camp on the north bank," Sumner said.

"Bridger said they were peaceful," Applegate replied.

"So am I," said Sumner, "until some shorthorn decides to test my patience."

"Bridger said the Shoshone are friendly to whites," Lou said, "and I trust his judgment. If there's trouble, it'll come after some of those men belly up to that saloon bar."

"A saloon?" Sarah Applegate exclaimed. "Jesse, you should have told them to stay out of there."

"I'm through telling them—or *trying* to tell them—anything," said Applegate hotly. "Since leaving the Missouri, I've told them no hell-raising in camp, for any reason. Besides, some of these unmarried young hellions are grown men and their own parents can't control them. How am I supposed to do any better?"

Kage and Dub hadn't concerned themselves with the conversation. Their eyes were on the Halleck and Wallace wagons. Supper fires still smoldered, but there was no sign of activity. Applegate understood the concern of the two cowboys, and when he spoke, there was a half smile on his weathered face.

"The Halleck and Wallace ladies have made their choices," Applegate said, "and they're sticking to them. The Halleck, Wallace, Applegate, Higdon and Quimby families will be driving to the trading post in the morning."

But Lou Spencer's misgivings regarding the saloon were well-founded. Most of the younger men had gone to the trading post for the sole purpose of patronizing the saloon. Some of those who drank had witnessed the disgrace of Sandlin and Pender, and recalling the spectacle, began to laugh them down.

"Laugh, you damn mule-heads," Juno Pender snarled. "Them damn Texas skunks will bleed just like anybody else when we put some lead in their guts."

"Or in their backs," somebody suggested.

There was a roar of laughter, and what had been only wishful thinking in the minds of Barney Sandlin and Juno Pender hardened into a grim, fiery determination.

13

~~~~~

Fort Laramie, Wyoming Territory. August 5, 1843.

*T*he Applegate party's first night near the trading
post was peaceful enough except for some drunken
shouting from the single men who had spent too much
time in the saloon. The following morning, a Saturday,
many men with wives and children drove their wagons
across the river, within a few hundred yards of the trading post. Dillard Sumner and his six men saddled up and
rode in, Sumner hoping to spend some time with the
mountain man, Jim Bridger.

"I got nothin' against a man wettin' his whistle a time
or two," said Sumner as he and his comrades dismounted before the saloon, "but go easy on the panther
juice. There'll be enough of them young varmints from
the wagon train endin' up owl-eyed, without us addin' to
the noise."

While the saloon had an adequate supply of wine and
whiskey, beer seemed to be the mainstay. There were
three kegs mounted behind the bar, all of them tapped.
It was much too early for most saloon patrons, and there
were only two men in the place; one behind the bar and
the other before it. The latter was Jim Bridger, nursing a
half-empty mug of beer. He turned as the cowboys approached the bar, recognizing Sumner.

"Wal, Mr. Sumner," said the mountain man, "it's a mite early fer normal folks to be bellyin' up."

Sumner laughed. "Much obliged for the compliment, but I got to confess there's some that don't consider Texans normal."

It was Bridger's turn to laugh. "You boys order up your poison. Then we'll set a spell."

Bridger turned to an enormous round table that was likely used for poker. With his moccasined foot, he hooked the rung of a chair, drew it out and sat down. Sumner and his companions, each with a mug of beer, dragged out chairs and sat down. Bridger had met none of the other cowboys, and Sumner quickly introduced them.

"This is the biggest saloon I ever seen," said Tull Irvin. "I reckoned it would be inside the tradin' post."

"Was, at the beginnin'," Bridger said. "But it got so rowdy when men was drinkin', gamblin', an' raisin' hell in general, folks just wantin' to buy goods at the tradin' post took to complainin' about the commotion. Then word come that all them emigrants was on the way, an' the owners of the post knowed there'd be women an' children. So they built the biggest damn saloon in the territory, leavin' the original post to nothin' but trade goods. Suits me. A man needs someplace where he can drink, cuss, an' fight without some female gettin' all upset an' flusterated."

"I reckon there's room here for all that," Sumner said. "We'd like to hear some more about this South Pass, some three hundred miles west of here."

"Can't tell you nothin' good," said Bridger. "The trouble spot we're talkin' about ain't the pass itself, but a rocky ridge *near* the pass. They was some military surveyors out here last fall, an' they come up with a damn fearsome report on this Oregon Trail wher' it crosses the ridge. Accordin' to them, this ridge is more'n seven thousant feet above sea level, an' the trail climbs more'n a thousant feet in maybe five miles."*

"There's been two trains ahead of us," Tobe Hiram said. "How'd they make out?"

"Poorly," Bridger said. "Some of that ridge—a good part of it—is nothin' but rock. Solid granite. Nothin' fer wagon wheels to grip, an' they slide off humps an' rises, bustin' wheels an' axles. Wagons got to cross in single file. One at a time, in fact, takin' the teams from two wagons just to git one acrost. Them wagons was loaded too heavy, an' folks has left all manner of things behind. They's cook stoves, beds, tables, chairs, cookin' pots, sacks of flour an' beans, piles of clothes, books, an' God only knows what else. Some of the ladies throwed out other stuff so's they could take their granny's china plates an' glassware, only to have it busted all to hell crossin' that granite ridge."**

"It be hell, I reckon," said Indian Charlie.

"That an' worse," Bridger replied. "Ever'body didn't make it. From that last party, five wagons didn't even try. Them folks just give up, an' I passed 'em as I rode back to Laramie. They'll git here in maybe another week, on their way east."

"God," said Kage Copeland, "ain't there some better place to cross?"

"Not that I know of, if yer goin' t' Oregon Territory. If you was to drive far enough south, there might be a better crossin', but you'd end up in Californy."

"From what you've seen," Sumner said, "and with all the problems, how long do you reckon it'll take us to cross sixty wagons?"

"Maybe a week," said Bridger, "if yer lucky."

* This was the point—a few miles southwest of the present day town of Atlantic City, Wyoming—where the Oregon Trail crossed the Continental Divide.

** This hazardous crossing is still marked, 150 years later, with broken glass.

"We're obliged for what you've told us," said Sumner.
"Lou Spencer and his riders will be ridin' in after we get
back to the herd. I reckon they'll want to hear the bad
news from you, instead of secondhand from us. Are
there any other dangers we've overlooked?"

"There's a camp on the north bank of the Platte,
maybe ten miles west of here," Bridger said, "maybe
fifteen men. They're no-accounts an' thieves, feedin'
off'n emigrants. They'll steal yer horses, yer cows, yer
sheep, an' anything else they reckon they can git away
with. They look like the kind that's been run off from the
other places, settlin' here 'cause they's no law."

"We're obliged for the warning," said Sumner. "Texans has got a habit of makin' and enforcin' their own
laws when there's a need. Maybe we'll drop by and show
this bunch of coyotes the error of their ways."

Bridger laughed. "Now I *know* I got to ride as far as
the Black Fork with you sandy varmints."

"We'll count on that," Sumner said. "Now I reckon
we'll slope on over to the tradin' post and have a look at
all the civilized finery."

As Sumner and his riders left the saloon, a dozen of
the single men from Applegate's party rode in on horses
and mules. Among them were Sandlin and Pender. The
saloon had no actual porch, there being only dirt for the
floor, but a shake roof overhung the front door. Sumner
and his riders stood away from the door, under the roof,
their eyes on the men as they entered the saloon. Sandlin and Pender looked straight ahead, ignoring the cowboys. The Texans were mounting their horses when Indian Charlie spoke.

"Them get drunk. Fight no be finish."

"I reckon it is," Kage Copeland said, "long as we
watch our backs."

"Dark come," said Charlie.

It was a profound statement, and none of them appreciated the truth of it until the fight erupted anew. This
time in the darkness, with the roar of Colts . . .

* * *

Jap Buckalew continued his uneasy alliance with Suggs, Gerdes, and the Schmidt brothers. There was little talk, for Buckalew's devious mind was busy with various schemes he might employ to steal the gold and the cattle from Applegate's party without getting himself shot dead. Suggs and Gerdes had nothing in common with Rufe and Jenks Schmidt except suspicion and animosity, so there was only the plodding of the oxen and the rattle of the wagons to break the silence. Only around the supper fire, when Buckalew studied the map, was there any conversation.

"Damn it," Suggs complained, "we should of been at Laramie by now. How much farther?"

"Less'n a hunnert miles," said Buckalew. "Eight, nine more days, I'd say."

"Lemme have a look at that map," Suggs demanded, "unless you ain't trustin' us to see it."

Buckalew ignored the insult, passing Suggs his copy of the only map that had been available to the emigrants. Gerdes leaned over Suggs's shoulder.

"I dunno where'n hell you got the idea Fort Laramie was halfway," said Gerdes. "I ain't an educated man, but Laramie looks a damn sight closer to Independence than it does to Oregon."

"That's how I see it too," Suggs said. "If this fool map means anything, we might be halfway when we get to South Pass."

"What the hell difference does it make?" Buckalew snarled. "We'll be there when we git there. I figger Everett's bunch is less'n two days ahead of us, an' I look fer them to lay over for two er three days at Laramie. With near two hunnert wagons, I'd say it'll be a while for all them folks to take advantage of whatever the place is got to offer. When we know we're gittin' close, Suggs, I'll want you or Gerdes to ride ahead an' find the Everett wagons, so's we don't stumble on 'em. While they're all layin' over, we'll circle wide an' git ahead."

"By God," said Gerdes, "if there's a tradin' post, there'll be whiskey—maybe the last anywhere between here an' Oregon—an' I ain't about to pass it up."

"Me neither," Suggs said.

"I ain't said we was goin' to," Buckalew all but shouted. "I said we was gonna git ahead of Landon Everett's wagons, damn it. We'll git well beyond Everett's party an' then ride back to the tradin' post. I got a horse an' you got horses. Anything wrong with that?"

"Yeah," said Jenks Schmidt. "Me an' Rufe ain't got horses."

"Well, bless my old granny's pantaloons," Suggs said. "I reckon you an' Rufe will have to mount a pair of them varmints pullin' your wagon."

"I reckon we won't," Rufe replied hotly. "We'll git past Everett's wagons, but not so far we can't walk back to the store."

"I said we'll git *well* beyond Everett's wagons," Buckalew growled. "You stop 'fore we do, count yerselves out of any plans I'm makin'."

Buckalew, Suggs, and Gerdes all had their thumbs hooked in their pistol belts, suggestively close to the butts of their Colt revolvers. Recognizing the proximity of death, Jenks and Rufe said nothing, avoiding any hostile moves. The disagreement ended, but whatever trust the Schmidts had gained, they had just as swiftly lost. They were eyed suspiciously, and neither had any doubt that they'd just outlived their usefulness to the treacherous trio with whom they traveled. The Schmidts spread their blankets as far from their companions as they could, and it was far into the night before Rufe felt it was safe for a whispered conversation with his brother.

"It's time we was makin' plans of our own."

"We go agin' 'em, they'll kill us," Jenks said fearfully, "and we'll lose out on what they're plannin' to steal."

"Hell," Rufe hissed, "they ain't sharin' nothin' with us. They figger to use us an' then shoot us when they don't need us no more. If'n this tradin' post is big an' got whiskey, I look to find some men thereabouts that might jist take to the idea of joinin' up with us in goin' after that gold an' them cattle."

"Outlaws an' killers, maybe," said Jenks. "You think they gonna do us any better'n these killers we tied in with now?"

"Not fer a minute," Rufe said, "but we can't take on that bunch of Texans without help. We git our hands on the gold an' the cows, we'll do to them that's helped us what they'd of done to us, an' we'll do it first."

As he had promised, Landon Everett called a meeting before supper suggesting that his party—men, women, and children—bed down in their wagons, however cramped and uncomfortable they might be. Finished, he awaited their complaints, and there were many.

"Hell, Landon," a man shouted, "we'd have to unload half our goods at night and load 'em again the next mornin'. Ain't we got no other choice?"

"Yes," Everett said wearily, "you can go on sleepin' under your wagon and risk gettin' your throat slashed."

"We need another wagon boss, one that can protect us."

"Get one then," said Everett coldly. "I'm done with it."

That silenced them, but not for long. Men cursed, women reprimanded them, and children cried. Landon Everett said not a word, making no attempt to quell the uproar. Eventually it died to an uneasy murmur as they looked at one another uncertainly. It was Will Hamer who finally spoke, angrily and loud enough for all to hear.

"Landon's too kind to say this, but I ain't. It's time you done somethin' for yourselves, instead of lookin' to the wagon boss. Landon ain't God, so he can't be everywhere at the same time. He's told us what we got to do, and that's all you got any right to expect from a trail boss. Some of you are lookin' at Landon like you've

elected him sheriff, like he owes you protection. Well, by
God, this is the frontier and there ain't no law except for
our loaded guns. I'm tellin' you what Landon should
have told you when this killin' started. He's doing the
best he can, and any one of you that thinks he can do
better is welcome to the job. Those of you that ain't got
the guts to do what's got to be done, maybe you'd better
just turn your wagons around and get the hell back to
where you come from."

The women, with the exceptions of Mattie Everett
and Quilla Rowden, were shocked. Will had spoken
roughly, swearing at them as though only men were
present. The men—especially those who had made the
most demands on Landon Everett—were embarrassed.

"Well," Will demanded, not letting them off too easily, "who wants to be wagon boss?"

"Damn it, Will," said Joseph Rowden, "Landon's
done all he could, all anybody could do, and I ain't
wantin' another wagon boss."

"Me neither," a dozen men shouted in a single voice.

Will Hamer said no more, for Landon Everett nodded
to him and held up his hand for silence. He got it.

"Will spoke for me when I should have been speaking
for myself," Everett said. "I have tried—foolishly perhaps—to keep as much harmony within our party as I
could. No more. People, I am tired of scolding you like
you are disobedient children. I have only this to say. If
you have no respect for my judgment and continue to
disobey my orders, then I refuse to continue as wagon
boss. I am done. Finished. Those of you wantin' rid of
me, raise your hands."

Those who had complained the most refused to look
at him, and not a hand was raised. It was no vote of
confidence, and the weary wagon boss knew it. They
simply had no alternative. When Everett spoke, it was
without satisfaction, without emotion.

"Starting tonight—if you have to unload every damn
thing you own—I want all of you inside your wagons

except for the men on watch. From now on, any of you disobeying my orders are subject to being expelled from the wagon train. If there are any of you—be it one man or a hundred—who cannot or will not accept such discipline, you are invited to withdraw from this party immediately. You may then do as you please."

Everett said no more. The die was cast. The wagons had not yet been circled for the night. He had purposely called them together prior to that, intending to give them the same ultimatum Will Hamer had, but Will had surprised him by saying it first. While Everett might not have been quite as harsh on them, he now realized they had been told exactly what they needed to hear. Following Will's hard words, he knew he had nothing to lose, and that had prompted him to demand their compliance or their withdrawal from the wagon train. Without a word the men returned to their wagons and began circling them for the night.

"Come on, Will," said Everett. "Let's position our wagons and get ready for supper."

When Dillard Sumner and his riders returned to the herd, Sumner told Lou Spencer and his outfit of the conversation they'd had with the mountain man, Jim Bridger.

"He might have told you all he knows of the trail ahead," said Lou, "but I reckon we'll set with him a spell. The rest of the boys are wantin' to meet him."

"Even if he tells you no more than he's told us, it'll be well worth your time," Sumner said. "He's some kind of man."

"Lou," said Kage Copeland, "as we was leavin' the saloon, Sandlin, Pender, and some of their friends was goin' in. Them shorthorns get enough in 'em, one Texan might look just like another."

It was a breach of Texas etiquette, subject to being taken as an insult, if one man seemed overly protective of another. It was Kage Copeland's diplomatic way of telling his friends to be careful, to watch their backs.

"Thanks, Kage," Lou said. He mounted his horse, following his riders west along the Platte River.

"I wonder," said Waco as the outfit rode toward the trading post, "what Bridger's doin' here. You said he's got a post of his own, somewhere west."

"I heard he was buildin' one," Lou said. "When he rode out to meet Applegate, Dill, and me, he said he could tell us somethin' about the trail from Laramie to Bear River. Accordin' to Applegate's map, the Bear flows south from eastern Idaho into northeastern Utah Territory."

"I reckon we wouldn't be nosin' into the man's private business, then," said Waco, "was we to ask him where his post is. If it's anywhere close to the route we're takin', might be a welcome place to lay over for a day or two."

"Hell," Red Brodie said, "you know it'll be somewhere along the Oregon Trail. Why else would a man build a tradin' post in this godforsaken part of the world?"

They could see the enormous trading post beyond the saloon, and the horses and mules tied to the hitch rail were assurance enough that Sandlin, Pender, and the other young emigrants were still at the bar. Lou and his riders dismounted, half-hitching the reins of their horses to the other end of the hitch rail.

"It's been a while," said Lou, "so belly up. Just lay off the hard stuff."

He didn't elaborate, nor did he need to. It was difficult enough staying alive on the frontier, without being owl-eyed from rotgut whiskey. But for an occasional beer, Lou Spencer was not a drinking man. The front and back doors of the saloon stood open and a cool breeze swept through from the northwest. There were ten other men with Sandlin and Pender, and at first they seemed determined to monopolize the bar. Grudgingly they gave way, allowing the cowboys to order their beer.

Lou ignored the bar, making his way to the table where Jim Bridger sat, his flop hat tipped over his eyes.

"Dillard Sumner and his boys met you here early this morning," said Lou by way of conversation. "Back so soon?"

"Hell," Bridger said, tipping back his old hat, "I never left. What else is they fer a man to do? Amble around in that tradin' post fer a while an' they figger you got to buy somethin' fer the privilege. This is the same damn beer I started with."

Lou laughed. He dragged out a chair and sat down, and as his riders did likewise, Lou introduced them to Bridger. When all the howdying was done, the riders became silent, allowing Lou to take the lead in the conversation.

"Sumner and his boys passed along what you told them about the trail ahead," said Lou, "so we won't ask you to repeat it. We heard talk back in Independence that you aim to build a tradin' post somewhere west of here. I been wondering if it would be ready in time for us to lay over there for a couple of days. With that hard climb ahead of us at South Pass, I'm of a mind to suggest that Applegate's party not replenish their supplies here, but wait until we reach your post."

"The post is already built," Bridger said. "Three gents I done plenty of trappin' with helped me build the place last fall, an' they wintered with me. They're lookin' after things there now until I git back. I aim to be open fer business by the end of August. You'll be crossin' the Black Fork River where my place is, an' that's four hunnert miles west of here."

"You'll be ready long before we get there," said Lou. "Without the cattle stampedin' and without any busted wagon wheels and axles, we're two and a half months away."

"That an' more," Bridger said. "I'll ride with you a ways, but then I got to move on, so's I can git there ahead of that bunch of emigrants that's ahead of you. I rode in here the day your wagons showed up, so's I could leave word about my post on the Black Fork. Like I was tellin' Sumner, they's five wagons from the bunch ahead of you that never even tried to git across South Pass. They jist turned around an' headed back."

"They'll be meeting other wagon trains headin' west," said Lou, "and they'll spread the word about South Pass."

"Damn right," Bridger said. "I'm countin' on that, countin' on them folks thinkin' like you do. They'll lighten them wagons all they can, waitin' until they reach my post 'fore addin' to their supplies."

"If I ain't bein' meddlesome," said Waco, "where and how are you able to get trade goods to stock your post? I'd bet my saddle you ain't haulin' 'em across South Pass."

Bridger laughed. "Safe bet, cowboy. Mine's comin' from northern Californy. Them Mormons that's been run out of someplace back east has took to settlin' down south of here, in Utah Territory. No towns or nothin', and there's a freight outfit from northern Californy that's wagonin' supplies to 'em. Them Mormons is a standoffish lot, an' they've took to gatherin' maybe eighty-five mile southwest of my place. Biggest damn salt lake you ever saw."*

"So you made a deal with 'em to freight in your supplies," Waco said.

"Fer a while," said Bridger. "Freighter's wagon boss figgers it'll be just a matter of time till these Mormons gits their own wagons an' starts to haulin' fer theirselves. I ain't sure where that'll leave me."

"We wish you well," Lou said. "If the fur trade holds up, you could likely headquarter all the trappers near your post."

* The settlement became the town of Salt Lake City, Utah Territory, in 1849, and eventually the capital of the state of Utah. In 1853 the Mormons overran Bridger's post.

"Trappin' won't last much longer," said Bridger regretfully. "These rivers an' mountain streams is about trapped out. Time was you could ride from the Rocky Mountains west to the big water an' not see a dozen men. Now you're seein' the beginnin' of the end. I got nothin' agin' these folks that's headin' fer Oregon Territory, 'cept they're bringin' more civilization with 'em than I kin tolerate. Last time I was in St. Louis, they was sodbusters all over Missouri, some of 'em dribblin' over into Kansas an' eastern Nebraska Territory. We git Oregon Territory settled, an' damn it, East an' West is bound t'meet. They won't be no more frontier. God, I hope I ain't alive to see it."

"Hell," Red Brodie said bitterly, "some of them damn fools in Applegate's bunch is bringin' sheep. Give the varmints twenty years and there won't be a bunch of grass from Independence to the ocean."

"Red's stretchin' it a mite," said Vic Sloan. "Thirty sheep ain't likely to take over the world. My God, we got eight thousand Texas cows."

"Red's right," Sterling McCarty said. "Wouldn't matter if they was just two of the woolly varmints, long as they was one of each kind. When we get on into the mountains, I hope the grizzlies get the whole bunch. That is, if they ain't too partic'lar about what they eat."

They all laughed at that, even Bridger. There was some commotion as Sandlin, Pender, and their friends departed the saloon. Some of them—Pender and Sandlin included—took full bottles of whiskey with them.

"I ain't likin' the looks of that," Waco said when the men had gone. "There'll be some hell-raisin' in camp tonight."

There would indeed, and nobody was going to regret it more than Juno Pender and Barney Sandlin.

14

Fort Laramie, Wyoming Territory. August 5, 1843.

Lou Spencer and his companions rode on to the trading post, leaving Jim Bridger in the saloon. A dozen of the emigrant wagons were drawn up near the post, but there were no horses or mules. Evidently Sandlin, Pender, and their friends had ridden in for the sole purpose of visiting the saloon. Dismounting, the cowboys went inside, immediately sighting Jesse and Sarah Applegate. That meant Jud, Sandy, and Vangie were somewhere within the huge store. Vic Sloan winked at Lou, speaking softly.

"Let's go find Sandy and Vangie."

"Later," Lou said. "I want to talk to Applegate."

Quickly Lou told the wagon boss what Bridger had said, cautioning them not to overload their wagons before the formidable South Pass crossing.

"You'll need supplies for another four hundred miles," said Lou. "Jim Bridger tells us he'll have his trading post in operation well before we get there. The less you have to buy here, the less you'll have to haul across the mountains between here and Bridger's place."

"That makes sense to me," Applegate said, "but I wish we'd known it a bit sooner. Some in our party have already bought enough to see them the rest of the way to Oregon Territory."

"Those who haven't already loaded up, advise them to travel as light as they can," said Lou. "Bridger says that trail over South Pass is hell, and I get the feelin' he ain't stretchin' it a bit."

Except for Vic Sloan, the rest of Lou's outfit had scattered about the huge store. Lou and Vic went looking for Sandy and Vangie Applegate, suspecting the two girls would be together, which they were. There was a big glass case in which jewlery was displayed, and it had captured the attention of both the Applegate girls.

"Damn," Sloan said, pausing. "I can tell you what's on their minds, lookin' at that kind of stuff."

"You don't have to tell me what's on their minds," said Lou. "I reckon I know as well as you."

Sloan grinned. "You ain't exactly broke. You aimin' to buy Sandy one of them rings she's admirin'?"

Lou grinned back at him. "I reckon that's none of your damn business."

When the Applegates were ready to return to camp, Lou and his men rode along behind the wagon. It was still early afternoon, and Waco approached Lou with a request.

"Nell—the Widow Hayden—wants to visit the tradin' post, and she ain't wantin' to go alone. Any reason why I can't or ought not to ride in with her?"

"None I can think of," said Lou, "long as you're back before dark."

Nell Hayden had a saddle in her wagon, and Waco saddled one of her mules. Nell and Waco rode out, to the admiring—and perhaps envious—looks of Waco's comrades.

"By God," Red Brodie said, "I've knowed ol' Waco near 'bout all my life. He's got enough sand to face a tribe of Comanches was there a need for it, but I never knowed he had enough to rope him a filly as purty as that."

* * *

When Dillard Sumner and his men rode out at dusk to
begin the first watch, the Applegate camp was quiet.
There was none of the drunken shouting and laughter of
the night before. Lou had told Sumner of the ample
supply of whiskey Sandlin, Pender, and their friends had
taken from the saloon.

"I think," Sumner said, trying not to be too obvious,
"we'll all ride closer together tonight. We got the Platte
River holdin' the herd to the north."

"We've had the Platte to the north of the herd ever
since we left them soldiers' tents at Kearny," said Dub
Stern. "I reckon me and Kage will pair up like we've
always done."

"Damn right," Kage Copeland said.

Sumner said no more. He had tried, but Kage and
Dub had immediately suspected what he had in mind.
Already the purple sky bloomed with millions of silver
stars, twinkling with varying intensity, and later there
would be a full moon. Had it been anywhere but the
western frontier, the stubborn pair of cowboys could
have been accused of rank insubordination, but Dillard
Sumner understood the unwritten code as well as they.
No western man embroiled his friends in a fight he considered his own, even if it cost him his life. When the
riders began nighthawking, Kage Copeland and Dub
Stern rode well ahead of their companions. Not being
bunched during the day, the herd was considerably
strung out. At one point the riders were within forty
yards of the northernmost side of the wagon circle. Sumner silently cursed himself for not having had the riders
bunch the herd well away from the shadowy hulks of the
wagons before sundown.

"Moon come," said Indian Charlie, riding alongside
Tobe Hiram.

Hiram said nothing, nor did he need to. The glow on
the horizon had become a ticking clock. Outwardly there
was no change, but every rider was tense, awaiting they

knew not what. The minutes dragged on. Finally, above a distant tree line, appeared the silver edge of the rising moon. Having begun its ascent, it rose rapidly, silvering the gray canvas of wagons, lighting the faces of the cowboys. There was no sound except the soft thud of their horses' hooves and the peaceful ripple of the nearby Platte River. Suddenly, as they neared the northern edge of the circle of wagons, the night erupted with gunfire. There were four rapid shots. Kage, in the lead, took a slug in his left arm, while another burned its way across Dub's right side, just above his belt. But the third and fourth slugs found only empty air, as Kage and Dub rolled out of their saddles, drawing and cocking their Colts as they went. In a zigzag run the pair of cowboys headed for the circle of wagons. The shooting had been near enough to spook the herd, and steers were bawling, surging to their feet.

"Bunch them," Sumner shouted. "Bunch them from the east."

It was a perilous situation. With the longhorns strung out along the river, the herd might stampede east or west. Sumner and his riders would be able to head them from an eastern run, but in their frustration they could always stampede westward. It was unlikely they would run north, crossing the Platte, but to the west nothing stood in their way unless Lou Spencer and his riders could reach the far end of the strung-out herd in time.

While it was almost two hours before Spencer and his outfit were to begin their watch, on this night Lou had taken the precaution of having every rider saddle and picket his horse. Within seconds of the gunfire the nine Texans were in the saddle. While they knew not what had taken place at the farthest end of the strung-out herd, the shots had come from there, and that meant Sumner and his men were involved. While Lou and his riders were unable to aid Sumner and his outfit, they could reach the western end of the herd, preventing a stampede in that direction.

"They're on their feet," Lou shouted as they neared the herd. "Bunch the varmints and move 'em down-river."

The outfit followed Lou's lead, every man knowing the risk they took. If Sumner and his riders, for any reason, failed to head the longhorns at the farthest end of the strung-out herd, Lou and his riders were in fact *starting* a stampede.

Kage and Dub reached the shadows of the wagons without drawing any more fire. The wagons were circled three deep, with the wagons belonging to the Sandlin and Pender families on the farthest side of the circle. If it had been Sandlin and Pender who fired the shots, they hadn't dared cross the moonlit area within the wagon circle. If they were to return to their own wagons without being seen, they had to work their way around the circle, staying within the shadow of the wagons. Piles of harness lay on the ground beside every wagon, while loose double trees dangled from chains. Movement wouldn't be easy without some sound, and when it came, Kage and Dub fired. They aimed low, lest their slugs strike someone within the wagons, and while the lead found no target, it had the desired effect. Two Colts cut loose, firing at the muzzle flashes, but Kage and Dub had dropped to the ground. There was a veritable drumroll of thunder as the cowboys returned the fire. Each man fired three times; once at the muzzle flash, once to the left, and finally to the right. Depending on whether he fired right- or left-handed, it was the most effective means of wounding or killing an enemy. The cowboys held their fire, and none was returned. The camp was awake. Women and children cried out, while men shouted inquiries. Finally there came the booming voice of Jesse Applegate.

"This is Applegate, and I'll personally shoot the next man who fires a shot. What's happened here? Somebody speak up."

"This is Kage Copeland, and Dub Stern's with me,"

Kage shouted. "Somebody from within the wagon circle tried to ambush us. We chased them back among the wagons and traded some lead. I think we salted 'em down. There's two of 'em somewhere between the wagons, almost directly across from where we are."

"There may be some risk havin' a look at 'em," said Dub Stern. "They could be playin' possum, aimin' to shoot anybody comin' close."

"We'll risk it," Applegate said. "I won't spend the rest of the night in doubt."

With Sumner and his outfit working the herd from the eastern end, and Lou and his riders bunching them from the west, the longhorns settled down. Lou rode around the milling cattle and rode forward to meet Dillard Sumner.

"About what we was expectin'," Sumner said. "Two guns cut down on Kage and Dub. Don't know if either of 'em was hit, but they was in good enough shape to go after them that started the fight. I'd say it was them firin' that last volley. From all the commotion and carryin' on, I'd say Kage and Dub finished what somebody else started."

But by the time Spencer and Sumner reached the inner wagon circle, Applegate seemed to have things under control, and no explanation was needed. Barney Sandlin and Juno Pender lay on their backs, apparently dead. Sumner ignored them and everybody else, his concern being for Kage and Dub.

"Light as it was, they couldn't have missed," Sumner said. "How bad?"

"Upper left arm," Kage said, "but it missed the bone. Bleedin' some."

"Right side," said Dub. "Burnt one across my ribs. Bleedin' a mite, hurtin' like hell."

Sarah Applegate already had a fire going, a pot of water on to boil. Applegate turned to Lou and Dill, and even as he spoke, there was the bitter weeping of women within the Sandlin and Pender wagons.

"Sarah will see to the wounds of your cowboys," Applegate said. With a sigh he focused his attention on the dead men lying within the shadow of the wagons. Two men stood over them in silence. Bart Sandlin and Jabbo Pender. Each man had lost his only son. For the moment they were in shock, and Applegate didn't wish to contemplate what might be their later reaction. He said nothing, for there was nothing he could say. While he was sorry the incident had taken place, he felt no pity for Barney Sandlin and Juno Pender. He would save that for their parents. But the Sandlin and Pender families had made a decision. It was Bart Sandlin who finally spoke.

"We'll be leavin', come daylight. After we've buried our dead."

"All right," Applegate said. "I'll do anything I can to help."

"We don't want your help," Jabbo Pender said sourly.

Kage and Dub had peeled off their shirts, and Sarah had brought the medicine chest from the Applegate wagon. Dorrie Halleck and Rosa Wallace had left their wagons and timidly approached the fire, their eyes on Kage and Dub. It was too much for Bart Sandlin and Jabbo Pender. They stomped toward Rosa and Dorrie, shouting as they came.

"You damn little tramps," Sandlin bawled, "this is all your fault."

Suddenly they froze, for Jesse Applegate stood before them, a cocked Colt in his hand, steady, unwavering.

"This is a tragedy that's gone far enough," said Applegate, "and I'll not see it pushed any further."

Without a word Sandlin and Pender returned to their wagons. When they returned, they brought blankets to cover their dead. Kage and Dub, their wounds attended, were buttoning their shirts. Sarah Applegate closed the lid of the medicine chest and poured what was left of the boiling water on the fire.

"We're obliged, ma'am," Kage said.

"Mr. Applegate," said Lou, "the herd's settled down.

I reckon we can secure the camp for the rest of the night. You'd better get everybody back to their wagons if you can. We'll be takin' the trail west at first light."

Western Nebraska Territory. August 6, 1843.

With Landon Everett's emigrants taking refuge in their wagons, there was no disturbance during the night. With the dawn, however, there was much grousing and grumbling as men were forced to rearrange their loads for the day's travel.

"God," Will Hamer said, "I've never been so glad to get out of a wagon in my life. It wasn't meant for a man to sleep with his head between his knees."

"Sure as hell wasn't," Buck Embler agreed, "and I didn't."

Landon Everett laughed, upon them before they knew it. "It's better than waking up dead, and it was your idea. Accordin' to the map, we ought to be reaching Fort Laramie sometime tomorrow afternoon. We'll lay over for some rest, and visit the trading post."

Everett made that same announcement to everybody at breakfast, and it seemed to revive their lagging spirits. Tomorrow, they reasoned, whatever happened in between, there would be time for rest and an opportunity to view whatever civilization Fort Laramie offered. But sometime during the night, the killer struck again, taking advantage of an opportunity Landon Everett had overlooked. Men were harnessing their teams, preparing to move out, when Everett became suspicious of a lack of activity around Upshur Hiddenbrandt's wagon. Hiddenbrandt was in his fifties, an old man for the time and place. Sometimes he didn't bother with breakfast, barely rising in time to take the trail with the rest of the wagons. But this morning he was unusually late. Some of the men saw Everett enter the Hiddenbrandt wagon, and all activity came to a standstill when Everett emerged. He was shaken, and it was a while before he could speak.

"Upshur's dead. His throat slashed like the others. We'll be here awhile. There's a grave to be dug and words to be said."

Nobody spoke. The shock was total. When they looked at Landon Everett, it was without anger, for none remained. There was a kind of hopelessness in their eyes. What more could Everett do? What could *any* of them do?

"Landon," said Will Hamer, "Buck and me will dig the grave."

"Thanks, Will," Everett said.

"Landon," said Joe Rowden, "Upshur was travelin' alone. What about his wagon and teams?"

"One damn thing at a time," Everett said wearily. "I'll need some help gettin' him ready for the burying."

"Leave it alone, Landon," said Gus Shondell. "Jasper, Grady, and me will do it."

"Thank you, Gus," Everett said. He felt a little guilty because Shondell and his sons had been on his list of suspects.

Somehow they got through the short service. Will Hamer and Buck Embler remained to fill in the grave. It was time to consider the problem of what was to be done with Upshur Hiddenbrandt's wagon and teams.

"Upshur must have some kin somewhere back in Ohio," Everett told the gathering, "but I'm of no mind to go through his belongings this morning, and I'd not expect any of you to. We'll take the teams and the wagon to Laramie, and there we'll search the wagon for next of kin. The wagon and teams can be sold and the money sent back to any kin Upshur left behind. Some of you folks with more than one son, will you allow one of them to lead Upshur's teams on to Laramie?"

"You can have one of my boys," said Jules Dewees. "Hamby or Isaac."

"Isaac, then," Everett said. Again he felt a stab of guilt, for Jules, Hamby, and Isaac had been on his list of suspects.

A somber Landon Everett led out with his wagon, and the others fell in line.

As Jap Buckalew had requested, Cope Suggs had ridden ahead to learn how far they were behind Landon Everett's party. Buckalew and the Schmidts had already unharnessed their teams for the night when Suggs rode in.

"Hell's fire," Buckalew growled, "you been gone long enough. What'd you do, join 'em fer afternoon tea?"

"Yeah," said Suggs amiably. He purposely said no more, for he had begun to enjoy irritating the impatient Buckalew.

"Well, damn it," Buckalew all but shouted, "what did you learn?"

"They buried somebody this morning," said Suggs. "New grave."

"You ain't told me what I sent you to find out," Buckalew said angrily. "How damn far are they ahead of us?"

"I'm a mite tired of you bellerin' at me like I was a stable hand," said Suggs.

"Please, Mr. Suggs," Buckalew said sarcastically, "tell me how far Landon Everett's wagons are ahead of us."

"Wal," said Suggs, pausing and seeming to ponder, "I'd say they ain't more'n a day ahead, if that far."

Gerdes laughed and the Schmidt brothers said nothing. Landon Everett had expelled them from his group, daring them to get too close. They had that much in common with Buckalew and his pair of gun toters, but that's where it ended. Jenks and Rufe Schmidt would part company with Buckalew, Gerdes, and Suggs somewhere beyond Fort Laramie, even if they had to shoot the troublesome trio while they slept.

Eastern Wyoming Territory. August 7, 1843.

By the time it was light enough to see, Bart Sandlin and Jabbo Pender had begun digging a pair of graves on a rise three hundred yards south of the circled wagons.

While Jesse Applegate had said nothing to discourage his party from attending the burying, none of them had chosen to. They had been on the trail long enough to have seen the Barney Sandlin and Juno Pender ambush for the cowardly thing it had been. Nothing was said, but it seemed the air had been cleared, a burden swept away. Having buried their kin, Sandlin and Pender harnessed their teams and turned their wagons eastward along the Platte, back the way they had come.

"How are you gentlemen feeling?" Applegate inquired of Kage and Dub as the cowboys gathered for breakfast.

"A mite stiff and sore," said Dub. "Like some hombre dragged a hot brandin' iron across my ribs."

"I'm just mighty glad I'm right-handed," Kage said. "Won't get much use out of that arm for a few days."

Nothing more was said, but Dorrie Halleck and Rosa Wallace managed to share a moment with the two wounded cowboys before the day's drive began. As the herd moved past the saloon and trading post across the river, a single rider splashed his horse across the Platte to join them: Jim Bridger.

"We reckoned you'd forgot about us," said Dillard Sumner when he and Lou rode ahead to meet the mountain man.

Bridger laughed. "Not much. Had me about all the civilization I can stand fer a while. Heard all that shootin' last night, an' I was wonderin' if I'd told you wrong about them Shoshone bein' friendly. Sounded like they was attackin'."

"Hell," Sumner said, "we ain't near as worried about heathen Indians as we are about some of them civilized varmints in the wagons." He then told Bridger of the twin shootings of the night before, of the cause, and finally of the Sandlin and Pender families pulling out and returning east.

"Just as well," Bridger said. "I'd say most of these pilgrims comin' west is got no idea what they're gittin' into. Them that ain't strong enough, it's best they git out 'fore they git in too deep. Fer a lot of years there won't be no law 'cept what a man carries on his hip, an' it won't be a damn bit stronger than how quick he can pull iron an' how straight he kin shoot."

"Best we can tell from Applegate's map," said Lou, "we shouldn't have a water problem. Where the Platte turns south, there's a confluence with it that we'll be able to follow all the way to South Pass."

"That's the Sweetwater," Bridger said. "After leavin' the Platte, you'll be follerin' the Sweetwater mebbe two hunnert an' twenty-five miles. My God, that stretch along the Sweetwater would be some kind of range. A man could take a few cows an' build hisself a empire."*

"You make it sound mighty tempting," said Sumner.

"Yeah," Lou said. "Some of this herd still belongs to me and my riders. If we don't like Oregon Territory, we can always drive 'em back to Wyoming Territory and settle along the Sweetwater."

"I'd welcome some Texans," said Bridger. "Them Mormons to the south is buildin' one hell of a congregation, an' they're startin to git on my nerves."

By Lou's estimate, Applegate's party had traveled a good ten miles west of Laramie when they stopped for the night. The wagons were circled and all seemed peaceful enough until one of the cowboys from the first watch—Pete Haby—rode in with word from Dillard Sumner. It was dark, but still early enough for Lou Spencer and his outfit to be awake.

"Lou," said Pete, "Dill wants you boys to saddle up an' come a-runnin'. Some riders crossin' the Platte, headin' this way. Just dark enough so's we couldn't be sure how many, but looks like a dozen or more."

"Sounds like that bunch I was warnin' Sumner about," Jim Bridger said. "The night 'fore I rode into Laramie, I

* Book #2 in the Trail Drive Series, *The Western Trail*

snuck up on their camp. Fifteen of 'em I saw, an' they looked like a bad lot. I'll ride along."

Lou and his riders, accompanied by Bridger, followed Pete Haby back to the herd, a little more than half a mile west of the wagon circle. Sumner and his remaining riders had fanned out, facing the fifteen mounted men, who had reined up fifty yards distant. Lou's companions spread out, siding Sumner's outfit. Bridger remained with Lou, and the two of them reined up next to Dillard Sumner.

"Now," said Sumner, as though resuming a conversation, "the rest of our outfit's here. Tell us again what you want."

In the dim starlight it wasn't easy to see the men or their horses. The lead rider had a full beard and wore buckskin, and it was he who spoke.

"Like I was sayin', the beavers is gettin' damn scarce, and they ain't enough fur trappin' to keep a man in plug. We got a hankerin' to ride on to Oregon Territory, but we're a mite low on grub. We're willin' to help with the cows from here on, just fer our feedin'."

It was clear that Sumner hadn't trusted these men, that he had avoided declining their offer until the odds were more equal. Lou spoke.

"We're working for wages ourselves, and we don't need help with the cows. As for grub, we can't commit to that, because we're bein' fed by the owners of the herd."

"Then I expect we'd best talk to the owners of the herd," the persistent leader said.

"No," said Lou. "You'd be welcome to a meal or two, but these people can't afford to feed you all the way to Oregon when we have no work for you."

"You might regret them words," the stranger said angrily. "It's a long ways from here to Oregon, an' they's any number of things that could happen, leavin' you short-handed. Men could git killed on the trail."

"They could," Lou said coldly, "and if they do, you

just be damn sure you and your bunch ain't nowhere close. Now ride."

They reined their horses around and rode back the way they had come. It was Jim Bridger who broke the silence.

"They'd work for nothin' an' steal you blind. They's been trappers that was caught robbin' other men's traps, an' they was run out. I'd not be surprised if that ain't been what's happened to this bunch. They're lookin' fer somethin' that'll put some gold in their pockets, an' they're figgerin' your cows is fair game."

"That's kind of what I thought," Sumner said. "I can't believe they won't follow, gun us down some dark night and try to take the herd."

"Our fault if they do," said Waco. "We been warned."

"Wrong," Lou said. "*They've* been warned."

"*Si,*" Indian Charlie said. "Dead hombres no need cows or gold."

Jim Bridger laughed.

15

Landon Everett's party reached Fort Laramie the day after Applegate's group had departed, and were just as dismayed to discover there was really no fort.

"Some map," Will Hamer said in disgust. "At Fort Kearny there was three tents and a few soldiers. Fort Laramie's just a couple of log buildings. What else ain't we been told?"

Buck Embler laughed. "Maybe there won't be no Oregon. We'll go right out of Idaho Territory and into the ocean."

"After a long hard day, the two of you know how to make a man feel lots better," Landon Everett said. "At least Laramie has a trading post."

"You don't know that," said Will, grinning. "We know one of them's a saloon, 'cause it has a sign on the front you can read from two miles off. The other buildin' don't say anything."

The conversation died. Quilla Rowden had unharnessed Caleb Vandiver's teams and stood looking across the river at the distant saloon. Many of the others—especially the women—had taken note of Quilla's obvious interest in the saloon, and there was some shaking of heads.

"We're no more than two hours shy of sundown," Everett said. "We're new to this country. We've already seen an Indian village on the other side of the river. I don't want any of you going to the saloon or the trading post after dark, and I don't want everybody leaving the wagons at the same time. We'll lay over here long enough for all of you to purchase any needed goods and supplies. Nobody leaves camp today. Daylight or not, I want a dozen men here in camp at all times. You can change watches at noon. I'll take the first watch in the morning until noon, and I'm asking for volunteers to join me. We'll need a dozen more for tomorrow afternoon."

The men crowded around, and Everett wrote their names on a tablet in the order of their watch. They were eager to volunteer, for this was their first opportunity for supplies since leaving Independence. In a way, it was a crucial test, for Everett didn't know how many men would pass up the trading post for the saloon. He looked at the tablet, finding that Buck and Will had agreed to take the first watch with him the next morning. He beckoned to the pair, and they joined him.

"Since we'll have plenty of time in the morning," said Everett, "I'd like for the two of you to help me search Upshur Hiddenbrandt's wagon for some evidence of kin. We're not taking the wagon or the teams any farther. When I go the trading post, I'm going to sell for whatever I can get. Then when we finally reach Oregon Territory, I'll return the money to Upshur's kin."

"The oxen ought to bring fifty dollars apiece," Will said, "and the wagon a hundred. My God, that's four hundred dollars. The murderin' varmint that's been cuttin' throats would kill you for half that."

Landon Everett said nothing, but Will's dire prediction had given him an idea, a possible means of trapping a killer. He would need Mattie's help, for she must play a convincing role, coming up with some logical reason why Everett must spend at least a few nights outside the wagon. Despite how little he actually received for Upshur's teams and wagon, it might be enough to tempt the killer. All he had to do, then, was wait, and when the time came, fight for his life.

It seemed the entire camp was up and about before dawn, excitement running high as everyone prepared to see what Laramie had to offer. Nobody seemed to notice as Landon, Will, and Buck made their way to the wagon that had belonged to Upshur Hiddenbrandt.

"I'll be glad when we're done with this," Will said. "Makes me nervous, goin' through a dead man's belongings."

There were the expected things: cooking utensils, provisions, a wagon jack, and a tin of axle grease. Finally they came upon a trunk, and it was locked.

"Damn," said Buck, "we buried the key with Upshur."

"Gus Shondell wrapped Upshur for the burying," Everett said, "and Gus told me Upshur's pockets were turned inside out. Drag the trunk back near the wagon gate while I get somethin' to force the lock."

Everett returned with an iron poker and broke into the trunk by prying loose the screws that secured the hasp to the cedar wood. At first the trunk seemed only to contain old books, the covers virtually in tatters. Everett removed them one at a time, stacking them on the floor of the wagon box. Beneath the books there was an assortment of papers and letters. The papers were receipts for debts paid, bearing only Upshur's name. The letters were in a neat bundle, tied with string. Everett divided them into three piles, and the men began searching for a name and an address.

"My God," said Buck, "some of these letters was postmarked ten years ago. Whoever wrote 'em could be dead by now."

"Let's hope not," Will said. "Every one I've looked at so far came from the same woman, and there's only a first name: Vanessa."

"That's how it is with those I have," said Everett, "but

here's one postmarked in 1840. There's a Columbus, Ohio, return address on the envelope, but no name."

"Handwritten, looks the same as on all the others," Will said. "Maybe there's a name inside."

"There is," said Everett after looking at the letter. "Vanessa."

"A sister, maybe," Buck said. "Since that's all we've found, you'll have to go with it, and we'll just hope she's outlived Upshur."

"But for the selling of the teams and wagon, we've done all we can do," said Everett. "I'll keep the letters and return them to Vanessa with the money. We'll let the rest of his belongings go with the wagon. Might bring a little more at the sale. When we go to the trading post this afternoon, I'll need one of you to hitch Upshur's teams to the wagon and bring them along."

"I'll do it," Buck said. "Me and my missus can ride back with Will."

Following the departure of the undesirable group of men, Lou Spencer and his riders returned to the wagon circle. Lou explained the situation to Jesse Applegate and the action the Texans had taken.

"You'll get no argument from me," said Applegate. "With the herd out of the picture, there's little left to tempt them, unless they steal our oxen. Of course, there's the sheep belonging to the Garner and Malden families."

Lou Spencer laughed in spite of himself. "We'll see to the herd, but Garner and Malden will have to look after their sheep."

Applegate, aware of a cowboy's dislike for sheep, had warned Garner and Malden to bed down their thirty animals as far from the longhorns as possible. As a result, the Texans kept their horse remuda and the cattle ahead—west—of the wagon circle, while Garner and Malden wisely kept their sheep behind—east—of the camp. It was an arrangement that had worked well until this particular night. Well into the second watch, somewhere to the east, came a thunder of gunfire. It was too distant to disturb the herd, but Lou Spencer wouldn't ignore it.

"Come on, Waco," he shouted. "Rest of you stay with the herd. This could be a diversion to draw us away."

Dillard Sumner and his outfit were of the same mind. Lou and Waco met them riding hard, bound for the herd.

"Stay with the herd," Lou shouted. "Waco and me can handle it."

It was sound thinking, for if the thunder of gunfire had been only to draw the cowboys away from the herd, Lou and Waco were wasting their time. As it turned out, the uproar had nothing to do with the anticipated return of the band of renegades. Lou and Waco reined up amid the nervous bleating of sheep and the angry shouts of men.

"What'n hell's goin' on here?" Lou bellowed, striving to be heard above the clamor. "Why all the shooting?"

"Damn bear stole one of our sheep," a man shouted.

"Is the bear dead?" Lou asked, ignoring Waco's poorly suppressed mirth.

"Hell no," the angry voice responded. "We couldn't see the varmint in the dark."

"Settle down," said Lou. "He won't be back tonight."

"God A'mighty," Waco said, "if they couldn't see it, how'd they know it was a bear? If they'd actually seen the varmint their shootin' would of woke up ever'body in Wyoming Territory."

"Likely a grizzly," said Lou, "and with all his gruntin' and growlin', I reckon even a tenderfoot would know what he was. The wagon circle's a lot closer than the herd, and we'd better tell them nothin' was lost but a sheep. Close as Applegate was to the commotion, it must have sounded like a war goin' on."

Lou and Waco reined up a hundred yards from the camp. "Texans ridin' in," Lou shouted. As expected, Applegate and every man in his party stood beside their wagons with drawn guns.

"A bear grabbed a sheep," said Lou.

Applegate sighed. "Thank God that's all it was. We expected worse, with all the gunfire. Did they kill the bear?"

"No," said Lou, "and with all the shooting, it's a miracle they didn't shoot one another. You'd better have some words with them in the morning and tell them not to be so damn quick on the trigger when they can't see what they're shootin' at. After this, they'll get spooked at the least sound, firing at shadows, and somebody's likely to be killed."

"My God," Applegate said, "you're right. A sheep, a cow, an ox, or a horse isn't worth a man's life."

When Lou and Waco returned to the herd and told the cowboys what had caused the disturbances, there was a unanimous lack of sympathy.

"Damn," said Sterling McCarty, "ain't they no decent game in these parts? Grizzly must of been starved, snatchin' one of them woolly varmints."

"Amen," Red Brodie said callously. "That bear will take sick an' die before daylight. Why, you could turn a hunnert of them woolly locusts loose an' wipe out the bear population to the last grizzly, all in six months."

"You could be sympathizin' with the grizzly a mite soon," said Lou. "He could decide he likes cow better than sheep, and we'll end up shootin' at him."

"Mebbe so," Indian Charlie said seriously, "but I bet Mejicano silver-mounted saddle if we all empty our guns, we get at least one slug in him."

"Damn, Charlie," said Dillard Sumner, "I didn't realize you had so much confidence in our gun throwin'. Whose slug would that be?"

"Mine," Indian Charlie said, serious as ever.

"Sumner," said Waco, "turn his horse toward camp and slap it on the rump. Another minute and we'll have to shoot the stuck-up little varmint, lettin' some of the wind out of him."

After a moment of laughter, the cowboys parted. Lou and his riders resumed their nighthawking while Sumner and his outfit rode back toward the wagon circle to resume their interrupted sleep.

The morning after Landon Everett's party circled the wagons for a layover at Laramie, Buckalew, his four companions, and their two wagons swung several miles to the south. Thus they passed Everett's wagons without being seen, and despite Rufe and Jenks Schmidt's determination to break away, their plans were thwarted by the ready guns and sharp eyes of Suggs and Gerdes. By the time Buckalew called a halt, they were well beyond Laramie and sundown was little more than an hour away. Suggs and Gerdes had shifted their attention to Buckalew, and it was Suggs who spoke.

"You can do what you want, but Gerdes an' me is ridin' back to that fort an' git some whiskey."

"Go on," Buckalew said amiably, "and when you ride back, bring me a couple of bottles. Since ol' Rufe an' Jenks ain't got horses, I'll jist set here an keep 'em comp'ny till you git back."

The implication was clear enough. The Schmidts were not to be allowed out of Buckalew's sight, for they knew too much. While Landon Everett had hanged their brother Ab, the Schmidts just might hate Buckalew enough to get word of his plans to somebody in Everett's party. Buckalew waited until Suggs and Gerdes had ridden out before he spoke to the Schmidts.

"Since they's jist the three of us, I'd be more comfortable with you boys rustlin' the supper."

Rufe and Jenks said nothing, but set about preparing the meal. There was no chance for them to discuss their plight with Buckalew observing their every move. They both were armed with Colts, but neither was especially handy with his weapon so they waited. When supper was ready, the desperate pair filled their plates and hunkered beside their wagon, getting as far from Buckalew as they could.

"Hope we ain't hurt your feelings none," Rufe said, "but it makes us sick in our guts, settin' close to you."

Buckalew laughed. "Bothers me the same way when either of you git too close. Jist so's you stay close enough fer me to see you."

It was already dusky dark. While Buckalew could see the Schmidts, they were far enough away to speak softly without being heard.

"We got to git away from here," Jenks whispered desperately. "When it gits dark enough, let's leave ever'thing and run fer it."

"Like hell," Rufe whispered back. "We'd need horses, an' with Suggs an' Gerdes gone, they's only one. Besides, them varmints might come after us. We'll make our break after they git back, later on tonight."

"Damn it," said Jenks, "then there'll be three of 'em."

"Yeah," Rufe responded softly, "an' maybe all drunk. I want them two horses Suggs an' Gerdes is ridin', an' we'll take Buckalew's nag with us."

"What about our wagon an' grub?"

"Damn the wagon an' grub," Rufe hissed. "First we save our hides, an' then we go from there."

As he had promised, Buck Embler harnessed the teams that had belonged to Upshur Hiddenbrandt to the wagon and led them to the trading post.

"Just leave them harnessed, Buck," Landon Everett said. "I'll move the wagon and unharness the teams wherever they're to be kept, after I've made the best deal I can."

Everett found the post swarming with men and women from his party, and the three men representing the establishment very busy. Finally he was able to talk to Amos Conrad, but found the man unenthusiastic.

"We just manage this outpost for Sublette and Campbell," said Conrad. "None of us has the authority to buy anything. Goods are freighted to us, and we must give an accounting for everything sold. If I bought your teams and wagon, I couldn't account for the money and I'd end up being responsible."

"There's no way I can take them any farther west," Everett said. "Go out and have a look at them. Then make me an offer and buy them yourself."

While Amos Conrad was a cautious man, Landon Everett was a persuasive one. Conrad agreed to at least look at the teams and wagon.

"This outfit would sell for near five hundred dollars in Independence or St. Louis," said Everett. "Maybe more."

"I won't argue with that," Conrad conceded, "but this ain't St. Louis or Independence. Anybody wantin' teams and a wagon will already have them by the time they get this far."

"Wagons break down and oxen die," Everett argued. "You could ask and get a hundred dollars each for these oxen, and then there's the wagon. After comin' this far, who can afford to go all the way back to Independence?"

"Maybe you got somethin' there," said Conrad. "How much you asking?"

"I'm askin' four hundred," Everett said. "It's worth more."

"I ain't got four hundred to spare and wouldn't risk it if I did," said Conrad. "Two hundred."

"No," Everett countered. "Three fifty."

"Two fifty," said Conrad.

"Three hundred," Everett said, "and no less. You can easily double that, without even trying."

"If you'll take fifty dollars in trade," said Conrad, "you got a deal."

"I can do that," Everett said, relieved. The difference would come out of his pocket when he sent the proceeds to Upshur's next of kin, but Mattie was already gathering needed things to replenish their supplies. He would be lucky to escape the trading post for as little as fifty dollars. He and Conrad returned to the store and Everett wrote out and signed a bill of sale for the teams and the wagon. No sooner had he concluded the deal than Will Hamer arrived with distressing news.

"Landon," said Will, "you'd best get down to the saloon as quick as you can. Quilla Rowden's been there since the place opened. She's drunk as hell and killin' mean. She pulled a Colt on the barkeep, forcin' him to bring her another bottle of whiskey."

"Damn it," Everett said, "why didn't some of the men warn the people who operate this saloon that Quilla is a woman?"

"Because they're our younger unmarried men," said Will, "and they don't like Quilla. You can't blame the barkeep. She was already soused before he learned she was female. My God, with her hair cut short, wearin' that old flop hat and swearin' like a bull whacker, she looks more like a man than some of the men do."

They found the rowdy Quilla with her back to the wall, and three bottles on the table before her. Two of them were apparently empty, and she had just upended the third and was drinking from it. Everett ignored the sly looks of some of the men, all of whom were giving Quilla plenty of room. The barkeep raised his eyebrows as Landon Everett approached.

"Don't let that woman have any more whiskey," Everett said.

"I wouldn't of let her have none, had I knowed she wasn't a man," the barkeep said sullenly. "Why don't you just stand wher' you are till she's killed that bottle, and when she pokes that Colt in your face, then *you* tell her she ain't gettin' no more panther juice."

"I'll do better than that," said Everett. As he approached the table where Quilla sat, she slammed the bottle down, fixing bloodshot eyes on the wagon boss.

"Quilla," Everett said quietly, "get up. You're going back to camp."

"When I'm damn good an' ready," Quilla snarled, "an' I ain't ready."

"Get up," said Everett in a dangerous tone none of the emigrants had ever heard him use.

Quilla laughed, a drunken cackle. "Make me, damn you, if you can."

With remarkable swiftness she had a Colt in her hand, but Everett was ahead of her. The toe of his boot struck the underside of the table and it was upended with a crash, taking Quilla, her chair, and the whiskey bottles with it. The Colt roared once, the slug sifting dust down from the ceiling. Before she could untangle herself and get off another shot, Landon Everett had caught her wrist and forced the Colt from her hand. She just lay there swearing at him, making no effort to rise. Everett took both her hands and dragged her to her feet, but this time she was too quick for him. She drove the toe of a heavy boot into his groin, and the sickening pain that swept over him allowed the drunken woman to free her hands. She didn't attack like a screeching, clawing cata-mount, but fought like a man. She caught him in the belly with a vicious left and followed it with a right to the point of his chin. The blows slammed Everett against the wall and he hung there, for he needed the support. Quilla seized the back of a chair, smashing it against the wall when Everett slid to the floor. He sprang at her and they went down in a tangle of arms and legs. Everett was on top and he fought to pin down her arms, but with phenomenal strength she humped him off and reversed their positions. She dug her thumbs into Everett's throat and he felt himself blacking out. His hands were free and he swung his right fist as hard as he could, slamming it into Quilla's left ear. It broke her stranglehold, and Everett pressed his advantage, throwing her off him. She had recovered and was coming after him again when he got his hands on the Colt she had dropped. He swung the muzzle of the weapon against Quilla's head with enough force to drive her to the floor, flat on her back, unconscious. Landon Everett got to his knees and finally to his feet.

"I regret . . . having to strike a . . . a woman," he panted, "but there was no . . . other way."

"God Almighty," said Will Hamer, "you should of done that sooner. She would have killed you."

The barkeep seemed struck dumb by the spectacle he had witnessed. He finally brought Everett a wet towel, and the wagon boss accepted it gratefully, wiping his face and neck.

"I ain't disputin' nobody's word," the awed barkeep said, "but are you gents dead sure that's a female? I've seen many a man that couldn't of put up a fight like that."

"Bring me something—anything—to bind her hands and feet," Everett said.

The barkeep hurried to comply, quickly returning with several lengths of heavy brown cord. Everett rolled Quilla over, belly down, and tied her wrists behind her back. He then got her feet together and tied them securely, wrapping the heavy cord around half a dozen times, just below her boot tops.

"Will," said Everett, "go get your wagon. We're going to take her to camp and pile her under Caleb Vandiver's wagon until she sobers up."

"Just like that?"

"Just like that," Everett said, "with word to the men on watch to ignore her swearing. From there we're going to find her parents—Joseph and Flora—and they're going to do whatever they must to keep that damn troublesome female away from that saloon until we move out."

The shot within the saloon had attracted attention, and while Will was gone after his teams and wagon, some of the men from the trading post entered the saloon. Among them was Buck Embler.

"My God," Buck said, "what happened here?"

"Quilla," said Everett. "Will's bringing his teams and wagon. We're taking her back to camp to sober up. While we're gone, there's something I'd like you to do. I've sold Upshur's teams and wagon to the trading post, but there's something I want you to get from that wagon. . . ."

"Hold it," Buckalew snarled, cocking his Colt.

"Damn it," Rufe Schmidt complained, "we ain't set-tin' here no longer. We're turnin' in."

"Go on," said Buckalew, "but you're spreadin' yer blankets there by the wagon, so's I kin see you."

The Schmidts did as he commanded, but they didn't sleep. They waited for Suggs and Gerdes to return, hopefully drunk, bringing a bottle for Buckalew. It was very late when they finally rode in.

"Took you long enough," said Buckalew. "You bring me some whiskey?"

Suggs laughed. "Confound it all, I told Gerdes we was forgettin' something."

"Damn the both of you," Buckalew shouted.

"Watch your tongue," said Gerdes. "Here's your damn bottle."

The Schmidts watched covertly, noting with satisfac-tion that not only had Suggs and Gerdes bellied up in the saloon, they had brought with them more than the bottle they had promised Buckalew. The moon had risen, and by its light and that of the stars, they could see the trio drinking the whiskey from the bottles. It was almost an hour before Buckalew, Suggs, and Gerdes sought their blankets. Drunk as they seemed to be, the three had been cautious enough to bed down uncom-fortably close to the Schmidts. It would be difficult for the desperate pair to reach the horses, saddle them, and escape undetected.

"We'll wait till midnight," Rufe hissed, "jist to be sure."

But they didn't have that much time. Suddenly one of the horses nickered and Buckalew sat up.

"Git up," he snarled. "Somebody's after the horses."

Suggs and Gerdes rolled out of their blankets and got to their knees. Buckalew was already on his feet, his Colt in his hand. There was a blaze of gunfire from the darkness and the trio died without firing a shot. Rufe and Jenks Schmidt cowered in their blankets, terrified. Before the echoes of the shooting faded, a voice spoke.

"You varmints there by the wagon git up. Do it slow, keepin' yer hands empty."

Having no choice, Rufe and Jenks Schmidt stumbled to their feet.

"Let's just kill the varmints, Tate," said a second voice.

"No," Rufe cried desperately. "They ain't no friends of ours. We was waitin' fer 'em to git drunk enough so's we could take the horses an' run."

"You ain't takin' no horse," said Tate. "We are, an' we ain't of a mind to leave nobody alive who kin say we took 'em."

"Hold off a mite, Tate," said a third voice. "There's nigh two hunnert wagons circled back yonder, acrost the river from the tradin' post, and sixty more a day ahead of these pilgrims. Somethin' damn funny here. I'm wonderin' why these varmints an' their wagons is driftin' along in between. Could be they know somethin' we'd ought to be knowin'."

"Maybe," Tate said, cocking his Colt. "Talk."

Rufe's voice trembled as he told them of Ab being hanged and of his and Jenks's expulsion from Landon Everett's party.

"Them three you gunned down," said Rufe, "was figurin' some way of takin' that herd of Texas cows."

The voice belonging to Tate laughed coldly. "An' I reckon the pair of you wasn't."

"Hell no," Rufe lied. "Five of us agin' sixteen gun-slingin' Texans?"

"I kin believe that," one of the unseen party said. "They ain't got the sand of a pair of yellow coyotes."

"Them three we shot down was fightin' men," Tate said. "What'n hell would they of wanted with a pair of varmints like you? You got ten seconds to tell me why I oughn't blow the two of you to hell."

"Gold," Jenks Schmidt shouted wildly. "Them wagons ahead, one of 'em has gold, an' we know which wagon it is."

"Wal, by God," said Tate admiringly, "you come up with jist the right words to save your scruffy hides. You'll be ridin' them horses after all, at least for a while. There's fifteen of us, an' we can take the cattle *and* the gold, if they *is* any gold. If they ain't, then there's one damn thing you varmints can count on. You'll be plumb sorry them sodbusters didn't hang the pair of you from the same limb as your no-account brother."

16

The men who had remained with the wagons watched in amazement as Landon Everett and Will Hamer lifted the hog-tied Quilla from the wagon. She was still cursing them as they rolled her—none too gently—under Caleb Vandiver's wagon.

"What's wrong with her?" Gus Shondell asked.

"Drunk," Landon replied. "Will and me are goin' back to the trading post for Joseph and Flora. When they get here, see that they don't turn her loose until she's sober. Even then, I want her kept in camp. She's not to go near that saloon again."

"We'll watch her," Jules Dewees said. "Did you have any luck gettin' the tradin' post to take Upshur's teams and wagon?"

"Yes," Landon said, "but they didn't want to. I had to let it all go for three hundred dollars."

"Damn it, Landon," Will said as they started back to the trading post, "you shouldn't have told them how much you got for the teams and wagon. Now everybody will know, includin' the skunk that's been murdering men for the gold in their pockets. You'll be risking your life just standing watch. Now you'll have to get in your wagon come dark, and stay there."

"No," Everett said. "Starting tonight, I'm bunkin' under my wagon until the killer comes lookin' for this three hundred in gold. I want you and Buck to see that everybody knows, but not a word as to my reason for comin' out of the wagon at night. Mattie and me will see to that."

"Of all the crazy ideas I ever heard—"

"This is the worst," Everett finished.

"You're damn right it is," Will replied. "Mattie will never—"

"Mattie will do as I say," Everett said. "We're goin' to lay this problem to rest before we leave here, and this is the only way I know."

Will said no more, knowing the futility of trying to change Landon Everett's mind once he had decided what he must do. They parted company at the trading post, and Everett went in search of Joseph and Flora Rowden, parents of the rowdy Quilla. Finding them, he wasted no words. He told them of the troublesome woman's disgraceful conduct in the saloon, warning them not to turn her loose until she was sober and manageable.

By the time Everett found Mattie, she had accumulated enough provisions and goods to more than double the fifty dollars Everett had promised to spend in the store. Mattie said not a word until they were trudging beside their teams, on the way back to camp.

"Something's wrong, Landon. What is it?"

"Mostly Quilla Rowden," Everett said. He then told her what he'd been forced to do, binding Quilla and then hauling her bodily back to camp.

"Dear God, Landon," Mattie said, "she could have killed you, and still might. Do you honestly believe Joseph and Flora can keep her away from that saloon?"

"No," Everett replied, "but what was I to do with her? Dog drunk, she's as hard to handle as any man, and stronger than some."

Everett dreaded telling her of his plan to trap the elusive killer, and the longer he delayed telling her, the more difficult the task would become.

"Mattie," he finally said, "come suppertime, you and me are goin' to do a thing we've never done before. We're goin' to have one hell of a fight, and you're goin' to kick me out of the wagon."

"What?"

Swiftly, he told her his plan, and just as swiftly she disagreed.

"Landon, I won't do it. Wagon boss or not, you're risking your life for these people, and not one of them has the right to ask that of you."

"Nobody's asked me," Everett said. "I'm taking it upon myself. I want to end this ordeal before we take the trail again. These damn wagons never were meant to be living quarters, and we lose an hour every morning while we all reload what we've dragged out to make room for ourselves."

The argument dragged on. With a sigh she finally gave in, bowing her head in resignation when it became obvious he wouldn't back down.

"Mattie," he said, draping an arm over her sagging shoulders, "don't you worry. I can protect myself, and I'll be ready. Better that I stay awake for a night or two than for us all to squat in these wagons, wide-awake from here to Oregon."

His attempt to draw a smile from her failed, and even to his own ears his laughter sounded weak and forced. It trailed off, leaving only the thumping of the hooves of the oxen and the rattle of the wagon.

One hundred thirty miles west of Laramie, North Fork of the Platte. August 14, 1843.

"I'm wonderin' why we ain't met them five wagons that turned back from South Pass," Jim Bridger said, as he and the Texans finished breakfast. "I got to be back at my place before the end of the month, so I'll be leavin' you folks this mornin'. Them wagons must of run into trouble. I'll see kin I be of any help."

"When you meet them," Applegate said, "tell them that when we meet, I'd like them to spend a night with us. I want to know anything they can tell us about the trail ahead."

"I'll give 'em the word," Bridger said. He rode out well ahead of the herd and was soon swallowed up by distance.

"We're goin' to miss him," Sumner said. "Wish he could of been with us when we cross this South Pass."

"What he told us about it wasn't encouraging," Applegate said.

The next afternoon, two hours before sunset, they met the five wagons Bridger had been expecting. Indian Charlie and Alonzo Gonzales headed the horse remuda, and when Lou waved his hat, the riders began milling the herd. That would be signal enough for Applegate and the lead wagons.

"Come on, Dill," Lou said. "Let's ride out to meet them."

They were the very picture of dejection. Silent men led their teams, their women and children strung out beside or behind the wagons. They reined up, waiting for the cowboys to reach them.

"This is the Applegate party," Lou said. "I'm Lou Spencer and this is Dillard Sumner. The rest of our riders are with the cattle, and the wagons are behind the herd. All of you are invited to stay the night with us, if you're of a mind to."

"We're obliged," said the man with the first wagon. "We're the Kittrell family. The Murchison, Saunders, Evans, and Hunter families are behind us. Bridger said you was comin'. We had all manner of trouble. Busted wheels, axles, and God, you name it."

The bedraggled people seemed half starved and Applegate waited until after supper before questioning them about the trail ahead. Much of their trouble had been the result of their falling behind the rest of their party.

"Three of us lost a child," Murchison said, "and that was bad enough. Then there was just one breakdown after another. By the time we got to this South Pass, it just seemed impossible. None of us cared a damn whether we ever saw Oregon or not, so we turned around and started back."

Applegate listened somberly, asking fewer and fewer questions, until the conversation died almost entirely. The five weary families returned to their wagons. After a hearty breakfast the following morning, they went on their way. Applegate set about harnessing his teams, and the rest of his party followed his example. Gloom reigned over the camp, and anxious to be free of it, the Texans rode out to bunch the herd for the trail.

"I never seen such long faces," Waco said. "You'd think the whole bunch just found out they ain't no Santa Claus."

Del Konda laughed. "You mean there ain't?"

"Nobody ain't told the Widow Hayden," Red Brodie said. "Ever' mornin', there's ol' Waco, harnessin' her teams. I reckon when she gits to this god-awful South Pass, she won't have no trouble at all. Waco, he'll put them teams an' wagon in his hip pocket, set that gal on his saddle an' just ride 'em on across."

"I been wonderin'," Sterling McCarty said, "when Waco's goin' to git a little somethin' fer all his attention to that woman."

To their total surprise, Waco laughed.

"What'n hell's happened to *him*?" Red Brodie wondered.

"He's done a mite of growin' up," Lou said. "I know at least two other hombres that could stand a dose of that. Now let's get them cows movin' and give Applegate's bunch some catchin' up to do."

Nobody knew what had started the ruckus between Landon and Mattie Everett, but before it was done, the entire party knew about it. There was much shouting back and forth and considerable swearing from Everett. Mattie was doing her part so convincingly, Everett hoped she never truly became angry with him.

"I think I'll go back to sleeping under the wagon for a while," Everett bawled, loud enough for most of the camp to hear.

"I don't care if you sleep on *top* of the wagon," Mattie responded hotly. "Just leave me alone."

That ended the "argument," and to make it all the more convincing, Will Hamer and Buck Embler spent some time with Everett, apparently urging him to remain in the wagon. But Landon Everett went ahead with his plan. This time he didn't spread his blankets beneath the big wagon, for if he had to fight for his life, he didn't want to be crowded. He folded a blanket, placed it behind his head, and leaned against one of the wagon's rear wheels. Because of the large number of wagons, they were circled five deep, and Everett's wagon was the fifth one, on the inside of the circle. He had purposely chosen this position so that the four wagons beyond his own would provide perfect cover for the killer. When it became dark enough, he removed the blanket he had placed behind his head and quarter-folded it with another. He then placed the thick pad between his back and the wagon wheel. While it wasn't perfect, it offered him some protection against being knifed in the back before he was able to defend himself. Occasionally, several of the men on watch came within the wagon circle. Normally they patrolled the outside perimeter, and Everett realized they were concerned for his safety.

Time dragged, and the only sound was that of the footsteps of the men on the second watch. While there was total silence from within Everett's wagon, he didn't doubt for a moment that Mattie lay wide-awake, her worried eyes on the gray wagon canvas above and her ears tuned to any conflict that might cost Landon Everett his life.

Everett awoke with a start, painfully aware that such

slumber, however brief, might become permanent. He desperately needed to stand, to walk, but he dared not. If he was to tempt the killer, he must seem to doze. What he judged to be an hour passed. Dawn was less than three hours distant, and if anything was going to happen, it must be soon. Fighting sleep, he forced himself to concentrate, to think. Quilla Rowden had been released from her bonds at suppertime. Everett had stared at her, hoping there might be some shame in her eyes, in her demeanor, but there was none. She glared back at him, and if there was anything in her hard eyes, it was hatred. . . .

The first warning—when it came—was so slight, Landon Everett could easily have charged it to his imagination. It was the faint rustle of cloth against wood, perhaps the underside of a wagon box. Almost too late, Everett rolled to his left as the knife was driven into the blankets that had shielded his back. But the assailant had made one mistake. The thrust, as Everett had planned, came between the spokes of the wagon wheel, and the blade of the knife became entangled in the blankets. Everett got to his knees, his hand on the butt of his Colt, just as the attacker freed the deadly knife. Before Everett could fire, the shadowy figure launched itself from under the wagon, the upraised blade of the knife glinting silver in the faint starlight.

Everett caught the arm with the descending blade and they fought for the weapon. His assailant, unbelievably strong, kneed him in the groin, and as nausea swept over him, the knife came uncomfortably close. Try as he might, Everett couldn't break the killer's grip on the knife. Like an arm wrestler seeking victory, Everett suddenly slammed the unyielding arm to his left, and it smashed hard against the heavy iron tire of the wagon wheel. There was a grunt of pain and the hand loosed its grip on the knife. Everett had his hand on the shaft of the weapon when a fist was driven hard into his nose and mouth. Flung backward, he still gripped the knife.

Dazed, seeking to defend himself, he brought the weapon upward just as his opponent lunged. The killer's body came down on him hard and Everett drove the deadly blade in as deep as he was able. There was a groan and he could feel warm blood on his hand, but it was over. Landon Everett lay there panting, the taste of blood in his mouth, too exhausted to move. The sound of the scuffle had brought men on the run who had been on watch, but Mattie was there first.

"Landon!" she cried. "Landon!"

"All right, Mattie," Everett replied. "All right."

Will Hamer and Buck Embler were among the first to arrive. Quickly they rolled the dead body off the wagon boss. Prepared for she knew not what, Mattie had matches and candles. Several were quickly lighted. Nobody was prepared for the grisly sight that greeted them. Quilla Rowden lay on her back, a knife driven deep in her chest, the front of her shirt soaked with blood.

"Great God Almighty," Will Hamer said in a whisper.

Within minutes the entire camp had been aroused and most of them had gathered around, nobody knowing quite what to say or do. Joseph Rowden, Quilla's father, found his voice first.

"You killed her," he shouted angrily. "You killed Quilla."

"Not until she tried to kill me," Everett said quietly. "Just as she killed three other men."

"You can't prove that," Rowden snarled. "You dragged her out of that saloon yesterday, tied hand and foot. If she was after you, it was because of that."

"No," Everett said. "She killed for gold, and that's why she was after me. I set this up, letting it be known I had three hundred dollars from the selling of Upshur Hiddenbrandt's teams and wagon. If you want proof, Mr. Rowden, I think we'll find that in your wagon. In Quilla's trunk. I expect you'll find a key in her pocket."

"No," Rowden said. "No."

"Just so I'm not accused of any tricks," Everett said,

"one of you take that key from her pocket. Then we'll open Quilla's trunk."

Not a man moved to do his bidding, not even Joseph Rowden. It was Mattie Everett who searched the dead Quilla and came up with the key. Silently, she passed it to Everett, and without a word being spoken, the entire party made its way to the Rowden wagon.

"Now, Mr. Rowden," Everett said, "none of us want to go rummaging through your wagon. Please get in there and drag Quilla's trunk out here on the tailgate so we can open it."

In the dim candlelight, Rowden took one look at some of the grim faces surrounding him and did as he'd been told. Mattie had passed around the candles and half a dozen were quickly lighted before Everett unlocked the mysterious trunk. It proved to be two-thirds full, most of its contents concealed between layers of old newspapers. But the very first thing they saw when the lid was raised was an impressive array of gold coins. All eagles and double eagles. There was a gasp from those who were close enough to see, and angry shouts from the many who could not.

"What is it? What's in there?"

"Gold," Everett told them. "Eagles and double eagles. Pile it all out in the wagon box, Will, and count it."

"Don't prove nothin'," Joseph Rowden growled. "Quilla was never one to spend much. That's her life's savings."

"That's not the proof I'm looking for," Everett replied. "When those three men were killed, their pockets were turned inside out. There was more taken than just their gold. We'll search the rest of that trunk, if we have to."

"There's six hundred and forty dollars in gold," Will said.

"Dig down a little more," Everett said.

Will removed the next layer of folded newspaper, revealing what appeared to be individually wrapped items.

Using his knife to cut the string, he began opening the parcels. Three of them contained pocket watches. In the fourth was a gold wedding band and a man's diamond ring. In the fifth there was a single brass key.

"That's enough, Will," Everett said. "Let me have that key."

Will did so, and Everett held up the key, speaking so the entire gathering could hear.

"Yesterday," the wagon boss said, "I sold Upshur Hiddenbrandt's teams and wagon at the trading post. I kept something from Upshur's wagon, and to be sure nobody could accuse me of trickery, I had Buck Embler remove it. Tell everybody what it is, Buck."

"It's the lock from Upshur's trunk," Embler said. "Upshur's pockets had been picked clean and there was no key, so we pried the hasp from the wood. The lock is still locked."

"Take this key, Buck," Everett said, "and see if it will open the lock."

Men and women surged forward, trying to see.

"Slide that trunk back in the wagon, Will," Everett said. "Then I want you and Buck to stand up there where everybody can see what Buck's about to do. Pass Will a couple of those candles."

When both men were in position and Will held the lighted candles close, Buck used the key, and the lock from Upshur Hiddenbrandt's trunk opened easily.

"That's my proof," Landon Everett said. "While I can't prove that Quilla committed all the murders, this is proof enough she killed Upshur. Are there any of you who want to argue the point?"

"No," they shouted with a thunder of voices.

"Then all of you get back to your wagons," Everett said. "We'll be here one more day and then we're moving out."

Slowly they turned away, leaving only Will, Buck, Landon, and Mattie. Joseph and Flora Rowden stood with bowed heads, and the silence that followed was painful. Landon Everett finally spoke.

"I did what had to be done," he said, "and I'm sorry it turned out this way. Come daylight, we'll dig a grave and help with the burying."

"No need," Rowden said dully. "You've done enough."

On the Sweetwater, 180 miles west of Laramie. August 20, 1843.

The Texans bedded down the horse remuda and the herd of longhorns less than an hour before sundown, while Applegate's party circled their wagons. While waiting for supper, Applegate spread out the trail map. Lou Spencer, Dillard Sumner, and several other riders gathered around.

"Tomorrow," Lou said, "we'll be crossing the Platte. It turns south just a mile or so ahead."

"According to the map," Applegate said, "that's where the Sweetwater flows into it. We'll be following the Sweetwater to within a few miles of the Bridger outpost."

"That's good news," Sumner said. "From what Bridger told us, once we reach the joining of the Sweetwater and the North Fork of the Platte, we'll be a hundred twenty-five miles from South Pass and two hundred seventy-five miles from Bridger's post."

"We've made a hundred and eighty miles in thirteen days," Waco said. "If our luck holds, we'll reach South Pass before the end of August."

"From what Bridger told us about South Pass, the crossing could cost us every day we've gained," Applegate said.

But South Pass wouldn't be the only delay. Fair weather and plentiful water from the Platte had lessened the need for rain and had diminished their fear of storms and lightning. Not since the Little Blue had there been the torrential rain that resulted in a prairie axle-deep in mud. But far to the west, dirty gray clouds were gathering, and as skies darkened from blue to purple, lightning crackled across the horizon.

"Maybe just heat lightning," Black Jack Rhudy said hopefully.

"Storm be coming," Indian Charlie said. "*Malo* knee, she hurt lak hell. Before mañana, she rain lak hell."

"He's likely right," Del Konda said. "We're overdue for one of them god-awful storms with sixteen kinds of lightnin'."

"We'll be keepin' an eye on it," Sumner said. "I reckon we'll know by midnight. If this is a bad one, it'll take every man of us to hold the herd. Even then, only if we're damn lucky."

As the night wore on, the lightning came closer, accompanied by distant thunder. The wind swept out of the west, so moist it dampened their skin and clothing like a fog. When midnight came, Lou and his outfit rode out for the second watch. But Dillard Sumner had reached a decision.

"We'd better stick with you," Sumner said. "She's gonna blow."

Rufe and Jenks Schmidt didn't get a good look at their questionable companions until first light, and what they saw did little to reassure them. The fifteen men looked like the very dregs of humanity. They were bearded, dirty, and boasted the most formidable array of weapons the Schmidts had ever seen. Every man carried at least one Colt revolver, while some had two. Most of them had long knives thonged to their belts, and there was a .50 caliber Sharps buffalo gun slung from every saddle. Some of the men wore buckskins while others were clothed in rough shirts and trousers, often patched but seldom washed. The Schmidts recognized Tate by his voice, and he didn't even bother introducing his companions.

"Leave your horses saddled," Tate told them. "We'll stop to eat and then we'll go on. I aim for us to catch up to them plow pushers and their cattle sometime tomorrow night."

"Tate," one of his companions said, "we got a right to know when you aim to take them cows an' the gold. Assumin', of course, that this pair of varmints ain't lyin', an' they really *is* some gold."

"Jessup," Tate said, "I ain't made up my mind how and when we'll make our move. When I reckon it's time for the rest of you to know, I'll tell you."

Tate's response didn't set well with his companions, and even as the men began preparing breakfast, some of them cast dark looks at their sharp-tongued leader. The Schmidts exchanged covert looks. Rufe had at first been angry with his brother for divulging the existence of the gold, but now Rufe felt that might work to his and Jenks's advantage. Clearly these men were thieves and killers, and, as such, they didn't trust one another. Before learning of the gold, concerned only with the rustling of the Texas cattle, there had been some unity among them. But the very mention of gold excited a man's greed, distorted his perspective, and set the evil side of his nature to pondering a means of taking all the riches for himself. The Schmidts held their silence, accepted the food offered them, and the seventeen men rode on in pursuit of the Applegate party.

Three hours before first light, the storm struck with all its fury. The wind rose to a shriek, bringing rain in torrents, raising some hope among the cowboys that they might be spared the terrible lightning and earth-shaking thunder that so often terrified a drowsing herd. But the thunder and lightning didn't spare them. Even as the cowboys circled the nervous cattle, trying to calm them, they could sense what was coming. The thunder rumbled ever closer and the lightning seemed to light the universe in a continuous golden glow. There was a sizzle as it struck somewhere close, and there followed a clap of thunder of such proportions that it set the horses to rearing and nickering. While most of the cowboys struggled to gain control of their mounts, the terrified longhorns were off and running, eastward along the Platte River. The outfits came together, galloping after the thundering herd. But the herd was gone and they faced another problem. Lou Spencer fired his Colt, getting the attention of the riders, rallying them to him.

"The horse remuda!" Lou shouted.

It was enough, and barely in time. Wheeling their mounts, they kicked them into a fast gallop. While the thunder had diminished, the rain and the lightning had not. In a flash of lightning, through the driving rain, they could see the horse herd coming. Lou drew his Colt and began firing, and the rest of the riders quickly followed his example. It was thunder of a different kind, and the galloping horses discovered they were running toward it instead of away from it. The lead horses cut sharply to the south, and the cowboys pressed their advantage, forcing the animals into a horseshoe turn. Trailing the slowing herd came Alonzo Gonzales and Indian Charlie.

"Damn," Waco shouted in mock anger, "we thought you hombres was goin' to hold the horse remuda."

Indian Charlie laughed. "We don't do no worse than you hombres. Where the *vacas* go?"

"I reckon they must of run off while we was helpin' you *pelados* head the horse remuda," Waco said.

"Waco," Lou said, "shut up. It's damn near impossible to head a herd in the dark, with thunder and lightning right on their heels. We were almightly lucky to have headed the horses."

"My God," Dillard Sumner said, "I just hope them wild-eyed varmints had the sense to split when they reached Applegate's wagons. If they didn't . . ."

His voice trailed off, but every rider knew exactly what he meant. They bunched the horse remuda, left Alonzo and Indian Charlie with it, and then rode ahead toward the circled wagons. The rain had slacked a little, but not much. Ahead, excited by the wind, flames leaped and sparked. The fire had been started beneath a canvas shelter that had been erected beside one of the wagons. Applegate, Higdon, and Quimby waited. A two-gallon coffeepot hung suspended from a three-legged iron spider. There seemed to have been no damage to the wagons as a result of the stampede. The cowboys dismounted.

"I hope nobody was hurt," Applegate said. "We were concerned."

"So were we," Lou said. "We managed to head the horse remuda, but that was all we could do. We expected the stampede to slow before it reached your wagons, and hoped when it did, the herd would split. But you can't ever be sure when it comes to cows."

"It had slowed considerably by the time it got to us," Higdon said. "I don't think you'll have to ride too far, rounding them up."

"It wasn't unexpected," Quimby added. "Most of us were awake and up. With all the thunder and lightning, we weren't surprised."

"Have some coffee," Applegate said. "This will cost us some time, but rather than complain about that, we should be thanking the Almighty that we haven't had more of these storms."

"You're right," Dillard Sumner said. "This bein' new territory to us, we don't know what its weather habits are, but we could of had this thunder and lightning two or three times a week. We'll be in our saddles at first light, gatherin' 'em as quick as we can."

17

Quilla Rowden was buried at dawn. Her father and brother had dug the grave, while her mother wrapped Quilla in blankets. Most of the men and women of the party had sympathized, but watched the lonely ritual from a distance, heeding Landon Everett's suggestion that the family be left alone with their grief.

"What are they going to do now?" Mattie wondered. "Will they go on to Oregon with us?"

"No reason they shouldn't," Everett said. "That's partly why we're laying over an extra day. I thought they'd need some time to accept this."

"I'm sure they will," Mattie said, "and I doubt that one day and a night will be enough. I think you should speak to Joseph tonight."

"I intend to," Everett said. Whatever Quilla Rowden had been, whatever she'd done, Everett knew he'd been responsible for her death, and he doubted her family would look beyond that. He dreaded speaking to Joseph Rowden, for he was in an awkward position. He found himself hoping the Rowdens would go on to Oregon.

Most of the emigrants took advantage of the extra day, loading up with extra supplies. The Rowdens were loading up too, and nobody knew whether it was for the journey to Oregon or for a return to Independence. Everett waited until after supper before approaching the

Rowden wagon. Rowden saw him coming and went to meet him.

"Joe," Everett said, "for whatever it's worth, I'm again saying that I'm sorry, and I hope you'll be going on to Oregon with us."

Rowden looked at him from watery, reddened eyes. "Do you honestly think we'd be welcome?"

"As far as I'm concerned, you are," Everett said, "and any man that says otherwise will have to answer to me. All of us are responsible for our own actions. You couldn't help what happened, any more than I could."

Landon Everett had never been close to Joseph Rowden, but somehow he'd chosen the proper words. Rowden swallowed hard before he finally spoke.

"Landon, I . . . we . . . we'd like to go on to Oregon, but only if . . . if . . ."

"Then we'd like to have you," Everett said, meaning it.

"You didn't let me finish," Rowden said. "I want you to take the gold, Landon. All of it. Those men must have had families, and I want you to divide it equally among their kin."

"But some of it rightfully belongs to you," Everett said, "whatever part of it that was Quilla's, and we have no way of knowing how much that was."

"That's why I want you to take it all," Rowden said. "Flora and me, we'd never lay a hand on any of it."

"Then I respect yours and Flora's feelings," Everett said. "Gather it up in something—a saddlebag, if you have one—and once we reach Oregon, I'll do my best to return it to the next of kin."

"Thank you, Landon," Rowden said. "That eases some of the burden. Just give us some time for . . . the rest, and we'll go on with you."

Mattie was waiting, and she saw the answer in his eyes before he spoke.

"God, Mattie," he sighed, "I felt like I was totin' an anvil around on my shoulders and somebody just took it away. I never expected to speak to Joe Rowden again, or have him speak to me."

"He must have felt the same way," Mattie said. "His burden may have been even more terrible than yours, and when you freed yourself, you freed him. Despite all that's happened, I believe he and Flora will sleep tonight."

"I know damn well I will," Everett said, "and I'm invitin' you to join me. Under the wagon."

Their first day back on the trail, they sighted the two wagons, and with sundown less than an hour away, Everett gave the order to circle the wagons. That done, most of the party focused their attention on the wagons ahead. Some of the oxen had wandered far upriver.

"The rest of you get the supper fires going," Everett said. "I'll take Will and Buck and we'll ride up there. Something looks all wrong."

As the three riders approached, a pair of buzzards flapped sluggishly into the evening sky. The bodies of Buckalew, Suggs, and Gerdes—what was left of them— lay where they had fallen. Wolves had been there well ahead of the buzzards, and the scene might have been something out of a nightmare. It was a long moment before any of the three recovered from the shock enough to speak.

"One of the wagons was Buckalew's," Will said, "and with them mismatched rear wheels, the other had to belong to the Schmidts. From the looks of it, the Schmidts gunned down Buckalew and his men, took their horses and lit out."

"Just one thing wrong with that picture," Buck said. "I don't think the Schmidts—one at a time or together— was fast enough or brave enough to have done this."

"I feel the same way," Everett said. "We'll leave the horses here and look around some. Then we'll bury what's left of them. There should be some shovels in the wagons."

"My God," Will said when they found the tracks, "there was a small army. Way the horses was millin' around, we can't be sure how many riders there was. Let's find their tracks where they rode out."

They had no trouble finding the trail, following it until it crossed the Platte. There they turned back.

"Eighteen horses," Everett said. "Buckalew had a horse, and so did the two men riding with him. With the Schmidts riding two horses and leading the third, that means there were fifteen men in the party that did the killing."

"The tracks tell us that," Will said, "but they don't tell us the most important thing. Why didn't these men just gun down the Schmidts like they did Buckalew and his friends?"

"You're overlookin' somethin' else," Buck said. "How come this pack of hell-raisers took Rufe and Jenks along with 'em? They ain't the kind of men you'd want for friends, if you'd known 'em forty years."

"That's the God's truth," Will admitted. "I wouldn't trust them Schmidts as far as I could flap my arms and fly."

"I expect those men have some use for Rufe and Jenks," Everett said, "and it may be best if we never know what it is. Let's get those shovels and get on with the burying, while there's still daylight."

When Everett, Will, and Buck returned to their camp, they found supper in progress. Everett walked to the center of the wagon circle, and conversation ceased. He quickly told them what he, Will, and Buck had discovered.

"The wagons and teams have been abandoned," Everett said. "Provisions and tools are in the wagons, and there are a dozen oxen grazing along the river. I see no reason why we shouldn't take the oxen and anything from the wagons we can use. Does anybody disagree with my thinking?"

"Not where Buckalew and his men are concerned,"

Gus Shondell said, "but I doubt we'll see either of them again. Not alive, anyway. I don't suggest that any of you go against your feelings. You can take what you need from what's obviously been abandoned or you can leave it like it is. I won't fault you either way."

"Well, hell," Jules Dewees said, "we ain't even halfway to Oregon, and I can't see leavin' perfectly good oxen to be et by wolves or taken by others no more derservin' than we are. I'll take two of the critters and fasten 'em behind my wagon on lead ropes. We know Buckalew and his friends ain't comin' lookin' for theirs. If the Schmidts show up wantin' their teams, we just give 'em back."

"Good thinking," Will Hamer said. "I'll take two."

"So will I," Buck Embler said.

"I have a suggestion," Everett said. "Since these oxen belong to none of us, we'll take them all as common property, to be used by any one of us if they're needed. If one of your animals should die or be killed, you take one of these we're about to claim."

There were shouts of approval, and Landon Everett sighed. God only knew what lay ahead, but for tonight he could rest easy.

The band of renegades with whom the Schmidts rode were less than an hour behind Applegate's wagons when Tate bid them stop for the night. As darkness drew near, lightning on the western horizon and a cooling west wind warned of the coming storm.

"They'll be rain 'fore mornin'," Tate said.

Some of the men started a fire and set about readying supper. When it was ready, it was eaten in silence. The men began taking their rolls from behind their saddles and shaking out their blankets. Each roll included a man-size length of canvas in which the blankets had been secured. It was the only protection a rider had in wet weather. The Schmidts, however, had only their blankets. Cramped as it had been, their wagon had kept them dry when the rain came. Jenks started to say something, caught Tate watching him and quickly changed his mind.

The Schmidts spent a perfectly miserable night hunched in their sodden blankets. But the night was shorter than any of them expected. The rain slacked before dawn, the wind swept away the clouds, and stars blossomed in a purple sky. Suddenly the renegades found their camp overrun with grazing, bawling cattle.

"Roll out," Tate shouted. "We got us some ridin' to do."

Rufe Schmidt laughed. "Fast thinkin'. Them Texas gun throwers will be lookin' for their cows come daylight."

"Saddle your horses," Tate snarled. "I won't tell you again."

The Schmidts did as they were told. Tate led out, crossing the Platte to the north bank, and the others followed. They rode beyond a rise and into the timber, well beyond the river. From there, Tate led them westward.

The Texans rode eastward along the Platte as soon as it was light enough to see. Almost immediately they began finding bunches of cattle.

"May not be too bad," Dillard Sumner observed. "Slowed 'em down some when they come up on all them circled wagons."

"*Vacas* no remember why they run," Indian Charlie said.

"That's pretty much the truth," Lou agreed. "Besides, they won't stray far from the river. There wasn't enough rain last night to fill the wet weather streams and water holes."

But as they continued along the river, the cattle thinned out and their optimism dwindled.

"We ain't come even close to eight thousand head," Waco grumbled. "Damn it, the varmints fanned out."

"It's startin' to look that way," Sumner said. "Why don't we round up the bunches between here and Applegate's camp, and let the others wait awhile?"

"That's about all we can do," Lou agreed. "Give 'em three hours in the sun, and let's hope they drift back to the river for water. If they don't, we'll have to track them down. Like Waco said, they've fanned out, and with the river blockin' 'em to the north, I reckon they're somewhere to the south."

It took less than two hours for the cowboys to round up the longhorns grazing along the river. Lou rode in and reported to Applegate.

"We got a little more than twenty-five hundred," Lou said. "There wasn't that much rain last night, and we're expectin' the others—some of 'em, anyhow—to return to the river for water. If they don't, we'll have to ride south and beat the bushes."

"How long?" Applegate asked.

"Two days, maybe," Lou said, "dependin' on how far they've drifted. If they come back to the river to water, then we may have 'em all by sundown tomorrow. Will you have some men ride out and keep those we just drove in bunched?"

"Yes," Applegate said. "Use all your riders for the gather."

The sun had the desired effect, and before sundown the Texans had driven another three thousand head upriver, bedding them down with those they'd gathered earlier. Applegate and five other men were watching the herd, and the wagon boss was greatly encouraged with the arrival of an even larger herd.

"We'll ride the river again in the morning," Lou said. "There'll likely be some more that'll wander in durin' the night. After that, we'll have to ride after them that's missin'. Might be some springs or permanent water holes south of here that we don't know about."

But come dawn, the cowboys were disappointed to

find a little more than five hundred longhorns grazing along the river.

"Damn stupid varmints," Tull Irvin growled.

"They not be so *estupido* they no find water," Indian Charlie said.

"We'll just leave this bunch along the river and go after the rest of them," Lou said. "We'll ride south five miles and fan out in a line a hundred yards apart, east to west. From there we'll ride north, heading them toward the river."

Nobody argued with Lou's strategy, nor did they question the next move should this fail. They would ride even farther south, repeating the procedure until they had the remainder of the herd.

Will Hamer, Buck Embler, and four other men from Landon Everett's party caught up the dozen oxen that had drawn the wagons belonging to Buckalew and the Schmidts. Secured in pairs by lead ropes, the animals willingly followed the wagons. Traveling five abreast, the wagons again took the trail. Leading out were Landon Everett, Ezra Higdon, Jonah Quimby, Will Hamer, and Buck Embler. Mattie Everett walked beside Landon, saying nothing, thinking. When she spoke, it was to ask a question.

"Landon, what have you decided about that band of men who shot Buckalew and his friends?"

"Nothing," Everett said. "What's to decide?"

"Why didn't they kill the Schmidt brothers, instead of taking them away?"

"I don't know," Everett replied. "Rufe and Jenks might have turned bad and went along because they wanted to."

"I don't think so," Mattie said. "Those men have some use for Rufe and Jenks, and that's why they're still alive. What could the Schmidts have said or done that would have spared their lives?"

"For God's sake, Mattie," Everett said, exasperated, "I don't know."

"Landon," Mattie said, unruffled, "something's going to happen. I can lead the teams. Please take your horse, catch up to Jesse Applegate, and warn him about those men."

"Mattie," Everett said, striving to hold his temper, "Applegate can take care of himself. My God, he has sixteen Texas gunmen by his side day and night. Besides, I don't think he'd take kindly to any of us being concerned about his welfare. Like a damn bunch of greenhorns, we listened to Buckalew, remember? We booted Applegate and the others who owned cattle to the rear of the train, to the cattle column. They left us at the Missouri in all of our ignorance, and they've been ahead of us ever since. Frankly, I don't have the gall to face Applegate, especially with any advice."

"Not with advice, Landon," Mattie said patiently. "You'll be warning him. Please, Landon. Jesse Applegate would do the same for you, and I believe you are as big a man as he is."

"If Applegate hated my guts—which he may—I'd warn him if I thought he was in danger," Everett said angrily. "What *is* this, Mattie, a premonition?"

"I don't know," Mattie said. "Perhaps it is. I'd never ask you to do anything like this, Landon, if something hadn't touched me."

"Take the teams, then," Everett said. "I'll want to tell Higdon and Quimby, and I think Will and Buck should know."

Everett said nothing of Mattie's fears, telling his companions only that he believed Applegate should know of the band of men who had killed Buckalew and his friends.

"Maybe one of us should ride with you," Will said. "If that wolf pack is up to no good, what's to stop them from gunning you down from ambush?"

"Nothing," Everett said, "but would it help our cause

or that of Jesse Applegate if you rode with me and they gunned us *both* down?"

"I guess it wouldn't," Will conceded, "but if there's danger for Applegate, there may be danger for you."

"I'll risk it," Everett said. "It's daylight, and I can ride there and back before dark. They can't be that far ahead of us."

Everett dropped his saddle from the wagon and released his horse from the lead rope looped over a rear wagon bow. Quickly, he saddled the animal and rode out, kicking the horse into a fast gallop.

Well north of the Platte, several miles west of where they had spent the night, Tate reined up. When he dismounted, the rest of the riders did likewise, the Schmidts being the last.

"Norton, you an' Jacobs scrounge up somethin' that'll burn an' start us a breakfast fire."

"If it ain't askin' too much," Jacobs said, "maybe you could tell us just where'n hell we're goin'."

"I'll tell you when I'm ready," Tate said shortly, "and maybe I'll be ready after breakfast."

With that, Tate allowed his hard eyes to linger on the Schmidts, and the Schmidt brothers had the uneasy suspicion that whatever Tate had in mind was definitely going to involve them. Norton and Jacobs used their knives to cut dry limbs from the underside of a wind-blown cedar and soon had a fire going. Breakfast was started and finished quickly, each man receiving a cup of hot, black coffee and three rashers of bacon. Tate poured what remained of the coffee on the fire. Their horses had remained saddled, ground-hitched and grazing. All eyes were on Tate, and finally he spoke.

"We ain't more than a few minutes' ride behind them plow pushers and their wagons. While that Texas bunch is beatin' the brush lookin' for them cows that scattered durin' the storm, it'd be a good time for us to work our way close to that bunch of wagons. Maybe close enough for this pair of shorthorns to point out them wagons that's carryin' gold."

"Yeah," Norton said. "Now we know how to git rid of them Texans. All we got to do is scatter them cows all over hell's half acre. Whilst they're all out cow huntin', we stick up them farmers an' take the gold in our own good time."

"Won't do you no good," Jenks Schmidt said sullenly.

"It won't, huh?" Norton snarled. He was closest, and he snatched a fistful of Jenks Schmidt's shirt. In his right hand, under Schmidt's nose, was a cocked Colt.

"What he means," Rufe said desperately, "is that you can't just take the gold an' ride away. Why you think them cowboys ain't haulin' all that coin around in their saddlebags? You'd need a wagon, an' them Texas gun-slingers would be all over us 'fore sundown."

"Turn him loose, Norton," Tate said.

Reluctantly, Norton did, and then he, like the rest of the unsavory band, turned angry eyes on Tate. Tate laughed and then spoke.

"Well, by God, this mule-headed farmer's outthinkin' us. He's brung up somethin' that's a problem, but the kind of problem I'm likin'. Who'd ever of thunk we'd come up on so much gold, prime for the takin', that we'd need us a wagon to haul it?"

"Hell," Jacobs said, "it's a problem jist as long as it takes us to bushwhack them Texans. That bunch of farmers wouldn't have the guts to come after us if we stole their gold *and* their women."

Again Rufe Schmidt became alarmed at the turn the situation was taking. With the Texas riders out of the way and the gold in the hands of Tate and his men, the Schmidts would have outlived their usefulness. For sure, they wouldn't be allowed to share the gold. Their payoff would come in lead. Rufe played his last card.

"They's a hunnert an' forty more wagons not more'n two days behind them that's got the gold," Rufe said. "It's them that's catchin' up that kicked us out after hangin' our brother Ab, an' he didn't do nothin' near as bad as the takin' of the gold we're after."

"They didn't scare you too bad," Tate said, "unless you been lyin' to us about goin' after that gold for yourselves. Maybe you better turn your tongue loose an' tell us more about how you was gonna take that gold an' them cows."

"We wasn't goin' after the gold or the cows," Rufe said, "until all them cows an' the wagons was acrost the mountains. We wasn't goin' to ambush them Texans till they had the cows 'most to Oregon Territory. Then we'd of took the gold, a wagon an' mule teams, an' some extry mules to spell the first teams."

"Hell," Norton snarled, taking a step toward Rufe, "we'll be forever—"

"Shut up, Norton," Tate said, dangerously low.

Norton froze in his tracks. Tate still had control, and he spoke to the rest of the men, ignoring the red-faced Norton.

"By God," Tate said, "it's time some of you done less talkin' an' more listenin'. Maybe this pair of pelicans ain't dumb as they look. What's wrong with waitin' till we got the worst of this damn trail behind us, 'fore we take the cows and the gold? If that ain't reason enough, Bridger's post will be open. With the fur trade playin' out, there'll be a dozen or two of them damn trapper friends of his whilin' away some time. You all saw Bridger ride west with them cowboys when they left Laramie. Now, was we to ride anywhere close to Bridger's post, how do we explain us ownin' all them cows, and what we done with them Texas riders? While them emigrants mightn't have the sand to come after us, they'd go whinin' on Bridger's shoulder, an' he's got pull with the Federals in Washington. He'd set the damn army on our trail."

What Tate was saying wasn't nearly as important as what he wasn't saying, and but for the Schmidts, every man there understood only too well. It had been

Bridger's influence with the fur trappers that had driven out Tate and his band of thieves. They dared not ride anywhere near Bridger's post, and if they were so much as accused of any kind of thievery involving the Texas cattle and emigrant gold, Jim Bridger wouldn't hesitate to send a posse of trappers, every man with a noose on his saddle. Tate well knew, as did his companions, that they must be far beyond Bridger's post before making their move. Far enough that they could dispose of the cattle, divide the gold, and lose themselves before Bridger got word and sent men to investigate.

"I never been to Oregon," Jacobs said, "but I been to California. Hell, I ain't wantin' to start no cattle ranch. Oncet we git far enough beyond the Bridger post, why don't we grab them cows an' the gold an' light out fer California?"

"Jacobs," Tate said, "that ain't a bad idea. You sure you know the way?"

"Yeah," Jacobs said. "We make our play in Idaho Territory, an' turn southwest, maybe 275 miles beyond Bridger's post."*

"Why wait so damn long?" Norton demanded. "Fifty mile t'other side of Bridger's post we kin make our move an' cut straight acrost northern Utah Territory."

"Damn right," Jacobs agreed. "Straight through Mormon country. Bridger's already had trouble with 'em. They'd pick us clean as Christmas geese. Now the trail I got in mind swings southwest through northern Nevada Territory, takin' us straight to a little place called Winnemucca. They was already doin' some minin' when I was through there, an' I hear there's some others now, south an' west of there. We can sell some of them cows to the miners, and the rest in California. Now who the hell wants to go to Oregon?"

"California," they shouted. "California." But their leader had doubts.

* Near the present-day town of Twin Falls, Idaho

"Jacobs," Tate said grimly, "you'd best know what the hell you're talkin' about. You've talked us into somethin' I ain't sure of, some territory that I never been in. If you ain't right, this is the last chance you'll ever get to be wrong. You won't be seein' California, Oregon, nor nowhere else."

"I know what I'm talkin' about an' where I'm goin'," Jacobs said sullenly, "an' I ain't about to ride from here to there with the whole damn lot of you scratchin' and clawin' at me. If you ain't satisfied with my idee, then say it now an' we'll go on to Oregon Territory, like you been plannin'."

"I'll go with the majority," Tate replied, "but if you ain't givin' us the straight of this trail, then I reckon I'll have a majority when it's time to call your hand."

For the time being, they were in agreement, and the Schmidt brothers sighed with relief. Their lives had been spared—at least, they hoped—until Tate and his companions decided to take the cattle and the gold.

As he rode to catch up to Jesse Applegate's train, Landon Everett felt like a fool. What was he going to tell Applegate? That Mattie believed they were in danger as the result of some female premonition? No, he decided. He would tell Applegate of the three dead men, of the disappearance of the Schmidts and of the fifteen renegades who were on the loose. Everett had ridden what he believed was thirty miles when he began seeing longhorn cattle grazing along the river. Obviously it was only part of the herd, and it was a moment before he understood the why of it. The herd had been scattered. Landon Everett knew nothing about Texas cattle, and his first thought was that the fifteen men he was riding to warn Applegate about had somehow scattered the cattle. What better means of separating the Texans from Applegate's emigrants? But none of the cowboys were in sight, and Everett rode on, westward along the Platte.

"It was considerate of you to warn us," Applegate said

after Everett had related his reason for catching up to them. "The thunder and lightning night before last stampeded the cattle. We'll be here the rest of today and perhaps tomorrow, until the riders gather them."

"We're a good three days behind you," Everett said, "and I suppose it serves us right. I . . . I . . . damn it, Jesse, we were fools for takin' Buckalew's advice, pushin' you and your folks back into that confounded cow column. When I say I'm sorry, I believe I'm speaking for everybody that took bad advice."

"No hard feelings, Landon," Applegate said. "You didn't realize—and neither did we—just how valuable these Texas cowboys would become. Some of Buckalew's advice was solid. As you can see, we're stranded here until the herd can be gathered."

Landon Everett rode back the way he had come, and those who'd gathered to hear what he had to say scattered. Sarah Applegate waited until she and Jesse were alone before she spoke.

"You didn't tell him we already were aware of the men he came to warn us about."

"I didn't want him thinking he had ridden to warn us for nothing," Applegate said uncomfortably. "What we *didn't* know was that these renegades had murdered three men and taken the Schmidt brothers with them."

"I believe Landon's party would unite with us, if you had made the offer," Sarah said. "But for that wretched Buckalew and his cow column, we would still all be together."

"If Everett's wagons catch up to ours, I won't discourage them," Applegate said, "but neither can I forget they forced us out upon the advice of a man who knew as little—if not less—about the trail than any of us."

18

On the Sweetwater, 125 miles east of South Pass.
August 24, 1843.

*T*hree days after the stampede, a hundred longhorns
were still missing. Lou Spencer and Dillard Sumner took the time before supper to talk to Applegate,
Higdon, and Quimby.

"We rode nearly ten miles south of the river," Lou
said, "and I don't believe we could find another hundred
of the varmints if we camped here for another week.
We'd best take the loss and move on, I'm thinkin'."

"I'm leanin' in the same direction," Sumner said.

"Far as I'm concerned," Applegate said, "the search is
over. My God, we have to cross the Rockies before first
snow."

"You got no argument from me," Ezra Higdon said.

"Nor me," Jonah Quimby quickly added.

"Tomorrow at first light," Lou said, "we'll take another ride along the river, just in case some more of 'em
have wandered back. Whatever the case, we'll take the
trail in the morning."

"Good," Applegate said. "Let's concern ourselves
with getting across the mountains and on to Oregon.
Once there, we'll share the loss equally."

After supper there was almost an hour of daylight left.

Kage Copeland and Dub Stern took advantage of it, inviting Dorrie Halleck and Rosa Wallace for a walk beside the river. Lou Spencer winked at Sandy Applegate. They would wait until Kage and Dub returned, for they would be riding the first watch. Vic Sloan grinned at Lou, a fair indication that he and Vangie would accompany Lou and Sandy. They would keep their distance, however, and Lou was grateful that Sloan had taken an interest in the younger girl. Later on, when he and Sandy were alone beneath the stars, he mentioned it to her.

"Thanks to old Vic," Lou teased, "I see Vangie don't follow you around anymore. They must be gettin' serious."

"Perhaps too serious," Sandy replied. "Haven't you noticed Vangie's gaining some . . . around her middle?"

"My God, no!" Lou gasped.

"My God, yes," Sandy replied.

"Damn it," Lou growled, "if we could wait, why couldn't they?"

"That's what Ma wanted to know," Sandy said.

"She . . . knows? Does . . . anybody else?"

"Of course she knows," Sandy said, "and the rest of the women know too, unless they're walking around with their eyes shut. Women always know. Ma and Vangie had words, and she swears Vic's going to claim her, once we reach Oregon."

"God, I hope so," Lou said. "Your daddy . . . does he . . ."

"I doubt it," Sandy said. "Ma likes Vic, just as she likes you, and I think she'll trust his good intentions. She'd trust yours too."

"I don't doubt she would," Lou said, "and I'm obliged to her for thinkin' well of Vic. He's a Texan and his word is good as gold. But there's somethin' Vic ain't considerin'. We don't know what's ahead of us. What if somethin' happened to Vic? Where would that leave Vangie?"

"But it's something *you* have considered," she said softly. "If it was me . . . instead of Vangie . . . and something happened to you . . ."

"It's something I must consider," he replied. "We've been fortunate so far, but there's a chance all of us won't reach Oregon alive."

She came to him then, and it was a moment he would never forget even if they never shared another. . . .

But the moments Vic Sloan and Vangie Applegate were sharing weren't quite as tranquil. Vangie sat on the riverbank while Sloan was at a loss as to what he should say or do. He walked away, came back, and finally sat down beside the girl.

"Oh, God," she sighed, "there's Sandy, Dorrie, and Rosa. Why did this have to happen to me?"

"But it ain't been that long," Sloan said. "Maybe it ain't . . . what you think. How can you be so sure?"

"I . . . I can't talk about that," Vangie said, "but there's . . . ways. We . . . a woman always knows."

"I've told you before and I'm tellin' you now," Sloan said, "soon as we get to Oregon, we'll stand before a preacher. Don't you trust me?"

She laughed. "You ask me that, when I . . . I'm . . ."

"That was a fool question," he said. "I'm sorry."

She turned to him, her hands on his shoulders, and even in the dim starlight he could see the tears on her cheeks.

"Nothing's changed about the way I feel," she said. "God, Vic, it's just taking so . . . so long to get to Oregon. We're not quite halfway. We'll be on the trail another three months, or perhaps longer. By then I'll be so . . . so . . . Lord, Vic, everybody will know I . . . we . . ."

"I reckon they will," he agreed, "and there's no help for that, but I'll stand beside you, whatever happens."

She took comfort in that, and Sloan held her as she wept, unsure as to the possible consequences when "everybody" *did* know.

The following morning at first light, Dillard Sumner, Tobe Hiram, Waco Tilden, and Black Jack Rhudy rode back along the Platte, and to their surprise another twenty-five longhorns grazed along the river.

"Damn it," Black Jack swore, "just where in hell has them varmints been holed up for the last two days?"

"When it comes to cows," Waco said, "you don't never question the wheres and the whys. Let's just run the varmints in with the rest of the herd and get back on that Oregon Trail."

Two days behind Applegate, Landon Everett had been slowed by a rash of wagon breakdowns. There were two smashed wheels and a broken axle, all in the same afternoon.

"My God," Will Hamer said, "let's call it a day before a fourth wagon gets busted."

"I can't see that we have any choice," Everett said. "Replacin' the two wheels wasn't so bad, but the Shondells don't have a spare axle. We'll have to fell a tree and make do."

"No help for it when a wheel slips into a hole or slams down on a rock," Buck Embler said. "Damn near ever'time an axle breaks, it's where she goes through the wheel hub. Some people's too stingy with the grease, and the friction of the wheel eats into the wood of the axle. Wear it down enough and it don't take nothin' to break it."

"I expect you're right," Everett said. "I thought everybody was aware of that before we left Independence."

"Wouldn't hurt if they was made aware of it again," Will said, "and I'd start with Gus Shondell. Them boys of his, Jasper and Grady, is plenty old enough for some firsthand experience in the fine arts of takin' an ax and shapin' a wagon axle from the trunk of a tree."

"I've suggested that," Everett said. "The rest of us will circle our wagons, leavin' a place for Shondell's. I'll ride back and help them with the axle. We don't have that much daylight left, and I don't want to lose any time in the morning."

"Landon," Will said, "you nurse this bunch like they was all wet behind the ears and you're their old granny."

Landon Everett laughed, took the lead rope that controlled his teams and gave the order to circle the wagons.

Without getting any closer to the Applegate wagons, Tate led his men to the north. He said nothing regarding their destination, and there were no questions. As they rode farther and farther beyond the Sweetwater, the land became more rugged, with arroyos cutting deep gashes in the slopes. Without hesitation, Tate led them into an arroyo that deepened until it ended at what seemed solid rock. It was forty feet high, blocking the westering sun, but at its base was a small spring whose runoff was soon swallowed up. But as the riders drew nearer, the Schmidts could see that to the left of the spring a narrow slash a dozen feet high angled away into the canyon wall. They reined up, dismounted, and Tate finally spoke.

"I'll get some provisions from our cache. Reynolds, you and Hawkins rustle some wood and get a supper fire going. Rest of you unsaddle the horses."

When Tate backed out of the narrow entrance with a gunnysack of food, he found that his own horse and those belonging to Reynolds and Hawkins still bore their saddles. Tate dropped the sack and turned on them in a fury.

"I said, by God, to unsaddle the rest of the horses. Ain't I been talkin' loud enough for you hombres?"

"Too damn loud an' too damn often," Norton said.

"We got near three hunnert miles with nothin' to do but start cook fires an' unsaddle hosses. I can't see they's no hurry. Fact is, I can't see why ever'body can't unsaddle his own hoss."

Without haste, Tate drew his Colt, and Norton's left earlobe vanished in a spray of blood. Tate stood with his back to the arroyo's stone wall, the Colt steady in his hand. He allowed his cold eyes to touch every man before he spoke.

"As I recollect," he said, "we made our plans on what we aim to do. Now them of you that's changed your minds, them that ain't got the patience, then you just deal yourselves out. Mount up and ride."

Nobody moved except Norton, who had managed to reach his bloody ear with one end of the bandanna he wore around his neck.

"All right," Tate said, pointing the muzzle of the Colt at Norton, "you unsaddle them three horses and do it quick. Next time you—or any of the rest of you—don't obey an order, you'd best pull your iron. This is the only warnin' you'll get from me."

Norton scrambled to his feet and with fumbling fingers began unsaddling Tate's horse. Hearing the shot, Reynolds and Hawkins had gotten close enough to hear Tate's words. Silently they began gathering the wood they'd dropped. Quickly, silently, the Schmidts exchanged looks. They had been looking—and hoping—for trouble among their captors, allowing them an opportunity to escape. But now Jenks and Rufe were reaching the same gloomy conclusion. If they were to escape, it would be at the risk of their lives, against the guns of every one of the renegades. In a show of contempt, Tate had allowed them to keep their revolvers, but to what avail? Had they been gunmen—which they were not—they were impossibly outgunned. The Schmidts hunched down, seeking to look as meek and frightened as possible. It was one of the few things they did well.

* * *

South Pass, Wyoming Territory. September 2, 1843.

Applegate's party made better time than they had expected. The days had been hot and sunny, but already the nights had become chill. It was warning enough that the snow that would render the mountain trails impassible wasn't too distant. Two hours before sundown the horse remuda and the herd reached the bend in the Sweetwater where it swung down from the mountains to the north.* Lou Spencer had long since told Indian Charlie and Alonzo Gonzales to count on a last camp before leaving the river, and Indian Charlie waved his hat. Lou was riding point, and passed the signal to the rest of the riders. When the leaders had been headed and began to graze along the river, Lou and Dillard Sumner rode back and met the wagons. It was time for a talk with Applegate.

"Tomorrow we'll be leaving the Sweetwater," Lou told the wagon boss, "and we'll likely reach South Pass. We're close enough now to ride ahead and see if this crossing is as bad as Bridger says it is. Do you want to ride with Dill and me?"

"Yes," Applegate said. "I think we should ride all the way across this South Pass. Perhaps we can learn where other wagons have had trouble and find some way around it."

"Another thing to consider," Sumner said, "is that after today we won't have a river runnin' alongside us. Bridger said there's a spring on the far side of the pass. The wagons that don't make it across may have to double back to the bend in the Sweetwater for the night's camp."

"Then we know where the next water is after crossing South Pass," Applegate said, "but on my map there's no more water for more than fifty miles."

* The Wind River Range

"Bridger didn't know the name of that river on your map," Lou said, "but the miles are about right. We'll be followin' that unnamed stream for maybe twenty-five miles until it forks in with the Green. Once we cross the Green, it's maybe twelve miles to Black's Fork, and we'll follow it the rest of the way to Bridger's post."

Again Bridger had been right. Lou, Dill, and Applegate rode not more than three miles before reaching the foot of South Pass. Even as they rode, they became aware of the increasing elevation, for the horses were already lathered.

"We'd best stop here and rest the horses," Lou said as they neared what seemed the foot of the dreaded climb.

It didn't look promising. There was plentiful evidence as to the difficulty earlier emigrants had faced. A cast-iron cook stove leaned drunkenly on three legs. Books, some of them leather-bound, were scattered carelessly. A heavy cedar trunk lay on its side, its lid sprung open, ladies' fancy goods spilling out. There were chairs, brass bedsteads, sacks of flour, spades, hoes, axes, and the broken remains of three wagons. There were the bleaching skulls of horses, mules, and oxen, their bones a macabre litter after buzzards and wolves had gotten to them. Finally, there was no mistaking the four grassed-over mounds with their crude wooden crosses.

"My God," Applegate said, aghast, "this is terrible."

"Bridger warned us," Lou said, "and he didn't stretch it. The horses are rested. Let's ride on across and find that spring on the other side."

The first few hundred feet of the trail across South Pass was especially difficult, for the soil had eroded, leaving almost solid stone underneath. The shod hooves of the horses slipped repeatedly on the stone, and the animals became skittish. The riders dismounted and led their mounts until the trail began to level out.

"Perhaps that's the worst of it," Applegate gasped.

"And perhaps it ain't," Dillard Sumner said. "See that next rise? This damn thing is a series of plateaus, the next one as bad or worse than the one we just climbed. You seen all them skint places on the rocks ahead of us, I reckon, and you seen how our horses was slippin' and slidin'. It's purely goin' to be hell, Mr. Applegate, when them iron tires goes slidin' off of that rock. There'll be busted wagon wheels a-plenty, and if the west slope is anything like what we're climbin', then you'd as well ready yourself to lose some wagons on the way down."

Applegate shook his head, the enormity of it taking his breath away. As the trail seemed to level out, they could see the next steep slope rising a few yards ahead of them.

"One thing for sure," Lou said while they again rested the horses. "You won't cross more than one wagon at a time. Like Bridger said, it'll take all the oxen from the wagons just to get one across."

There were places where it became impossible to move straight ahead, and the wagons had veered north or south along a hogback until there had been a break wide enough for the train to again move west. Sometimes the only way had been over enormous boulders, and there were the remnants of wagon wheels where they had slid off, smashed to bits when the weight of the wagon had come down on them. Finally the trio reached what surely seemed the crest of the deadly pass. Again they stopped to rest themselves as well as the horses.

"Great God," Applegate groaned, "if we can't cross the confounded thing on horseback, how in thunder will we ever get the wagons across?"

"Lighten the loads and double up the teams," Lou replied. "It'll be one hell of a climb to where we are now, but like Dill said, goin' down the west slope may be the hardest of all. You'd best take a look at every wagon, with attention to leather brake pads and brake handles."

"I intend to," Applegate said, "and I need to do that before dark. If I'm to do that, I must start back immediately. The two of you will have to check out the west slope and find the spring at the foot of it."

The Texans nodded and Applegate turned back. It seemed the enormity of this undertaking hadn't fully sunk in until the wagon boss had actually seen the treacherous trail for himself.

"We'd best push on," Lou said. "We don't know what the rest of it's like."

"I feel safe in sayin' it won't get no better," Sumner replied.

The cowboys rode on, often walking their horses. They weren't encouraged by the downward slope, and as Sumner had warned, it might prove the most hazardous of all.

"Damn," Sumner swore as they started down, "look at them wheel marks. A wagon toppled over along here."

"Yeah," Lou said, "and I reckon that tells us something."

"Thick leather brake pads and strong brake handles won't make much of a difference with the hooves of the horses and mules slippin' and wagon wheels skitterin' about like they was greased." Sumner shook his head.

The scene became even more grim as they proceeded down the west slope of the pass. There were more bones of mules and oxen and the ruins of two more wagons.

"It's a thing I've never seen happen," Sumner said, "but I can see it in my mind. The teams can't hold back the wagons because their own hooves are slippin' and slidin' just like the wagon wheels. Them easterners has got sand, but I doubt they've ever come up against somethin' like this."

"Neither have we," Lou said, "but that's never stopped us. If extra teams can draw the wagons up that eastern slope, then why can't those extra teams act as a brake, easin' 'em down the other side?"

"By God," Sumner exclaimed, "that's the answer. We yoke extra teams to the rear of each wagon, keepin' 'em far enough back so they got solid ground under their hooves. Movin' 'em backward a little at a time, they can slow the wagons without dependin' on the hand brake."

"We'll have to depend on that," Lou said. "With the teams unsure of their footing, wagon wheels sliding, I think the hand brake will be less than useless. These people who crossed South Pass ahead of us must have counted on that, and we can see how far it got them."

Eventually the cowboys reached the bottom of the west slope, and a little more than a mile beyond, they found the spring. They allowed their horses to rest, watered them, and then began the journey back across the pass.

"If you could turn this thing around," Sumner said, "swappin' east slope for west, there wouldn't be a *centavo*'s worth of difference. One's just as damn steep as the other."

"That's how I see it," Lou replied. "I reckon it took us three-quarters of an hour gettin' across. If nothing breaks, we can double that for each of the wagons."

"God Almighty," Sumner said, "that's near ninety hours. Startin' at first light and workin' till dark, we might get ten hours of daylight a day. Goin' by that, we'll be here at least nine days. Already it's so cold at night I'm usin' every blanket I got and wishin' for more. There'll be snow in these mountain passes before the end of the month."

"Time's runnin' out," Lou agreed. "There won't be time for us to linger at Bridger's post."

When Lou and Dill reached the wagons, it was near suppertime. Applegate wanted their thoughts on the crossing of South Pass, and after he had heard them out, he spoke.

"I'd like for you to go out there in the wagon circle," he told them, "and tell the entire party what you've just told me. Don't spare them. Tell them what we must do. They'll listen, for I've told them what we've seen, what they can expect."

Lou Spencer didn't waste words. What hit them the hardest was the number of days that might be needed to get all the wagons across.

"My God," Ezra Higdon exclaimed, "it'll be like the crossing of the Missouri all over again. Landon Everett's party will be right behind us, all of them giving us hell."

"Maybe not," Lou said. "Everett's party has nearly four times as many wagons. Once they see what we've seen, I think they'll be glad to wait their turn. If all of you keep your heads and don't panic, we might cut back on the crossing time."

"You and your riders intend to help us, then," Jonah Quimby said.

"We aim to try," Lou said, "if you'll take good advice. We hired on to move cattle, not wagons, but we don't hanker to be caught here in the mountains when snow flies. If you're still here, we'll be here too."

The cowboys hadn't been very sympathetic the night a grizzly had taken one of the sheep, and their owners, Garner and Malden, hadn't forgotten.

"I don't like your attitude," Garner said. "Are you sayin' we can't get over this pass without your help?"

"No," Lou said bluntly, "but I am sayin' it might take you twice as long and you'll likely smash up your wagon or kill some of your oxen. If you don't want any help gettin' your wagons across, then let all the other wagons go ahead of you. Then you can cross any way you damn please. There ain't much of a trail, and in some places, no trail. We don't want what there is blocked with dead oxen and busted wagons."

"Why, you damn high-handed cow nurse," Malden bawled, "you can't—"

"He can," Applegate said. "I've seen the trail, and I'm ready to listen to his and Sumner's advice. Whether or not you take it is entirely up to you, but you *are* going to listen."

Lou nodded to Dillard Sumner, and Sumner quickly told them of his and Lou's plan for getting the wagons down the hazardous west slope. When Sumner had finished, he and Lou stepped aside, leaving it to Applegate to settle any disagreement.

"If anybody has a better idea, I'd like to hear it," Applegate said.

There was only silence. While Garner and Malden looked as disgruntled as ever, neither spoke. The pair seemed not to realize or care that they were viewed with some contempt for having thrown a fit over a single sheep.

"In the morning at first light," Applegate said, "the riders will take the cattle over the pass. Those of you with livestock other than your teams, you'll take your extra livestock right behind the cattle. Then we'll decide the order in which the wagons are to cross."

Tate had remained in camp, sending Jacobs to scout the positions of the two wagon trains. It was late afternoon when Jacobs finally returned.

"Took you long enough," Tate growled.

"You didn't tell me I had to be back at no certain time," Jacobs growled back. "I took my time."

Jacobs continued taking his time, unsaddling his horse and pouring himself a cup of coffee before he spoke.

"First bunch of wagons is at the foot of South Pass," Jacobs said. "I'd say they'll start the crossin' tomorrow. Rest of 'em—near two hunnert wagons—is two days back."

"Damn it," Norton said, "somebody break out the cards. We'll still be settin' right here when snow flies."

"Shut up, Norton," Tate snarled.

"Cattle up ahead," Will Hamer shouted.

"Applegate's riders didn't find them all, then," Everett said. "Maybe an hour of daylight left. After we've circled the wagons, some of you with a horse saddle up and come with me. No reason we can't round up those cows and drive them on ahead of us. There should be enough sons and daughters in our party to keep them moving until we catch up to Applegate's party."

Everett, accompanied by Will and Buck, rode almost a

mile westward along the river. They counted fifty-five grazing longhorns.

"They've stayed put this long," Everett said, "no reason for them to wander away during the night. We'll gather them in the morning and start them ahead of the wagons."

"I hope Applegate appreciates this," Buck said. "We kicked him out to rid ourselves of cattle, and here we are roundin' them up ourselves."

"I look for us to catch up to Applegate at South Pass," Everett said, "and I'm thinking more and more about scuttling that 'cattle column' foolishness. We started out together, and I'm more and more of a mind for us all to reach Oregon together."

"I believe that would be in the best interests of us all," Buck said. "We got no excuse except that we listened to Buckalew, but how long have we got to go on payin' for that? A man makes a mistake, admits it, and you go on from there."

"That's the Christian way of lookin' at it," Everett said, "but let's not speculate on it just yet. It will depend on how Applegate feels. Christian or not, I'm not the kind to shove my way in where I'm not wanted."

At first light, Everett, Will, and Buck rode out and bunched the cattle in preparation for the day's journey. Already the drovers were there afoot. Sol Menges had sent his son, Daro. Jules Dewees's sons Hamby and Isaac were there, while Gus Shondell had sent Jasper and Grady.

"Just keep them moving well ahead of the wagons," Everett advised.

The longhorns were trailwise and readily loped ahead. Everett, Will, and Buck returned to their wagons and the caravan moved out.

Not quite twenty-five miles ahead of Everett's party, the cowboys had just begun moving the cattle over South Pass. Behind them—at a considerable distance, thanks to Applegate—came Garner and Malden with their twenty-nine bleating sheep. Following the sheep came a mixture of horses and mules, some thirty head in all. That left only the wagons and the teams drawing them.

"We'll take my wagon across first," Applegate said.

"Why?" somebody shouted. "I say we draw lots."

"And I say we don't," Applegate snapped. "I'm sending my wagon first so we can test this method of getting down the west slope. If anybody's wagon gets smashed, it'll be mine. We'll use three teams of oxen for each wagon to cross. That's extra teams to get a wagon to the summit and extra teams to slow its descent down the west slope."

"I'll unhitch my teams," Ezra Higdon said, "and hitch them in front of yours. Maybe they'll be enough to get us up there."

"Then I'll follow with my teams," Jonah Quimby said. "You'll need them to slow your wagon on its way down."

"No," Applegate said. "Once we're ready to go down, we can unhitch Ezra's team and use them to anchor the wagon and ease it down. When my wagon reaches the bottom, I'll bring my team back to the top. We'll use them to ease Ezra's wagon down. We'll swap teams often enough not to exhaust any of them."

"On to Oregon," they shouted as Applegate's teams began the ascent.

19

"I swear," Will said, after their first day of following the fifty-five strayed longhorns, "I can't see why Buckalew thought them cows would slow us down. We've had to hustle to keep up with them."

"I expect we've all learned a lot since leaving Independence," Everett observed.

The wagons had been circled for the night, and most of the men lingered over a last cup of coffee. Everett was studying the trail map.

"We can't be too far from South Pass," Buck Embler said. "Remember them five wagons we met, the folks that didn't even try to cross? I would of liked for us to have met them near sundown, so we could have had them spend a night with us."

"I had the feeling they didn't want to talk about it," Everett said, "so I didn't insist. We did well today, and if we do as well tomorrow, I think we'll reach the bend in the Sweetwater. That should put us practically at the foot of South Pass."

"If this South Pass is all that tough," Will said, "it'll take a while to get across. Suppose we get there and find Applegate's wagons ain't all made the crossing?"

"We'll wait our turn," Everett said. "I'm kind of hoping they will still be crossing. We don't know what we're up against, and perhaps we can all learn from them. We must give those Texas cowboys credit. They're frontiersmen, and if there's a safe way of getting those wagons across, I believe they'll find it."

"Since we'll be leavin' the Sweetwater this side of the pass," Will said, "and the map don't show any water for maybe fifty miles beyond, every wagon that crosses the pass will be without water, waitin' for the others to cross."

"That's another reason I'm hoping Applegate's wagons won't all have made the crossing," Everett said. "From what I learned at the trading post, those Texans made friends with Jim Bridger, a trapper and mountain man. Bridger rode west with them and has a trading post of his own somewhere beyond South Pass. Those cowboys have a herd to look after, and they'll be concerned with finding water after the crossing. I see no reason why Applegate wouldn't share such information with us."

"Before we leave the Sweetwater," Buck said, "we'd best have a talk with Applegate."

"I intend to," Everett said. "If they haven't crossed all their wagons by the time we get there, I expect we'll find them camped near the bend in the Sweetwater. When we sight their wagons—assuming that we do—that's when we'll circle ours. We can then ride ahead and see what progress they've made and perhaps learn where they expect to find water after their wagons have made the crossing."

Applegate's wagon was the first to take the rugged trail across South Pass, and the wagon boss quickly learned why they had been advised not to load their wagons at the trading post. Slowly but surely the double teams of oxen drew the wagon up the treacherous slope. Wheels slid off rocks, chunking into washouts and holes, and after reaching the first plateau, Applegate rested the teams. Sarah, Sandy, Vangie, and Jud Applegate trudged beside the teams. When the wagon finally reached the crest, Lou Spencer and Dillard Sumner were there.

"Here's where we unhitch the front teams and harness them to the back of the wagon," Lou said. "We'll wrap the trace chains around the rear axle. Do you have bolts and nuts to secure the chains?"

"Yes," Applegate replied, "and I also have hooks."

"No hooks," Lou said. "I've seen them come loose. I suspect that's what those other folks used, and it cost them some wagons."

Dillard Sumner had unhitched the first teams of oxen and led them into position behind the wagon. Lou looped the heavy trace chains over the axle, pulled the chain tight against itself, and ran a bolt through the links where the chain came together. A nut secured the hitch. Finished, Lou turned to Applegate.

"Dill will back the team down from behind," Lou said. "Just take it slow with the front team. I'll ride the wagon box, using the brake if and when I need to."

The descent was worse than they had expected, for there were places so narrow the wagon was forced into ruts and over rocks that tilted the vehicle precariously to one side or the other. But the team hitched to the rear of the wagon made the difference, and Lou used the brake sparingly. Slowly the wagon was let down, and when it reached the bottom, Applegate reined up the teams. Quickly Lou and Dill removed the chains from the wagon's rear axle and Applegate urged his teams forward.

"Straight ahead," Lou shouted. "The cattle, the horse remuda, and extra livestock are beyond the spring. We'll circle the wagons on this side of it."

Lou and Dill began the climb to the crest of the pass, Sumner leading the extra teams of oxen.

"We'll let down one more wagon with this team," Lou said, "and let them rest a while. I reckon we stretched the time a mite. It didn't take as long as we figured."

"No," Sumner agreed. "If the rest of them do as well as this one, we'll cross 'em all in three days. Maybe less. The teams and wagons will work out pretty good. We'll be the ones catchin' hell, hikin' up and down this damn mountain. A man's a fool to fall into a job of work he can't do from his saddle."

"Before we're done with this," Lou said, "I'll likely be agreein' with you. But we won't be doing it all. There's sixteen of us, and I figure we can work four of us at a time. Soon as one wagon starts up the slope, the next one can come right behind. Two of us can hitch the back-down team, take the wagon down, while two more of us can be readying the next wagon at the top. I told Waco and Vic to join us as soon as Applegate showed up with his wagon."

Sumner laughed. "I reckon Waco will be here with bells on, wantin' to have a hand in gettin' the Widow Hayden across. She's got mule teams, and so have three or four others. No way we can mix them with oxen."

"No," Lou said. "I've already spoken to Applegate, and he's talked to the owners of the mule teams. There's a place for mules, but not here. This calls for the patience of oxen."

The Higdon and Quimby wagons crossed without mishap, and by the time the sun was noon-high, ten wagons were safely across.

"God," Sumner groaned, "my feet are killing me. It's time we watched the cows and four of them other jaybirds walked this slope for a while."

"They been told," Waco said. "I told McCarty, Brodie, Copeland, and Stern to relieve us at noon."

"Waco's done," Vic Sloan said. "He's got the widow across."

"At least the widow's belly ain't swelled none," Waco growled.

Waco was tired, irritable, but it was a cruel thing to have said. Sloan's eyes turned hard and his lips were a thin line as he sidestepped his horse nearer Waco's.

"Vic," said Lou, "whatever you aim to do, don't."

Sloan swallowed hard, his hand on the butt of his Colt.

"Sorry, amigo," Waco said, not sounding sorry at all. "You tend to your business and I'll tend to mine."

The moment passed as McCarty, Brodie, Copeland, and Stern reined up. Lou and Dill once again climbed the slope to be sure the new riders understood the procedure for lowering the wagons. With the eleventh wagon safely on the west side of the pass, Lou and Dill mounted their horses and rode back to the herd.

"This crossing of South Pass is goin' entirely too well," Sumner said. "I reckon we'll catch hell from some other direction."

"I won't argue with you on that," Lou replied. "Waco and Vic learned cow together, and you saw 'em at one another's throats."

"It's been a long drive," Sumner said, "and we're just maybe halfway. I reckon all the boys are a mite touchy, and I wish they'd back off on all the hoorawin' where women are concerned. I believe Sloan will do the right thing, once we get to Oregon. Hell of it is, time ain't on his side."

"No," Lou said. "On this trail, time is the enemy of us all, and in more ways than one."

Landon Everett and his party could see the upper slopes of South Pass long before reaching it. Their progress had been even better than expected, and at least two hours of daylight remained. When at last Everett could see wagon canvas in the distance, he reined up his teams.

"Rein up," he shouted, "and circle the wagons."

It was much too early for supper, and Everett saddled his horse. Ezra Higdon and Jonah Quimby said nothing, but there were questions in their eyes. It was time for a decision regarding the possible reuniting of their wagons with those of Applegate's, and Everett didn't want that decision to be his alone. He spoke to those who had gathered, including Higdon and Quimby.

"I'm going to ride ahead and speak to Applegate," Everett said, "and if some of you want to come with me, please do so. I'm going to suggest that we bring all our wagons together again. Do any of you object to that?"

"I ain't objectin' to it," Gus Shondell said. "But why? Ain't we doin' all right on our own?"

"So far," Everett agreed, "but after we cross South Pass, there'll be long stretches of trail where the rivers aren't nearly as well defined as they have been. For instance, after we've crossed South Pass, there's more than fifty miles with no water showing on the map. I'm going to tell you something, those of you who haven't figured it out for yourselves. We were fools, allowing Buckalew to convince us that the owners of cattle should be cast out into that infernal cow column. The truth is, Applegate and his cow column have been ahead of us since we crossed the Missouri. Those Texas cowboys have seen to that, just as they'll find water where our map shows none. Applegate has an advantage that we're lacking, and if he and his people will have us, I'm saying we should combine our party with his."

"I'll join you in a talk with him," Ezra Higdon said.

"So will I," Jonah Quimby said.

Most of the party had heard, and shouted their approval. Higdon and Quimby saddled their horses, and with Everett leading, the trio rode toward the few wagons ahead of them.

"Only a dozen wagons," Quimby said, amazed. "They'll have the rest of 'em across sometime tomorrow."

"Won't help our case any," Higdon replied. "God knows how long it'll take to get all of ours across, and for every day it takes us, it'll cost Applegate and his people a day on the trail. I won't blame 'em if they tell us to go to hell."

"Nor will I," Landon Everett said, "but I'm counting on Jesse Applegate to be a bigger man than that."

The trio reined up at one of the wagons whose teams still grazed along the Sweetwater. A man stepped down from the wagon box, his hand on his Colt.

"We're looking for Jesse Applegate," Everett said.

"On t'other side of the pass," the teamster said.

Everett, Higdon, and Quimby rode on, reaching the foot of the pass in time to follow a wagon being drawn up the slope by double teams of oxen. Finally the three riders were forced to dismount and lead their horses over the steepest part of the incline. Reaching the plateau just before the descent of the western slope, the double teams were reined up. Lou Spencer and Dillard Sumner unhitched the first teams, leading them to the rear of the wagon. Landon Everett and his companions watched in amazement as the two cowboys faced the teams away from the wagon and fastened the trace chains securely over the rear axle. Their task finished, Sumner mounted the wagon box while Lou took the lead rope of the backward-facing teams of oxen.

"A remarkable idea, Mr. Spencer," Everett said.

Lou Spencer seemed to notice the three for the first time, saying nothing.

"We're looking for Jesse Applegate," Everett said, uncomfortable with Lou's silence.

"There's a spring two miles west of the foot of the pass," Lou said. "I reckon you'll find him there."

"We'll follow you down," Everett said. "I want to watch that wagon."

Lou Spencer didn't respond. He stepped wide, waving his hat, and the man in control of the lead teams lurched them and the wagon into motion. Lou backed the teams of oxen slowly, matching the gait of the lead teams, keeping the chains taut. The wagon tilted dangerously from side to side as it was forced across protruding rock, but it remained upright. When it reached the bottom of the slope, the cowboys unhitched the teams of oxen from the wagon and it rumbled off. Everett, Higdon, and Quimby followed.

"I see what you mean about those Texans," Quimby said. "Who would ever have thought of that?"

"I don't believe they had to discard anything from the

wagons either," Higdon said. "All those things littering the eastern slope look to have been there a while."

As Everett and his companions rode among the wagons that had already been driven near the spring, Everett spoke to people he knew. Applegate had seen them coming and walked to meet them.

"Step down," Applegate said. "We have coffee now, and there'll be supper within the hour."

The trio dismounted, and Everett wasted no time getting to the point.

"Jesse, we're on the Sweetwater, a few hundred yards beyond the last of your wagons. We brought fifty-five head of your cows we found grazing along the Platte. Now I want to speak to you about something I've already discussed with my people."

"Much obliged for fetching the cows," Applegate said. "Now what's on your mind?"

"We made a big mistake back in Independence, when we allowed Buckalew to create that cursed cow column. I have conceded that, and the rest of the folks in my party agree. They also agree that it would be in our best interest if your wagons and ours again became a single caravan. So I'm asking, Jesse, as humbly as I can."

Having seen the trio ride in, some of the cowboys and others within Applegate's party had gathered, listening. Applegate surveyed the faces of those who had heard Everett's request, and found some resentment there. That told him this could not be a hasty decision, and he answered accordingly.

"I can't give you an immediate answer, Landon. Just as you talked to your people, I must talk to mine. This is the fifth of September, and while we're new to the West, you need not be a westerner to sense the coming of the winter. There will be snow in these mountains soon, and you have three times as many wagons as we do. Every day that we wait for your wagons to cross the pass, we'll be losing a day on the trail. I don't mean to be unkind, but in fairness to my party, we'll have to consider that."

Lou Spencer and Dillard Sumner brought only one more wagon down the slope after Landon Everett and his companions had ridden away. They mounted their horses and rode toward the gathered wagons near the spring, arriving just as Jesse Applegate was responding to Landon Everett's request. While Lou and Dill hadn't heard Everett's request, Applegate's response gave them some idea as to the issue at hand.

"I can understand your position," Everett said, "and I'd not want you to go against the wishes of any of your people. You still have some wagons to be brought across the pass. Will that be enough time for you to reach a decision?"

"I think so," Applegate replied. "As you've seen, the method we're using to get the wagons safely across takes some time. We had no idea how to begin, and we owe Mr. Spencer, Mr. Sumner, and their riders for this ingenious means. Any delay and they're as much at risk as the rest of us of being caught here in these mountain passes when snow flies. I think it only fair that I ask their opinions before I speak to the rest of the party."

Quickly Applegate repeated Landon Everett's request. When he finished, Lou was the first to speak.

"Mr. Everett," Lou said, "you saw us bring that wagon down the slope. I reckon it looked easy, but only because we planned ahead. We didn't overload our wagons at the trading post. Did you?"

"Well, I, ah . . . fear we did," Everett admitted. "I believe if there was a problem, we could unload some of the goods, cross with what we could safely handle, and return for the rest."

"You've seen all the discards of those who have gone ahead of us," Lou said. "They might have taken the time to return for what they'd left behind, but they didn't. We purely don't have that choice. You have near two hundred wagons, loaded to the bows. It'll cost us a week if we wait for you to cross South Pass just once, and longer if we have to wait for you to repair broken-down wagons.

When overloaded wagons lurch off rocks and drop into chuck holes, axles and wheels break. We're not bein' unreasonable, Mr. Everett, when we insist on your folks lightenin' them wagons."

"That's a logical argument, Landon," Applegate said. "I'd need your word that you're willing to lighten those wagons. Do that, and I'll consider your request to join us for the rest of the journey to Oregon."

Everett sighed. "You have my word, Jesse. I'll talk to my folks tonight and get back with you early in the morning."

There seemed nothing more to be said. Everett, Higdon, and Quimby mounted their horses and rode back toward South Pass.

"God," Higdon said, "my missus will raise hell. We'll have to leave her cook stove behind."

"Better that than food and provisions," Quimby said. "You can cook over an open fire if you have to, but not if you got no grub."

"It's a hard choice," Everett said, "but a necessary one. The truth is, Applegate's had some better guidance and advice than we've had. While I feel we can adopt their means of getting our wagons safely across South Pass, there is no denying the truth of what Spencer said. We'll have to leave behind whatever it takes to lighten the wagons."

While Landon Everett presented the hard choice to his people, Jesse Applegate gathered his party and told them of the proposal. To Applegate's disgust, it was Garner and Malden, owners of the sheep, who voiced the strongest objections.

"We got eleven more wagons to git across," Malden said. "Tomorrow we'll be ready to move on, and I'm favorin' doin' just that."

"Me too," Garner shouted. "We don't owe them people nothin'. Hell, they run us off. Let 'em pay for their mistake."

"They have, I think," Applegate said, "and they have

admitted they were wrong in cutting loose from us. When a man admits his mistake, you don't go on holding it over his head."

"Jesse's right," Joseph Rowden said. "It takes a heap of forgivin'. I'd just want to be dead certain they take some of the load off'n them wagons, so we don't lose any time on breakdowns. Are we goin' to take their word, or do we look at their wagons 'fore we start?"

"I have already spoken to Lou Spencer and Dillard Sumner about that," Applegate said. "I'll let them answer that question."

"In the morning," Lou said, "before we move any of our wagons, we'll ride over there and get Mr. Everett's answer. If they've agreed to our condition, then Dill and me, with the rest of our outfits, will spread out and take a quick look inside all those wagons. Mind you, none of this is to our liking, tellin' a man what he can keep and what he can't, but takin' on two hundred more wagons is burden enough. Having them break down from overloading is more than we can stand."

"If they decide to accept our terms," Sumner added, "by the time the rest of our wagons are across, we'll have theirs ready to go. That means you'll have to bring the rest of your wagons across without us."

"We can," Applegate said, a little embarrassed, "now that you've shown us how."

"Jesse," Sarah Applegate said, "may I suggest something?"

When a man had made a decision, it was unusual— often unacceptable—for a woman to interfere. Applegate paused, his eyes meeting those of most of the Texas cowboys. Finding no opposition there, he spoke.

"Yes, Sarah. What is it?"

"Please talk to Mr. Everett again tonight, before his people begin discarding things from their wagons. Don't let them leave any food behind. We still have eleven wagons to be brought over the pass, and those wagons have not been loaded as heavily as they might have been.

Why can't they each bring some extra provisions from Mr. Everett's wagons?"

"Sarah," Everett said, "that would be swapping one overloaded wagon for another."

"Maybe not," Lou said. "Ma'am, it's not a bad idea. If there's an overload of provisions, we'll try and distribute the excess among our wagons still to be crossed."

As it turned out, while Sumner and his riders took the first watch, Lou and Jesse Applegate rode back across South Pass to talk to Landon Everett. It was already dark enough for Everett's men to be on watch. Lou and Applegate reined up a hundred yards away.

"Mr. Everett," Lou shouted, "this is Spencer and Applegate. We're ridin' in."

Lou and Applegate dismounted, looped the reins of their horses over the rim of a wagon wheel and made their way through the maze of wagons into the wagon circle.

"Landon," Applegate said, "we need to talk again. Have you reached your decision?"

"Yes," Everett replied. "We'll discard whatever we must to get the wagons over South Pass and on the way to Oregon."

"Good," Applegate said. "Let's have everybody gather around and I'll tell them all what we feel should be done regarding any overload."

Everett's people had already begun to gather. Silently they listened as Applegate talked, and if there was any resentment, it was in the faces of the women. When Applegate had finished, Landon Everett spoke.

"None of us want to leave anything behind, but if we must, I'd have to agree with Mr. Applegate. We shouldn't leave provisions we may need later. I suggest we accept the offer to distribute any extra provisions among Mr. Applegate's wagons. Do any of you disagree with that?"

Nobody disagreed.

"Our Texas riders have agreed to help you redistribute

your loads," Applegate said, "and they'll be here at first
light. Any of you whose wagons are drawn by mules,
you'll have to lead your teams across the pass. We must
use oxen to get the wagons across, and we'll need double
teams for each wagon."

After Lou and Applegate had ridden away, it was Applegate who finally spoke.

"I felt a bit guilty telling them they must discard some
of their belongings. We were fortunate to have Jim
Bridger warn us against overloading our wagons at Laramie. It took Sarah to remind me that those people had
probably bought provisions for the rest of the journey to
Oregon."

"Somethin' to consider," Lou agreed. "There'll be
provisions at Bridger's post, but not for them that spent
all they had at Laramie."

"Precisely," Applegate said.

South Pass, Wyoming Territory. September 10, 1843.

Applegate's people, with time on their hands and eager
to be on their way, threw themselves into the task of
getting the wagons of Landon Everett's party across
South Pass. By the time one wagon started down the
west slope, another was right behind it, while a third had
already begun the ascent from the east.

"Thank God," Everett said, his eyes on the sun.
"We're going to finish today. Five days. I can't believe
it."

Jesse Applegate laughed. It was the first time he'd
laughed—or felt like it—in weeks. He had feared there
were suppressed hard feelings among Everett's group
that might surface later, but as the men had come together in a joint effort to get Everett's wagons safely
over South Pass, it seemed to bring them all together.

"If our luck holds," Applegate said, "we're about a
week away from Jim Bridger's post. From there, if these

maps are correct, we'll be about seven hundred and fifty miles from Oregon City."*

When the wagons again took the trail the next morning, they were in columns of four behind the longhorns and the Texans' horse remuda. Leading the columns were Jesse Applegate, Landon Everett, Ezra Higdon, and Jonah Quimby. It would be their first day on the trail where there would be no sure water awaiting them at the end of the day, and the Texans had planned accordingly. Lou Spencer trotted his horse alongside Dillard Sumner's.

"Take the point, Dill," Lou said. "I'm ridin' ahead to look for water. Tomorrow it'll be your turn."

As Lou had hoped, with the mountains to the north, there was no shortage of water. He had ridden an estimated fifteen miles when he came upon a swift-running clear creek. He rode back, passing the word to the horse wranglers, the riders with the herd, and finally to Applegate and Everett.

"If we can make fifteen miles today," Everett said, "then why can't we do as well tomorrow and the day after?"

"There's more reasons than I could name if I started now and talked till sundown," Lou said.

When Lou had ridden away, Applegate laughed.

"He's not very optimistic," Everett observed, a little resentfully.

"No," Applegate agreed, "and I'm learning to appreciate that more an' more. This frontier is unpredictable, and that's the only thing you can count on."

But the days came swiftly, the nights grew cold, and unbelievably, there were no disabled wagons. Four days west of South Pass they forded the Green River, circling the wagons on the west bank. Applegate was jubilant.

Landon Everett laughed. "We *did* average fifteen miles a day," he said.

* Oregon City was platted in 1841, incorporated in 1849.

"According to the map," Applegate said, "we're only forty miles east of Black's Fork and Bridger's post."

But the Texans didn't share the excitement. They had ridden enough trails to know that when all seemed secure, hell was about to bust loose. The trouble started around the supper fire, when Vic Sloan approached Sarah Applegate.

"Ma'am," the cowboy asked, "where's Vangie?"

"In the wagon," Sarah replied. "She's very sick."

20

For two days Vangie Applegate was kept within the confines of the wagon, and despite Vic Sloan's anxiety, he dared not inquire as to her condition from any of the Applegates. Instead, he appealed to Lou, who in turn talked to Sandy.

"It's . . . her condition," Sandy explained reluctantly. "She's sick every morning and she won't eat. She's just . . . weak, mostly."

The third day after the last wagon had crossed South Pass, Vangie was able to walk beside the wagon. But she still looked pale and she lagged.

Jim Bridger's trading post. September 13, 1843.

Bridger's trading post proved to be half the size of its counterpart in Laramie, but was sufficiently stocked to meet the needs of emigrants on the Oregon Trail. While Bridger had no saloon, he sold whiskey, and there were a number of trappers or former trappers who spread their blankets near the post on what seemed a regular basis. Bridger greeted the Applegates and the Texans enthusiastically, and was introduced to Landon Everett, whom he had not met.

"Glad you folks is all pulled together," Bridger said. "This ain't no time fer small parties. Them damn Mormons is still congregatin' jist a skip an' a jump south of here, near the big salt lake. They been layin' out in the brush, some of 'em, an' throwin' lead at us."

"Why?" Everett asked.

"God knows," Bridger replied. "Pure cussedness, I reckon. Maybe we're jist too close to 'em. You folks had best keep an eye to the south, though. They's a hell of a lots more of you than they is of us, an' if they's seein' us as a threat, they're likely to git mad as hell at the sight of so many wagons."

"We won't be here more than a day or two," Applegate said. "We want to put these mountains behind us before the snow falls."

"If'n you don't git slowed down," Bridger said, "you'll be into Oregon Territory in another month. Then it jist depends on how far west you hanker to go."

The mountain man's words were welcome. Applegate's party, having kept their wagons light for the crossing of South Pass, bought provisions at the Bridger trading post. The day before the caravan was to again take the trail west, Jesse Applegate and Landon Everett took advantage of the last hour of daylight to study the trail map. Lou Spencer, Dillard Sumner, and some of the other riders gathered around.

"I figure it at seven hundred and fifty miles from Bridger's post to Oregon City," Applegate said. "Fifty days, if we average fifteen miles a day."

"You can't count on that," Dillard Sumner observed. "Bust a wagon wheel or axle and there goes a day."

"Yeah," Waco said, "and we got more'n two hundred chances."

"Hell, Waco," Red Brodie said, "ain't you learnt every wagon's got four wheels? We got near a thousand chances."

"*Dios,*" Indian Charlie groaned, "why must you remind us? Let us do as the Mejicano. Let mañana take care of mañana."

"Charlie's right," Lou said. "Tomorrow we might bust

a wheel on every wagon in the train, but gettin' spooked over it today won't change a thing."

The trail west. September 15, 1843.

Bridger had told the Texans of a creek a day's travel west, and Lou saw no reason to doubt the mountain man's word. They pushed the horse remuda and the herd, reaching the stream well before sundown.

"Bed them down," Lou told his companions. "I want to talk to Applegate and Everett."

"From here on," Lou told the wagon bosses, "until we're well beyond that Mormon settlement, I want you to double the guard around the wagons."

"You think they might come after us, then," Everett said.

"I don't know," Lou replied, "but we can't afford to take the risk."

"He's a cautious man," Everett said after Lou had ridden away.

"They all are," Applegate said, "and it's a habit I'm cultivating within myself."

On the third day after departing Bridger's post, a few minutes after the wagons had taken the trail, the Mormon attack came from the south. A rifle slug killed one of Applegate's lead oxen while a second shot felled one of the animals drawing the Higdon wagon. A dozen other shots ripped through wagon canvas or struck splinters from wheel spokes or wagon boxes.

"Rein up," Applegate shouted, "and take cover."

But it was over as swiftly as it had begun. Lou Spencer had galloped to the rescue with three other cowboys, but there was no more fire.

"Two oxen down," Applegate said as Lou, Waco, Tobe Hiram, and Pete Haby dismounted.

"This could be the beginning for somethin' more serious," Lou said. "I reckon we'd ought to ride that bunch down and teach 'em the error of their ways."

"There were more than a dozen shots fired," Ezra Higdon said, "and I'd say there was a man for every shot. They wouldn't have been able to reload that fast."

"I have the feeling they could have killed some of us as easily as they did the oxen," Applegate said, "and I'm wondering why they didn't. Perhaps they are expecting riders to come after them and are planning an ambush."

"That's how the Comanches do it," Waco said. "Raise just enough hell to get some riders on their trail, then lay back and cut 'em down from ambush. These varmints know this country, and we don't."

"That's how I'm inclined to see it, Mr. Spencer," Applegate said. "I'm not doubting that you and your riders are familiar with such tactics, nor do I doubt your abilities to take care of yourselves. Those men could just ride back to their settlement and you'd never find the guilty ones. Meanwhile, we would be losing time we cannot spare. We have extra oxen. Let us push on and put this country behind us as quickly as we can. As you suggested yesterday, we will continue to double our watch for as long as we're in this territory."

Lou said no more. He mounted and rode out toward the herd, his three companions following.

"I didn't mean to jump in there ahead of you, pard," Waco said apologetically, "but them shots looked like a trick to pull some of us into the brush country to the south. If they try that again, I reckon we'll have to go after them. But like Applegate says, there's always the risk of an ambush, and we could kill two or three days, only to have them lose us."

"I understand Applegate's thinking without having you explain it to me," Lou said shortly, "but I've always been the kind that, when some skunk throws lead at me, I throw it back, and the sooner the better. There's always some risk of an ambush, but that's never stopped any Texan worth his salt."

Nothing more was said until the Texans caught up to the herd and horse remuda. Lou quickly explained what had happened, concluding with Applegate's decision. There was much grumbling among the outfits, for they, like Lou, disagreed with Applegate's wish to just move on. The horse remuda moved out, the herd followed, and the drive was again under way. The two dead oxen were dragged away and quickly replaced. Applegate gave the order and the wagons rumbled on. Far ahead, Dillard Sumner trotted his horse alongside Lou's.

"You should of suggested they skin out them two oxen," Sumner said. "We could of had fresh beef tonight."

"That would have taken time," Lou said sourly. "Time we can't spare. I don't care a damn if that bunch has to live on fatback and beans from here to Oregon Territory."

Sumner laughed. "I do believe the Senor Applegate's been rubbin' your fur the wrong way. Why don't you just turn the cat around, leave him be, and let him get neck-deep in trouble on his own?"

"Ah, the hell with it," Lou replied. "He gets in over his head and it'll be up to us to throw him a rope. You done any thinkin' about how they'd have got them wagons across South Pass if we hadn't offered to help?"

"Considerable," Sumner said with a grin. "Time they was done, there'd of been enough splintered wagons on the west slope to have kept the next wagon train in firewood for a while."

"Take the point," Lou said. "I'm ridin' ahead to look for water before somebody decides I'd best be doin' something else."

Lou found suitable water and was riding back to meet the herd when again he heard the distant rattle of gunfire. He kicked his horse into a gallop, knowing he couldn't reach the scene in time. When he met the horse remuda, the animals were at a standstill. The longhorns were milling under the watchful eyes of less than half the cowboys. The first rider Lou reached was Waco, and he looked properly remorseful.

"Damn it," Waco said, "you was right. I reckon they cut down more than a pair of oxen this time."

"We'll let Dill and the others find out," Lou said. "I'm damn well through handin' out advice that ain't wanted."

Dillard Sumner had taken with him Tobe Hiram, Pete Haby, Red Brodie, Del Konda, and Josh Bryan. They reined up and dismounted near Applegate's wagon, for that's where it seemed all the commotion was. Sarah Applegate sat with her back to a wagon wheel, the bloody left sleeve of her dress stripped away, as several other women treated her wound. But that wasn't the worst of it. Jesse Applegate stood with his Colt in his hand, apparently unaware that he held the weapon. His head was bowed, his eyes on the blanket-covered form at his feet. Landon Everett had seen the cowboys ride up and he made his way to them.

"How bad?" Sumner asked.

"For Applegate it couldn't be much worse," Everett said. "Sarah's been shot in the arm, and that's young Jud under the blanket. He was hit in the throat, and my God, it almost ripped his head off."

"You don't need us here, then," Sumner said. "We'd best ride the length of the train and see if anybody else has been hit. Did they take any fire?"

"Some," Everett said. "I wish you would ride back that way. I may be busy up here for a while. Jess has all the grief he can handle, without takin' on any more."

The Texans hadn't met all of Landon Everett's people, so Dillard Sumner and his riders didn't know Jules Dewees by name. A much younger man—likely a son—had his arm around the shoulders of his father, and the two of them stared helplessly at the bloodstained blanket covering a dead man. One of a pair of men Sumner had often seen with Landon Everett stepped forward and spoke.

"I'm Will Hamer, and this is Jules and Isaac Dewees.

That's Hamby under the blanket, Jules's youngest boy. He was shot in the back."

"Take charge of things here," Sumner said, "and do what you can. There may be others. Applegate's wife is wounded and his son's dead."

Sumner and his companions rode on, but it seemed the only other casualty was Widow Hayden. Nell Hayden lay facedown, a blanket covering her from the waist. There were no men present, and the women who had gathered ceased what they were doing as the Texans reined up.

"Ladies," Sumner said, "we just rode back to see who was hurt and how bad. Is there anything we can do?"

The women seemed embarrassed and said nothing. Finally it was Nell Hayden herself who spoke.

"It isn't proper to ask where I've been hurt, and even less proper for me to tell you. Just tell Waco he may have to drive the wagon from here on to Oregon."

The cowboys grinned at one another, appreciating the woman's cleverness in telling them what they wished to know. They rode back the way they had come, and by the time they reached the Dewees wagon, they could hear shouting somewhere ahead.

"Applegate," Josh Bryan predicted. "He's been cut deep and he's swapped his hurt for a hell of a mad."

"I expect you're right," Sumner replied. "We'd as well go see what he's hollerin' about. The state he's in, I purely hope he ain't gonna go throwin' orders around like lightnin' bolts."

But Applegate was doing exactly that, or attempting to. With a look in his eyes akin to madness, he didn't even wait for Sumner to dismount before making his wishes known.

"Go get Mr. Spencer," Applegate said. "Tell him I must see him at once."

Sumner nodded and rode out, his companions following. They had conquered South Pass and it had seemed that the worst of the trail might be behind them, but now

Dillard Sumner wasn't so sure. The five riders scattered, returning to their duties with the herd, while Sumner rode to find Lou. The longhorns and the horses were grazing, so the cowboys who hadn't accompanied Sumner rode to attend his meeting with Lou. Quickly Sumner related the startling turn of events, saving until last the message he had promised to deliver to Waco.

"Great God Almighty," Lou said when Sumner had finished. "This morning he was ready to ignore those troublesome Mormons. Now I reckon he's ready to gun them down to the last man."

"Might be best for Waco if we don't hurry on to Oregon," Sumner said, with a hint of laughter in his eyes. He waited for the anticipated explosion from Waco, and it let go on schedule.

"Now just what'n hell is that supposed to mean?" Waco bawled.

"It means the Widow Hayden had some lead burn her across the seat of her britches," Sumner said. "She asked me to tell you that you might be drivin' her wagon from here on to Oregon."

"Damn you, Dillard Sumner," Waco said, "you ain't got no consideration for a lady at all, talkin' like that. I reckon I better go. . . ."

"I reckon you'd better stay here with the herd," Lou said. "Come on, Dill. I think we know why Applegate's pawin' the ground, but we'll have to listen to him tell us."

Applegate wasted no time. He seemed anxious to bury his grief by throwing himself into something else. He barely waited for the two cowboys to dismount before he spoke.

"Mr. Spencer, I owe you an apology."

"You owe me nothing," Lou said.

"I happen to disagree," Applegate said sharply. "Had I listened to you, two lives might have been saved and others would not have been wounded."

Lou was uncomfortable with Applegate's bitter self-analysis, and kept his silence. Applegate took that for agreement and began suggesting possible plans of attack.

"Whoa," Lou said. "I don't trail a bunch of killers unless I have a say as to how it's done."

"I feel the same way," Sumner quickly added.

"We'll do it your way," Applegate said. "I don't care, as long as I am there for the finish. There's less than two hours of daylight, we must reach water, and we have dead to bury. I think we must wait until dawn before taking their trail. Then we must follow with every man who owns a horse and gun."

"You're dead wrong," Lou said. "They're countin' on us waiting for dawn. That allows them enough time to return to their settlement, and instead of us facing the dozen or more who cut down on us, we'll end up facing a hundred, with no idea as to the guilty. Dill and me will take maybe six riders and go after them tonight. You're welcome to ride with us, but don't bring more than two or three other men. I'll send the horse remuda and the cattle on to the nearest water. Have Landon Everett take the wagons and follow. Have him circle the wagons tight, and be damn sure he assigns a double watch."

"All right," Applegate said, "but there's the dead. . . ."

"Put them in the wagons," Lou said. "You can bury them in the morning, but we must go after their killers tonight. It's that or just forget it."

"We're going after the killers," Applegate said. "Jules Dewees wants to go, and I'd like to have Buck Embler and Will Hamer with us. We'll be ready in fifteen minutes."

"Dill," Lou said, "I want you to take the herd on to water. Send another rider to help Alonzo with the horse remuda. I want Indian Charlie with me. Send me Kage Copeland, Dub Stern, Waco, and Vic."

"There'll be only ten of us," Applegate said doubtfully as Sumner rode away.

"Mr. Applegate," Lou said impatiently, "I can understand you wanting to take every armed man who can ride, but they'd make more noise than a bunch of shirttail young'uns at a Sunday picnic. Now find the three men you aim to take with you, and have them here by the time my riders get here."

Applegate hurried away. Lou felt a timid hand on his arm and found a tearful Sandy Applegate beside him. He allowed the stern face he had worn for her father's benefit slip away, replacing it with a smile for the girl.

"Lou," she said, "you told me . . . so many times . . . that some of us wouldn't make it, but he . . . was only a boy, Lou. Not even . . . seventeen . . ."

"I know," Lou said. "About the same age as the Dewees boy."

"You're riding after them? Tonight?"

"Yes," Lou said. "Tomorrow will be too late."

"Please, please be careful," she begged. "I . . . I've had all the hurt I can stand."

Lou turned away, not wishing to have Sandy dig any deeper into his plans. Sarah Applegate still sat with her back to the wagon wheel, her wounded arm bandaged, staring dully at nothing. Jud's blanket-wrapped body had been taken to the wagon, and that meant the wounded Sarah would have to walk. Lou knelt beside the stricken woman.

"Sorry, ma'am," Lou said. "How do you feel?"

It was a foolish question and he was immediately sorry. Sarah Applegate spoke without even looking at him.

"I feel like it's the end of the world, and I don't care. I don't care."

Lou returned to his horse and waited until Applegate returned. With him was Jules Dewees, Buck Embler, and Will Hamer. The four men led their horses and said nothing. That suited Lou, for there was no point in going over his plan twice. He would wait for his own riders and speak to them all as a group. They didn't have long to wait, and even as the cowboys dismounted, Lou began speaking. The Widow Hayden was there, looking uncomfortable, but Waco had time only to tip his hat.

"I don't much expect an ambush," Lou said, "and the unexpected ones are the worst. Indian Charlie will be riding ahead of us to be sure all or some of 'em don't double back. If they're part of that bunch Bridger spoke of, I'd say they're a hundred miles from home. I figure they put off that last attack until late in the day because they reckoned we wouldn't pursue them after dark. Thinkin' that way, I look for them to spend the night on the trail instead of makin' that long ride in the dark. We must catch them before they return to their settlement. Any questions?"

"Suppose we find them," Applegate said. "How do we approach them?"

"Shooting," Lou replied. "We'll talk about that before we move in."

The ten of them mounted and rode out, Indian Charlie taking the lead. Charlie quickly found the positions from which the marauders had fired, and eventually the place where they had all come together before riding south.

"They no hide tracks," Charlie said. "Fo'teen hombres."

"They don't expect us to follow or they ain't scared of us," Waco said.

"In either case it's their mistake," Lou replied grimly. "Charlie, if you see any sign of an ambush, find where they're holed up and report back to me, *muy pronto*."

Charlie rode ahead, Lou and the others holding back to give him distance.

"We don't have much time before dark," Applegate observed.

"We won't need much," Lou said. "We know these varmints have a village to the south, and if they don't light a shuck for home, it likely means they aim to hole up and raise some more hell. After we follow 'em a ways, learn what gait they're ridin', we'll know what they're plannin' to do."

The westering sun sank below the horizon, leaving in its wake a crimson aura to meet the purple of approaching night. They rode in silence for more than three miles. Finally, Kage Copeland spoke to nobody in particular.

"They're ridin' at a slow gallop. That usually means a long ride."

"It does," Lou agreed, "and in this case, proof enough they're heading for their home diggings. They're not pushing their horses, but they aim to get far enough ahead to lose us in the darkness."

It was well past sundown and the first stars were winking silver when Indian Charlie rode back to meet them.

"They stop soon," Charlie said. "Wait." With that, he was gone again.

Will Hamer laughed. "He don't talk much, does he?"

"You don't have to," Dub Stern said, "when you can read sign like he does. He can track a Comanche across solid rock. If this bunch he's trailin' knowed what they're up against, they'd be ridin' all night, thankful for the chance."

Charlie soon proved the truth of Stern's words. In little more than an hour he returned, his speech as brief as ever.

"Creek," Charlie said. "Mebbe fi' mile. Moonrise, we find."

While there was only a half moon, adding to the light of the stars, it was enough. The ten men rode south, Indian Charlie in the lead. Finally he reined up and the other riders gathered around.

"They sleep this side of creek," Charlie said softly. "Split fire."

"Waco," Lou said, "take Vic, Dewees, and Hamer with you. Charlie, you take them across that creek somewhere above the renegade camp, bringing them back down on the other side of it. The rest of us will cover the camp from this side. Charlie, you set the pace. The rest of us will fire when you've opened the ball. Shoot to kill."

"No warning, then," Buck Embler said.

"As much as they gave us," Lou replied. "It's a bullet or a rope, and since they've fired on us twice, I reckon we know them well enough to skip the formalities."

They were at a disadvantage, the wind being from the northwest, and Charlie had taken that into consideration. The horses were picketed far from the creek, all the attackers advancing on foot. Applegate stepped on a dead limb and it broke with a resounding crack.

"Careful, damn it," Lou hissed. "That could be heard for a mile."

They moved cautiously on. Suddenly a horse snorted and Lou held up his hand. They waited a moment, then continued until they could hear the chuckle of the creek. As was usually the case near water, there was a profusion of underbrush and clutching briars. Towering pines filtered out most of the light from moon and stars, slowing their progress even more. When Lou could finally see through the underbrush that shrouded the riverbank, he found that they had veered too far up- or downstream, for the sleeping men they sought were not there.

"We've missed them," Lou whispered to the men following him. "We'll go upstream a ways."

Had Lou and his men been on course, they would have been in position ahead of Indian Charlie's band. Now Lou wasn't so sure, although Charlie and his followers had farther to go. Now Lou had to face the possibility that he was *already* too far upstream, and that he was taking his men even farther out of position. Lou knew that if he'd guessed wrong, Charlie's group might open fire before he and his companions were ready, all but destroying the effect of the planned crossfire. Just when Lou was convinced he'd made the wrong move, a gust of wind wafted a spark from a dying campfire.

"A little farther," Lou whispered to the men behind him. He halted them finally with a wave of his hand. The farthest bank of the creek was in deep shadow, and he was unable to count more than nine sleeping men. It all depended on Indian Charlie and his men to go after those lost in the shadows. Lou noted with approval that his companions had done as he'd told them, and were strung out in a line along the riverbank. Now all they had to do was wait for Indian Charlie to open fire. Although they were expecting the shot, it came with an abruptness that jangled their already taut nerves. His Colt ready, Lou cut loose, while the thunder to his right told him his companions had followed his lead. There was some activity among the men who slept within the shadow of the trees, but Lou and his men were unable to choose a definite target. There was no return fire, and in less than a minute the thunder faded to silence. Lou and his men waited. He who spoke too quickly invited lead. Indian Charlie was in a better position to have seen what had taken place, and it would be up to him to shout a warning or an all clear. But when the call came, it was Waco who spoke.

"Lou, it's done. Three of 'em got away."

"Where's Indian Charlie?" Lou asked.

"We kind of had a change in plans," Waco said. "Some of that bunch was in shadow so deep we couldn't see a damn thing. Charlie left us to do all the gun work while he snuck over yonder and cut their horses loose. He thought some of 'em might get away, and while we might not prevent that, we could see they had one hell of a walk."

Lou laughed. Indian Charlie was a half-breed who spoke poor English, but he was a Texan born and bred, with a sharp eye and a quick mind. It was the very thing Lou Spencer would have done, given similar circumstances.

"My God," Applegate said, "ten men dead. What have we done?"

"What we had to," Lou replied. "Thanks to Charlie's quick thinking, we have a chance to put this country behind us before word gets back to that Mormon settlement."

"I'm not all that sorry they escaped," Applegate said. "They've more than paid for what they did to us."

"You'd be sorry enough if they wasn't afoot," Kage Copeland said. "If they had horses, they'd ride back to that settlement and return with enough men to kill us all. With a good horse, a man can ride seventy miles in a day. We got to be satisfied with them that escaped bein' afoot, but I'd feel a mite better if they was layin' dead with the rest of 'em."

Waco and his men crossed the creek and they all began the long walk to their horses. Indian Charlie was there waiting for them.

"Charlie," Lou said, "you are one *bueno* hombre. Let's ride."

∽☙∼

21

Western Wyoming Territory. September 18, 1843.

*D*illard Sumner and the riders remaining with the herd had taken it and the horse remuda on to the next creek, and Landon Everett had followed with the wagons. While there were no fires, it seemed nobody within the wagon circle was asleep. Lou and his riders were immediately challenged by one of the men on watch.

"Mr. Applegate," Lou said, "I'll leave it to you, Mr. Dewees, Will, and Buck to tell your folks what happened. We'll all be here at first light to pay our respects, if that's all right."

"Very much so," Applegate said, "and much appreciated."

Lou and his companions rode out to the herd, identifying themselves as they drew near. The men who had remained with the herd paused in their nighthawking duties to hear Lou's report of the attack. He was quick to give the half-breed, Indian Charlie, full credit for loosing the horses.

"It's in our favor, them bein' afoot," Sumner said, "but we can't be so sure they're the only bunch of hell-raisers. I think, until we're maybe five days into Idaho Territory, we'd best have some outriders to the north and the south of this train."

"I think you're right," Lou said. "I should have done that, following the first attack yesterday morning. My fault, because I lost my patience with Applegate."

"Aw hell," Waco said, "it was Applegate's damn fault, not wantin' to go after them varmints, and I agreed with him."

"Still my fault for giving in to him," Lou said. "Lose your temper and it clouds your judgment. On the frontier, when you're not playin' with a full deck, somebody dies."

There was no breakfast the following morning until Hamby Dewees and Jud Applegate had been laid to rest beside the creek. Landon Everett read the Word from a tattered old Bible, and though he kept the service mercifully short, it took its toll. None of the Applegates wanted breakfast, and Applegate had to help the pale, weeping Vangie back to the wagon after the burying. Lou allowed the Applegates as much time as he could. Finally he sought out Landon Everett and they went to the Applegate wagon.

"Mr. Applegate," Lou said, "for the next week or so I need six good men who have horses and sharp eyes. Even if it means sons, daughters, or wives handling the teams."

"For what purpose?" Applegate asked.

"So that what happened yesterday won't happen again," Lou said. "Three of these men will be strung out to the south of the wagons and three of them to the north. These outriders are to warn you with a pistol shot at the first sign of attack. If those four men who escaped our ambush are afoot, we should have time to get beyond their reach. But we can't be sure their horses headed for home. If they ran two or three miles and stopped to graze, those four men could reach the Mormon settlement today. By tonight they could be on their way here with a hundred armed men. Yesterday we gam-

bled, and you know what we lost. I won't have it happen
again."

Applegate sighed, rubbing his reddened eyes. "I
know. God, how well I know. Landon, I trust your judgment. Choose the men, see that they understand their
duties and that they take their positions when we move
out this morning." Applegate turned away, dismissing
them.

"He's been cut deep," Lou said. "Mr. Everett, I'm
glad you're with us."

"Selfish of me," Everett said, "but so am I. Now let's
go talk to the outriders. Their wives will have to take
over the teams, but I want two of those men to be Will
Hamer and Buck Embler. Then I want Isaac Dewees,
brother of the boy who was killed. Sol Menges can spare
his son Daro, and I'm sure Gus Shondell will let us have
Jasper and Grady."

"Talk to them," Lou said, "and get them in position. A
rider north and south of the first wagons, one north and
south of the last wagons, and one north and south mid-
way of the train. Have them ride well out of rifle range
of the wagons, so that anybody approaching the train
must ride through their lines."

Everett hurried away. Lou found the rest of the cowboys finished with breakfast and ready to ride, with the
exception of Vic Sloan. He stood looking dejectedly at
the Applegate wagon, to which Applegate was hitching
his teams.

"Mount up, Vic," Lou said. "With Sarah hurt, and
then the burying, she won't be feelin' very sociable."

"I reckon not," Vic said. "I just wish there was somethin' I could do."

"We did all we could last night," Lou said. "The rest
will take time."

The horse remuda took the trail first, followed by the
longhorns. Lou didn't slow the drive in deference to the
wagons. Despite yesterday's tragedy, the drive must go
on. Lou trotted his horse alongside Dillard Sumner's.

"I've been havin' all the fun," Lou said, "so I'm willing to share with you. On the map there's an unnamed creek or river, and Bridger said it's just across the line in Idaho Territory. I don't doubt it's there, but we need to know for sure how far. You're welcome to ride on ahead and have a look at it. While you're there, ride it a ways to the south, keepin' an eye out for tracks. I don't know who'd be up there ahead of us, but after yesterday, we can't be too careful."

"I'll have a look," Sumner said, "and I hope there's no recent tracks."

Tate's garrulous band of renegades chafed at the delay, as the big wagons were laboriously taken across South Pass. Rufe and Jenks Schmidt had not been accepted, but by staying out of the way and out of the conversation, had been tolerated. The men were camped on the Sweetwater, in the mountains north of the pass. They had been content to gamble for a while, but charges of cheating had led to cursing and fighting. Just short of gunplay, Tate had taken the cards, and some of the men still eyed him in surly disfavor. He returned their irascible stares, daring them to cross him. They were waiting for one of their number, Jessup, to return with a report on the crossing of the wagons at South Pass.

"Where'n hell is he?" Norton demanded. "He could of rode to Laramie an' back, long as he's been gone."

"Won't make no difference to you if he don't git back 'fore morning," Tate growled. "That's slow work, gittin' them wagons across the way they're doin', and we ain't movin' from here till they're done."

"If we ain't goin' after 'em till they're in Idaho Territory," Jacobs demanded, "why don't we ride on an' wait there? It's some warmer there, and its cold in these damn mountains."

"You know what a hell of a time Bridger's had with them Mormons," Tate said, "and it ain't just him. They're poison mean, and they'd cotton even less to us than they do him. That's just one more good reason for lettin' that wagon train go on ahead of us. If them Mormons is spoilin' for a fight, let 'em cut down on the eastern tenderfeet and their wagons. That'll keep ever'body busy while we ride in from the north."

That silenced them for a while, and eventually Jessup rode in. Before he spoke, he unsaddled his horse, turning it loose to roll and graze.

"Well," Tate said, "did you see anything worth talkin' about?"

"Maybe," Jessup replied, "but nobody's gonna like it."

"Damn it," Tate said, "talk."

"You reckoned they'd be maybe three days gettin' them wagons over the pass," Jessup said. "Well, you kin add another week to that. That bunch of wagons we been follerin' has growed some. Damn near two hunnert more of 'em has caught up, an' by God, they're joinin' forces."

"Jessup," Tate snarled, "this ain't no time for hoorawin'. Just how'n hell do you know they come together?"

"Because it was you that rode down there last time," Jessup said, "an' it was you that told us they wasn't more'n a dozen wagons left to cross. I just seen near two hunnert more wagons near where the Sweetwater bends south, an' I watched some of 'em bein' took across the pass to join them on the other side. Now what the hell else can you make of that?"

"If that's how it is," Tate said grudgingly, "it's a little longer fer us to wait. It don't change nothin' else."

"Hell's fire," Norton said, "it adds another two or three hunnert men with guns. That don't mean nothin' to you?"

Tate tried to control his temper. "Damn it, Norton, it means we got to use our brains more'n our guns. We been outgunned from the start, even without them gunthrowin' Texans. First we stampede the herd. Then, when them cowboys is scattered from hell to breakfast roundin' 'em up, we cut down on 'em with our Sharps buffalo guns. With them out of the way, you think we can't take whatever we want from them easterners?"

"I reckon we can," Norton conceded, "but I don't aim to be here next spring, huntin' for all them damn cows. If there's gold, I say we take it and rattle our hocks fer California. To hell with the cattle."

"We'll talk more about that when the time comes," Tate said. This was no time to fight among themselves. Tate said no more, allowing them to shout one another down, agreeing and disagreeing. He wouldn't interfere unless one of them pulled a gun.

"It's a good fifteen miles," Dillard Sumner said when he had returned from his quest for water. "No tracks except from the wagons and animals that passed ahead of us. Right smart of a river there too."*

"Will there be a problem fordin' it?" Lou asked.

"No," Sumner replied. "It's deep in places, but there's shallows too."

Lou rode back to meet the wagons. It might push them to reach water before dark, and he wanted both wagon bosses to be aware of that. Much to his surprise, Sarah Applegate, her arm bandaged, trudged beside the wagon. Sandy walked behind her. Lou longed to speak to the girl, to ask about Vangie, but thought better of it. Sarah Applegate walked with her head down, her bonnet shading her wan face. Lou dismounted, and leading his horse, walked beside Applegate. Applegate listened gravely as Lou talked.

"Oxen seem to have just one gait," the wagon boss said, "and that's slow. We will do the best we can."

Disturbed, Lou mounted and rode eastward beside the wagons rumbling westward until he met Landon Everett's wagon. He tipped his hat to Mattie, dismounted,

* The Bear River

and walked along beside Everett. Quickly he related what he had just told Applegate.

"What did Jesse say?" Everett asked.

"Very little," Lou said, "and nothing worth repeating. There's no fire in him."

"I know," Everett replied. "His son's death hurt him like nothing else could have. I wonder if he even cares whether he reaches Oregon or not."

"I hope he does," Lou said. "That's the surest way not to make it. Are all the outriders in position?"

"Yes," Everett said, "and we're all a bit more comfortable because of them. I just wish they'd been out there yesterday."

"So do I," Lou replied. He rode forward to catch up to the herd, and when he passed the Applegate wagon, the oxen plodded along as before. When Lou caught up to the drag riders, Kage Copeland waved his hat.

"How far to water?" Kage shouted.

"Fifteen miles," Lou shouted back. "Keep 'em bunched and step up the gait."

Lou relayed the same orders to the flank and swing riders as he again rode to join Dill Sumner at point. Sumner eyed him questioningly but said nothing. They were two of a kind, each respecting the other's right to speak or to remain silent.

"I told all our boys to pick up the gait," Lou said.

"What about the wagons?" Sumner asked.

"I told Applegate and Everett it's fifteen miles to water," Lou said. "Landon Everett understands, but I reckon Applegate don't give a damn if it's fifteen miles or fifteen hundred. If he wants to spend tonight in dry camp, that's his problem, but by God, we're taking our horse remuda and these ornery longhorns on to that river."

"His boy gettin' killed likely took the spirit out of him," Sumner said.

"I reckon it did," Lou replied, "but unless he aims to shoot himself, he's got to think of the living. I'll ride

ahead and speed up the horse remuda so's they don't
end up with longhorns proddin' them in the behinds."

Alonzo Gonzales and Indian Charlie saw Lou coming
and dropped back to meet him.

"It's near fifteen miles to the river," Lou told them.
"We'll drive the herd as hard as we can. Stay well ahead
with the horses, and when you reach the river, herd them
upstream a mile or so. Them longhorns will be almighty
hot, thirsty, and cantankerous when they smell the water, and I don't want the horses in the way."

By the time Lou rode back to the tag end of the herd,
he could no longer see the dust of the oncoming wagons.
Kage Copeland, Dub Stern, Black Jack Rhudy, and Josh
Bryan were at drag.

"We're runnin' away and leavin' them wagons," Black
Jack said.

"Their problem," Lou replied. "This herd is our responsibility, and I don't aim to nurse these damn cows
through a dry camp tonight."

"This would be a prime time for them gun-totin' Mormons to jump the wagons again," Dub Stern said.

"Not likely," Lou replied, "but if they should, there
are outriders to warn the train. They've become too de-
pendent on us. For all we know, the next attack may be
against the herd, and we could end up fighting for our
lives."

"Yeah," Black Jack agreed, "they look to us for help,
but if we was to get hit unexpected by a bunch of gun
throwers, we'd all be graveyard dead before them folks
with the wagons knowed anything was wrong."

"That's about the way I see it," Lou replied. "We'll
throw in and help when we can, but not at the expense of
wrasslin' eight thousand thirsty longhorns all night."

The sun was no more than an hour high when a west-
erly breeze brought the thirsty herd the smell of water.
The lead steers lurched into a bawling, horn-clacking,
thirst-crazed gallop, and the rest of the herd fell in behind them. There was only one thing the Texans could

do, and they did it. They got out of the way and let the longhorns run.

"God," Waco said, "I hope Alonzo and Indian Charlie got them horses all watered and out of the way."

"They know as much cow as any of us," Lou said. "They're *bueno* hombres."

When the longhorns had been watered and taken beyond the river to graze, there still was no sign of the lagging wagons.

"They should of been here by now," Sumner said. "You reckon some of us ought to ride back and see if somethin' went wrong?"

"Oh, hell," Lou said wearily, "I reckon we got to. Dependin' on them for grub, we don't eat till they get here. Come on."

It was almost dark when they finally met the wagons, the oxen plodding along with seemingly no change in their gait. Applegate seemed a little less indifferent.

"How much farther?" he asked.

"Another hour," Lou said, "unless you pick it up some."

Applegate said nothing, and the cowboys rode back along the trail until they met Landon Everett's wagon. Everett greeted them with some enthusiasm.

"The horse remuda and the herd are bedded down for the night," Lou said. "You're another hour away."

"Thank God we're that close," Everett said. "You talk to Jesse?"

"Barely," Lou said. "We're goin' back up front and give the lead wagons somethin' to follow."

Reaching the lead wagons, Dill and Lou trotted their horses ahead. Some of the other teamsters, taking heart, began shouting questions. It seemed to have some effect on Applegate, and in less time than Lou had estimated, they heard the bawling of a cow somewhere ahead. There were shouts of excitement from some of the wagons.

"By God," Sumner growled, "I hope that bunch of shorthorns has learnt somethin' from this."

Lou laughed. "Don't bet your saddle on it."

"If Applegate ain't shook the dust out of his tail feathers by the morning," Sumner said, "I think we ought to have us some serious talk with this Landon Everett. I know him and Applegate had a fallin' out over that damn cow column business, but things has changed. I say if Applegate's so strung out he can't or won't do no better, then he should let Everett take the lead."

"I'm inclined to agree with you," Lou replied. "Applegate owns most of the herd, and we hired on with him, but we'll never reach Oregon with him draggin' his feet. I reckon we'll have to talk to Everett, and if nothing else, he can take it before all these people."

"I hope it don't come to that," Sumner said. "If it does, we're likely to end up with Applegate havin' a burr under his tail, on the outs with Everett again."

"Maybe not," Lou said. "Everett seems to have learned more on this trail than Applegate has."

When finally the wagons arrived and were circled, Lou and Dill sought out Landon Everett while supper was being prepared. Everett listened while they talked. When they finished, he was silent for a long moment.

"I can understand your concern," he said, "and I share it. I'll talk to Jesse tonight. Perhaps I can suggest that I shoulder some responsibility, and have him accept it in the spirit in which I intend to offer it."

When the Texans rode in for breakfast, Lou looked for some change in Applegate, but if there was, he saw no outward evidence of it. There was one favorable change. Vangie, looking pale and weak, had left the wagon and was trying to eat. For the first time in days, Vic Sloan was able to talk to her, and he wasted no time in doing so. Before Lou could speak to Landon Everett, the wagon boss shook his head.

"He's still touchy, where I'm concerned," Everett

said. "I made it a point to mention that the map shows only major rivers, and that there will be days perhaps longer than yesterday before we reach water."

"His will still be a lead wagon, then," Lou said.

"Yes," Everett replied, "but we compromised, in a manner of speaking. We traveled four abreast all day yesterday, and unless the terrain becomes too rough, I see no reason why we can't continue. Higdon and Quimby will remain in the second and third wagons. Jesse has agreed to bump the fourth wagon back to the second rank, allowing me a lead position."

"That's worth something," Lou said. "Higdon and Quimby have always been practical men, as best I could tell. Talk to them, playin' heavy on the need to keep the wagons moving. Tell them what I'm about to tell you: that we're going to get the horse remuda and the herd to water, whatever it takes. Should there be trouble of any kind, it won't help your position if we're miles ahead of you."

"I'll tell them," Everett said, "and at first opportunity, I'll talk to Jesse again."

There was jubilation among Tate's hardscrabble band when finally the last wagon was safely across South Pass.

"Since they took on all them other wagons," Tate observed, "the lineup may be some different. Tomorrow, after they take the trail, we'll find out jist where that wagon with the gold is. That's when we fin'ly git some good out of this pair of plow pushers." He turned his hard eyes on Jenks and Rufe Schmidt. "You varmints still claimin' there's a pile of gold coin in one of them wagons, I reckon?"

"Yeah," Rufe muttered uneasily.

"They better be," Norton snarled.

"Damn right," the rest of them shouted.

"Tomorrow, then," Tate said, "some of us will ride within sight of them wagons, takin' these two jaybirds with us. They're goin' to point out the wagon with the gold. From then on we stay one day behind till we reach the place where we'll stampede the herd."

The Schmidts kept quiet until late that night, when they finally were able to communicate in whispers.

"God," Jenks whined, "what we goin' to do? They ain't said nothin' about us sharin' the gold."

"They don't aim to share nothin'," Rufe said. "Once they know which of them wagons is carryin' the gold, we're dead."

"We'll tell 'em the wrong wagon," Jenks said hopefully.

"Don't be a damn fool," Rufe replied. "They wouldn't know it was the wrong one till after we was dead. Only chance we got is that all of 'em won't be ridin' with us, an' we can make a run fer it."

"Tomorrow, then?" Jenks asked fearfully.

"Tomorrow," Rufe said. "We duck our heads an' ride like hell."

The Schmidts slept little, awake long before Tate and his men arose. Breakfast was eaten in silence. Only then did Tate speak.

"Me an' Norton will ride in and let this pair of varmints point out the wagon that's carryin' the gold."

"I'm goin' too," Jessup shouted.

"We'll all go," the others shouted.

"No," Tate said, his hand on the butt of his Colt.

They snarled their discontent, but Tate stood firm and wore them down to silence. Clearly they didn't trust their leader, and he knew it.

"Damn it," Tate said, "I know what you're thinkin', and there ain't no way me an' Norton can move in on that gold without the rest of you. Now pull in your horns. We'll be back here in maybe two hours."

The renegades rode out, forcing the Schmidts ahead of them. They didn't follow the trail, but rode parallel to it, several miles north of the moving wagons. Suddenly to the south there came the rattle of gunfire.

"Rein up, damn it," Tate growled.

The Schmidts needed no second invitation. The four of them sat their saddles, listening. The shooting had ceased and did not resume.

"What'n hell you make of that?" Norton asked.

"I dunno," Tate said, "unless it's that bunch of Mormons that's been ridin' up here shootin' at ever'body. Reason enough for us waitin' till we're in Idaho Territory before goin' after that gold."

"Maybe you're right fer a change," Norton said sarcastically.

"Ride on," Tate said, his eyes on the hesitant Schmidts.

They were far enough north of the trail for the terrain to have become more mountainous. They reached a boulder twice the size of a house, and when the Schmidts rounded it, they were momentarily out of sight of Tate and Norton. The desperate pair kicked their horses into a run, but their captors reacted swiftly, their Colts blazing. Jenks Schmidt rolled out of the saddle, a slug in his back. Rufe escaped the lead, but his horse was hit and quickly threw him.

"Touch that pistol an' you're dead," Tate said.

Carefully, fearfully, Rufe got to his feet. Jenks lay on his back, his eyes closed, groaning. Blood soaked his shirt just above his belt buckle.

"He's bad hurt," Rufe cried. "Do somethin' fer him."

"Good idee," Norton said. Trotting his horse forward, he deliberately shot Jenks Schmidt through the head.

"We don't need but one of you varmints no-how," Tate said. "Now you," he said, turning to Rufe, "git on that horse an' don't make no funny moves."

"Maybe we better ride north a ways," Norton said. "That bunch with the wagons could of heard the shots. They might be sendin' somebody back to have a look around."

"Ain't likely," Tate said. "Them Texans might of been

curious enough, but they're far enough ahead not to have heard. Let's ride."

But Rufe Schmidt's eyes were on his dead brother. These men were ruthless, and he would live only long enough to identify the wagon with the gold. Suddenly he sidestepped his horse into Tate's mount, seized the startled renegade, and the two of them slid to the ground in a tangle of arms and legs. Norton had his Colt out but couldn't get a clear shot. Tate and Rufe fought like madmen. Tate straddled Rufe, but Rufe broke loose, throwing Tate free. But for Rufe Schmidt it was a fatal move. Norton fired twice and Rufe lay still, the front of his shirt a massive pool of blood.

"You gun-happy damned fool," Tate bawled. It was a bad move, for Norton already had his Colt cocked. His teeth bared in a wolf grin, he shot Tate twice in the belly. Tate lay on his back, the blood pumping out, his lips moving.

"You . . . double-crossin' bastard . . ."

Norton laughed. "You should of kilt them farmers when we gunned down their three pardners. Now I got to tell the rest of the boys them plow pushers shot you, an' I shot them. I reckon that makes me the head of the pack, huh?"

Tate's eyes were open but they were empty. Norton was talking to a dead man. Leaving the bodies where they lay, he mounted his own horse and caught up the reins of the other two. He didn't know what had become of the wounded animal, and didn't care. He rode toward the distant camp, prepared to assume command.

Southeastern Idaho Territory. September 19, 1843.

The sun was noon-high, and Lou was surprised to see Will Hamer riding to catch up to the herd. Hamer slowed his mount and came quickly to the point.

"Landon sent me," Will said. "A saddled horse just caught up with us and looks to have been shot. Bad wound on his rump. Mort Padgett's wagon is back near the end, and it was Mort who first saw the horse. That kind of fit in with what Mort's missus said. Remember that mornin' them Mormons first shot at us? Just a little while after that, Mort's missus swears there was shots back up there toward the mountains, to the northeast. Mort told her she was hearin' things. An echo, maybe. Now he ain't so sure. Everett thought you'd want to know."

"He's right," Lou said. "Jim Bridger told us there's a band of renegade trappers in these mountains. I think this is a job for Indian Charlie. I'll have him ride down our back trail a ways."

"I'd like to ride with him," Will said.

"That'll be up to Charlie," Lou said. "He's up ahead, with the horse remuda. Come on."

"By God, that's how it was," Norton said. "They kilt Tate an' I shot the two of 'em. Now I'm takin' over this here outfit, unless there's some bull of the woods with a better idee an' the sand to back it up."

"How you aim to find the gold?" Jacobs wanted to know. "Must be near two hunnert an' fifty wagons."

"The gold's somewhere in one of them lead wagons," Norton said. "Got to be. A man with that kind of money ain't gonna be the tail end of a train."

"So you aim to just bust open ever' wagon till you come to the right one?" Jessup said.

"Why not?" Norton said. "Once we git rid of them Texas cowboys, who's to stop us? Why, I reckon we won't have to do no lookin' at all. Suppose we grab us some of them females? What we do to them will depend on just how long it takes fer somebody to tell us where that gold is. Give 'em two more days, and we'll scatter them cows from hell to breakfast. That'll scatter the riders, and that's when we pick 'em off one at a time, with our Sharps .50s."

* * *

Lou sent Black Jack Rhudy to help Alonzo with the horse remuda, as Will Hamer and Indian Charlie followed the back trail. It was near suppertime when Will rode in alone. By then everybody was aware of the mystery horse and of the efforts of Will and Charlie to backtrail it. There was no keeping it from them all, and Will didn't try.

"Three dead men," he announced, "two of them the Schmidts. There was four riders, and one of them rode north. Charlie's trailing him."

"A falling out among thieves," Applegate said. "How can it affect us?"

"I think those thieves are following us with mischief on their minds," Lou said. "The one Charlie's trailing will likely lead him straight to the rest of them."

"Even so," Applegate said, "we have no proof they're trailing us. What would you have us do?"

"Load your guns and be ready," Lou said, his eyes meeting those of Landon Everett. "We'll be prepared to stop them if they come after the herd, but the wagons are your responsibility. Double and redouble your guard tonight and every night until we settle this. We'll know more when Charlie returns, and I look for him sometime tonight."

Lou called all the riders together after supper, after they had ridden back to the herd.

"When it's your turn to sleep," Lou told them, "don't take off anything but your hats. Keep your horses saddled and picketed. We'll circle the herd, nighthawking as usual, but on both watches I want two men for outriders. I want them two miles out, circling the perimeter. If that bunch comes after the herd, they won't be as cautious until they're close by. I want as much warning as we can get. We can't afford another stampede, because our time is gettin' short. Keep your Colts fully loaded, and if you have an extra, stick it under your belt."

"I'll be one of the outriders on the second watch," Waco said.

"Then you'll be riding with me," Lou said. "Dill, your outfit has the first watch. Pick your outriders."

"I'll be one of them," Sumner said. "Any volunteers for the second?"

"Me," Tobe Hiram said.

Two hours into the first watch, Indian Charlie rode in, accompanied by Dillard Sumner. It was a tribute to Sumner's vigilance. He had already spoken to Charlie, whose English was limited, so Sumner relayed the information to Lou and his riders.

"Fourteen men," Sumner said, "and assuming the dead man was once part of the bunch, that's likely the renegades Bridger was talkin' about. Somethin' just don't add up, though. Why did them varmints take the Schmidt brothers in and then gun 'em down, along with one of their own men?"

"We may never know," Lou said. "As Applegate put it, a falling out among thieves, I reckon. Dill, I believe that bunch is after us, with ideas of taking the herd. Charlie's the best tracker we have. If it's all right with you, I'd like for him to get back to that camp, and when that party moves out, follow them. I look for them to head west, and when they do, Charlie is to ride wide of them, get back here and warn us."

"I'll go along with that," Sumner said. "Charlie, you hear?"

"*Sí,*" Charlie said. "They ride mañana."

"That means, if they follow, we can expect them tomorrow night or the night after," Lou said. "Ride, Charlie."

Indian Charlie caught up a fresh horse, mounted, and rode out.

"I'm ridin' back to the wagons," Lou said. "They should know what we have learned."

"Applegate don't seem to think there's a problem," Sumner said.

"I don't care a damn what Applegate thinks," Lou

replied. "I aim to talk to Landon Everett and Will Hamer."

While Lou made it a point to speak to Everett and Hamer, others, including Applegate, had gathered around. Applegate seemed to have regained much of his spirit, and it was he who had a question.

"Do you expect these ruffians to attack the wagons or the herd?"

"If I had to guess," Lou said, "I'd say the herd, but you can't afford to guess. They could stampede the herd and keep us here a week, attacking the wagons while we're scattered all over the territory rounding up cattle. We're in no position to spend any more time gathering a stampeded herd."

"If you're that sure they're going to stampede the cattle," Ezra Higdon said, "some of us should arm ourselves and side you."

"We're obliged," Lou said, "but we can take them, if need be. We're used to the ways of the Comanche, and this bunch can't hold a candle to them. If they come after us, we have an edge. Indian Charlie will warn us well before they get here, and we'll be waiting for them before they ever get close enough to spook the herd. All of you be ready to move out at first light, and let's get as many miles behind us as we can."

No explanation was necessary, for even as Lou spoke, a chill northwesterly wind whipped about them, scattering fallen leaves before it. Ominous gray clouds gathered far to the west, and there was little doubt that what they'd bring to the higher elevations would not be rain.

The night passed uneventfully, and again Lou rode out the next morning seeking water. When he returned, it was with grim news.

"The river—if that's what it is—runs dry in places. Hell, this is a creek. The next decent water is a spring, with a runoff, and it's a good fifteen miles or more."

"We can get there with the horses and the herd," Sumner said. "Trouble is, will them wagons make it?"

"That's their problem," Lou said. "I aim to tell them what they're up against. That's all I can do."

"Wrong," Waco said. "You can bring back some grub and coffee for supper. I ain't of a mind to fight off a bunch of damn rustlers on an empty belly."

There were shouts of approval from the rest of the riders, and Lou had to concede their request wasn't unreasonable. On a trail drive, good food and hot coffee was often the only bright spot in an otherwise miserable day or night.

"I'll speak to Applegate," Lou said. He suspected it might well rub the wagon boss the wrong way, suggesting that the Texans had little confidence in the wagons reaching water in time for supper. The hell with it, Lou decided. There was more at stake here than Applegate's pride.

"The map says there's a river ahead," Applegate protested.

"I don't care a damn *what* the map says," Lou replied hotly. "Saddle up a horse and go see for yourself. It's a creek, and by God, it's dry."

"He's right," Everett said, seeking to avoid a confrontation. "It makes no difference what the map says if there's no water. Is the terrain such that we can travel after dark?"

"Yes," Lou said, "but come sundown your animals will be almighty thirsty. That west wind, if there's even a hint of water, could stampede every ox, horse, and mule you own."

"Then we'd better step up the gait some," Jonah Quimby said.

"I agree," Ezra Higdon said.

"I'm for that," Landon Everett agreed. "Jesse?"

Applegate was in a poor position, and the look he gave Lou Spencer said he didn't appreciate it. Lou said nothing, awaiting Applegate's answer. His was a lead wagon, and the gait of his teams must conform to that of the others.

"I shall see that my teams do as well as the others," Applegate said stiffly. "Is there anything else?"

"Yes," Lou said. "We want grub and coffee for supper tonight, in case you don't make it. There's a possibility we may be facing that band of outlaws, and we ain't of a mind to do it on empty bellies."

"I'll take care of that," Higdon said, hoping to avoid an angry outburst from Applegate. "We have an extra coffeepot, utensils, and eating tools."

If Applegate took offense, he concealed it and said nothing. Lou took the food and utensils Higdon had supplied and rode back to the herd. It was near sundown when Indian Charlie rode in, and he quickly confirmed all Lou's suspicions.

"Hombres come," Charlie said. *"Lento."**

"I reckon that tells us what we need to know," Sumner said. "They aim to hit us late tonight, likely in the early mornin'."

"Dill," Lou said, "you and your boys take the first watch as usual, except for Charlie. I want him staked out three or four miles east of here, so he can ride back and tell us when they're movin' in. We're downwind, and that's against us. Before it's good dark, I'll take my outfit back yonder a ways and we'll set up our positions. You're likely right. I look for them to wait until sometime in the mornin', but if they don't, I'll send Charlie for you after he warns us. If nothing happens before midnight, the rest of you move on back and join us for the fight."

The horse remuda and the herd reached the spring Lou had found, and there was time before dark for the Texans to prepare their supper and douse the fire. After eating, Charlie again saddled up and rode out. The westering sun dipped beneath a cloud bank, painting the sky

* Slow

in shades of pink and red. Sumner and his riders began saddling up for the first watch.

"Dill," Lou said, "keep the horses and the herd bunched and well to the east of the spring and the run-off. When you hear the wagons coming, ride out and meet them. I want them well beyond the spring. We're ridin' out to take up positions for the ambush, and we'll make it distant enough so the shooting won't spook the herd."

"Shouldn't be a problem," Sumner said. "Wind's been out of the northwest all day."

Leaving Sumner and his riders with the herd, Lou and his companions chose a boulder-strewn plateau where they took refuge. It was an hour past dark when they finally heard the distant rattle of wagons.

"Well, by God," Waco observed, "they finally made it."

"They're learning," Lou said.

"Nothin' left but shootin'," Waco observed. "Seems like wherever you take a herd of cows, there's always some varmints that's got to be shot along the way."

"Yeah," Red Brodie agreed, "an' you don't take this many cows anywhere without fightin' for 'em, be it Injuns or outlaws. Hell, let's git done with it an' go on to Oregon."

Midnight came and went, and they saw or heard nobody except Dillard Sumner and his cowboys, come to reinforce the ambush.

"I reckon all the wagons made it," Lou said.

Sumner laughed. "Yeah, but I got the feelin' Applegate had a big burr under his tail. He didn't say howdy, go to hell, nothin'."

"I've learned some things about him I don't especially like," Lou said. "He has trouble livin' with a decision unless he makes it."

"You'd better get used to it," Sumner laughed, "if he's gonna be your daddy-in-law."

"I don't aim to live in his shadow," Lou said. "He gets

his back up, I'll ride so far away, it'll take him three days to smell my smoke."

The wind was still out of the northwest, and conversation dwindled as the night dragged on. By the stars it was nearing three o'clock when Indian Charlie arrived. He was afoot and they heard not a sound until he spoke softly from the darkness.

"Pass the word to the others, Charlie," Lou said quietly.

Charlie drifted away like a shadow. The moon had risen, and with starlight, it would be enough. The ambush had been carefully arranged, for there was virtually no cover on the slope ahead. The rifle having its limitations, needing the rapid-fire capabilities of the Colt revolver, Lou had arranged for none of the Texans to fire until the attackers were within pistol range. They came riding out of a stand of trees, three hundred yards distant. Somewhere to the west a cow bawled, and the oncoming riders paused. But the sound seemed to reassure them, and they came on. A hundred yards. Eighty. Sixty. Forty.

"Fire!" Lou shouted.

The thunder of Colts ripped the stillness. Every man was hit, but some were only wounded. They reined their horses around, trying to escape, but a second volley cut them down. The silence that followed seemed even more profound than ever. The Texans waited, lest some of the downed men be playing possum, lying wounded with a Colt ready. Indian Charlie made the first move. Having reloaded his Colt, he stepped out among the dead with it in his hand. There was no movement except from some of the riderless horses wandering near the foot of the slope.

"That's it," Lou said. "Let's round up those horses. We can use them in our remuda."

"Kind of spooky, robbin' the dead," Vic Sloan said, "but why don't we take their guns and ammunition? Might be somethin' those wagon folks can use."

"Might be somethin' *we* can use," Sterling McCarty said. "Some of them hombres had saddle guns."

"Rider comin'," Waco said. "Somebody from the wagon camp."

"Landon Everett!" a voice shouted.

"Ride on in," Lou replied.

"We heard the shooting," Everett said, dismounting.

"It's finished," Lou said. "Any trouble on the trail?"

"None that we couldn't handle," Everett replied. "I just wanted you to know that I . . . we appreciate how you handled that situation yesterday. Jesse has been . . . difficult since his son was killed. It was the right thing to do, taking the herd on to water and leaving us to make it on our own. Perhaps I shouldn't say this, but Jesse had come to lean heavily on you and your riders. I saw that when he allowed you to take the responsibility for getting all of the wagons across South Pass."

"He's been under an almighty lot of strain, I reckon," Lou said, a little uncomfortable. "I've heard that the first part of the journey is the worst. If we can reach Oregon Territory before the first snow, things should ease up some. As all of you have learned, we can't always depend on that map for water. The rest of the way, one of us will be riding ahead, looking for water. Keep those wagons moving like you have fifteen miles to water every day. Some days will be easy, and those days when it *is* a long ride to water, it won't seem impossible."

"I believe you," Everett said, "and I'll talk to Higdon and Quimby."

Everett mounted and rode back the way he had come. Lou joined his men in collecting the weapons from the dead outlaws, and when that was done, he and his riders rode back to the herd to finish the second watch. At dawn all the Texans returned to the circled wagons for breakfast. Sandy Applegate made it a point to join Lou for the meal, while Vangie, stronger now, sat with Vic. To the astonishment of just about everybody, Waco took his plate and joined the Widow Hayden on the seat of her wagon. Sarah Applegate was recovering from her wound and seemed cheerful enough, but Applegate himself had nothing to say. Once the drive got under way, Lou rode ahead to look for water.

The third day following the ambush, the long dreaded snow began, but during the night it changed to a cold rain.

"I don't know whether to be thankful we missed the snow or to cuss the mud," Buck Embler complained. Indeed, the rain was a blessing and a curse.

Wagons became stuck in the sloughs, requiring the use of two or three teams of oxen to free them. The rain continued for three days before letting up, and because of the slowing of the wagons, they managed barely ten miles a day. They cooked and ate under canvas, and virtually nobody slept because of the excessive water and mud.

"Damn," Waco said, "the farther west we go, the worse it rains. It's no wonder there's an ocean out here."

"It could always git worse," Red Brodie said. "Look back yonder."

Far behind them, in the upper reaches of the Rocky Mountains, there was snow.

"Yeah," Del Konda said, "and I'll bet it's neck-deep to a tall Indian up there on South Pass."

Finally they arose to the glorious rays of the rising sun in a sky so blue it almost hurt their eyes to look at it. By noon the mud had begun to harden, the oxen's hooves took hold and the wagon wheels ceased to slide. For the first time in many nights the supper fires burned bright and there was laughter in the camp. Water had ceased to be a problem, for all the streams ran bank full and there were wet weather springs in abundance as a result of the three-day rain. Although Vangie Applegate was often too sick for breakfast, she felt better by the end of the day. Lou spent most of his evenings with Sandy, and slowly but surely, Jesse Applegate regained his good humor and sensible demeanor.

* * *

Oregon Territory. September 30, 1843.

"According to the map," Applegate said, "we'll cross a substantial river before we pass into Oregon."

"The Snake River, accordin' to Jim Bridger," Dillard Sumner said, "and before we get there, we'd best ride ahead and see if there's a problem fordin' it. After all the rain, it may be bank full, with backwater."

It was Lou who rode out, found the Snake and located a shallow place where the wagons could cross.

"That's got to be the Snake," Lou said, "crooked as it is. We'll pitch camp this side of it and cross in the morning."

Reaching the river well before sundown, they gathered on the east bank and in jubilation looked into the wilderness that lay beyond. There were pines that stood so tall it was difficult to see their lofty tops. On the west bank someone had driven one end of a broad slab of wood into the ground. Scrawled on the wood in black paint were the words *Welcum to Oreygun.* Sitting atop the crude sign was the horned skull of a cow.

"While it's still light," Lou said, "let's take another look at that map. The Snake River is a pretty definite landmark, and we should be able to get some idea as to how much farther we have to go."

Applegate spread out the map and as many of them as found room gathered around to study it.

"Near as I can figure," Applegate said, "we're about three hundred and thirty miles from Oregon City."

"Oregon City," Buck Embler said. "That's all anybody in Independence ever talked about. If the whole territory's open for settlement, then there's no reason some of us can't settle on the other side of the river if we want."

"No," Applegate said, "I see no reason why you can't, but I can think of many reasons why you shouldn't want to. The areas recommended to us are in the Willamette

Valley and along the Columbia River.* They're near the coast and convenient to goods brought in by incoming ships. It may be years before eastern Oregon Territory is settled."

"You got a point there," Will Hamer said. "Settle too far inland, and you got to travel over three hundred miles to Oregon City for supplies, or damn near the same distance back to Bridger's post."

"I reckon I'll settle closer to the big water, then," Embler said.

The following morning, the cowboys took the horse remuda across the river first, following with the herd. The crossing Lou had chosen was wide enough, but there was only a portion of the bottom that was solid. The longhorns hit the river a dozen abreast, and some of the animals on either side of the column went neck-deep in water. The cowboys had to ride downstream from the floundering cattle and force them to a low bank where they could climb out. Meanwhile, the column had been narrowed to four abreast, and the rest of the animals crossed without incident. Lou rode back across to speak to the wagon bosses before the wagons began crossing.

"I reckon you saw the problem we had with the herd," Lou said. "That means there's enough solid bed for one wagon at a time. Try to cross them two abreast and you'll lose one. Does everybody understand that?"

"I do," Applegate said. "I also think we'll be all day crossing this many wagons. How far do you plan to go today, after we've crossed?"

"No farther than the west bank," Lou said. "As you cross the wagons, take them just far enough beyond the river to circle them. Once we cross the Snake, the map doesn't show decent water for another seventy-five miles. We have to find a lot of springs and creeks in that

* These areas are located to the south and east of the present-day city of Portland.

distance, and on the frontier you never leave sure water with sundown starin' you in the face."

Applegate's prediction was close. Despite the solid riverbed, being able to cross just one wagon at a time slowed them down considerably. As a result, their first night in Oregon Territory was spent just across the Snake River. But water seemed plentiful enough, despite the fact that government men had seen fit only to show major rivers on the map. Dillard Sumner was the first to scout the trail ahead, and in his enthusiasm rode more than twenty miles.

"She looks good," Sumner reported. "There's creeks and springs where we don't even need 'em."

While the nights were cool, the days were dry and sunny. There was very little underbrush to obstruct the trail. For mile after mile they were in the shade of the towering pines. There were times when day seemed like twilight.

"My God," Landon Everett said, "a man could set up a sawmill somewhere near the coast and ship lumber all over the world."

Many of the settlers who had embarked on the journey to Oregon were, for the first time, seeing the potential of the territory. Around the supper fire there was talk of farming and ranching, of homes to be built, and the flame of hope that had beckoned them westward burned brighter than ever.

"It all looked pretty damn dismal when we got to South Pass and saw so much that had been left behind," Will Hamer said. "It looked like everything folks held dear had to be cast aside to rot, that all of them—and all of us—would have to start over. But a man has to see this land not for what it is now, but for what it can be."

"Amen," Jesse Applegate said. "Within a few years the sailing ships will be docking, bringing with them all the things—and more—that we tried to bring across the Rocky Mountains by wagon. My dearest wish is that all of us may settle along the river and in the fertile valleys south of Oregon City."

Oregon Territory, 150 miles west of the Snake River. October 10, 1843.

"By God," Dillard Sumner cried excitedly when he rode back to meet the herd, "there's a village on the west bank of that river up ahead."

"Aw hell, Dill," Waco chided, "you been too long on the trail. Who'd settle way the hell out here?"

"I dunno," Sumner replied, "but somebody has. I saw two cabins, and cows grazin' along the river."

"You should have ridden over there and talked to them," Lou said.

"We'll all be there well before sundown," Sumner said. "We'll bed down the herd along that river, and then some of us can ride across and see who they are."

Lou rode back and met the wagons, taking word of Sumner's discovery.

"They'd almost have to be from the train that left in April, just three months ahead of us," Applegate speculated. Makes me wonder why they settled this far from Oregon City."

"Kind of puzzling," Ezra Higdon agreed. "They're a good two hundred miles inland."

Curiosity speeded their progress. When the herd had been bedded down and the wagons circled, a party prepared to cross the river to meet the people who inhabited the cabins. Applegate chose Landon Everett, Ezra Higdon, and Jonah Quimby to represent the settlers. Lou asked Dillard Sumner, Waco, and Vic Sloan to accompany him. Only two cabins were visible from the river, but as the riders topped a rise, they could see two more cabins. Near one of the cabins, four men labored, raising what appeared to be a log barn. When the men became aware of the approaching riders, they dropped their tools, wiped their brows and prepared to greet the newcomers. Each man wore a belted Colt. The riders reined up and Applegate spoke.

"We left Independence in early June, bound for Oregon City. Are you from the party that left in April, ahead of us?"

"Yes," one of the men said, "we got here in July. Ride in an' get down."

They did, and Applegate introduced his party.

"I'm Uriah Belton," said the man who had spoken to them. "This is Elton Bernard. Next to him is Jefferson Williams, and finally, the Reverend Pendleton Reeves. His missus was killed when he lost his wagon at South Pass."

"Sorry," Applegate said. "The journey has been difficult for us all."

"That it has," Belton replied. "That's why some of us settled here. Elton, Jefferson, and me, we all had sick babies, and our women just didn't feel up to fightin' the trail any farther. Reverend Pen's been thinking of going back to Ohio, but I believe we've coaxed him into staying."

The settlers seemed friendly enough, and without considering how Applegate might react, Vic Sloan had a question for the preacher.

"Reverend, could you—would you—read from the Book for a man and woman wantin' to marry?"

"Why, yes," the minister replied. "I'd be glad to."

Jesse Applegate looked as though he was about to say something he might later regret, but Lou Spencer was a jump ahead. Laughing, he slapped Vic on the back, congratulating him. It was contagious, and the others joined in. Landon Everett, Ezra Higdon, and Jonah Quimby had taken Vic's side in a friendly conspiracy that had spared the cowboy embarrassment at the hands of Applegate. Landon Everett winked at Lou and took control of the situation.

"Why don't you folks ride across the river in the morning and join us for breakfast? I'm sure the rest of our people would like to meet you, and the Reverend Pen can do the marrying while you're there."

Applegate and his companions were crossing the river to their camp before Vic Sloan finally got up the courage to speak to Applegate.

"Sir," Vic said, "before I spoke to the preacher, I should have asked your permission. I'm askin' it now, before I speak to Vangie."

"You leave me little choice," Applegate said. "You have my permission."

Oregon Territory. October 12, 1843.

Beneath the stately pines, Vic Sloan and Vangie Applegate stood before the Reverend Pendleton Reeves and said their vows. Men laughed, women wept, and when the time came for the ring, Vic was embarrassed. From a coat pocket the preacher took a thin golden band.

"Here," he said. "This belonged to my late wife, and I'd be proud if you'd wear it."

All too soon the friendly gathering was over and Applegate prepared to take the trail west. The four families who had settled along the river hated to see the newly arrived emigrants go.

"I'd like for you to settle here with us," Uriah Belton said. "Some day there'll be a town here."*

"Sorry," Applegate said, "we're bound for the Willamette Valley, and it's another two hundred miles."

The Texans led out with the horse remuda and the herd of longhorns, while the string of wagons lumbered along behind. Bound for Oregon City, at the end of the Oregon Trail. . . .

Oregon Territory. October 28, 1843.

It was near sundown when the cowboys and weary emigrants stood looking at the lush Willamette valley

---

* The town of La Grande, Oregon, was founded in 1861.

below. To the west there was the silver, red, and gold of a rainbow, and beyond that, the setting sun shot glorious rays of red and pink into a cloudless blue sky. Sandy Applegate stood beside Lou, while Vangie stood beside Vic. Nell Hayden stood beside Waco, and when he spoke, it was for them all.

"My God," said the cowboy reverently, "it's as near the Promised Land as any of us will ever see in this world."

Some of the emigrant women wept while men shouted and fired their pistols. But the cowboys who had hired on with Higdon and Quimby were solemn, for they had little awaiting them, except for Kage and Pete. They now stood with their chosen companions, Dorrie Halleck and Rosa Wallace. Dillard Sumner spoke for the rest of his forlorn outfit.

"She was some trail," Sumner said. "I wouldn't take nothin' for having rode her once, and I wouldn't ride her again for a thousand dollars."

"Por Dios," said Indian Charlie. "What we do now? Our work be finish."

"Not unless you want it to be, Charlie," Ezra Higdon said. "Jonah and me aims to join our herds and build us a ranch. You boys file on the lands joinin' ours and throw in with us on shares. Hell, there's enough here for us all. How about it?"

"Nobody in Texas ever made me an offer like that," said Sumner. "Deal me in, and let's take these longhorned catamounts home."

There were shouts of agreement from the rest of Sumner's riders, and grins from Lou Spencer and his outfit. Waco's jubilation got the best of him and he kissed Nell Hayden long and hard, aware of the hoorawing and not caring. The darkness would hold off a little longer, and they set out for the valley below.

EPILOGUE

❧❧❧

*J*esse Applegate became wagon boss of the so-called "cow column" that left Independence in 1843. Applegate settled in the Willamette Valley, and in the years to come attained considerable political prominence in Oregon.

Fort Kearny, named for S. W. Kearny (often misspelled as "Kearney" on early maps), did not become an actual "fort" until 1848. Eventually—from a few tents— it became a full-fledged fort on the Platte River to protect the Oregon Trail. The fort was abandoned in 1871.

Fort Laramie, on the west bank of the Laramie, was two miles above its juncture with the North Fork of the Platte. The "fort" was actually founded in 1834 as a trading post owned by Sublette and Campbell. It came into the possession of the American Fur Company in 1836, and in 1849 became a U.S. military post. In subsequent years Laramie became a major stopping place on the Overland Trail. The fort was garrisoned until 1890.

Fort Bridger was a supply post founded by James Bridger in 1843, and it became a station on the Oregon and other trails. From 1853 until 1857 the Mormons took possession of Fort Bridger, but retreated into Utah with the coming of government troops. Following the Mormon retreat, Bridger leased the fort to the government, and it was garrisoned until 1890.